"LET ME GO"

He stared down at her for several moments. "You hurt me."

"Good."

"Are you supposed to hurt the one who saves your life?"

She rolled her eyes. *Am I actually having this conversation?* "Probably not." He raised one dark silver brow in question and she growled in annoyance. "You can't be serious."

"Of course I am."

She glared at him, but said nothing.

"I'm waiting."

Dammit. If she didn't say anything, he'd keep her like this for ages. And having this fiend so close to her barely clothed body was making her extremely uncomfortable. Finally, she spit out, "I'm sorry if I hurt you."

"That was . . . better. I suppose. And yet—"

"Yet what?"

He settled down against her, and that was when Talaith realized he'd placed himself between her legs. The only thing between them at the moment was her very thin and worn nightdress.

"I don't feel you really mean it."

"What?"

"You say the words, but you don't *mean* the words."

"Really? Well, I mean these . . . *get the bloody hell off me!*"

<u>BOOK YOUR PLACE ON OUR WEBSITE</u>
<u>AND MAKE THE</u>
<u>READING CONNECTION!</u>

We've created a customized website just for our very
special readers, where you can get the inside scoop on
everything that's going on with Zebra, Pinnacle and
Kensington books.

When you come online, you'll have the exciting
opportunity to:

- View covers of upcoming books

- Read sample chapters

- Learn about our future publishing schedule
  (listed by publication month *and author*)

- Find out when your favorite authors will be visiting
  a city near you

- Search for and order backlist books from our
  online catalog

- Check out author bios and background information

- Send e-mail to your favorite authors

- Meet the Kensington staff online

- Join us in weekly chats with authors, readers and
  other guests

- Get writing guidelines

- AND MUCH MORE!

Visit our website at
http://www.kensingtonbooks.com

ABOUT A DRAGON

G.A. AIKEN

ZEBRA BOOKS
Kensington Publishing Corp.
http://www.kensingtonbooks.com

ZEBRA BOOKS are published by

Kensington Publishing Corp.
850 Third Avenue
New York, NY 10022

All Kensington titles, imprints, and distributed lines are
available at special quantity discounts for bulk purchases for
sales promotion, premiums, fund-raising, educational, or
institutional use.

Special book excerpts or customized printings can also be
created to fit specific needs. For details, write or phone the
office of the Kensington Special Sales Manager: Attn. Special
Sales Department. Kensington Publishing Corp., 850 Third
Avenue, New York, NY 10022. Phone: 1-800-221-2647.

Zebra and the Z logo Reg. U.S. Pat. & TM Off.

ISBN-13: 978-1-4201-0374-8
ISBN-10: 1-4201-0374-1

First Zebra Printing: December 2008
10 9 8 7 6

Printed in the United States of America

To my dad,
the angriest dragon of them all.
You have no idea how much I miss you.

———

Dear Reader:

You know, it's not every day that you get the chance to write about someone so blindingly arrogant, so irritatingly superior that you can't believe anyone would find him attractive. And yet, for every dragon, there is a mate. But someone like Briec the Mighty needs more than just a typical female to keep his arrogance in check. He needs Talaith.

Originally published in 2006 under the title "The Distressing Damsel," ABOUT A DRAGON is one of those stories that is very close to my heart. I've always loved dragons, but there's something extra special about Briec and his mighty arrogance.

Like Talaith, I fell for this silver dragon who's not quite sure why humans exist. He's endearing. Like the large dog in your yard that won't do anything you say, but who you still love anyway.

And Talaith . . . well, Talaith is a dangerous woman with lots of secrets. But, as typical with most dragons, when it comes to what they want, Briec won't stop until he finds out everything about the dark beauty with the acid tongue.

This is Book 2 in my Dragon Kin series and I hope you enjoy it and the little teaser to brother Gwenvael's story.

Chapter 1

"Come with me," he ordered.

Big brown eyes slowly looked up at him in surprise. Then she muttered, almost to herself, "Good gods, the trees have started moving on their own."

"Pardon?"

"Nothing. Just referring to your rather . . . unholy size."

He glanced down at his human body. He actually found it small, almost puny . . . like most humans. And he found her downright tiny.

Shaking his head, he decided to figure all that out later.

"Come with me." He smiled. "I desire to have you."

How could he not? She was beautiful. Clearly from Alsandair, her soft brown skin told him of many ancestors living under the hot desert suns. Her hair, though, was darker than the few desert people he'd seen over his long lifetime. Almost black and a riot of soft, silky curls, reaching down her back and swaying against what he considered an amazing ass.

"That's . . . uh . . . charming. But I'm almost positive my husband would have a problem with that." She tried to walk around him, but he stepped in front of her.

"Husband?"

"Aye. Husband."

"The slow-witted one that's been following you? I thought he was your servant."

She snorted, then quickly looked down at the ground. Covering her mouth with one small hand, she remained silent for several seconds. Finally, she focused on him again, but he could see the laughter in her eyes. "Yes. That's the one. But he is my husband. Not my servant. Although some days . . ." He expected her to be insulted for her mate. She wasn't. Good. It gave him hope.

"Well, you deserve better than that. You deserve me. So come with me."

Her smile was slow in coming, but once it turned into a full grin, he thought his weak human knees would give out. He'd never seen anything so beautiful before.

"My, my. That's a lot of arrogance you have in that very large body. How do you fit your head through doors?"

"I'm arrogant because I know I can offer you more than that rodent? Is that arrogance or honesty?"

She shook her head. "Who *are* you?"

"Come with me and find out."

"No. No. I'll not be traipsing off with any strange knights this day. Although I appreciate the offer."

She walked around him, muttering to herself, "I'll have to write this day down in my diary."

He could let her go. Any other human female he would have. But he found her absolutely fascinating. Maybe it was the way she snarled at the baker who initially refused to serve her. She'd been getting similar treatment all over the market. They all seemed to fear her, but he wasn't sure why. Magick surrounded her, but it was untapped—almost stagnant. Something a typical human peasant would never know or see. Nor was she marked as a witch like his sister and so many other females with power. Nothing marred that beautiful face. So why they all seemed to hate her, he had no idea.

"Wait."

She stopped and turned to face him. "Yes?"

"You're not safe here."

"Well, that's a new approach."

"I'm not joking. Do you not see it?" He glanced around at the vendors watching them. "They despise you. They fear you."

He knew fear like that. He saw it every time he flew over a town or spotted a battalion too close to his territory. To be quite honest . . . he loved that fear.

Her smile faded and she pulled the worn cloak she'd recently put on tighter around her. She deserved better than those ugly clothes. She deserved the finest silks and wool to drape that body.

"You think I don't already know that? You think you're telling me something new and shocking?"

"Then why do you stay?"

He saw it. In her eyes. A deep weariness, coupled with fear. "Because I have no choice."

"You always have a choice."

"Perhaps knights such as yourself do. But I am not that lucky."

The one she called husband walked out of the local tavern and glared at the pair of them. "Come on," he barked at her.

"Aye," she called back. She looked at Briec and smiled. "I've enjoyed our conversation, knight. It's been nice talking to someone who can—"

"Create full and complete sentences?"

That grin returned and, for a moment, his heart actually stopped beating. "No. It was nice to finally meet someone whose arrogance is only rivaled by the arrogance of the gods. Now, if you'll excuse me"—she leaned in and whispered good-naturedly—"my servant awaits."

She winked at him and walked away. And he knew right then it didn't matter who she bound herself to, he'd have her . . . at least until he was done with her.

* * *

She placed the food in front of her husband, and turned to walk away. But he grabbed hold of her wrist and dragged her to his lap. She didn't fight him. She knew she didn't have to.

His lips touched her neck and she forced the repulsion back. She decided to think about other things to distract her and immediately, strange violet eyes came to mind. She didn't know they'd built men that size in these insignificant little Northern towns. For sixteen years she'd lived here and it seemed like any man taller than her left the village to become a soldier or a castle guard. The remainder were not very tall nor very handsome.

Ah, but that knight . . . by the gods, he was absolutely magnificent. Covered from head to toe in that expensive black cape, all she could see were those beautiful violet eyes and that face. Gods, that face!

Outrageously arrogant, too. But it amused her. Mostly because she didn't have to live with that every day. If she did, she might kill him in his sleep—once she was done with him, of course.

Still, she should have never spoken to him. Strangers didn't come through this little village often and it had gotten worse in the last three years. Even with one of the main travel roads cutting close by, less than a day's foot travel away, the traders and travelers who once came often, came no more.

Those in the village recently started to blame her for the lack of outsider gold. Of course, lately they'd been blaming her for everything. A cow died . . . her fault. A child caught the brain fever . . . her fault. One of the village women twisted an ankle . . .

Apparently everything was her fault. My, she never knew she had such awesome powers.

Aye, their lack of kindness made speaking to the strange knight from parts unknown easy, but a dangerous chance to take. He would feel no need to protect her or respect the bonds of her marriage bed. Yet, she simply couldn't help herself. He'd been so outrageously ridiculous he made her smile. And, the gods knew, she didn't smile often.

She doubted she'd see him again, but he would be a nice memory to hold on to.

Finally, her husband pushed her away with an angry snarl. "*Evil bitch, what have you done to me?*"

She strained herself trying not to sigh in annoyance. This conversation had become tiresome ten years ago, now it neared intolerable.

"I know not of what you speak, husband."

He stood, knocking the chair over in the process. "Lying bitch! You've hexed me or something! I get near you and . . ." He gritted his teeth and glanced down at his groin.

"I don't understand, husband." She barely reined in her sarcasm. Barely. "From what I understand many of the ladies have been lucky enough to find out what a steed you are in bed. I assumed you'd merely tired of me."

Then he was there, his hand raised. She didn't flinch, which is what he wanted. But she knew he'd never follow through. He'd only hit her once and quickly learned never to do it again. Of course, since then, he'd looked at her like a demon incarnate.

Just like now.

Unwilling to take the risk, he turned over the dining table and stormed out into the night. Tomorrow, he'd return with muttered apologies and it would all start once more in a month or two.

For sixteen years this had been her life and it would continue to be her life until told otherwise.

With a sigh, she righted the table, cleaned up the mess, ate a little of her own dinner—without the herbs she'd put in her husband's meal—cleaned the grime of the day off her body, put on her white nightdress—after securing the dagger tied to her thigh—and finally crawled into bed.

As she drifted to sleep she thought of violet eyes and arrogant men in chainmail.

Chapter 2

They dragged her from bed before the two suns even rose over the Caffyn Mountains. She fought as best she could, but the noose they'd wrapped around her throat cut off her ability to breathe, weakening her. And they bound her hands tightly with coarse rope because they feared she'd cast a spell on them. She had none to cast, but what really annoyed her was her inability to get the dagger still tied to her thigh.

Of course, only she would get an entire town to try and kill her. *Nice one, idiot.*

Strong men threw the end of the rope over a sturdy branch and slowly pulled her off her feet. They didn't want her to die too quickly. They wanted to watch her hang for awhile, and it looked like they'd prepared a pyre for a good, old-fashioned witch burning.

Lovely.

The man she called husband screamed at her. He screamed how she was a witch. How she was evil. How they all knew the truth about her and now she would pay. If she weren't fighting for her life, she'd roll her eyes in annoyance.

But what truly galled her . . . what set her teeth absolutely on edge—other than choking to death—was that the goddess who sent her here all those years ago was the same one leaving her to die.

She thought the evil bitch would at least protect her until she finally accomplished what she needed her to do. What she'd been training to do since she was sixteen.

But Talaith, Daughter of Haldane, had learned long ago that no one was to be trusted. No one would ever protect her. No one would ever do anything but use her. Eventually she'd learned to trust no one but herself.

Of course a few allies might have helped you this day, Talaith.

She coughed and squirmed in her bonds, praying her neck would finally just break. She would definitely rather not die by burning. Talaith never considered flame a witch's best friend.

As she wondered what it would take to snap her neck using her own body weight, she saw him.

He stood out like a jewel among pigs. Her arrogant, handsome knight, still in his chainmail with the bright red surcoat over it, but without the black cape he wore that shielded part of his face and hair from her sight. She wasn't sure if it were her imagination or if her impending death had made her sight untrustworthy, but he had—*silver?*— yes. He had glossy silver hair that reached past his knees. But it wasn't the silver hair of an old man. This beauty couldn't be more than thirty winters. At most.

Gods, and he was a beauty. The most beautiful thing Talaith had ever seen. Well, at least she'd leave this world with something pretty for her last vision.

He walked up to one of the townsfolk and motioned toward her.

"She is a witch, m'lord!" a woman—whose child Talaith saved from a poisonous snakebite the year before— screamed. "She's in league with demons and the dark gods."

She wished. At least the dark gods protected their own.

The knight stared at her for several moments. If she

could, she wouldn't have been too proud to beg for mercy.
But, even if she could speak, she wouldn't bother. Those
cold violet eyes of his told her it would have done no good
anyway.

*If only you'd fucked him like you wanted to, he might feel
slightly obligated to help you. But you had to be a hard
bitch.*

Of course, according to her husband, she was always a
hard bitch.

With a bored sigh, her knight turned and walked away,
disappearing into the surrounding woods.

Typical. Even a brave knight wouldn't help her. Every
day her life grew more and more pathetic.

"Die, witch! Die!" *How lovely.* Her own "dear" husband
started up that endearing chant. The bastard. She'd meet
him on the other side when his time came and she'd make
sure he suffered for eternity.

The noose tightened a bit and she felt more of her life slip
away while they continued to pile extra wood around the
stake.

*Funny how one's mind plays tricks when so close to
dying.*

For instance, if she didn't know better, she'd swear that
was a giant silver dragon ambling out of the forest. An enormous, amazing creature, with a silver mane of hair that
gleamed in the morning sunshine and nearly swept the
shaking ground at its feet. Two massive white horns sat atop
its head and a long tail, with what looked to be a dagger-
sharp tip, swung lazily behind him.

Silently, he stood behind the townspeople. So focused on
her, they were completely unaware of his presence. *Who
knew I could be so fascinating as to distract an entire town?*
Of course, they could also be ignoring the dragon because
it was simply a figment of her imagination. A dream of a
grand rescue that would never come.

Her fantasy dragon leaned forward and nudged Julius the

baker with the tip of his snout. Julius glanced behind him, nodded and turned back to her. Then he froze where he stood . . . just before he pissed himself. That's when his wife glanced at him and behind him. She screamed, grabbed her son, who had been seconds away from throwing a rather large rock at Talaith, and ran. Soon after, the rest of the townsfolk caught sight of her fantasy dragon, screamed and bolted away.

She frowned. Perhaps she still had enough of her power so she could conjure the image of the beast, but somehow she doubted it.

The dragon shot out a few flames at the retreating humans, but nothing to do any real harm. Finally, it stared at her for several moments, turned and walked off.

Unbelievable. Even my rescue fantasies are disasters.

But as she wondered if her afterlife would be as pathetic as her current life, the dragon's tail whipped out. The tip cut through the rope that hung her from the tree, and she dropped.

Expecting her ass to hit the unforgiving ground at any moment, she tensed in surprise as the tail wrapped itself around her body and held her.

Now that the noose was not so tight, her senses slowly came back to her. That's when she realized a tail really did have her. A tail attached to an enormous dragon casually walking through the forest. She tried to move out of its grasp, but the tail pinned her arms—with her still bound wrists—against her body. And her noose still tight enough she couldn't call for help.

Of course, who would she call? Her husband? Probably not. Lord Hamish, ruler of these lands? If she had the strength, she would have laughed at that.

No. It looked as if she was going to be the breakfast of a monster.

As the dragon made it into a clearing and suddenly took

to the air—with her still wrapped up in its tail—Talaith had only one thought . . .

Typical.

Briec the Mighty, second oldest in the House of Gwalchmai fab Gwyar, second in line to the throne of the White Dragon Queen, Shield Hero of the Dragon Wars, Lord Defender of the Dragon Queen's Throne and, as far as he was concerned, the only sane one of his kin, headed to a nice, quiet spot. Some place by water would be nice. It would be at least two days before he made it back to his den, but he wanted to take a good look at his prize. Preferably without the puffiness that comes with being hung from a noose.

True, his sister awaited the information he had about Lord Hamish, which wasn't much. But when he decided to stay in the village, he'd passed the minute bit of information on to one of the Garbhán Isle soldiers waiting outside Madron lands. As it was, Briec couldn't believe he'd run an "errand." For his brother's bitch, no less. She'd actually sent him to find out if Hamish was preparing to make a move on Garbhán Isle. From what Briec could tell, Hamish wasn't planning anything. Still, he was Briec *the Mighty* sent to do this menial task. Really he should have killed the woman when he had the chance. But his brother Fearghus seemed so fond of her. Although for the life of him he couldn't understand why.

Scarred and insane that one, and Briec would rather spend his long years with a nest of vipers.

Yet, he'd never seen his brother so . . . well . . . happy. The crazy cow made him smile. Cranky, unfriendly, "kill you as soon as look at you" Fearghus the Destroyer smiling. It confused Briec.

Briec himself wasn't unhappy. But he wasn't *that* happy either. And lately he'd been wondering how one achieved that level of happiness. He wondered if it had to do with Fearghus's human female and if the same would work for him.

When he saw his dark beauty in the village, Briec thought, *Why the hell not?*

He'd returned to the village early that morning to sniff her out, destroy her husband if he interfered and take her home with him. But Briec never expected to find the entire town trying to execute her while turning the event into a family gathering.

And they called dragons "monsters."

Besides, he'd reminded himself at the time, *if you rescue her she'll be grateful.* According to his younger brother Gwenvael there was nothing more accommodating than a grateful human female.

Briec looked down, the two suns glinting off a large lake catching his eye. A perfect place for taking a little break and getting to know his new human.

They landed by the water's edge and Briec immediately released her from his tail. As he expected, she pulled herself into a tight ball. Her eyes tightly closed, her entire body shaking. Dragonfear. No, Briec didn't understand it, but he respected it. Dragons were awesome beings, so humans should quake in fear. At least for a little while.

Briec yawned and glanced around the dark bit of forest he discovered. It was nice. Shame a cave wasn't nearby. Although he hated the thought of moving. After two hundred and sixty-two years, he'd collected quite a lot of treasure. Besides, he liked his den.

As he was wondering how long before the dragonfear might take to wear off, Briec saw movement out of the corner of his eye. Turning his head slowly, he watched the human, her hands still bound but hurriedly pushing her fingers between the noose and her throat, scrambling up to her feet. As she moved toward the trees, Briec whipped his tail out, slamming the tip into the ground right in front of her. She reared back and fell on her adorable ass.

"Going somewhere, little human?"

* * *

G.A. Aiken

Talaith stared at the silver spike planted in front of her. That silver spike a mere tip to the longest tail she'd ever seen. Slowly, she looked over her shoulder at the dragon.

By the gods—he's huge! She felt the panic again. The dragonfear. One of the most unpleasant feelings she'd ever experienced. It dug deep into her gut and spread out, immobilizing her limbs, her ability to speak and think. All she wanted to do was scream and cry and beg for eternal darkness so she didn't have to look at it anymore.

"Take deep slow breaths," it told her. "It will calm you."

Calm her? Slow breaths? Instead she sucked in a breath to tell it to go to hell, but ended up sending her late-night snack spewing across the dragon's foot.

Staring down, it muttered, "Oh, that's just vile."

Talaith's eyes narrowed and suddenly she found her voice. "And yet, I feel remarkably better," she sneered.

Ah, and look . . . she'd found her stupidity, too. *You're mouthing off to a dragon, Talaith.* Well, she never could curb her tongue.

Although, she wasn't lying. She actually did feel better. Perhaps getting sick relieved the tension the dragonfear caused. She didn't know, but when the dragon's violet eyes settled on her, she was grateful she hadn't had a big snack the night before.

"Hhhmm. A sense of humor." He cocked his head to the side. "That actually might annoy me."

She frowned, ignoring the teasing sound to that oh-so-low voice and, with heavy sarcasm answered, "Oh, well, that'll keep me up nights."

Had she lost her mind? What was she doing? Her husband always said she had the most vicious tongue he'd ever come across. But she couldn't help herself. Some days it was her only defense.

"Seems the dragonfear is wearing off, little human."

"So it would seem, enormous dragon." She cringed when

he showed rows and rows of large fangs. *Good gods is that his smile?*

"Well, we can't stand here all day marinating in your sick."

Sitting back on her heels, her stomach finally settling, she said, "Sorry. Does the smell ruin a good meal for you?"

"As a matter of fact, it does."

"Well, isn't that just too—*Aiyee!*"

The dragon's tail wrapped around her waist, lifting her off the ground. "So perhaps we should get you clean then, eh?" Then the bastard flung her into the lake.

She screamed until she hit the water and went under. Forcing herself not to panic or drink too much of the lake, Talaith kicked her legs hard trying to get back to the surface. As she broke through, she saw the dragon glide into the water, his head and body disappearing from her sight.

He was coming to eat her! Her lust for survival swept through her, knocking out any fear, and she turned and did her best to swim to the other side with her hands still bound.

She knew she didn't have a chance, though, and wasn't surprised when he grabbed hold of her waist. That's when she started fighting, kicking, and thrashing. He would still make her his morning meal, but she'd make sure she didn't go down easy.

"Calm yourself, woman."

"Let me go!"

"*I said calm down!*" He yanked her to him and Talaith immediately froze. That did not feel like any dragon.

She looked down and saw an arm wrapped around her waist. Although it was the biggest arm she'd ever seen in her entire existence, it was still not the forearm of a dragon. It was human.

Terrified of what she'd find holding her, Talaith turned her head and peered behind her.

"Feeling calmer now, m'lady?" he asked while grinning.

Talaith took a deep breath as she stared at her beautiful

knight. "As a matter of fact . . . no. I'm not." Then she growled, "So get your bloody hands off me."

"But I like having you in my arms."

That did it. She couldn't take anymore. Not another second. This was all simply too much for one woman to take. With a feral snarl she swung her bound hands at his face. He roared in anger, but released her to cover his right eye. She took her chance and swam toward the shore. She'd just dragged herself out of the water when he came charging up behind her.

Talaith got as far as the line of trees before she felt his hands, still human thankfully, on her. They grabbed hold and yanked her back. She slid, hitting the ground, her knees scraping across rocky dirt. She tried to pull away again, but his firm hold merely tightened, then he flipped her over. She tried kicking him, but he pinned her down with his own body. As human, the man was simply *enormous*.

He grabbed her bound wrists and pushed them above her head, keeping her in place.

"*Stop fighting me!*"

"*Not in this lifetime!*"

He gave a short roar and Talaith froze. She closed her eyes, the dragonfear making a sudden and rather unpleasant return. Yet it didn't last this time. Going as quickly as it came.

Once gone, she opened her eyes and looked at the dragon hovering over her in human form.

Oh, he's absolutely perfect. Talaith blinked. *Nice one, Talaith. Any other frightening thoughts about the dragon's perfect body before he has you for dinner?*

Yet she simply couldn't help herself. He truly was perfect. His long silver hair framed a ruggedly sculpted face. A hard, square jaw with high cheekbones and a long nose that had clearly been broken before. He had a full bottom lip she could see herself spending hours sucking on and matched with his thinner top lip, she knew with all her heart it would feel absolutely wonderful having him kiss every inch of her. Add in those nothing-but-trouble violet eyes and Talaith felt herself slipping into a very dangerous place.

She fought for control. "Let me go!"

He stared down at her for several moments. Then he took his free hand and felt the not-even-swelling right side of his face, by his eye. "You hurt me."

"Good."

"Are you supposed to hurt the one who saves your life?"

She rolled her eyes. *Am I actually having this conversation?* "Probably not." He raised one dark silver brow in question and she growled in annoyance. "You can't be serious."

"Of course I am."

She glared at him, but said nothing.

"I'm waiting."

Dammit. If she didn't say anything, he'd keep her like this for ages. And having this fiend so close to her barely clothed body was making her extremely uncomfortable. Finally, she spit out, "I'm sorry if I hurt you."

"That was . . . better. I suppose. And yet—"

"Yet what?"

He settled down against her, and that was when Talaith realized he'd placed himself between her legs. The only thing between them at the moment was her very thin and worn nightdress.

"I don't feel you really mean it."

"What?"

"You say the words, but you don't *mean* the words."

"Really? Well, I mean these . . . *get the bloody hell off me!*"

"Yes. Those I do feel you mean."

"What do you want from me?" He looked down at her face and that's when she felt his oh-so-human erection pulsating hot and powerful against her sex. "Oh, not in this lifetime, dragon!"

"Perhaps. And yet—" He sniffed the air. "It smells as if your body has other ideas."

"What you smell is fear."

"No. I know fear. It has a subtle difference, a little more tangy. What I smell at the moment, however, is anything but fear. No, m'lady. I smell lust."

"You do not!"

He leaned in closer, his nose brushing against her jaw, her cheek, the side of her neck. He took another deep breath, letting it out on a groan.

"Sorry, little human. But I most certainly do."

Talaith closed her eyes again. She got the feeling she could yell at this dragon until the end of time, and he would still do what he wanted with her. So, she put her pride away and gave one last-ditch effort.

Softly, she asked, "Please. Please get off me."

Instantly, the dragon's expression changed from laughing amusement to deep concern. He moved away from her, releasing her wrists.

Fighting back tears she would never allow to come, Talaith awkwardly pulled herself to a comfortable sitting position. Her arms hugging her knees tight, her wrists still bound. That's when the dragon finally removed the noose from her neck and the rope from her wrists.

"I should have taken these off sooner."

Startled, she looked up to see him toss the rope away before grasping her wrists and gently massaging them. *I guess I could pretend that's an apology.* Although from what she knew of dragons . . . not likely.

"And remind me to put something on your throat, or that rope burn will hurt something horrible come tomorrow, if not sometime tonight." He tilted her head back with his forefinger under her chin, examining her wounded neck closely. "It still may scar, though."

It amazed her exactly how beautiful this man was. From his extremely long body rippling with well-defined muscles under smooth tan skin to his excessively wide shoulders and back tapering into a narrow waist. All of it the definition of male perfection.

Talaith's eyes traveled farther down. She couldn't help herself. And once she saw it, his erection, she couldn't tear her eyes away. She couldn't even be bothered to study those massive thighs of his.

He cleared his throat and her gaze snapped back to his face. His grin had returned, more powerful than the last time. Because now he caught her looking. "Like what you see apparently."

That wasn't a question.

She'd always heard dragons were arrogant, but she didn't realize to what extent until this particular dragon. And she had to admit it annoyed the living hell out of her.

In answer to his statement, she shrugged and lied, "I've seen better."

Now both eyebrows peaked in surprise, but he still said, "Liar."

Oh, and she was. A big, fat, dirty liar.

"If that will help you sleep tonight, dragon."

"Actually, m'lady, you'd—"

She cut him off as soon as she realized where the conversation was leading, "Don't say it."

He nodded. "As you wish."

Carefully she pulled her hands away from him and again wrapped her arms tight around her knees. "What do you want from me, dragon? Honestly. No more games."

The dragon stretched that long, magnificent body out on the ground beside her, resting on his side. He didn't bother covering himself up, and she realized he probably wasn't aware exactly how naked he truly was in human terms. Dragons may lay around naked, but not humans.

"I've never been with a human before. I've been with dragon females who were human at the time. But never a full human."

She scratched her head in confusion. "Why would dragons
. . . uh . . . *be* with each other as human?"

"We find it entertaining."

Talaith nodded in understanding, then she realized exactly
what the dragon was telling her. On occasion she could be
a tad slow catching on to things.

"Are you saying . . ." She cleared her throat, but it didn't
help. That was panic choking her at the moment. Nothing
to really do about panic. "You want to bed . . . me?"

"We can do it in a bed, if you wish. I told you all this yesterday."

"No." This couldn't be happening. No, no, no.

"Why not?"

Think, Talaith. "Well, first off I'm bound to another."

"Ah, yes. To the man who tried to kill you."

"Well—"

"Let's see . . ." He laid out flat on the ground, his big hands
behind his big, fat head. "What were his exact words again?
Ah, yes. 'Kill the witch. Burn the witch.' Didn't he hand a
child a rather large stone?"

"All right. All right." *Bastard.* "Forget that."

"Forgotten."

"In the end, I am human. And you"—she looked at him
from the top of his beautiful head to the bottom of his gar-
gantuan feet—"are clearly *not* human."

"So? I can shift into human, as I've done here. And you
seem quite pleased with my form."

"It was one look."

"Yes. But it spoke volumes, m'lady."

Talaith ran her hands through her wet, tangled mass of
curls. She'd give anything to have a comb or brush. She'd
give anything to be dry. "I am not a lady."

"Perhaps. But you're no mere peasant either."

Working hard to keep her face neutral, she asked, "Why
would you say that?"

He shrugged nonchalantly as he stared up at the two suns.

"I can just tell." He sighed in boredom. "I don't want to talk anymore."

Good. His voice had begun to drive her mad with wanting. "Fine."

He looked over at her. "Come." He motioned to his throbbing hard shaft, currently pointing at the suns and, if she was not mistaken, calling her name. "Ride me."

Yes, m'lord! "What? *No!*"

"Are you going to be this difficult all the way back to my den?"

Uh-oh. "Why are we going to your den?"

"That's where you'll live, of course. You know, until I'm done with you."

Finally, all fear—and lust—of the dragon left her, and Talaith's mouth dropped open in shock at his pure arrogance.

"You rude, arrogant bastard!"

"Excuse me?"

She pushed herself to her feet. "You heard me. I haven't survived sixteen years with that idiot, simply to become the plaything of a monster."

"I am not a monster. I'm a dragon. You humans should be worshipping us."

"Shame it's more fun to hunt your kind then, isn't it?"

The dragon sprung to his feet. "That is not something I'd joke about if I were you, little human."

"I won't stay."

"You will. Whether you bed with me or not. You will stay. You're mine by dragon law."

"I am not governed by dragon law."

He grabbed her arm and yanked her over to him. Talaith rose up on her toes, forced to by the way he pulled her.

"Now that I've saved your life, little human, it *belongs* to me. And that means you are governed by the laws of *my* people."

Because she didn't know what to say about that, Talaith said the first thing that came to mind.

"I hate you."

He snorted a laugh. "Hate is a human emotion. It means nothing to me."

The dragon released her by pushing her away from him.

"I'll go find us some breakfast. Try and leave, m'lady, and I'll make sure you regret it when I find you." His eyes narrowed. "And I *will* find you."

Then he stalked off into the woods, leaving Talaith alone.

Good. Now I can panic in peace.

Was it really supposed to be this hard? Did his brother have to fight this hard to get *his* human mate to submit? Of course, Briec wasn't Fearghus. His brother probably seduced the crazy female. Briec didn't waste time with seduction. Why bother? Either she wanted to be with him or she didn't.

Simple. Logical. Of course, humans didn't strike him as the most logical of beings.

He stopped by a tree, putting his hand against the rough bark so he could lean against it. Glancing down, he willed his human cock to behave. Unruly thing. Especially around this particular female.

He wished it was simply because she was gorgeous, even when heaving her meal on his talons. Unfortunately, it was more than that. He found her mean and funny and very smart. A potent mix for his lust.

Still, she hated him. Her exact words. For humans, apparently, that was quite important. As was love. Both of those emotions so foreign to Briec, he'd never actually used the words in a sentence.

It bothered him he should care whether this woman wanted him or not. He was Briec the Mighty. Females clamored for his attention. No one had ever dismissed him so quickly or eagerly before. And no one had ever outright rejected him. How dare a *human* reject him. If he thought it would bother her, he'd go back and destroy her entire village. But he knew better. She wouldn't care. She didn't belong there and they both knew it. Why she stayed there for so long, he would find out. He intended on finding out everything about this difficult, mean-spirited, beautiful woman.

Briec's hand dug into the tree, tearing the bark from it as a large jackrabbit raced past him. He stared at it for several seconds then shot a ball of flame, roasting it on the spot.

It gave him small satisfaction, but it would do for now.

Chapter 3

By the time Briec got back to their camp, the female sat huddled by some wood, desperately trying to start a fire by banging two rocks together. Her entire body shook and she cursed steadily at her efforts.

"What are you doing?"

She didn't even glance at him. "What does it look like I'm doing?"

"Banging two rocks together."

She muttered more curses that nearly singed his ears, then growled, "I'm trying to make a fire. I'm freezing."

He spit a small bit of flame at the kindling. It burst to life as the woman squealed and stumbled back away from the bonfire.

"What in all that is holy do you think you're doing?"

"You would have never gotten that fire started on your own. And you are of no use to me if you get ill. You humans don't heal very well from sickness."

"Perhaps. But we don't heal well from burns either, dragon."

He grunted, unwilling to admit the truthfulness of her words. "Seems you've recovered well from the dragonfear."

Now that the fire had calmed to a dull roar, she squatted

next to it, warming her hands. "Prefer me quaking and crying, eh?"

"Not at all. Wouldn't mind you a little less viper-tongued, though."

"I'm sure you wouldn't. But I just don't think I can manage that." She glared directly at him, looking him right in the eye. "At least not for *you*."

Good gods, he'd never known someone so ready at every turn to be so blatantly rude to him before. Apparently the dragonfear his kind relied on so much was not nearly as powerful as promised.

Deciding not to get into another fight with her, he dropped the three rabbits he'd caught. These he'd left raw, assuming she'd want to cook them herself.

She stared down at the carcasses then back up at him. "And what do you want me to do with that?"

"Whatever you humans do to your meat. Skin it and cook it, yes?"

With more angry muttering, she pulled up her painfully boring nightdress and Briec noticed for the first time she had a sheath tied to her shapely leg. A sheath that held a very sharp and well cared for blade.

As she went about skinning the animals, Briec settled against a tree opposite from her.

"Do you always go to sleep with a blade tied to your leg, m'lady?" Since he'd assumed by her dress that those peasants dragged her from her bed. Of course, why humans went to sleep wearing clothes he'd never understand. She'd have to stop that once they began bedding together. He wanted that naked body pushed up against him. He'd be damned if some ugly material lay between them . . . ever.

"Yes."

"Did your husband not think that odd?"

"He didn't know."

Briec, a being easily bored by nearly everyone, found himself irrationally intrigued by this woman.

"How could he not know?" She didn't answer, instead focusing all her energy on the rabbits. Only one possible way came to mind of how the man wouldn't know about that blade. "Did he not bed with you?"

Without looking up, she murmured, "Not for many years."

It galled Briec how ridiculously happy that little admission made him. "And how did you manage that?"

Unless the man was blind, there would be no way he couldn't want this woman. Briec wanted her the second he saw her.

"I don't understand your question."

"If I remember correctly, you said something about the two of you being together for sixteen years. That's a very long time for a husband not to—"

"Couldn't he have just grown tired of me?"

"Of course." *If he were a complete and utter idiot.* "But males of most breeds still have moments when they take that which is most available. So I'm not sure how—"

She threw the skinned rabbit down on the ground and turned that dark, angry gaze his way. "Herbs. I put certain herbs in his food."

"You poisoned him."

"No!" She actually had the nerve to appear insulted when she was the one putting herbs in the man's food. "Understand, he bed many others, it would have been cruel to deny him that, but anytime he came near me, he'd lose his . . . uh . . ." Once again she glanced at his lap. Seemed she couldn't stop herself from staring at it. "Well, you know. With the herbs and a very simple spell it was surprisingly easy."

"If you didn't want him, why did you stay?"

"I don't want to discuss this anymore." She picked the rabbit back up and finished cleaning it. "It's none of your business what I did or didn't do with my husband."

"Were you with others?"

"Other what?"

"Other males."

She rolled her eyes. "I didn't want the one I had. Why would I bother with another?"

"Because at our core, we're all animals in need."

Her head snapped up at his bald statement. For a split second, he saw a heat in her eyes that nearly burned him to embers. But, just as quickly, she hid it. He guessed she'd been hiding much her entire life. He looked forward to stripping away all the layers of protection she'd wrapped around herself.

"I don't know what your needs are, dragon. And I don't want to know."

"Really?" Dramatically, he sniffed the air again, and she glared at him.

"Would you stop doing that!"

"I could. But where would the fun be in that?"

Fun? He thought this was fun? Nightmares were made of this. Tales of terror to scare children into behaving. She was not having fun. Dammit.

Standing up, Talaith went in search of a sturdy stick. "Tell me, dragon. Are you planning on forcing me to bed with you?"

"No." He said it so casually. Like she didn't just ask him if he had intentions of raping her.

She crouched down, moving a small pile of twigs and branches around until she found what she needed. "Then you and I will not be—"

"Oh, yes we will."

The branch held tightly in her fist, Talaith stood and turned quickly to face him. "No. We will not."

He snorted a laugh, his eyes rolling. "Why do you deny yourself?"

"Oh. Is that what I'm doing?" His arrogance made her head want to explode.

"Aye. To both of us."

Marching back to her rabbits, Talaith again crouched by the fire. She picked up one of the carcasses and brutally shoved the stick through it. She didn't even have to sharpen the end to a point with her knife.

"You, dragon, are the most—"

"Amazing being you've ever met." It wasn't a question from him. It was a statement.

"I was going to say the most arrogant son of a bitch."

He blinked. "Well, that's rude."

"Personally, I find you—"

"Shush." He waved his hand.

For a moment, Talaith truly thought her head might explode. Through gritted teeth, she snapped, "Did you just *shush* me?"

"Aye. I want to take a nap before we move on." He settled back against the tree, closing his eyes. "And I find your constant chatter quite annoying."

Talaith looked around desperately. *When did everything become blood red?* Because at the moment, everything appeared blood red.

"And don't try running off anywhere." One eye opened and focused on her. "Although it might be fun to chase you down." He smiled as he again closed both his eyes and seemingly drifted off.

Unable to think of anything else to do, Talaith stuck her tongue out at him.

"And don't stick that tongue out at me," he teased in a low, sing-song voice, "or I'll find a good use for it."

Startled, she immediately closed her mouth and turned back to her rabbit. But when she heard his deep chuckle from across the flames, she knew at that moment she really did hate him.

Briec only slept an hour or so. The suns hadn't moved far through the sky. He glanced around the camp and panic swept through him. Gone. She was gone. But then he heard her gasp and a startled, "Ack!"

Before he could move, she stumbled out of the forest pulling her nightdress down. He really would have to get her something better to wear than that. He'd begun to despise it.

"What's wrong?" he demanded as he quickly stood, ready to blast anyone who may have touched her or tried to harm her.

She opened her mouth to answer but closed it again.

"Well?" he pushed.

She shrugged. "Bugs."

"Did you say bugs?"

"Yes. And don't look at me like that." She glanced around the forest. "I don't like"—she shuddered—"being outside."

She walked closer to the dwindling fire. "I was off taking care of . . . uh . . . some things when something suddenly crawled on me."

He stared at her and she angrily folded her arms across her chest. "I don't need to be judged by *you*."

"As you wish."

She perked up. "Really? As *I* wish? Then can I go home?"

"Yes."

She blinked in surprise and he smiled. "Home with me. Unless you hope to return to the noose."

"Oh, keep tossing that into my face," she snapped.

"If it gets me what I want."

She stormed up to him, looking fierce in her dirty nightdress and bare feet, gorgeous hair an out-of-control mane of curls, and pointed one small finger at him. "I. Detest. You."

Briec leaned down until their noses almost touched. "I. Don't. Care."

Screaming in exasperation, she turned away from him. He couldn't hear what she muttered, but he really didn't care.

"Let's be off. I want to get a few more leagues between us and that den of vipers you lived with before the suns go down."

"You're really insisting I go with you, aren't you?"

"Of course. You'll be safer with me."

"And how can I be sure of that?"

Briec walked over to her. Gently gripping her shoulders, he said, "I promise I won't hurt you."

"But you won't let me go either."

"Where exactly would you go? Clearly you're from Alsandair. I can tell by your color." He reached up and caressed her cheek, startling her. But he couldn't help himself. She had the most beautiful brown skin he'd ever seen. Flawless, even when outright cranky. "Do you have family here? Friends? Anyone who cares for you within a thousand leagues of this place?"

She tried to turn her face away at his words, but he wouldn't let her. "Trust me. I'll make sure nothing happens to you. And we'll at least get you some decent clothes."

"Fine."

He stared at her, but her face revealed nothing. She'd taken control of her emotions and hidden any feeling she had. She was good at that.

Realizing he'd gotten the most out of her he could, Briec walked away. When he was at a safe enough distance, he chanted the old spell of his people and his body shifted. He went from man to dragon in moments. She stared at him, looking duly horrified. It was no longer dragonfear. No, she simply found him a monster. He'd somehow have to get her over that.

With that last thought swirling through his brain, Briec the Mighty did something he never thought he'd do. He lowered himself to the ground as much as possible.

"Climb up."

Her eyes widened. "Climb up? Where?"

Briec sighed, annoyed he'd even think of allowing this. "On my back. Grab hold of my hair and climb up."

"Can't we walk? Or a brisk run is always nice."

"Woman, don't test me."

She glanced desperately around the forest, apparently looking for that last way out. But he didn't give her one.

"Unless you'd like to make our journey wrapped in my tail—"

Her head snapped around. "*No!*" she yelped.

"Then climb."

After another long pause, she finally walked over to him. With a deep sigh, she grabbed hold of his hair and hauled herself onto his back. She actually tried to sit sidesaddle. And he knew why. Except for that dagger she kept on her, she was naked under her nightdress.

"That won't work, little human. You'll need to straddle me." He heard her quiet moan of despair and fought back a laugh. Normally he would never revel in someone else's discomfort. But he knew what she was hiding as soon as she straddled his back. He felt it against his scales as if it were human skin she rested upon.

The woman was wet. Evidently she liked a good fight. Of course, so did he, when he found a worthy opponent.

Add in that heady scent of lust, and Briec knew he'd made the right decision.

She was his . . . until he was done with her.

Smiling, he unfurled his wings and took to the skies, all the while enjoying the feel of his little human clinging desperately to his back and hair, even as she insisted on squealing like a frightened mare.

Chapter 4

Arzhela, the goddess of Light, Love, and Fertility, glowered down at the lowered head of her priestess.

"What do you mean he took her?"

She heard the woman swallow before she answered. "He took her."

"Who took her?" And to be quite honest, she feared the response.

"A grotesque beast. A demon from the underworld. A blight upon—"

"*Do not test me, Mer'lle!*" the goddess's voice boomed across the temple built in her honor.

The woman trembled, and Arzhela reminded herself a frightened priestess was a useless one.

"Tell me what the villagers said, Mer'lle."

"It was a . . . dragon. A silver dragon, my goddess."

Arzhela turned from her priestess and stared at the gold statue made in her image. She took a deep breath and sent a silent call to her brothers and sisters, gods and goddesses of this world, to keep an eye out for her little protégé. She couldn't afford to lose Talaith now. She'd invested too much in the human, using her best priestesses to train her. Prepare her.

The time had finally come when she was to call on Talaith to perform her sacred duty. In fact, Arzhela would have called on her within the next week. Because after the coming full moon, another moon would follow. Among her pantheon, it was the time of darkness and despair. The time when a dark evil would force her priestesses to build up their protections around the villages while keeping all other Magicks and spellcasting to a minimum. Because it was the night the power of the dragon gods would reign supreme upon the land. To the dragon gods' brethren, the Moon of the Black Fire was a mighty and sacred time when their powerful witches worked their strongest Magicks. And a time that one of the dragon gods had been looking forward to for centuries. She knew all he needed was finally in alignment. All he wanted at the ready. Unless she could stop him. Unless she could destroy his plans. Which meant she must have that viper-tongued little rodent back.

And, if she had to, she'd rip the land apart until she found her.

It took them much longer than Briec anticipated to get to the next safe place he knew of on this route. By the time he decided to land, both the suns had set and he knew his little human must be freezing. He could hear her chattering teeth over the howling wind.

His feet touched solid ground as he landed, trying not to jar her any more than necessary. Glancing over his shoulder, he saw that she'd plastered herself to his back with her face buried against his neck. She'd dug her hands into his hair, her fingers clinging to big handfuls of the silver strands. She didn't even look up, instead choosing to tighten her legs around him . . . if that were physically possible. The woman had remarkably strong thighs.

He liked that.

"We're here."

"I don't care," she raged into his neck, her entire body trembling.

"Are you going to stay like that?"

"Yes."

"How long?"

"Forever."

Now why did he like the sound of that? Quickly, Briec pushed that ridiculous thought out of his head. "Listen—"

"No. I'm not moving. Ever. Again."

"As you wish."

"You keep saying that like you mean it."

Briec stifled a laugh and, remembering something his sister taught him many years before, cast a quick flame-protection spell around the girl. It was slight and would only last mere seconds, he thought for sure she wouldn't even notice, but her body stiffened and she said, "What are you up to anyway?"

Flames surrounded the pair and he shifted back to his human form, smiling at the fact he had this beautiful woman straddling his naked ass. He crossed his arms and rested his head on them, wondering how long it would take her to notice.

For nearly two minutes she didn't say a word. Then she moved around a bit, and her bare sex—hot and hungry—ground into his cheeks.

She gasped in horror and finally sat up straight. "What in holy—"

"I thought you weren't moving?"

"You tricky bastard. I *knew* I felt you cast a spell."

"Just a minor one. I'm surprised you even sensed it."

Her hands still tangled up in his long hair, he had enough room to turn over. Which he did quickly, before she could bolt off.

Briec caught her around the waist and pulled her tight against him, her pussy rubbing against his now healthy erection.

Panicked, she tried to get her hands untangled from his hair, but she seemed to be having quite a time of it.

"Let me go," she demanded as she yanked one hand and realized she still had his hair.

Wincing from the pain of that pull, he challenged, "I can't let you go. Because you've still got me." As he made the statement, making sure to sound sad and at a loss, he ground his hips up between her thighs.

This time she pulled his hair on purpose. "*Don't do that!*"

"Sorry. Accident."

"It was not." After a few more desperate struggles, she held her hands up in triumph. She'd finally untangled herself from his hair. But when she tried to jump off his lap, he tightened his grip on her waist.

"You're not going to leave me like this, are you?"

"*I most certainly am!*"

What the hell was going on? No man—or in this case male—had ever pursued her like this before. And he *was* pursuing her. With every look. Every word. Every devious thrust. And, to be quite honest, she had no idea how to handle it.

Talaith had loved only one man before and lost him at sixteen. After, they handed her over to the one she now called "husband." Since that man knew she was his as wife, he never bothered pursuing her. She had a feeling he wouldn't have appreciated it one bit if he'd been forced to either. Yet the more she fought the dragon, the more he seemed to be enjoying himself.

True, she could just give herself to him and get it over with. But something, that inner voice that had never steered her wrong all these many long years, told her she'd never recover from her time spent in this dragon's bed. And did dragons even have beds? Would she have to mate with him on the cave floor? None of that sounded very comfortable.

"This isn't fair."

"What does fair have to do with anything?"

"I'm tired and freezing. I can't fight you right now."

"Why does everything between us need to be a fight?"

Because she enjoyed it? No. Probably not a good idea to say that. She'd never get rid of him then. She could tell he liked their fighting just as much.

Shaking her head in exasperation, she snapped, "Everything between us? What are you talking about? We've known each other since this morning." She slapped at his tightening hands on her waist. "Stop that!"

Talaith pushed hard against his chest, but his arms wouldn't budge. Still, she kept trying. And, finally bored with the struggle she assumed, he released her. Since she didn't expect that, Talaith shoved herself backward and landed hard on the ground.

"Ow!"

He didn't even apologize as he sat up, staring down at her. Was he angry? She guessed not when he began to speak to his erection.

"I know. I can't believe she left us like this either. Cruel wench, isn't she?"

After the long, frightening, horrible day she had, this was not remotely how she expected to end it. And, against her will, she smiled.

"Look. Now she's laughing at us."

Desperately fighting a bout of laughter, she ordered, "Stop talking to it."

He shrugged. "Well, you won't talk to him . . . and he's feeling awfully lonely. And I think you hurt his feelings." Then he made it bounce twice in agreement.

Talaith covered her face and sighed. What exactly did her mother tell her the seven signs of madness were? Well, a dragon talking to his own shaft *had* to be one of them.

"Are you going to answer any questions this evening?"

"No." She wouldn't even look at him. For her, he'd shifted

to human when they'd first arrived and had remained that way ever since. Yet still she wouldn't look at him. If she didn't like him human and she didn't like him dragon, then what exactly did that leave?

"I don't understand—"

"Please," she sighed. "I am so tired. Can we not simply go to sleep?"

He gazed at her across the campfire and she did truly appear worn.

"Of course."

He patted the ground next to him. "Come. You can sleep here."

"Oh, you must be joking."

"No. I'm not. I don't have blankets for you. My body will keep you warm."

"I just bet it will," she muttered to herself. She seemed to do that a lot. Talk to herself. He found it . . . odd. To him she said, "Do I look that stupid to you?"

"You don't look stupid at all. I don't waste my time on stupid people."

"Well, that gives me ease."

"I'll make a promise to you. You'll sleep here and I promise nothing will happen except sleep."

"And you expect me to believe that?"

Briec, for the first time in a very long time, became a little angry.

Slowly, he pulled himself up and walked across the burning campfire, enjoying the warm flames briefly surrounding his body, until he stood over her. Brown eyes stared up at him, and he no longer saw any fear. Most likely because now she spent most of her time hating him instead.

"Are you questioning the word of a dragon, little *human?*"

She stood, looking much less fierce in her now filthy nightdress. "No. I'm questioning the word of you. *You* just happen to be a dragon."

"My promises are much more reliable than some human might make."

"You took me from my village—"

"I *rescued* you."

"—and now you won't let me go."

"I break no laws, m'lady."

"Dragon laws, which don't affect me."

"They affected you as soon as I saved you from those villagers."

She stared up at him for several more moments then, growling, she turned from him and stepped away. "Thank you, but I'll be fine on my own."

"You're being ridiculous."

"It's my right, or have I lost the ability to make all my own decisions?"

"Fine. Freeze in the night then. I don't care."

He turned from her and walked off into the woods, allowing his body to slowly shift back to dragon as he did so. He'd watch her and keep her safe, but he'd do it from a nice, respectable distance.

Briec didn't understand this woman. Not at all. Even for a human she seemed damn strange. Was it not a mere hour or so ago she'd been laughing and smiling at his jokes? And now she'd returned to treating him like he'd wiped out her whole family.

He stopped in mid-stomp. *Wait. Did I?* He thought long and hard, then finally shook his head. No. He'd never damaged any villages or towns in Alsandair. So, he realized, he could be quite righteous in his anger and started walking again.

He didn't have time for damn difficult women. Especially beautiful human ones. Perhaps the queen was right. Perhaps it was time to settle down with a nice dragon female. Pick a mate. Breed some hatchlings, if he absolutely must. He truly thought his older brother and heir to the Gwalchmai fab Gwyar throne would have taken care of the future heir situation for him so he wouldn't have to worry one way or the other. But choosing a human as his mate, Fearghus resigned himself to a life without offspring. Of course, Fearghus seemed to like so few beings, perhaps that was in everyone's best interest. Who knew what nightmare his brother would raise?

Briec settled his big body down and watched the woman from the trees, surrounding them both with a strong protection spell. She couldn't see him. He was too far away for her human eyes. He didn't know what he expected to see once she believed herself alone. But what he didn't expect was for her to sit on the ground, her knees pulled up under her chin, her long arms wrapped around her legs. Then she turned her head and rested her cheek against her knees. She made no sound. She didn't call for help. She didn't try to leave.

Still, even from this distance, he could see her tears. He closed his eyes and fought his desire to return to her. His desire to shift back to human and to get her to stop crying the only way he knew how. It was a hard fight, but somehow he won.

As he watched her, looking so alone and so despondent, he tried to figure out what this feeling was he suddenly had. Deep in his chest, burrowing its way up his body.

It was something he'd never felt before and hoped to never feel again—the feeling he'd done something wrong. And that somehow he should feel bad for it.

He shook his head. No. He'd done nothing wrong. He was a dragon and this was how things were.

His sweet little human would simply have to learn to live with it.

She knew he watched her. Even from this distance, she could feel his eyes on her. Tears streamed down her face, but she refused to wipe them. To show him any of her feelings.

He'd merely think she was sad anyway. That was far from the truth. Leagues away, in fact.

No, sadness wasn't her problem. Frustration. Pure frustration was her problem. Exactly how many others would take her from where she lived and order her to do their bidding? How many others would use her like she were some barwench awaiting their next ale order?

For sixteen years now, Talaith waited. Waited for the day when the goddess who claimed Talaith as her own would come and tell her exactly what she wanted from her. That's why she'd lived with that dullard she'd called husband all this time. That's why she stayed in this land that was not of her people. And why she'd lost her power. Because she had a price to pay.

Yet she never saw this dragon coming. And Talaith would bet all the gold in the universe her goddess never saw him either.

The dragons had their own gods and their gods protected them with a fierceness bordering on rabid. The gods of humans were less protective but there were many more humans to go around. Since one great battle eons ago, human gods and dragon gods could never fight each other because they could never enter the other's plane of existence. So they used their loyal worshippers to fight their battles for them, then sat back to enjoy the carnage.

Still, a very uneasy alliance had developed among humans and dragons over the last thousand years or so. It used to be if you left the dragons alone and ignored the occasional stolen cow or destroyed battalion, they stayed away from the villages and the humans. Those humans looking for glory, who broke the unspoken pact, usually brought the dragons' brutal wrath swiftly on some poor kingdom and king's head.

In the last few years, however, rumors had begun to spread through the small towns and villages. Rumors of more and more dragons seen taking to the skies. Although still no talk of any destruction or violence, fear had taken root and spread. Especially in Madron where Lord Hamish ruled with a brutal fist. The few rumors he allowed in her tiny village were that the dragons were once again killing randomly, destroying towns, villages, anything that might annoy them. But the armies of Madron were preparing for some kind of war against dragons . . . as if the humans could win. All humans truly had in their favor was their number. One of her teachers back in Alsandair compared humans and dragons to fleas swarming over a wolf. Enough could cause unbearable torment, but usually a good bath would wash them off.

Talaith never thought she'd ever see a dragon much less be taken by one. Taken so he could bed her. Clearly he didn't get out of his cave much if she was the best he could do. Perhaps she should speak of commitment and really scare him back to his lair. She almost smiled at the thought, but she knew her tongue would get the better of her.

He irritated her. Greatly. And when anger ruled her head that meant her mouth took over. Woe to those who ended upon the wrong side of that.

But who knew a being could be so bloody arrogant? And demanding? And rude? And gorgeous? And so well-endowed, he reminded her of a warhorse?

Lord Hamish roused his best men before the two suns rose. He had them dressed in travelers' robes, their weapons hidden, and divided into several groups so they could cover more area in the shortest amount of time.

"I want the little bitch back before the next full moon. Am I clear?"

"Aye, Lord Hamish," they answered as one.

"We've failed our goddess once. We'll not fail her again. Not if you hope to live."

They had failed her. Nine years ago. They'd failed her

and he'd been attempting to make it up to her ever since. What surprised him was that she didn't kill him when she'd discovered his failure. Instead, she'd forgiven him and told him if he continued to do her bidding, she'd reward him with more power than any human could ever hope to obtain. Since then she'd protected him from the Mad Bitch of Garbhán Isle. He shuddered to think he almost wed that demon-stain. She probably would have slit his throat while he slept. He never thought he'd meet anyone more insane than her brother. But she was *more* insane and the last three years of her rule proved it.

No. He'd never fail his goddess again. If for no other reason than Arzhela would be the only one who could protect him from the Blood Queen of Garbhán Isle.

"And the dragon with the woman, lord?" one of his men asked.

He didn't hesitate. "Kill it. But she lives."

And that's all he had to promise his goddess. He didn't understand what she needed this woman for. A peasant, from what he knew. A peasant and nothing more. But the goddess wanted her back and that's all he needed to know. So his men would bring her back alive.

What they did with her between Dark Plains and here . . . not really his concern as long as she returned breathing.

Chapter 5

Talaith thought for sure the goddess would come for her during the night. Of course, the sad truth remained she couldn't decide which was the lesser of two evils—the goddess or the dragon.

She wouldn't worry about that now, though. The suns had begun to rise and she knew the dragon would want to leave soon. Still, she felt safe and warm. Of course, now that she thought about it, that seemed strange. Because she fell asleep the night before with chattering teeth and her body pulled into a tight ball. It got so bad she almost called out for the dragon, but she couldn't. Her pride simply wouldn't let her.

Talaith forced her eyes open. Trees swayed over her as the wind blew. A storm was coming, she could smell it. Then why wasn't she freezing—or already frozen—to death?

She glanced down and realized a thick, shiny mane of silver hair covered her entire body. Her entire *naked* body. Glancing to her left, she saw the human form of the dragon stretched out next to her. Stomach down, one big muscular arm thrown over her waist; he'd pushed his own body right up against her side, his handsome face even more so in sleep.

He's got the longest eyelashes . . . oh, good gods, Talaith. Get hold of yourself.

Before she panicked, she closed her eyes and used the tiny bit of Magick the goddess allowed her to keep to search for anything the dragon might have done to her while she slept. After a few moments, she knew he hadn't done anything besides lay next to her all night. No spells cast. No charms of lust. And he definitely hadn't fucked her.

Knowing he hadn't broken his promise to her, she felt confident enough to turn and say, "Get your bloody hands off me!"

Without moving from his apparently comfortable position or opening his eyes, he calmly replied, "Don't get snappy at me, wench. I had to do something. Those chattering teeth of yours would have kept me up all night . . . and don't pull my hair."

She snatched her hand back before she got a firm hold on the silver strands. "Let me go." She squirmed, trying to get him to release her.

Instead, he groaned.

"You really need to stop doing that. Or, do it more."

"Doing what?" she demanded absently, desperately trying to reach the blade he'd left tied to her leg. Did he leave it because he knew how much safer she felt with it on? Probably not. That would require him to think about someone or something other than himself.

His grip tightened on her waist and his eyes opened, devastating her with one look from that heated gaze. "Stop squirming, woman, or I won't be responsible for my actions."

Eeek! "Oh. Sorry." She winced, realizing she'd apologized to the big oaf. "If you let me go—"

"I don't want to let you go." The hand on her waist now slid up and down her side, caressing her skin. "You're soft. All over."

This could easily get out of hand. Especially when she

had to fight her own desires. It had been a long time since she'd been with her husband or any man. If only the dragon were ugly or somehow repulsive. But he wasn't. Even his dragonform, which horrified her, still didn't disgust her.

"I think you need to—"

"You know"—he kissed her shoulder and she had to close her eyes and grit her teeth to stop from moaning—"you would have frozen to death last night if it hadn't been for me." His tongue flicked out and licked a small scar she had on her shoulder blade. "That's twice I've saved your life."

Her nipples peaked, and she had the intense desire to slap herself in the face. "This time doesn't count. I wouldn't be here if it wasn't for you."

He propped his head up with one arm while his other hand continued to move along her flesh, making her think things she knew for a fact were morally wrong. "You'd prefer I left you in that tiny trash heap you call a town?"

"No. But you could have dropped me off at any larger town between here and there."

Yawning and closing his eyes, he rubbed one leg against hers, which she was starting to find a tad disconcerting. "And leave such a sweet young thing to the tender mercies of those harsh streets? What kind of dragon hero would that make me if I did that?"

Dragon hero? It must be nice in his fantasy land. "Look, I . . . *stop that!*" she barked when he tilted his head a bit and rubbed her nipple with the tip of his nose.

The small and rather strange move sent shots of heat coursing through her entire body. "I don't need you or anyone else to protect me."

He stared at her breasts and her now painfully hard nipples. "But you're so soft and fragile."

Soft and fragile? The week before she'd dragged a lost cow out of a mud patch.

"I am not soft and fragile. I'm . . . I'm . . ."

Unable to continue, she watched him—with his mouth

hovering so close to her breast—knowing what he was going to do long before he did it. Still, she panicked like a young virgin when his mouth opened and his head lowered.

"I thought you said we had to get an early start," she spat out in a rush as his tongue just flicked the tip of her nipple. It took all her strength not to arch her back and beg for more.

The dragon paused and growled. Sleepy violet eyes looked up at her. "Is there not a moment in the day when you're not talking?"

"No."

He stared at her and for a bit she feared he'd ignore her and simply go back to amusing himself with her breasts. If he did, she wouldn't be able to stop him. Mostly because she really wouldn't want to.

Sighing, he instead pushed himself away from her and immediately she felt the loss of his body heat. Talaith pulled her legs up, wrapping her arms around them. His long hair slid across her bare skin, sending her heart racing, while he sat up.

"Fine. The sooner I get you back to my den, the sooner we can work this out."

Back to his den? Well, that didn't sound too good. "Work out what?" Her teeth started chattering again and he glared at her in annoyance.

He relit the dead pitfire with a blast of flame. "What do you think?" Absently he lifted his head and sniffed the air. He smiled. "Stay here."

Then he was up and disappearing into the forest.

With a shake of her head, she grabbed her discarded nightdress—struggling hard not to imagine him slipping it off her body while she slept—and tugged it back on.

Forcing herself up and moving, Talaith put more wood and twigs on the pitfire. She could be wrong, but she wondered if those really were screams and war cries she heard off in the distance. She couldn't be sure, so she decided not to worry about it since the sound never came closer.

Eventually the dragon returned. He had a large satchel over his shoulder and a beautiful black dress in his hand.

"Here. See if this fits. I can't stand you in that hideous nightdress anymore."

She glanced down at herself. "Besides the dirt—which I blame on you—what exactly is wrong with it?"

"It's dull and plain and boring. All the things you are not. So take it off and put this on. At least this will keep you warmer until we can get you better clothes."

Talaith took the dress from him. Made of the finest wool, she'd guess it cost more gold than all her dresses put together. Still, her rescuer had no pockets whether dragon or man, so where did he get this from?

"Where did you find this dress?"

He pointed back where he'd come from. "Caravan on the road."

Talaith shuddered. Now she knew those screams had been all too real. "Are you telling me you killed the girl whose dress this is?"

"No. That's not what I'm telling you. She ran away screaming. As did her rather plump handmaidens. The soldiers with her, though—"

She held her hand up. "Please don't."

"Don't feel bad for them. They're enemies of my brother's mate . . . I think. Maybe. Anyway, it was like two birds . . . one stone."

When she only stared at him, he held up the satchel. "Hurry and get changed so you can eat. They had bread and cheese."

Sighing, Talaith placed the dress down carefully and proceeded to turn her back to the dragon and remove her nightdress. Once naked, she quickly scooped the dress back up and hastily put it on, knowing the dragon watched her every move.

She tied the bodice and turned to face the dragon. "Well?"

He smiled warmly. And for the first time ever, Talaith felt beautiful. "Much better."

She reached for the nightdress, intent on washing it as soon as she could manage, but a small blast of fire beat her to it, destroying the garment in seconds.

She looked at the dragon, one eyebrow raised. "Was that *really* necessary?"

He shrugged. "I *really* hated that nightdress."

"I think I'm grasping that."

She was hungry. That's what she said. Even after the bread and cheese. So, a few hours into their flight, he landed in a clearing and now they walked through the forest toward a town so they could get her food. And the entire time she kept talking. Constantly.

Mostly it was complaining. But some of it was observations about everything. Constantly.

"Shouldn't you be living in a cave somewhere, waiting for virgins to be thrown at your feet or something?"

"Well, I—"

"I mean, exactly how long are we going to keep this lunacy going?"

"Look, I—"

"Did you ever consider how *I* might feel about all this? No. Wait. Don't bother answering that one. I can well imagine your feelings on what us lowly humans think."

She looked at him over her shoulder. "Well? Aren't you going to say something?"

When he only laughed at her, she stomped away muttering to herself.

"Don't be mad," he called after her. She stopped walking and turned to face him. "I'm just not used to so much . . . uh . . . conversation."

Her eyes narrowed. By the moment, she seemed to become less and less fearful of his dragonform. Shame she couldn't say the same about when he was human. "Are you saying I talk too much?"

"You *don't* think you talk too much?" He sauntered up to her, enjoying the view of her in her lovely new dress. Although nothing could quite beat how beautiful she was naked. Slipping that horrid nightdress off her the previous eve had made all he'd had to endure since taking her quite worth it. "Not that I don't enjoy the sound of your voice."

That surprised her. "You do?"

"Aye." He circled her, his tail sweeping in front of her. "You're beautiful. Intelligent. A little mean."

"I am not!"

"And clearly hiding something."

Her body tensed at that, but she didn't say anything. He slid his tail gently around her legs, enjoying the little shiver he caused her. "Aren't you? Hiding something?"

"If I was, do you actually think I'd tell you?"

"Fair point. Still . . ." He dragged his tail up her legs and across her ass.

She gave a little squeal and slapped at it. "Stop doing that!"

"You're much too smart and well-spoken to be some mere peasant. You say you can read and write. Therefore, definitely not peasant stock. You're from Alsandair, yet you have no family close by. I've never met a female from the desert lands who traveled this far north without another female or their kin. Add in that Magick—untapped, mind you—just pours off your body like rainwater and you make me think that perhaps you hide something."

She stood silent, staring straight ahead.

"Who are you really, little human?"

Dark eyes focused on his face. "I am a Nolwenn witch." It was an evasive answer, but it fascinated him nonetheless.

"Nolwenn witch? Here?" Now he was truly confused.

"Why in the world would a Nolwenn witch live with that buffoon you married?"

"My mother disowned me long ago. So . . . I . . . left. Came north."

Briec sat back on his haunches. "Disowned you? But Nolwenn witches can only have one child. Usually a girl, I believe."

"I know!" she snapped. "Do you not think I know my own people?"

"But what, little witch, could you have done to get your mother to disown the only child she would ever have?"

"I fell in love."

Ah. Now he understood. Nolwenn witches never mated for life. Only to breed and to satisfy inherent needs or for certain Magickal rights. They never took another as their mate. Instead their lives belonged to their demanding desert gods and the Magick.

"Your husband?"

"No. Another. And before you ask, he died. Long ago."

"Your mother wouldn't take you back?"

"I never asked."

"You are *fascinating*." She truly was. A Nolwenn witch? Here? He must introduce her to his sister, a white dragonwitch. Only their mother, the Dragon Queen, held more power than his sister.

Briec had another thought. "How old are you?"

She sighed. "Thirty-two winters. Soon thirty-three. Why?"

"You're a babe." Like dragons, Nolwenns weren't immortal, but they could live up to six or seven hundred years.

"Perhaps as dragons go, but witch or no, I'm still a human."

"I know. Tragic really."

"And why is that tragic?"

"Because . . ." He gave a little sniff of disdain. "Humans are so weak, annoying, whiny, and stupid." She opened her mouth to speak, but he cut her off. "But that's why I find you so fascinating. You're none of those things. Except annoying."

She huffed. Several times, in fact, before she turned and stomped off. She kept doing that, too. Stomping off.

"Were we done talking?"

"Yes."

He followed after her. "But I have more questions."

"You can stick your questions up your ass."

He slammed his tail in front of her. "I don't think I heard you, little witch."

"You heard me just fine and stop threatening me with that thing!" She kicked his tail.

By the gods, she was absolutely adorable!

"I wasn't threatening you. I was halting your progress. Trust me . . . you'll know if I'm threatening you. Now"— he settled back down—"where were we? Ah, yes. There's something you need to explain to me."

Sighing in resignation, she asked, "What?"

"Nolwenn witches are powerful from birth."

"Some. If all the proper spells are done before, during, and after the birth," she answered as she began to suddenly walk around him picking wildflowers. Seemed odd. She didn't exactly appear to be the flower-picking type.

"Yet although Magick surrounds you, it's not truly . . . harnessed."

"True enough." She walked behind him, still picking flowers. "I have not practiced or studied since I left Alsandair."

"I see. Well, perhaps I could—" He'd turned around to speak to her directly, but she was no longer behind him.

Briec glanced around, quickly realizing it wasn't that she was no longer behind him. She was no longer there.

The little bitch was gone!

Talaith crouched on the highest branch that could hold her weight. It hadn't been easy getting above him and out of his eye range so quickly . . . the beast was huge. She glared down at the big silver head of that arrogant idiot.

Irritating? I'm irritating? Did he have absolutely no concept of what a bastard he was? Clearly not, otherwise he would have let her go.

But he was "determined" to have her. No. No. No. That would not be happening. She'd done some strange and stupid things, but having a dragon between her legs would not be one of them.

Concentrating, Talaith slowed her breathing and heart rate. Dragons had amazing hearing, her trainers said, so she used all her skills to make sure he wouldn't hear her. She faded into the shadow of the branches and leaves, so his dragon eyes wouldn't spot her.

The only thing she couldn't control was his keen sense of . . .

The dragon sniffed the air, then looked right at her. "There you are, my little witch."

Dammit.

Before she could even think about climbing back down, he grabbed hold of the tree with his two front claws and shook it. Screaming, Talaith went flying. But that damn tail of his caught her seconds before she hit the ground.

"Now that was amazing, little witch. Tell me, where did you learn to move so fast and to disappear so well? In your little village after baking the morning bread?"

He laughed at his own joke, walking again toward town with her still wrapped up in his tail.

"Yes, I was right about you. You are *fascinating.* You and I will find such pleasure together, my little witch."

Could I hate him more? She thought about it for a moment. *No, I could not hate him any more than I already do.*

Chapter 6

The chatter in the pub they decided to go to for food was interesting, to say the least. Lots of talk about angry gods and horrible storms. Plus, they feared the coming of the Black Moon.

Of course that wasn't the correct name of the powerful moon, but she'd given up hope that the Northerners had any real knowledge of other cultures. Besides, she had bigger issues at the moment.

The only thing she currently worried about was getting away from one annoyingly determined dragon. He leaned back in the booth they'd luckily found in a quiet corner. She'd feared they'd have to sit out at one of the long tables on a bench. As it was, the dragon was hard to miss. Even with the hood of his black cape covering that silver mane of hair and the chainmail shirt and leggings he wore— apparently one in that doomed caravan had been close to his size—he received looks wherever he went. How could he not? He towered over everyone. Add in that he practically had to drag her along behind him, and the two of them stood out quite loudly to the general populace.

What she didn't understand, what she would *never* understand, is why she hadn't screamed yet. Why hadn't she yelled for help? They'd passed a magistrate on their way to the pub. One of the few towns that actually had one, and although he watched them with intense interest, she never screamed or tried to pull away. Instead, she only stared back.

Resting her chin in her hand, Talaith stared into her beer. She knew exactly why she didn't yell for help. He might get hurt. Even killed. She didn't want that. As much as she detested him—oh, and she did detest him—she still didn't want to be responsible for his death. She merely wanted him to let her go. But if the town turned on him before he had a chance to shift or if he shifted and took the town with him . . . she'd never forgive herself either way.

She could almost hear her mother whispering in her ear, "Talaith, Daughter of Haldane—you are an idiot."

And the dragon wondered why she didn't run back to her mother for solace. She, of all people, knew that welcome home would be less than pleasant.

"You're deep in your thoughts, little witch. What worries you?"

"You know if you keep calling me that someone will slash my face open."

He frowned in confusion. "That's no longer the law."

"Really?"

"Really. It has actually been against the law for about three years. Since the new . . ." he sniffed in that arrogant way he had and said, ". . . *queen* has been in power."

Talaith stared down at her mug and kept her face neutral even as her hand tightened around the cup. "A *new* queen?"

"Aye. The Butcher of Garbhán Isle is long dead. His sister took his head and his throne."

"I see."

"Did you not know of this?"

They told her it was coming—that *she* was coming—but no one had told her it had already happened. "No. Lord Hamish didn't allow information in or out of the towns without his express approval. Those spreading rumors were usually dragged away in the middle of the night to his dungeons."

The dragon rolled his violet eyes in barely concealed disgust. "I don't like that little man."

She finally smiled. "Only *you* would think him little."

"Very true."

She licked her lips and carefully asked, "Do you know the, uh, new queen?"

"I choose not to speak of her," he answered distractedly. He sat forward abruptly. "I itch to be off."

Talaith groaned, unable to hide her distaste for flying. "Can't we walk?"

"With storms coming? I think not, little witch. So drink up so we can be off. I grow weary of all these"—he glanced around—"humans."

"Trust me"—she sneered before tossing back her ale in one gulp—"that feeling has become mutual."

The townsfolk had been correct. A storm was coming. A bad one. Briec could smell it in the air. But it was moving fast, a lot faster than he was. Although he'd have no problems braving an ice storm, he couldn't do that to her. These humans and their frail skin, she'd freeze to death before he ever made it home.

So, grudgingly, he headed to the one safe place he knew of in a thousand leagues.

They landed inside the cave as the winds picked up and the first drops of rain and flakes of snow fell on his wings. Thankfully, she'd stopped squealing during this flight, but she insisted on keeping a brutal death grip on his hair.

"You can let me go now."

"Are you sure?"

He smiled at the trepidation in her voice.

"Yes. I'm sure. Unless you want me to shift to human while you're—"

"*No!*" She cleared her throat. "I mean, no need."

Her fingers untangled from his hair as he lowered himself to the ground so she could slip off.

She took several steps away from him, wrapping her arms around her body for warmth. "Is this your den?"

"No. But we'll never make it in this storm. At least you won't." And he wasn't willing to risk her.

"You sure we'll be safe here?"

"Aye." He moved away from her, heading deep into the cave. "You wait here. I won't be long."

"Yes," she called after him. "What fun I'll have standing around in this dank, dark cavern waiting around for *you.*"

Ignoring her sarcasm, Briec went to head off the trouble he knew was lurking around somewhere in this place.

After five minutes, the storm turned deadly. She couldn't remember seeing a storm this bad in all her years in this northern land. But when lightning bounced off two stones outside the cave only to ricochet inside and nearly take her head, she decided waiting around for the dragon's return might not be in her best interest.

Unsure what else to do, but knowing she couldn't just stand there, Talaith headed deeper into the cave. It didn't take much time to find a long corridor lit with torches. Sighing in relief at the soothing golden light, she strolled down the rocky path, almost able to ignore the massive bouts of thunder exploding outside the stone walls surrounding her.

She passed huge naturally formed chambers. Some were empty except for a big boulder or two, but as she moved along, she found the others filled with furniture, clothes, statues. Some chambers so large they held entire carriages. And one had gold coin and treasure from the dirt floor to her hip.

She paused at that one. She hadn't seen gold since she'd last been to her father's home, when she would sneak off to meet him. Smiling at the brief memory of, as her mother called him, "the one who gave me the seed which allowed for your presence," she again strolled down the hall. After a few more steps, she stopped. Froze, really.

How long had he been following her? Watching her? True, she could stand here forever, terrified. But hadn't she done enough of that for the last two days?

So, steeling herself against what awaited her, she slowly turned.

"Well, hello, pretty lady."

It spoke. An enormous gold dragon with a gold mane of hair that swept across the cave floor spoke to her.

Why not? This sort of thing must be common among those of us going insane.

Most people never met one dragon. Somehow Talaith had managed to meet two. Could her life be any more unmanageable? Probably not.

He leaned down a bit and sniffed her. "Ah, big brother's about, I see. Are you his gift to me?"

Talaith growled. She tired of arrogant, smirking dragons assuming she existed only to be their plaything. Actually, she'd grown tired of *everything* male. The entire male species merely horrid beings meant to do nothing more than destroy all that existed around them.

Enunciating each word clearly so there'd be no confusion, "No, you arrogant, half-witted bastard. I am not here for you."

Startled, the dragon sat back on his haunches. "I . . . uh . . ."

"What? Am I supposed to be quaking in fear of you?" Purposely keeping her voice low and controlled, she stepped closer to him. "Should I be sobbing and begging for mercy? Well, I'd rather burn in the farthest reaches of hell before I give you or that arrogant, half-witted brother of yours the satisfaction."

She thought for sure she'd die. Thought for sure she'd finally pushed her luck to the breaking point. Especially when he went down face first on the ground and repeatedly slammed his claw against the rocky floor, shaking the cave.

Surprisingly, though, death did not seem his purpose. Laughter, however . . .

Even more evident when he rolled that giant dragon body onto its back and laughed harder. Hysterically, almost. Powerful dragon limbs flailing and everything.

Eventually, her silver dragon charged in. She'd started to learn his different expressions and moods. Right now he appeared concerned.

He stared at the gold lying on the ground literally rolling around in laughter then at her. "What did you do?"

Incredulous, she snapped, "*Me?*"

The gold looked up at the dragon. "*She is going to make your life a living hell, brother!*" Then he exploded into another round of violent laughter, again rolling back and forth across the floor.

Growling, the silver grabbed the gold around the throat and picked him up, placing him on his feet. The gold hit him to get the silver claw off his throat. So the silver hit him back. They stared at each other for several seconds, then the battle was on.

Not bothering to look back, Talaith ran, praying she could avoid getting buried alive with two idiotic dragons.

Éibhear the Blue opened his eyes when she sat on his tail, which lay happily buried under Gwenvael's gold. He'd come to his older brother's den to wait out the coming storm and had settled his bulk under one of the many piles of gold Gwenvael had scattered around.

He'd always been good at disappearing. Especially for a dragon.

Still, he never expected to find anything as interesting as this among Gwenvael's treasures.

A woman. Human. Very pretty. And reeking of his big

brother's scent. Briec with a human? The queen wouldn't like this one bit. She'd barely learned to accept Fearghus's mate.

Slowly, so as not to startle her, he drew himself over to her until his snout rested by her leg. She didn't notice him right away, cringing every time the cave walls shook—*Briec and Gwenvael must be having one of their "discussions"*—or stones fell from the ceiling, just missing her head. He knew, however, the instant she became aware of his presence.

Her entire body tensed, her eyes closed, and she moaned in despair. "Exactly how much am I expected to take?" she asked no one in particular. Éibhear said nothing, figuring she'd look at him in her own good time. And, she did.

"Hello."

She sighed. "Blue. You're blue."

"I'm Éibhear the Blue." After eighty-seven years, he never tired of saying that.

"Of course you are." She rubbed her eyes with her fists. "Exactly how many more dragons are there?"

Éibhear wasn't sure what she meant or even if she was speaking to him, so he decided to ask, "Here, m'lady, or in the entire world?"

Without taking her hands away from her eyes, she snapped, "Why would I give a centaur's shit about the entire world?"

A known fact among their kind was that Éibhear was the most tolerant of his entire kin. He liked humans as a general rule and called many among them friend. That didn't mean, however, he had to let someone yell at him for no good reason.

Slowly, Éibhear moved away from her. But she didn't really notice until he pulled his tail out from under her and her butt slammed down hard with the pile of gold that had been covering him.

"Ow." Gorgeous, dark brown eyes turned to him. "What did you do that for?"

He shrugged. "I thought you wished to be alone."

Another crash came from deeper inside the cave and the walls trembled. She pulled her legs in tighter and wrapped her arms around her body. "No," she answered as she stared up at the ceiling, clearly terrified it would crash on top of her at any moment. "I do not wish to be alone. It will be nice to be buried alive with another. We'll keep each other company in the afterlife."

Taking a deep breath, she admitted, "I'm just so tired. I'm sorry if I offended you."

"Oh, you didn't." Éibhear wanted to put her at ease, so he laid the tip of his snout on her raised knees. "I completely understand."

Talaith stared down at the blue dragon snout lying dangerously close to her face. *Ah, well, this makes sense.* And although she should at least feel wariness if not outright terror at this dragon, she didn't. Something about him simply put her at ease. She couldn't explain it and, at the moment, she didn't want to.

"My brothers will stop anytime now," he said reassuringly. "Usually when one or the other starts bleeding."

"Aren't you worried?"

"About?"

"The sturdiness of this cave."

"Ah. This cave was here long before any of us were born, and will be here long after we go home to our ancestors."

Another loud bang shook the walls, and Talaith placed her hand on the dragon's head. For some unknown reason, she found it comforting.

In response, the blue snuggled in closer to her, sighing contentedly when she ran her hand through his hair. She couldn't resist—*it was blue!*

"What is your name, m'lady?"

Even the dragon who had her for nearly two days never

asked her that—as if he couldn't be bothered. "Talaith. I am Talaith."

"Very pretty name, m'lady."

Still stroking the silky hair, Talaith finally gave a very small smile. "I am no lady, dragon. Merely the only daughter of a merchant." *And the chosen one of a goddess who is to . . . hmmm, probably shouldn't mention that.*

"I've met many with rank. You're more royalty than most of them."

Laughing, "You don't even know me."

The enormous dragon lifted his head and beautiful silver eyes focused on her. As he looked her over, she didn't feel naked and uncomfortable at all, as she seemed to when the silver dragon did the same thing. No, she knew in her heart this dragon was simply assessing the situation before him.

His eyes narrowed dangerously. "Lady, what happened to your neck?" His snout gently brushed her throat where she'd hung from the town noose while they prepared the stake.

When she didn't cringe at him being so close, she felt quite proud.

Shrugging, "My entire village tried to hang me yesterday morn."

And as easily as he showed kindness, he grew angry. "Why would anyone do that to you?"

"Because I am a witch."

He sniffed with indignation. "Well, of course you are. I can see the Magick all around you. But what about your family? Was there no one to protect you?"

She couldn't help it, she chuckled. "My husband led them, Éibhear." *Gods, Talaith. That's not funny.*

He growled low and black smoke curled from his nostrils. "Do you want me to kill them? I can destroy a village you know. I can destroy them all."

"That is very, um, sweet of you. But do not waste your time. Leave them to their ignorance, Éibhear. I can no longer be bothered."

Staring a moment more, he nodded before placing his head back on her knees. "As you wish. But please let me know if you change your mind."

Talaith grinned as she hadn't in ages. "I will, Éibhear. I promise."

Gwenvael held up his claw. "Stop. Stop." He wiped his snout and looked at his gold talons. "Ack! Blood. I'm bleeding! Death comes for me!"

Briec rolled his eyes, annoyed beyond reason by his idiot brother's antics. "Oh, grow a spine."

Gwenvael roared and crouched down, prepared to charge him again, when Briec suddenly noticed his human had fled.

"Where's the woman?"

Immediately Gwenvael became distracted. One just needed to mention something female and he became distracted. Gwenvael's sexual prowess rivaled only by their grandfather's.

"I don't know." He glanced around. "She was standing here a moment ago."

Briec glared at his kin. "*You* scared her off."

"*I* scared her off?"

Letting out an exasperated sigh, Briec sniffed the air and followed her scent. Not surprisingly, Gwenvael followed right behind him. *Nosy bastard.*

"So where did you find her? She's quite lovely."

"At her village. And stay away from her."

He had the nerve to sound affronted, when he said, "Why, brother. I would never—"

"Don't bother. Fearghus already told me what you did with that mate of his."

"I was only playing. Honestly, none of you have a sense of humor."

"And from what I heard, neither did his mate. By the way, how is your neck? I heard she put a dagger to it."

"It's fine, thank you. And why don't you ever use her name?"

"Don't see a reason. She is of no consequence to me."

Briec stopped walking and again sniffed the air. Gritting his fangs, he turned to Gwenvael and together they said, "Éibhear."

Talaith glanced up as the silver and gold dragons stomped into the chamber. As soon as the silver saw her, his eyes narrowed, and she had the overwhelming desire to protect Éibhear.

"What the hell do you think you're doing?"

Éibhear, who'd shifted back into human and graciously put on a pair of black breeches out of respect to Talaith, fairly ignored his brother as he tilted her head back a bit more to get at her wounded neck.

"What does it look like I'm doing?"

"Don't backtalk me. I asked you a question."

"And I don't see the need to answer it. As it is, I'm so angry at you right now, I don't even want to see your face."

"What are you talking about?"

Unable to stop herself, Talaith sucked her breath in between her teeth and cringed. Éibhear's face softened as he looked at her.

"I'm sorry. This will only take a minute or so more." *By the gods . . . that voice!* She nearly envied the woman who would wake up every morning to that voice greeting her. Of course, the silver dragon's was nothing to sneer at. Only his made her think of dirty, dirty things.

"That's all right. I'm fine."

By sheer force of will, Talaith stood her ground while Éibhear gently smoothed on more cream. He said his sister, a fellow witch, had created it and that it would manage the pain of the rope burn on her neck. The blue dragon had been horrified when he realized his brother had not taken care of her wound. Of course, Talaith knew she would have never let the silver dragon get that close to her.

Plus it had completely "slipped" her mind that he'd asked her to remind him to care for her neck. The big bastard should have remembered without her reminding him.

All right, Talaith. Now you sound like a wife.

Éibhear motioned for her to lift up her hair as he moved around to get where the noose had dug into the skin behind the backs of her ears.

"Did you never think to treat this, big brother?"

By the startled look on the silver's face, followed by the glare in Talaith's direction, he remembered quite well their earlier conversation.

"She'd promised to remind me."

"Remind you?" Éibhear stood behind her, but she heard the annoyance and outrage in his voice.

The gold leaned back on his haunches and shook his head. "How could you? You bastard."

"Shut. Up."

The gold glanced at her and winked. *Cheeky idiot.*

"Fine," Éibhear went on. "I understand how that could slip your mind. But while I'm doing this"—he gently moved some of her stray hairs out of his way—"why don't you introduce us, big brother?"

"Oh. Of course." The silver cleared his throat, opened his giant maw to speak . . . but nothing came out.

Éibhear kept putting on the ointment, but the gold clearly expected his brother to introduce them properly. When he said nothing, the gold balked.

"*Are you telling me you don't know her name?*" the gold demanded.

"Well, I, uh—"

Stepping away from her, Éibhear closed up the jar of ointment as she released her hair. Her eyes began to water from the pain and she wondered about the logic of allowing

Éibhear to put that dragon-created junk on her human flesh. The dragon witch probably made it for something with scales.

Éibhear dropped the jar in a small bag he had with him. "He's had her since yesterday."

The gold's eyes practically exploded from his head, then he burst out laughing.

Talaith said nothing as Éibhear pushed her hair off her face to examine a small scrape on her forehead. But she knew the silver didn't appreciate the familiar move one damn bit. *Good.*

"It was an oversight," her kidnapper gave by way of explanation.

Éibhear's silver eyes locked on his brother. "*I* know her name. And I've known her about ten minutes."

"I'm Gwenvael the Handsome," the gold stopped laughing long enough to say. "At your service, m'lady." He made a low, sweeping bow and the silver brought his tail down on the back of the gold's head. "Ow! What was that for?"

"Accident," the silver snapped. He turned back to Éibhear. "This is none of your concern, baby brother. I saved her, therefore she—"

"If you say," she spit out between tightly clenched teeth, surprising them all, "I belong to you, one more time. I swear by all that's holy I will scream these walls down."

The three dragons silently stared at her. When she didn't back down or look away, the gold fell into another fit of laughter that caused the silver to roll his eyes practically to the back of his head.

"Hungry, m'lady?" Éibhear asked as he stood beside her. It suddenly occurred to her the pain no longer plagued her.

She almost sighed in relief, but instead said, "Starved."

He held his arm out. Like the rest of him, his arm was big and muscular. In fact, his human form was bigger than even the silver's. "Then let's get you fed."

She took his arm gratefully, and they headed toward the

exit. As she passed the silver, she stopped and looked up at him.

"And the name is Talaith, in case you were wondering."

With that, the pair walked off, but she could still hear the gold's hysterical laughter tormenting his brother.

After Briec slammed Gwenvael's head into the floor a few thousand times, he shifted into human, yanked on a pair of breeches and boots and went in search of his human.

Talaith.

A very pretty name. It fit her. And he probably should have asked her what her name was . . . he just didn't think of it. She'd never believe it, but the woman distracted him. To be honest, he was surprised he could remember his own name when in her presence.

Besides, it's not like she took a breath long enough during her constant chatter to allow him to ask her much of anything. Especially important questions like who the hell she really was. He had no doubt she was truly a Nolwenn witch, but she was much more than that. So very much more.

It didn't take long to track down the pair. Like all his kin, Gwenvael had set up several of the cave alcoves for the possibility of humans stopping by. He had several furnished with beds, chests for their clothes, bookcases. Whatever they may need. This particular chamber had a dining table and cooking pit. A lamb slowly roasted over the open flame while Talaith and Éibhear ate fruit, bread, and cheese. When he walked in she was laughing, turned in her chair to face his brother. She looked . . . comfortable.

He stopped before reaching them and tried to understand this awkward *new* feeling. No. He wasn't liking this one bit either. He felt it now every time he looked at her. The feeling that he'd give anything merely to hold her close.

Briec shook his head. Exactly what had this woman

done to him? Damn Nolwenn witches. Apparently even the untrained ones cast spells.

His brother and Talaith looked up at his approach. And as soon as she saw him, her smile faded and her laughter died. She sat straight in her chair, turning to face the table.

He frowned at Éibhear in concern, but his brother merely raised an eyebrow as if to say, "What exactly did you expect?"

Briec sat one seat over from Talaith. He grabbed a fruit, put his feet up on the table, and proceeded to eat while watching her. She fussed with her hair, scratched her wrist and hand, and basically appeared uncomfortable.

What the hell am I doing wrong? Éibhear and Gwenvael never seemed to have these problems with humans. Especially female humans.

"So have you eaten well?"

She nodded without looking at him. "Yes."

"What about that?" He motioned to the cooking meat.

Éibhear yawned and scratched the back of his head. "That's for later tonight."

Still Talaith refused to meet his gaze.

He motioned to the chamber exit with a nod of his head. In response Éibhear shook his head.

Briec barely caught his roar in time. "Éibhear, would you mind excusing us?"

"As a matter of fact, I would mind."

"Don't test me, little brother." His patience was waning. Had been since he'd first set eyes on this woman. He'd had a vain hope they'd make it back to his den this evening and he'd be between her thighs before the suns rose the following day.

Clearly that wouldn't be happening now.

Talaith laid her small hand over Éibhear's much bigger one. Briec's eyes narrowed, focusing on where their hands met. Another new feeling. Somewhat territorial, which belonged to all dragons when it came to their treasure, but something more. Something he didn't like one bit.

"It's all right, Éibhear," she assured his blue-haired bastard, baby brother. "I'll be fine."

"All right then. But call me if you need me."

If he didn't know the snot-nosed little cretin was being sincere, he'd rip out his lungs.

With one last glare at Briec, Éibhear left. Once alone, Briec dropped his feet to the ground. "Talaith—"

"Oh. So you're using my name . . . now that you actually know it."

Briec sighed. "I simply didn't think it was—"

"I don't even know your name," she cut in.

He blinked in surprise. "Really? I . . . I just assumed Éibhear would have told you by now."

"Is that his job then? To make sure everyone knows your name since you don't have the decency to introduce yourself?"

It appalled him he was allowing some human to speak to him like this. And it appalled him even more he cared he might have hurt her.

"Fine. My name is Briec. Briec the Mighty." He truly did not appreciate the snorted laugh that followed his statement. "What's so funny?"

"It just . . ." She cleared her throat. "It took me by surprise is all. I thought you'd be Briec the Silver like Éibhear is 'the Blue.'"

"I *was* Briec the Silver. When I was much younger. But once you make a name for yourself that usually changes."

"And what about Briec the Arrogant? That seems much more fitting."

"It's Briec the Mighty, little witch."

"Mighty, huh? Did you give yourself that name?"

"No," he practically spat in slow, measured tones. "I did not."

"I was just asking. No need to get testy."

He was glad to finally see her smile, he simply didn't appreciate it was at his expense.

"Talaith, understand, I didn't ask your name because—"

She turned suddenly in her chair to face him. "Are you physically unable to say you're sorry?"

That stopped him cold. "Pardon?"

"The words, 'I'm sorry.' Are you unable to speak them?"

Briec thought for a moment. "You know, I don't think I've ever said it." He thought a moment longer, then shook his head. "No. I've never said it before."

"Isn't it time you started? Just tell me you're sorry instead of making all these excuses."

He looked down into that beautiful face, torn between wanting the return of the cowering female paralyzed by dragonfear and this sarcastic, argumentative female he had the feeling he'd never recover from. "Is that really necessary?"

"Yes."

He bent his neck to the side and heard the bones crack.

"Here, Briec the Mighty, try it with me." She leaned forward. "I'm sorry, Talaith."

Suddenly Briec couldn't look away from those eyes. They snared him as sure as a war party's nets. When he finally said the words, he nearly whispered them, unable to find his voice. "I'm sorry, Talaith."

She blinked in surprise, most likely guessing she'd never get him to say it. She tried to pull away, but he slipped his hand behind the back of her neck and tugged her closer while he leaned over the chair between them.

"Briec?"

"Sssh."

He had to kiss her. Simply had to. He moved in closer, nearing his goal.

"So what's to eat?"

Briec's head snapped up at the sound of Gwenvael's voice. And before he could consider the consequences of his actions, he sent a ball of flame that shoved the dragon's human form completely out of the chamber.

As soon as he did it, he knew his mistake. He turned

around, black smoke still curling from his nostrils, to find Talaith staring at him. Her eyes wide, her mouth open.

"Talaith—"

She shook her head. "No. No. Everything's fine." Of course, she said that as she pried his fingers off her neck and leaned away from him.

Talaith no longer had the dragonfear, but that didn't mean she wasn't wary. She went back to her fruit and cheese as Briec desperately worked to control his human body.

Glancing at him out of the corner of her eye, she said, "Um, so, how long you think this weather will last then?"

Accepting his defeat for the moment, Briec shrugged. "I don't know. But hopefully not long."

Hopefully not long at all. His desire for this strange female was beginning to affect his normally logical mind.

And he didn't like it one damn bit.

Talaith stood at the mouth of the alcove and stared. "This is amazing," she murmured.

"Dragons like water. One of my brothers has a lake in his den."

She nodded as she examined the steaming hot springs. There were eight in varying sizes, replenished from an outside water supply according to Gwenvael. He'd bragged about them all through the delicious lamb dinner Éibhear made. The more he talked about it, the more she wanted to try them out. She hadn't had a bath since the dragon dunked her in the lake after she'd vomited.

"You going to get in or just stand there with your mouth open . . . drool coming out."

She glared at him. "Very funny." Talaith stepped inside, letting the light fragrant steam wrap around her. It was warm but not uncomfortably hot. Crouching down, she tested the water with her finger, relieved to discover it was hot but not searing—with dragons you could never be too sure, their idea of uncomfortably hot differing from most. With renewed eagerness, her fingers went to the ribbon tying her bodice together, quickly undoing it. But as she started to strip off her dress, Talaith realized Briec leaned back against the wall and watched her.

"Could you excuse me?" she asked.

"No," he answered.

"Will you not let me enjoy anything?"

"That's a bit unfair." He grinned. "I merely thought we could enjoy it together."

"Well, you thought wrong."

Briec sighed. "Do you really dislike me that much, little witch?"

"It isn't that I dislike you so much, big, fat dragon. It's that I don't like you enough."

"You're cruel." And she knew he teased.

"Aye. So I've been told. Too cruel for you." She put her hands on his chest and tried her best to shove the big ox from the chamber. "Find yourself a willing woman. A dragoness perhaps. Someone who actually finds you charming."

He took hold of her hand and brought it to his lips. "I'll leave you, little witch."

"Thank you—"

"For now."

Talaith bit her lip as Briec slipped her index finger into his mouth. His tongue swirled around the tip before gently sucking. His eyes stayed on Talaith's, unwilling to let her go.

Her sex went dripping wet, her strong legs went weak. Another minute of this exquisite torture and she'd be flat on her back without another word.

All I wanted to do was take a bath. Now all she wanted to do was wrap herself around Briec the Arrogant like a jungle snake.

Using the same control she possessed to slow her heart rate and calm her breathing, Talaith pulled away from the dragon. "Well, that was . . . interesting." She took a step back. "*Now* if you'll excuse me."

Briec nodded, turned, and began to walk away. Stopped abruptly. Sniffed the air. Looked back at her with a grin. *Then* he walked off.

She glared at his retreating form and thought about all the wonderful ways she could eviscerate the beast.

Moving silently so as not to wake the sleeping Talaith, Briec lay down outside the cavern Gwenvael gave her for a room. It had an enormous bed. A table and chairs of the finest wood. A pitfire built right into one wall. It was nice and he'd give almost anything to share that bed with Talaith. But she still resisted him. He had no idea why. She wanted him. He knew it. She knew it.

They could be spending the entire night making each other very happy until they both passed out from the pleasure of it. Instead, she fought him. Fought him and herself as far as he was concerned.

Yet what truly baffled him? What would most likely keep him up for the entire night . . . why he cared? And why he enjoyed her fight so very much?

She sighed in her sleep and he crossed his eyes at the images that were inhabiting his delirious brain. Of her under him, sighing like that when he made her come, and come . . .

Stop, Briec. You're only torturing yourself. Painfully so.

Briec rested his dragon head on his arms and prayed for dawn. Dawn would bring the suns and his way out of this nightmare. Because, he knew, once he got his lovely, sweet Talaith back to his den, she'd be all his.

Chapter 7

"Where the hell are the suns?"

Talaith's head snapped up from her book at Briec's angry shout somewhere off in the cave.

Gwenvael, who'd fallen asleep at the table, jerked awake, screaming, *"I never touched her!"*

Éibhear sighed in disgust. "You never fail to embarrass me." He placed a bowl of hot porridge in front of Talaith. Where he learned to cook, she'd never know, but she appreciated it. He even made normally boring porridge delicious.

Gwenvael glared down at the bowl of porridge thrown in front of him. "Porridge? You want me to eat porridge?" He looked up at Éibhear. "Has your mind slipped since last night? Where's that horse I found the other day?"

Talaith, unable to hide her shock and not really wanting to, stared at Gwenvael in horror.

Éibhear cleared his throat and glared at his brother. "The horse, idiot brother o' mine, is safe and *alive* somewhere else."

"Come on, Talaith," Gwenvael implored. "You don't mind if we eat—"

"Yes. As a matter of fact, I do mind."

He gave her what must be his best "imploring" face. "But, Talaith . . . my love."

"Gwenvael . . ." she mimicked back to him, ". . . my pain."

Éibhear laughed hard as Briec entered the chamber wearing only black breeches and boots. *Does he have to look so . . . tasty?* He sat in one of the chairs across from Talaith, threw his feet up on the table, pushed his porridge away and grabbed a piece of fruit. All while glaring at her.

She stared back, then said, "What are you looking at?"

He motioned to the ceiling with his hand. "Are you responsible for this?"

She glanced up at the rocky ceiling. It was actually kind of pretty with its sparkly shards hanging down. Of course, then she thought about those dropping on her head and suddenly they looked like dangerous blades. Shaking off the scary image, Talaith looked back at a still glaring Briec. "I didn't do anything to the ceiling."

"Not the ceiling," he barked at her. "The weather."

She crossed her arms in front of her chest. "Has being around dragons given me some kind of god-like status I am not aware of?"

Out of the corner of her eye, she saw Éibhear bend his head over his porridge, desperately shoveling it into his mouth while Gwenvael simply laughed out loud.

Briec ignored his brothers and pointed an accusing finger at her. "You are the witch."

"An untrained one, as you so eloquently pointed out. Besides, why would I play with the weather and risk angering the gods?" Like she didn't have enough of that to worry about in general.

"Perhaps because you don't want to leave. You seem so comfortable with my brothers, little witch."

She leaned forward, ridiculously angry and loving every minute of it. For some strange reason, she felt completely safe arguing with this dragon—odd. "Because your brothers haven't been pawing me or trying to see me naked."

Gwenvael shrugged his massive shoulders. "Actually—"

Annoyed with the very sound of his voice, Talaith grabbed one of the fruits from the bowl near her plate and threw it. Her aim, as always, unerring. The large, round, and juicy fruit slammed into Gwenvael's head with unrelenting force.

"Ow! What was that for?"

"Accident," she snarled.

"Nice aim," Briec grumbled. "For a quiet little wife."

She turned to look at him, one eyebrow raised in challenge. "Your point?"

He growled, and she grinned. Which did nothing but piss the dragon off. But before he could do or say anything else, Éibhear looked up from his empty bowl. "So!"

Startled by his near shout, they all stared at him. "Doesn't seem like the rain will let up. What would everyone like to do today since we're stuck inside?"

Talaith pointed at the book on the table next to her bowl. "I've got this."

"You read?" For some unknown reason, Éibhear seemed ridiculously happy about this.

"Aye."

"She's a well-read peasant," Briec drawled out.

"I know where there are more books." Éibhear jumped up and was out of the cavern in seconds.

"But I already have a book," she said to no one in particular.

"I guess he feels you need more."

Her eyes locked on Briec. "What I need is to be let go."

"Why would I do that? Have you somehow fulfilled your blood debt to me without my knowledge?"

"I never asked for you to save me."

"Most likely because of that rope choking the life from you."

"Oh!" She stood. "I *hate* you. Perhaps you should go fly in the rain and lightning will strike you dead!"

Grabbing her book and ignoring her growling stomach, she turned and stormed from the cavern.

* * *

Gwenvael leaned back in his chair, his hand under his shirt so he could scratch his chest. The other hand rubbed his forehead where the fruit had made a rather unpleasant temporary dent. "So what is your obsession over this human female, brother?"

"She's . . ." Briec struggled for words.

"Strange?"

Briec frowned. "Compared to what?"

His brother had a point. No one in the dragon world ever referred to the Gwalchmai fab Gwyar kin as normal.

"She doesn't trust me," Briec added.

"That one trusts no one."

"Fearghus's mate trusts him."

So that's what this is about. He'd wondered about Briec's sudden interest in a human female. Now he knew. He wanted what Fearghus had. But what Fearghus had with Annwyl was special. Very, very special. "That's different, Briec. Annwyl is . . . well . . . Annwyl. And would you start using her name."

"Why? She's of no consequence to me."

More like Briec still hadn't forgiven her for backhanding him during one of her rages. As far as Briec was concerned—the most powerful human queen known to this world in the last ten thousand years didn't exist for him.

"But you still want what Fearghus has."

Briec looked up from the bowl of fruit in front of him, horror written all over his face. "Good gods! I'd rather remove my eyes than spend a minute in that woman's bed."

Gods, his family could be literal.

"I don't mean you want Annwyl, idiot. I mean you want the kind of relationship Fearghus has with Annwyl."

Briec shrugged and went back to his fruit. He chose two. "He does seem . . ."

"Happy?"

"As much as Fearghus can be." True. No one referred to Fearghus the Destroyer as the life of anyone's party. Their grandfather, Ailean, still held that title. Even Gwenvael hadn't quite managed to pass that old bastard's excesses. Of course all that was before Ailean met their grandmother—Shalin, Tamer of Ailean. A title well earned and held until her final days.

"Look, Briec, if you want anything close to what Fearghus has, you'll need to change some . . . things."

"But she hasn't even seen my den yet." Briec grabbed a hunk of cheese and bread. "She might like it."

Gwenvael struggled not to slap his older brother in the back of the head. Although he and Briec were close—no matter how much they fought—he still found him frustrating. Mostly because his arrogance could fill up an entire city.

"I meant you'll need to change some things about *you*."

"Me? Change? For her?" Now Briec leaned back in his chair, arms crossed over his chest. "Why would *I* change for a human? Any human?"

"If you want to be between her legs without her crying and praying for death, you better change."

"What am I doing wrong?"

"Everything."

"Specifics, brother."

"Telling her she belongs to you when you haven't even bed her yet is always a bad idea."

"Why? She does belong to me by dragon law."

Silently, Gwenvael sighed. This would take longer than he thought. Briec could be so stubborn. Almost as bad as their father.

"Dragon law only works, brother, if you want her as your slave. If that's what you want, then throw our laws in her face at every opportunity. But if you ever hope to have her bed you willingly the way Annwyl does Fearghus—and from what I've been able to figure out, she drains his cock dry—then I suggest you take another tack."

"Are you saying I have to seduce her?"

Gwenvael stared at his older brother. "What did you think?

She'd be so grateful for your rescue, she'd drop to her knees to service you?"

Briec fell silent for a moment, then he answered honestly. "Yes. As a matter of fact, I was expecting that."

Gwenvael shook his head. "It amazes me we have the same blood."

Returning to the fruit and cheese in front of him, Briec muttered, "It amazes me I didn't strangle you at birth. And why am I eating fruit? Where's that horse?"

Arzhela stared down at the bowed golden head of her favorite loyal servant. Unlike that bitch, Talaith, Hamish of Madron came to her of his own free will. He wanted power and she could provide it . . . as long as he remained loyal to her.

As always, and like a good dog, he came when called.

"The time has come, my son."

As was proper, he did not raise his eyes to look upon her. So she couldn't see his face, but she could sense his smile, she made sure he understood—with her victory would come his power and ascension. "But there is much to be done. Is all prepared?"

"Nearly, my goddess. My best warriors have been dispatched to track down that peasant. And my army is nearly assembled. A few more details and we'll be ready for your command."

"Good." She reached down and like her favorite hunting hound, she petted his head. "I know you will not fail me."

"Never. My life is yours, m'lady. It has always been yours."

She grinned and she knew he couldn't see her fangs. "I know, child. I know."

Another set of books dropped at Talaith's feet. She cringed. "Éibhear!"

He stopped. "What?"

"I think I have enough books."

"You sure?"

Talaith glanced around at the piles and piles of books that now surrounded her. Perhaps thirty books altogether. "I'm sure."

"Well, if you're sure." He stared at the books, a deep frown on his handsome face. Clearly he didn't feel confident she had enough to entertain her. Exactly how long did he think she'd be staying?

"Mind if I join you then?"

"Uh—" was all she managed before Éibhear, grinning, grabbed one of the books and sat on the floor, leaning against her chair.

"It's nice that you're here, Lady Talaith."

Talaith barely stifled her laugh at the title he'd given her, knowing the blue dragon was being sincere. "Thank you, Éibhear."

"Are you very miserable?"

Truth be told, she wasn't miserable at all. Uncomfortable, yes. A tad wary, absolutely. And the sounds of Briec and Gwenvael constantly fighting had begun to seriously wear on her frayed nerves. But, other than that, she was hardly miserable.

Some might actually interpret her current feelings as rather . . . contented. Although that made no sense to her. Trapped in a cave with three human-eating dragons—she should be terrified beyond all reason.

But she wasn't.

"Lady Talaith?"

Smiling, she reached over the arm of the chair and patted one of Éibhear's enormous shoulders. "I'm not miserable, Éibhear. And you don't have to call me lady. I'm not, actually."

"Aren't Nolwenn witches royalty?"

Now she did laugh. "Hardly. We're very political, that's true. We've been the advisors of many kings and queens over the centuries. But no Nolwenn witch born has been of royal blood."

"Ah. Well, you still seem like royalty to me."

"You're very sweet."

"I know." He leaned his head back so he could look at her, his blue hair falling across her arms and legs. "I'm the nice one."

"Are you now? And Gwenvael? Which one is he?"

"He's the whore."

Enjoying the conversation immensely, Talaith relaxed back in her chair, her legs tucked up under her. The wool dress she wore had been waiting for her on a chair beside her bed when she woke up that morning. She didn't know which brother left it for her, and she wasn't about to ask . . . but even she had to admit it looked wonderful on her. "And Briec?"

"The warrior."

Unable to stop herself, she snorted. "Is he? Really?"

Éibhear eagerly turned around so he could rest his arms on Talaith's lap and lean in close. By the Dark Gods of Fire, she'd never seen arms that large before. "Really. He's fought great battles for many years."

"And who did Briec battle? Some of my poor fellow humans?"

Solemnly, Éibhear answered, "To be honest, Briec doesn't consider fights with humans as battles. I think he sees that more as hunting. Or a snack that runs."

"What a lovely thought."

"My brother's battled other dragons. Those who would dare challenge our mother's throne. And he's never been defeated. Not once. They've written songs about his conquests and . . . uh, Talaith that really hurts."

Talaith looked down to see she'd reached over and gripped a handful of Éibhear's hair. "Oh. Sorry." She released him, absently petting his head. "Did you say your mother's *throne?*"

"Aye."

"Your mother is, um, the Dragon Queen?" One of the most brutal and powerful killers in the known world and Talaith somehow ended up in her children's laps. *Good one, Talaith*.

"Aye. Queen Rhiannon of the House of Gwalchmai fab Gwyar. First Born Daughter of Queen Addiena. First Born White . . ."

"So"—she cut him off before the litany of his mother's titles forced her to stab herself in the neck—"you're actually *Prince* Éibhear."

"I guess." He rested his head on her lap and instinctively Talaith dragged her hands through his blue hair, which no longer seemed that strange a thing to do.

"And Briec is Prince Briec?"

"Aye." He snuggled in closer, his eyes drifting shut. "Now don't you feel special, Lady Talaith? You've been kidnapped by royalty."

Chuckling, Talaith continued to stroke Éibhear's hair. "Oh, aye. This entire kidnapping takes on a whole new meaning, my friend."

Éibhear sighed, relaxing into her. "My mother used to do that."

"Do what? Be sarcastic?"

"No, no. No one does that quite like you. I mean—" He yawned. A big one. "She used to stroke my head like you're doing."

"She doesn't anymore?"

"No. She says I'm too old." His voice began to fade.

"Perhaps, but that's no worry to me, now is it?"

He didn't respond and she leaned over to see Éibhear had fallen dead asleep.

Smiling, she relaxed back and started to again read her book while gently stroking Éibhear's head.

* * *

At first he'd felt nothing but intense jealousy while he stayed back in the shadows and watched the pair. Especially when his little witch began petting his baby brother's head like that. But Éibhear's words humbled him. He didn't know his little brother thought so highly of him. Or bragged about him so. And, of course, seeing Talaith's face when she found out they were royalty . . . well, one really couldn't put a price on that.

Still, it was the way she stroked Éibhear's head that fascinated him. Nothing lusty about it at all. In fact, it was very maternal and sweet and warmed his heart as nothing ever had before. Too often he and Gwenvael had to hurt those who would take advantage of Éibhear's good nature. Or mock him for being kind. But Talaith, she let him be as kind as he wanted and never made fun of him for it or tried to take advantage.

Now the question became, how did he get Talaith this comfortable with him but without her feeling maternal? There had to be a way to get her to soften toward him. But the only time she seemed unafraid of him was when they were fighting. Gods, but the woman did love to fight.

Of course, when Briec thought about it, so did he.

If he were remotely human, he'd never see or hear her heading toward one of the lower exits out of his cave.

He should let her go. It wasn't wrong Briec took her from that village because he was truly rescuing her. But not to let her go once he got her to safety—only Briec would think that was perfectly acceptable.

Still, leaving without letting any of them know bothered him. And Éibhear was so fond of her, too. Plus, Gwenvael truly enjoyed the way she tortured his older brother. He'd pay her to stay if she would keep that up.

Her body melded into the shadows—she'd changed into all black—and she moved silently. Yes, her skills truly did impress him and now Gwenvael understood why Briec seemed to constantly question her.

This woman was no mere peasant.

She stood a stone's throw from the mouth of the cave, but she wouldn't move. Her eyes scanned around. She sensed him. *Very impressive.* He waited, wondering how long before she caught sight of him. For another minute or so, she continued to search the area with her eyes. She knew he was there, she just didn't know where.

Finally, she stood up straight and her head fell back so she looked up at the ceiling—and him.

"Talaith."

Even though he kept his voice calm, because he felt no anger at her escape attempt—she wasn't *his* female—she still screamed. Like a banshee.

She ran, too. Right toward the exit and the ongoing storm outside. But he ran along the ceiling until he passed her, then he dropped down in front of her, shaking the cave walls and blocking her way out.

"Oh, no you don't." He sat back on his haunches and stared at her.

She quickly crouched before him, a dagger drawn, and inched back step by step. This was a woman who knew how to protect herself. He liked that. Weak females bored his kind, so Briec had chosen well.

"Move, dragon."

He fought his urge to laugh at her order. What exactly did she expect to do with that tiny blade? Especially with her usually powerful voice sounding shaky from fear.

"I can't. My brother would have my head."

"I don't belong to him."

"No, but you'll have to fight that fight yourself, beautiful. Now"—he motioned in the opposite direction with the tip of his tail—"go back to Briec."

"I'm not a dog. And what is wrong with your tail?" She frowned. "It's missing something."

Unwilling to discuss the betrayal of his kin and the day those bastard brothers of his cut off the tip, Gwenvael brought his tail up so he could wrap it around her waist and carry her back to his brother. But she latched onto it with one hand and used the other to plant her blade between her teeth. While Gwenvael was still trying to understand what the hell she may be up to, he raised his tail, allowing her to jump from it to his forearm. Next thing he knew, she climbed onto his snout and over the top of his head.

"What in bloody—"

Then he saw her dagger. How could he miss it? She aimed it straight at his eye. He swatted at her with his claw. He didn't knock her off, but it startled her enough she stabbed his head scant inches from her original target.

"*Aaaaaaarrrrrrrrgggggggggggghhh! You mad cow!*"

He didn't want to hurt her, but he had no choice. Especially when she yanked her blade back and took aim again.

Using his tail, he slammed her from behind, sending Talaith flying. She hit the ground with a grunt, but smartly rolled with the landing.

She ended up on her back, the dagger still clenched in her hand. He didn't wait for her to get up. He wrapped his tail around her, making sure her arms were pinned at her sides and headed back into his cave.

Morfyd the White, Dragonwitch of House of Gwalchmai fab Gwyar, First Born Daughter of Dragon Queen Rhiannon, Vassal to Queen Annwyl of Garbhán Isle, and Supreme Battle Mage to the armies of Dark Plains, picked herself up off the ground, unable to look any of the men in the eye who'd watched her trip over her own two big feet. After all these years, she thought she would have mastered her human body a little better.

Unfortunately . . .

"Are you all right?"

She winced at the humor-filled voice she now so easily recognized.

"Aye, Brastias." She took the hand of Queen Annwyl's general and second-in-command, allowing the man to help her up.

"Those feet of yours just came out of nowhere and attacked again, huh?"

She glared into his smiling face. "Keep that up, and I'll let the next battle wound you get go septic."

She brushed off the front of her white robes and desperately tried to ignore those strong hands of Brastias's brushing off the rear. With every pass over her ass, she practically purred.

"Honestly, Morfyd," he said with all sincerity, "are you sure everything is all right?"

"Aye. Just one of my brothers." She had felt a sudden and extreme pain in her head that ended just as suddenly. Not good, especially when it caused her to trip over her own two feet, but her brother still lived. That she knew.

Brastias frowned in concern. "Are they all right? Gods, it's not Fearghus is it?"

She shook her head, but couldn't help but smile. No one wanted to have *that* particular conversation with the queen should her mate be in distress.

Brastias took her arm and headed toward her tent. "Which brother then?"

She knew he could care less, but he always liked to find a reason to take her hand or arm and to escort her to her tent. Morfyd had to admit, Brastias did make going to war an almost pleasurable event.

She concentrated for a moment, feeling for those tendrils of Magick that kept the entire Gwalchmai fab Gwyar family continually connected. They could shut each other out at will and usually did—unless they were surprised. Clearly, something blindsided her kin. "Gwenvael, I think."

"Gwenvael? Really? Shocking," he said flatly.

Morfyd laughed. Brastias had been around her kin long enough now to know if there was trouble, Gwenvael would most likely fall head first into its lap. "I know. Unbelievably shocking."

They now stood in front of her tent and, as always, Morfyd desperately searched for a reason to invite Brastias in. It had been three years since she met the man and she still had yet to find a reason that didn't sound idiotic.

Would you like to come in and count my herb supplies, O tall, gorgeous one? By the Dark Fire Gods, you're pathetic.

"Bullocks this," she muttered.

Chuckling in surprise, "I'm sorry?"

She girded her loins. She could do this. He was only a human. A gorgeous, amazing, beautiful, human . . . but still a human. "Brastias, I was wondering if—"

Morfyd.

It was only her name, but it held enough power to drop her to her knees. Brastias held on to her arms, the power of the gods tearing through her.

Call to me, child. Send for me.

Shaking, Morfyd looked up into the extremely concerned face of Brastias as storm clouds appeared in the sky above his head.

"What is it, Morfyd?"

"Inside my tent," she gasped. "A large satchel. Fetch it for me."

Frowning, Brastias clearly did not want to let her go. But he had no choice. *She* had no choice.

"Please, Brastias."

He nodded, releasing her, and disappeared inside her tent. *Morfyd.*

Scowling, Morfyd raged, *"I hear you! Stop bloody calling me!"* She took deep breaths to calm her nerves, motioning to one of the young messengers who helped out during battle. "Boy. Come." Reluctantly, the boy moved toward her. "Go to the queen, tell her a storm comes. A bad one."

The boy glanced up in confusion. It had been a beautiful night, clear skies. But that was about to quickly change. Storms were heading their way. She'd hoped they would stay ahead of them, but it looked like that wouldn't be the case.

"Boy!" She watched as his large eyes snapped down to focus on her. "Do it *now*."

He nodded and ran off, relieved to be away from her most likely.

Brastias returned to her side. "Morfyd, what is it?"

More like who, but she didn't have time for that. Instead, she ignored the concern in his voice. "Help me up."

He did, easily lifting her to her feet.

"The bag." There was too much going on to bother any longer with niceties.

Brastias quickly handed the satchel to her. Turning away from her tent, she headed toward a river a bit away from camp. "You sure you don't need me to—"

"No, Brastias!" She stopped when she realized she'd snapped at him. Gods invading her body brought out that reaction. But the warrior had done nothing wrong.

She looked at him over her shoulder. "I'm sorry. I didn't mean to—"

"No need to apologize, Morfyd." He gave her a warm smile, never angry at her sudden and abrupt changes of mood brought on by the constantly shifting winds of Magick. "Go. We'll have food waiting for you when you get back."

And he knew she'd be fairly starving after working Magick. *The man is absolutely perfect.*

He smirked. "If we can find a cow laying around that is."

She glared at him before storming off. *Sarcastic bastard.*

"Why are you being so nice to me?"

"What?" Briec looked up from the game he'd been play-ing with Éibhear for the last hour. So focused on the pieces and his next move, Briec barely noticed Éibhear kept staring at him.

"I said why are you being so nice?"

"Can't I be nice to my baby brother?"

"No."

Briec chuckled, but it choked off when a bleeding, raging Gwenvael stormed in with a bruised, less bloody, but equally raging Talaith wrapped in his tail.

"What the hell is going on?" he demanded as Gwenvael tossed Talaith at his feet.

"That mad bitch stabbed me!"

"*You were in my way!*" Talaith yelled back.

Growling, fangs showing, Gwenvael moved on her. But Briec stepped between the two, staring his younger brother down, and baring his own fangs.

"I know, brother, you haven't lost your reason."

"She's crazy. You haven't had her yet. So I say we dine on her this evening before she kills us all in our sleep."

Although human males were fair game to his brother, there was no woman alive Gwenvael had ever "dined" on. At least not that way. And the way the big gold tried to look around Briec to glare at Talaith told him Gwenvael merely wanted to terrify her. Which was good. Because Briec's desire to protect this female—against his own kin, no less—confused him. He had no idea what he'd do if Gwenvael actually tried to hurt Talaith.

"Éibhear, take care of our brother's scratch, would you?"

"*Scratch? You call this a scratch?*" He pointed at the wound with his claw and it took much not to wince at it. "*She nearly took my eye out!*"

"Don't over-dramatize, Gwenvael," Éibhear chastised while helping Talaith to her feet by letting her grab hold of one of his talons. "When I'm done, you'll be fine."

"This is my den. I want her out."

Briec snorted a laugh before he had the chance to stop it

and he thought for sure Gwenvael would try to remove his head. But Éibhear grabbed Gwenvael's forearm.

"Stop it, Gwenvael." He motioned to his brother with his tail. "Come."

Éibhear walked off, dragging a glaring Gwenvael behind him.

Briec watched until he was sure Gwenvael was gone. What he found entertaining was that Talaith actually thought him distracted enough not to notice her attempt to sneak away.

He slammed the tip of his tail in front of her and she screamed, then kicked it.

"*Gods damn that thing!*"

"You harmed my brother, m'lady."

She turned to face him. "You said yourself it was only a scratch."

"I said that in the hope of keeping you from becoming his next midnight snack. I left that blade on you because I trusted you not to use it. Especially not to use it on my kin."

She had the decency to look a bit ashamed. "I didn't want to hurt him. I just wanted to leave."

Apparently he owed his brother much if he prevented her from leaving.

"Why?"

"Why what?"

"Why do you want to leave?"

"You are joking."

"No. I'm not. I want to hear your reasons. I want to know what it is about me and my brothers you find so horrifying you'd rather brave the wrath of the gods than stay here with us?"

Even deep within Gwenvael's den they could hear the thunder and lightning strikes dotting the land around them. This was not the kind of weather anyone, human or dragon, should be out in.

"You're dragons. Our most hated enemies."

He rolled his eyes and sat back on his haunches. "Honestly, little witch, I know you can do better than that."

She sighed. A great heaving sigh. And her shoulders dropped. She shook her head slowly, her brown eyes locked on the ground at her feet.

"I just can't stay."

If only he was as stupid as the one she called husband. If only he cared so little for anything but himself, he'd never know when she was lying.

Not that spending her life among scales and tails held much pleasure for her. But for the first time since that fateful day Arzhela and her priestesses came for her had Talaith felt content. Not quite happy, but she'd never really been a happy person.

As her mother used to joke—on those rare occasions the woman joked about anything—"Nolwenn witches and happy . . . words simply never used in the same sentence."

And she really didn't mean to hurt Gwenvael, but he'd given her no choice.

"Answer me, Talaith."

Damn that dragon voice. The way Briec said her name—it curled around her like a warm blanket. But she didn't dare look him in the eyes. Those violet eyes tore right through her.

"I simply can't stay, Briec."

"Does someone wait for you?"

Exasperated at his persistence, she glared at him and snapped, "Yes. In fact there's an entire army waiting for me. I intend to service them all. Happy now? Now can I go?"

"Are you incapable of giving me a straight answer?"

"Are you incapable of hearing me? I want to go. Now."

Flames flared around him and then were gone, leaving the man behind. And oh, what a man . . .

She didn't know which was worse—the dragon Briec who could eat her in one bite or the human Briec who she wanted to eat her in one bite.

"Why do you insist on arguing about everything with me?"

She'd angered him. Good. It was much easier dealing with an angry dragon than a considerate, caring one. "Why do you insist on not listening to me?"

"Even if I wanted to let you go, you still can't leave in this weather."

"I'll do as I like, you oversized, scaly bastard. And that means I'm leaving."

She turned to walk away, but Briec took firm hold of her arm and swung her back around.

"Don't walk away from me!"

"Get your hands off me before I slice you open like I did your brother."

She still had the blade in her right hand. And that was the hand Briec gripped and yanked to his throat, pressing the tip of the blade against the soft spot where his neck met his collarbone. "Then do it, little witch. Push your dagger home and run."

Talaith stared at the tip of her blade pressing against soft flesh. *Do it, Talaith. Do it.* She yelled the words at herself over and over. But she couldn't. She couldn't kill him.

"You can't do it, can you?" He didn't sound smug or arrogantly sure—he sounded shocked. "Can you?"

She didn't answer him. They both knew she didn't have to. Her hesitation revealed too much. Gave too much away.

"I—" was all she managed before he slapped her hand, and the dagger it held, away and gripped her face tight between his hands.

Briec yanked her up seconds before his mouth slammed down over hers. Not exactly how she imagined their first kiss, but this was so much better.

She whimpered and tipped her head to the side, her tongue dipping into his mouth and sliding across his. She felt his body tense, surprised by her bold reaction no doubt. Surprised and entertained. He pulled her tighter against his body and deepened their kiss, ravaging her mouth with his own.

Now this . . . *this* was a kiss. A kiss of the highest order.

The kind of kiss she'd dreamed about all her life, but never thought she'd experience. The kind she knew would make her willing to give up everything for a night in a man's bed. Except for Briec not exactly being a man, she was there.

After a few moments, the kiss gentled and Briec took his time exploring her mouth. Talaith let him, enjoying this kiss in ways she never thought she could. Her entire body screamed for his attention. Screamed to be taken and claimed. She wanted him. Gods did she want him!

Slowly, he pulled his mouth away from her and murmured, "I knew you wanted me."

Damn him! Talaith brought her booted foot down on his instep.

"Ow!" He stumbled away from her. "*What in holy hell was that for?*"

"For not half being an arrogant bastard."

She retrieved her blade from the floor and headed to the chamber she used as her bedroom, resigned to staying in this pit of despair at least until the weather cleared or Arzhela called to her.

"I hate you, Briec the Arrogant," she yelled over her shoulder. "You and all your kind."

"Really? It certainly doesn't *smell* that way."

She didn't respond. Why bother when he was right?

When she didn't show up for dinner, Éibhear went searching for her, Gwenvael trailing behind. Briec wouldn't speak of her and wouldn't go. Éibhear didn't know what happened between them after he and Gwenvael left, but it made Briec one cranky dragon.

They finally tracked her down at the springs. She sat on the edge of one, her small bare feet in the warm water and her hand firmly wrapped around one of his father's bottles of Fire Wine . . . *uh-oh.*

Sitting on either side of her, the brothers watched her

stare into the water and sway. Side to side. Side to side. Humming. It was kind of mesmerizing.

"Lady Talaith?"

Big, brown, and rather dazed eyes slowly focused on him. "Éibhear—" He waited for her to say something more but that seemed to be all she could manage.

"What are you doing, m'lady?"

She held up the bottle. "Drinking tea."

He smiled. "That's not tea, Talaith."

"I sensed that when I walked into the wall." She pointed to the spot, using the hand holding the bottle and almost slapping Gwenvael on the wounded side of his head. Luckily he moved quickly. "The wall over there."

She turned back around and that's when she saw Gwenvael.

"Gwenvael." She leaned against him, surprising both brothers. "I'm so sorry I almost killed you."

What Éibhear admired about Gwenvael was how he never stayed angry for long. And, unlike their father and Fearghus, he didn't bother holding grudges either. He preferred enjoying himself by making others miserable. He was very good at it.

"It's all right, Talaith. I'm sure you can make it up to me somehow."

Gwenvael winked at him over the top of her head and Éibhear rolled his eyes in disgust. No shame. His brothers simply didn't possess the ability to feel shame.

Talaith waved the bottle of wine in Gwenvael's face. "Oh no you don't, dragon. I may be a little drunk, Handsome the Gwenvael, but I'm not *that* drunk." *Handsome the Gwenvael?* Oh, she was so *very* drunk. "You'll not defile me with this"—she looked him over carefully—"gorgeous human body of yours."

"I know. You'll be defiled by Briec's gorgeous human body."

She punched him in the shoulder and Gwenvael actually

winced. "I will not. He's such a pushy, arrogant bastard. More than you, believe it or not."

"Oh, I believe it."

"But I have no desire to be . . ." She searched for words and Gwenvael decided to help her there.

"Fucked within an inch of your life?"

"Gwenvael," Éibhear warned.

"I'm just helping her."

"No." Talaith shook her head. "You're being a bastard. But I'm getting used to that. Besides"—she patted his shoulder—"you're such a cute bastard."

"Talaith," Éibhear said softly. "Perhaps we should get you back to your room."

"No. *He'll* be there. Lurking outside my chamber like a giant scaly watchdog."

"Briec would never force himself on you," Éibhear assured her. Because he knew his brother never would. To be quite blunt, he couldn't be bothered.

"I know. He can be so nice," she said sadly, "when he's not being an arrogant son of a bitch."

"If you know that," Gwenvael cut in, "I'm not sure why it would concern you where my brother slept. Unless it is your own control that concerns you, m'lady."

Talaith raised her hand and flicked Gwenvael's still-healing wound.

"Ow!"

"Don't irritate me." She hugged the bottle to her chest and sighed. "None of you understand. I'm trapped with no way out. I've been trapped now for sixteen years."

Éibhear and Gwenvael exchanged concerned glances. What was she talking about? At first, he thought she was still talking about Briec, but she'd only known him a few days. For some other reason she felt the need to leave. For a reason Éibhear knew she'd never share with them. Talaith had been keeping secrets for a very long time. He knew that even drunk, she'd still keep those secrets.

"I wish you'd let us help you, Talaith." He gently pushed her curly hair off her face. "At least let Briec." Briec would do anything for her, except neither of them had realized it yet.

"No one can help me, Éibhear. I've learned that all too well, my friend."

Somehow she pushed herself to her feet, the bottle still gripped in one hand and pressed to her chest. "I'm going to stagger to my room now."

"Talaith—"

"No. No. I'll be fine." She took several awkward steps, then stopped. "You. I knew you'd be lurking."

Éibhear turned to see Briec leaning against the entrance wall, his arms crossed over his chest. His human form looked casual enough, but Éibhear sensed his brother's concern. Briec would never admit it, but he cared about this lovely but strange woman who couldn't hold her drink.

"Come, Talaith. Let me take you to bed," Briec offered.

"I can manage well enough on my own, serpent." She walked toward him. "So just keep your claws off me." She hiccupped once and pitched forward. Briec caught hold of her before she landed face first in the dirt.

"Briec?"

"Don't worry, Éibhear. I'll take care of her." Briec lifted the unconscious woman up in his arms. "Thanks for finding her before she drowned herself."

Éibhear waited until he was sure Briec was out of hearing range, then turned to Gwenvael. "You're right, you know?"

"About?"

"She is going to make his life hell."

Gwenvael grinned, his wound seemingly forgotten. "I know."

Briec laid his drunken human down on the bed, finally prying the bottle of Fire Wine from her grasp. Even he didn't drink his father's homemade wine, but he had used it to clean rust off old armor.

He brushed Talaith's hair off her face and her brown eyes fluttered open. "Oh. It's you."

Did she have to sound so disappointed? "Aye. It's me."

"Come to take advantage of me in my inebriated state?"

"I try not to do that. Nothing worse than the morning-after sobbing."

She laughed while struggling to sit up. "I don't understand you, dragon."

"What don't you understand?"

"Sometimes you can be so nice, and I can almost forget how annoying you are. And then you open your mouth, and I remember *exactly* how annoying you are."

She finally found a way to sit up and, for a brief moment, he expected her to pitch forward again, but she managed to keep her seat. He watched her struggle with the ribbon tying her bodice together, which she managed to get completely knotted up.

Sighing, he kneeled in front of her and pushed her hands away. "At this rate, you'll be sober before you get your dress off."

He worked at untying the knots she created, but he could feel her eyes on him. Her words still startled him, though. "I like you on your knees, dragon."

Briec dug in and decided not to look at her, instead concentrating on the knots before him.

"I don't think you're necessarily better looking on your knees," she continued, "but I find you almost charming there."

"Talaith, I need you to stop talking now."

"Why? Am I shocking you?"

No. She wasn't shocking him. But she was making him hard. From this position, he could do all sorts of things to her and with her. But he wasn't about to take advantage of her while she was flying high on his father's homemade liquor. He liked his women sober and willing. Not passing out in the middle of it or, even worse, throwing up on him. Besides, hadn't she done enough of that already?

"Don't you want to fuck me, dragon?"

He dropped his head on her still-clothed chest. "Where did a nice witch like you learn words like that?"

"Did you forget? Peasant village. I know all sorts of words after living with those people. Want me to list them?"

"No!" He cleared his throat. "No," he said more calmly. "Just stay quiet . . . or pass out. Anything that will stop you from talking."

She stopped speaking.

Then she started again. "Does your dragon cock have scales?"

"That's it." He took firm hold of her bodice and ripped it in half. He pulled the dress down, practically flipping her off the bed in his desperation to get it off her. Once done, he tossed the ruined dress into the pitfire.

"Look!" She stood on the bed, arms over her head. "I'm naked!"

He grabbed Talaith to him—ignoring how good her warm flesh felt against his—and lifted her up off her feet with one arm. With the other, he dragged the fur covers back and dropped her onto the bed. He covered up her luscious body as quickly as he could manage.

"Go to sleep, woman."

He turned and walked several steps away. Stopped. Turned. And returned to her. She looked up at him and smiled.

"Big bastard." She giggled.

"Annoying harpie," he growled back. Then he leaned down and kissed her mouth hard. She moaned and her hands dug into his hair, clinging to him.

Unfortunately, he had to stop. He had to. Or he'd be inside her in seconds.

"I want you sleeping in the next two minutes," he ordered.

"Or what?"

He bared fangs, two long ones in the front. He hated doing it, mostly because they tore up his lip due to their size. But the crazy witch made him absolutely insane.

She shrunk away from him. "All right. All right. No need to get mean."

Moving toward the exit as fast as the erection pushing against his breeches would allow, he said, "Sadly, little witch, you seem to understand nothing else."

But by then, he could already hear her light snoring.

Chapter 8

For three straight days, the storms raged. Ice-cold rain beating down, brutal winds blowing, plus powerful lightning ensured Talaith wouldn't leave the dragon's cave.

And after her first thwarted escape and drunken escapade—*did I really stand on the bed and say "I'm naked"?*—Briec wouldn't let her out of his sight. So for three solid days she'd been stuck with him and his kin. Although, she did have to admit it had definitely been an interesting three days trapped in a cave with three related dragons who seemed hell-bent on torturing each other.

She thought for sure Gwenvael would never forgive her for what she did to him. But he healed fast enough and didn't seem to care, especially when irritating the living hell out of his brother clearly took precedence.

As soon as he realized merely being close to Talaith annoyed Briec, the gold dragon went out of his way to not only forgive Talaith, but to show her as much affection as he could manage.

It seemed Gwenvael enjoyed lounging around or on her. Of course, all this closeness only seemed to happen when Briec was in the vicinity. Gwenvael would stretch out beside her, sometimes human and sometimes dragon. As human,

Gwenvael would lay his handsome head in her lap, ignoring the fact she would be in the middle of reading something. As dragon, he'd lay his snout. Either way, when Briec found him it always turned ugly. She'd gotten to the point that as long as stones didn't drop from the ceiling onto her head, she didn't worry.

As for Éibhear, he couldn't seem to do enough for her. He made sure she ate well, had warm clothes, clean bedding, and books to read. He had to be the kindest being she'd ever known. Plus, very funny and very smart. She'd begun to call him Éibhear the Diplomat. He was the only one who could calm his brothers when they went into one of their arguments. He seemed to like everything and everyone peaceful.

Still, he did have his occasional mood changes, but he never directed those her way. His brothers received the brunt and they didn't seem to notice. Gwenvael finally told her that, among his kind, Éibhear was young. "Not yet a hundred," Gwenvael would tease, knowing to a human—even a Nolwenn witch with their long lives—that sounded strange. In a few more years Éibhear would finally grow into his true dragon self. She already mourned the loss of the sweet, endearing bear of a dragon who loved to make her laugh.

And then there was Briec.

After her little escape attempt and their kiss, he circled around her like a bird of prey. If his brothers got too close, he was there to move them. If she got lost in the enormous caverns and tunnels of Gwenvael's home—which, unfortunately, happened more than once—he'd find her and lead her back.

When he wasn't doing all that, he was looking for an argument. He absolutely loved irritating the hell out of her. He made sure to do it often, it seemed. Of course it didn't help that when he would start the fights, not only would she jump in with much enthusiasm, but the arguments invariably made her want him. Desperately. They both knew it, too. The way he'd stare at her. The way his nostrils would flare seconds before he'd say something else to aggravate her more, proved to her he knew exactly what he was doing.

Yet, she knew deep in her soul, all this did was kill time. Time until he could get her truly alone. Away from his meddling brothers. Talaith, however, lived in fear of that day. She didn't fear Briec. Not anymore. But she did fear her feelings for him. She'd been so young when she'd met her first and, up to this point, only love. A young, tall warrior with light brown eyes who treated her like a princess. They'd given each other everything, to her mother's great annoyance. But he'd died in battle and that's when her entire world changed.

But he'd been a mere boy. Barely ten and eight. Briec, however, was in no way young or inexperienced. Plus the fact he wasn't human still bothered her . . . a lot. Many would consider a mating between the two an abomination. Actually, Talaith would have felt that way, too—before she met Briec.

Now she dreamed every night about the big bastard. And in every dream they argued. Which normally wouldn't worry her. What worried her was waking up a sweating mess with her sex wet and her hand between her legs. Even in the darkness of the cave, she knew Briec watched her. He watched her moan and writhe on the bed and not once did he touch her. Although she sensed he wanted to . . . very much. She had to admit, she admired his strength of will. Most men she'd known wouldn't wait for her. Ones not remotely as powerful as Briec would have taken what they wanted from her whether she agreed or not.

He didn't. Which just made her like him more. And she hated him for it.

Finally, though, the rains and lightning stopped. At least temporarily since the clouds still hovered near. After much begging—and arguing—Briec finally agreed to take her

down to the closest village. But she had to promise she
wouldn't do anything "annoyingly stupid" like yell for help.
She grudgingly promised, because Arzhela still had not
called to her. Once that call came, she would do what she
had to, even break her promise to the dragon.

The town near Gwenvael's cave—where every local
woman seemed to know or know *of* the three brothers—
boasted a sizable market, and there were many items she
would have liked to purchase if she had any coin. But she
wouldn't ask the dragon for any money. Not in this lifetime.

Gwenvael grabbed her hand and dragged her over to one
of the dressmaker shops. "We should get you something
pretty."

"We? You actually plan to spend money on me?"

"No. That's my dear brother's job. But I can dress you as
the goddess you are. Especially because I have much better
taste than him."

Talaith laughed while he looked over the already made
gowns and the available materials. Gwenvael had grown on
her. True, she had no doubt he'd fairly leap between her legs
if she even gave him the merest hint she might welcome
him. But they both knew he'd only do it to annoy Briec.

Which was why she wasn't surprised when Briec suddenly appeared behind her, glaring at Gwenvael.

"What are you doing?"

"Picking out a dress for you to buy for your lady."

His lady?

"I am not his lady."

"She's not my lady."

Talaith glared at Briec over her shoulder. "What do you
mean I'm not your lady?"

"You just said you're not my lady."

She turned to face him. "I can say what I want. You, however, need to keep your mouth shut."

"You know as I begin to forget your peasant upbringing,
you seem to delight in reminding me."

"As you pointed out before, my upbringing was not that of a peasant. I am the daughter of a merchant."

"A sea merchant?"

Her eyes narrowed. Sea merchants held extremely bad reputations throughout Dark Plains and Alsandair. Rumors abounded that most of them were more pirates than merchants, their boats coming down from the Northland Sea and raiding seaside towns. "No, you arrogant—" She stopped speaking and looked down at the big hands holding a lovely dress up in front of her. Of course, leave it to Gwenvael to hold her dress up by taking a firm grasp of her breasts.

Before she could tell him to get his bloody hands off, Briec beat her to it. "Remove your hands, brother."

Gwenvael's large, strong body pressed against her back while his golden head leaned over her shoulder and stared down, she assumed, at the dress. "I wanted to see how this looked on her before you buy it."

"Remove your hands . . . or lose your hands."

Keeping his head firmly against her shoulder, Gwenvael lifted only those big gold eyes of his. "Now, now, brother. Temper, temper."

"Oh!" Talaith slammed her foot down into Gwenvael's instep.

"Ack!"

She pulled away from Gwenvael and quickly maneuvered around Briec before he could grab hold of her either, so her back faced the shop exit. "Both of you cut it out. I will not be tugged between you two like a . . . a . . ."

"Fine sweetmeat?"

"Delicious morsel?"

"Tasty tidbit?"

"Scrumptious delicacy?"

"Decadent delight?"

She held her hands up. "Stop. Stop."

"Good gods, brother." Gwenvael rested his hand on Briec's shoulder. "Is that a smile your lady wears?"

"I think so. But I'm not all that sure. I've seen so few on her face."

"It's beautiful, though."

"Aye," Briec answered, his eyes devouring her on the spot. "That it is."

She knew this was moments from getting horribly awkward. So she did the only thing she could think of. "Both of you are absolutely impossible. I'm leaving."

She rushed out of the shop only to crash into Éibhear.

"There you are, Talaith. Come. I've found a bookseller."

She barely managed a light squeal before the young dragon had her by the hand, and dragged her off across the square.

Eavan walked up to his commander. "You're not going to believe who I saw being dragged across the town square."

His commander turned one cold blue eye his way, the other lost in battle long ago, but said nothing. He was a man of few words.

"Our prize."

"The dragon?"

"Nowhere to be seen. She has aligned herself with a knight. Perhaps more. But no one that's a real threat to us."

His commander grinned. "Seems riches and glory will be ours soon, my friend."

Eavan returned his commander's smile. Riches and glory. What he'd always wanted.

Briec snatched the dress from Gwenvael's hands. "Stay away from her, Gwenvael. Especially her breasts."

"But they're magnificent, brother."

Gwenvael grinned and Briec debated ripping the bastard's head off. Of course it could make for tense dinner conversation with his mother, though.

What annoyed him more than he wanted to admit was the fact Gwenvael had damn near more physical contact with that impossible female than he did.

Gwenvael shook his head. "Get out now, brother. Really. Give her gold for her trouble and leave her here."

"No." He couldn't. No matter how much the rational side of him wanted to. She must have trapped him with, he was fairly convinced, a spell of some kind.

"You don't understand, Briec. You won't be getting rid of her anytime soon. You keep her now . . . you'll keep her forever."

Briec scoffed, "I have no intention of keeping that human harpy longer than absolutely necessary."

Catching the eye of a shop girl, Gwenvael proceeded to follow after her but not before throwing over his shoulder, "If you think getting your cock inside that woman will end this—you're dumber than Fearghus."

Briec already knew that, too.

"I'm falling!"

"Oh." Éibhear grabbed back half the books he'd piled in her arms. "Sorry."

Talaith smiled, and Éibhear couldn't help but envy his brother's choice of female. He thought Talaith was amazing. So pretty and sweet, with a wonderful sense of humor. Even drunk she was adorable.

Of course, she was also hiding something. But, as always, Éibhear's only concern was his family. As long as whatever her secret was didn't involve his family, he'd leave his brother to it. But if any of his kin were in danger, he'd smite the beauty where she stood.

"It's all right, Éibhear. But you do know I don't need all these books."

"You can never have enough books," he quoted Annwyl.

"I see." Talaith gave him that indulgent smile she seemed

to hold just for him. He wondered if Briec realized how nurturing she was. She'd make a good mother one day.

The shopkeeper slipped into the back to find a book Éibhear had been searching for, leaving them alone in the small, book-filled shop. "You are going to stay? With Briec."

She looked startled, then she looked resigned. "No, Éibhear. I will not."

"Will not or can not?"

"Both." She fidgeted and he realized how uncomfortable this conversation was making her.

"Besides," she argued, "your brother only wants me for as long as he wants me. I'm sure he will bore of me soon. Especially, if . . ." Her voice faded out.

"Especially if he beds you?"

She winced and nodded curtly. "It seems males of any species are no different."

He might agree with her if this were Gwenvael they spoke of. But Briec didn't waste his time on . . . well . . . anything. He bored easily and had an arrogance rivaled only by their father. If he only wanted to bed a female, any female, he would have left Talaith outside of her little town when she asked him to rather than spend a moment longer trying to lure her to spread her legs. Briec's determination to have this woman in his bed and life, however, told Éibhear that bedding Talaith a few times would not get her out of his system.

Still, beautiful as this woman was, she continued to remind Éibhear of a coiled snake ready to strike. As long as you left her alone, she'd leave you alone. But if you got too close . . .

"I'm starving," he announced, unwilling to obsess over Talaith and her secrets too much.

She grinned. "When aren't you starving?"

"I'm still a growing boy, you know. I'm barely even ninety winters old."

She stared up at him, horrified. "Good gods, Éibhear, do you mean you'll actually get . . . *bigger?*"

She didn't even have to turn around to know he stood behind her.

"You watch me constantly," she said over her shoulder as she continued to study the lovely jewelry the vendor sold. Silver remained her favorite because gold never looked very good against her skin color. Although she could never afford either.

"I want to make sure you don't try to slash any of my other kin."

"Your brother seems to have forgiven me about that."

Briec stepped up beside her. "My brother will forgive any female anything as long as he can stare at her breasts while doing it."

"You're too hard on him."

"And you are like every other female that allows him much leeway."

Frowning, Talaith looked up at him, but he would not face her. Instead he stared down at the jewelry as if considering each piece carefully. "I give your brother no leeway and never will."

"I didn't see you moving his hands away while he held that dress against you."

"First off, you didn't give me the chance. And second, you sound awfully jealous."

"Me? Jealous?" Briec finally turned and faced her. "*Of him?*"

"Don't yell at me," she replied calmly. "And yes, you sound very jealous of your brother. Like it's making you insane with rage."

"Why you evil little—"

"You two argue," Éibhear cut in, "while I starve to death."

His big hands rested on his lean hips. "If someone doesn't feed me soon, I will get cranky."

"Can this not wait until we're done," Briec snarled.

"No. You two argue constantly." Éibhear grabbed her hand and Briec's eyes narrowed at where their fingers touched. "Argue later. Feed me now."

Without another word, Éibhear dragged her off yet again, this time toward the local inn.

Talaith glanced back at Briec and she immediately understood the look on his handsome face. His patience waned—greatly. No, Briec the Arrogant wouldn't tolerate his brothers' interference much longer. And thoughts of what he might do when that patience ran out had her knees nearly buckling.

Glendower, Son of Glewlwyd stumbled out of the Great Hall of Garbhán Isle castle and into the arms of Eryi, captain of the guards.

"Ho, Glendower!" The man laughed. "Too much drink, my old friend?"

Not bothering to answer, he turned in Eryi's arms and grabbed the collar of the man's chainmail shirt. He yanked him out of the way as flames burst from inside the Great Hall and out the door, nearly singeing them both on the spot.

The two men, now facedown in the dirt, looked up at each other.

"What in all that's holy . . ."

Glendower, who had stupidly offered to be temporary Garbhán Isle vassal until the queen and her army returned, shook his head. Who knew suggesting the rotation of crops over to the south side of the castle grounds would cause the queen's consort to get so terse. "I believe our lord misses the queen . . . greatly."

"That woman," Eyri panted, "cannot return fast enough."

And Glendower most heartily agreed.

* * *

She'd been nervous since *they* walked in. Her legs under the table bounced incessantly. An already annoying habit he was hoping to break her of, but this was intolerable. And her eyes kept straying across the room to look at them.

Finally, Briec couldn't stand it anymore. "Is there a problem, Talaith?"

Her eyes snapped back to the three dragons sitting at the table with her. "No. Why?"

"I don't know. Maybe it's the way you keep staring at those four men over there."

Gwenvael leaned back as far as he could manage, trying to get his body comfortable in the tiny table setting. Clearly no one designed these inns with dragon patrons in mind. "Do you know them?"

Her hand strayed to the rope burn on her neck. It'd turned into a lovely shade of purple and green, but at least, according to her, the pain plagued her no more. "Um . . . I know of them." She shrugged. "They're soldiers. Lord Hamish's soldiers."

All three of the brothers turned and stared at the men.

"Don't stare at them," she whispered fiercely.

"They look like travelers or priests," Éibhear offered.

But Gwenvael shook his head. "They're much more than that, little brother. They're well-armed under those robes."

"Oh." Éibhear was silent for a moment. Then, in that Éibhear way, he said, "Let's kill them then."

Now all their attention turned to Éibhear.

"What? What did I say?"

Briec caught Talaith's eyes and they smiled at each other. Every once in awhile Éibhear reminded them all he was still a young dragon.

"They haven't actually done anything, pup," Briec somehow managed to say without laughing. "We can't just kill them."

"Clearly Talaith feels threatened. Isn't that enough?"

"No." Gwenvael chuckled. "That's not enough."

"Well, it should be," Éibhear grumbled as he took the rest of Gwenvael's meal as his own.

"Have they ever hurt you?" Briec asked. If her answer was "yes," then Éibhear would get his wish.

Talaith shook her head. "No. No. Nothing like that. I'm just wondering why they're here. Little far from Madron, wouldn't you say?"

She had a valid point.

"Aye. I know some who wouldn't like the idea of any of Hamish's men this close to Dark Plains." And Garbhán Isle. Fearghus became awfully testy when he thought that viper he called mate might be in danger. Of course, the woman had been out with her army for months. How Fearghus tolerated that, Briec didn't know. Simply thinking of Talaith leaving anytime soon gave him this very odd feeling in his chest. He didn't know what it was, but he knew he didn't enjoy it.

"I'd like to know how they got this far, in this weather," Gwenvael questioned before finishing the last of his ale.

"That only matters," Éibhear said while nearly inhaling the food off his plate as if he hadn't eaten in years, "if they're here to find Talaith. They may have already been traveling before the storms started."

"Well, little human," Briec asked softly. "Are they here for you?"

Instead of giving him an answer, Talaith said, "Perhaps we should just leave." Talaith looked like she'd give anything to be able to disappear into the dirt floor.

The three brothers glanced at each other. These men would follow but, of course, that worked out better for them in the end.

"Good point. Let's leave."

"No dessert?" Éibhear appeared fairly stricken and Briec couldn't help but laugh.

"I'm sure we'll find something back at Gwenvael's den to help with that sweet fang of yours."

He dropped gold on the table and held his hand out for Talaith. She stared at it as if she expected it to tear out her throat.

"Problem?"

She forced a smile he hoped never to see from her again, it held so little life, and said, "No. Of course not." Talaith stood without taking his hand and headed toward the door, pulling the hood of her cloak over her head.

Briec sighed as he followed his brothers out, knowing the men from the inn would be right behind them.

Good. He really wouldn't mind killing something tonight.

They'd looped behind the buildings and came at them from the front, multiplying from four to ten. Briec pushed Talaith behind him, the males facing off.

Suddenly she was ever so grateful to have the protection of Briec and his kin. True, the soldiers wouldn't kill her. She was too valuable. But she not only knew the reputation of the Madron soldiers, she'd seen it in action in her village.

She knew her trip back to Madron with these men would be . . . unpleasant. No. She had no intention of going with them. Her virtue may not be much but it was hers. And, unlike the dragon, she knew these men would honor nothing on their way back to Madron. Besides, Briec wouldn't let her go, which secretly made her smile.

Still, there was no way this wouldn't end without bloodshed.

"Hold, knights," one of them calmly stated to the brothers—no doubt fooled by their chainmail and surcoats, which they'd dug up in one of Gwenvael's caverns while discussing what they'd done to the men who once wore them. The soldier pushed his robes back so they could see the hilt of his blade.

As Gwenvael noted, they were well armed. "I believe you have something that belongs to us."

Something that belongs to them? Good thing the dragons stood between them. She'd kill them herself if she could get her hands around their collective throats.

"And what would that be, soldier?" Gwenvael asked with a smile. The brothers itched for this fight, their lust for blood flowing from them like honey.

"Give us the woman. We'll let you live."

No, they wouldn't.

Gwenvael motioned to Talaith. "This woman? Sorry, my brother got to her first. She's his prize. She stays with us."

The ten soldiers drew their swords and the three brothers watched them do it.

She waited for them to do something. Walking out of the pub, the brothers had decided that shifting to dragon would be a last resort, since doing so could wipe out the entire town in the process. Gwenvael apparently had many barwenches and whores he made use of when he was bored, and he was unwilling to risk losing them. Which left fighting the soldiers in human form. Talaith had never seen them fight, so she had no idea how good or bad they were. Which worried her. She didn't want Gwenvael or Éibhear hurt. And, she grudgingly admitted to herself, she felt even more so about Briec.

They all wanted this fight, though. Once males got this way, no use trying to get between them. So she stood and waited.

The one who'd spoken first lunged at Gwenvael, who easily grabbed hold of his sword arm and snapped it in two. She cringed at the screams that followed while Gwenvael twisted that broken arm with the sword still clutched in the hand and impaled the soldier with his own weapon.

Brutal, but very effective.

She stopped worrying at that point. She only had to see the fear on the remaining soldiers' faces as the three brothers moved forward. The men stumbled back so quickly, they almost tripped themselves.

Debating whether to sit down until they finished with their current prey, she only had time to gasp when a hand slapped over her mouth. She started to struggle, but an arm around her waist stilled her. Instead, she went limp and allowed the man holding her to drag her into the nearby alley.

Briec was *so* bored. He thought he may have a challenge, but how much of a challenge could ten humans be to three dragons? Even dragons in human form.

Eibhear lifted one of the soldiers up in both his hands, then dropped him onto his knee, snapping the man's back like kindling.

Briec rolled his eyes. His baby brother truly liked that move. What few knew, though, was their mother taught him that.

The three brothers stepped forward again, and again the remaining soldiers took several panicked steps back. That's when Briec stopped. As they'd advanced, the soldiers continued to move back . . . and away. He looked over his shoulder and snarled.

"Where is she?" he yelled. It was a late hour and the streets deserted, his roar ricocheting off the surrounding buildings. The soldiers stared at him, unwilling and—at least a little—unable to answer.

No more games. "Burn them," he snapped to his brothers.

He turned and traced his steps back while his brothers lit up the skies with their flames. He barely heard the screams of the dying men over the pounding thud of his heart.

If he'd lost her . . . if he'd stupidly allowed some trash to run off with his prize, he'd tear the land apart until he found her. Until he had her back right where she . . .

Briec stopped in his tracks. He watched Talaith walk out of a dark alley. She finger-combed her hair into place.

Smoothed down her dress. Took a deep breath, and moved toward him.

In the darkness, it took her a moment to see him. When their eyes met, he saw a myriad of human emotions pass over her face. Relief. Concern. Annoyance. And panic. Especially when she glanced back at the alley. But she forced a smile on her face and headed toward him.

"Done then?"

"We'll have to move quickly. The whole town will be out here soon."

She nodded and hurried off toward his brothers while he took several quick steps back to the alley and looked in. He smelled human male.

He moved forward and found the body lying beside a pile of trash. An old warrior, with one eye long missing. Briec kneeled down and looked closely. The corpse's one eye stared straight up. He appeared startled, but seemingly unharmed. Leaning closer, Briec stared hard at the man's neck. Even in this darkness, his dragon eyes picked up the small pinholes dotting the soldier's throat.

Briec raised an eyebrow in surprise. "Little witch, what skills you have."

The town's residents were so busy trying to put out the soldiers' remains and to stop the fire that singed a few of their buildings; they didn't even notice the four of them leaving. It took her a few moments once she caught up with Éibhear and Gwenvael to get her harried emotions under control. But by the time the dragons stopped blasting those soldiers with white flame, her breathing had returned to normal and she'd controlled her heart rate.

Not an easy skill, but one she'd learned well.

Now, with another storm moving on them quickly, they tromped through the forest toward a clearing so the brothers could return to their natural form and fly them back to the safety of Gwenvael's cave. How she hated flying.

They were silent for most of the walk until Briec muttered something to his brothers. They both nodded and kept moving, but Briec stopped. She stopped, too. She had to; he stood right in front of her.

He watched his brothers for a few more moments until they vanished in the dark of the forest.

"What are we doing?"

That's when he turned and grabbed her arms, forcing her up against a tree.

"Tell me what you did!"

Her eyes narrowed. If he'd asked her nicely she *might* have answered him. Not now, though. "There's nothing to tell."

"Don't lie to me," he growled low. His hands tightened on her arms and he pulled her up until she stood on her tiptoes.

And this . . . this was why she hated herself. She wanted him. More than she'd ever wanted him before. He yelled at her and all she could think about was having him take her, right there. Up against that tree.

Exactly what was wrong with her?

"Answer me, woman. Answer me right now!"

"Or what?" she snapped. "What exactly will you do to your *prize?*" she sneered the last bit and she knew she'd crossed the invisible line they'd been dancing around for days.

The black smoke curling from his nostrils really should have scared her more than it did . . . but it didn't. It only managed to make the wetness between her legs triple in quantity.

And he knew it, too. Knew she wanted him. His nostrils—the ones with the black smoke still coming out of them—flared just the tiniest bit. And she knew he knew.

She only managed an "eep," then he was kissing her. His tongue forcing its way past her lips and claiming her mouth.

She should cut his throat. She should yank her blade from her boot and cut his throat from ear to ear.

Snarling, she snatched her arms out of his grip, but only

so she could wrap them around his neck and bury her hands in his hair. His big hands now gripped her ass, pulling her tight against him and they both groaned at the contact. She could feel his erection through her dress. She'd already seen the size of it, and knew exactly what it looked like. Her imagination soared with the damage that beauty could do to her body.

Their tongues tangled and she was seconds from reaching for his shaft in the hopes of releasing it out of his leggings and inside her. But before she could grab hold, he pried her hands off his neck. Then he dropped her. She stumbled back, thankful for the tree. It kept her butt from landing on the hard ground.

He walked away from her, his back to her, his hands resting on his hips. Lightning flashed and thunder rumbled around them. Briec took huge gulps of air as if he'd run for leagues. For a moment, she thought he'd leave her in this forest—panting from the passion of that kiss. Leave her and all her damn secrets behind.

She wouldn't blame him, it was the smart thing to do.

"Let us be off, brother," Gwenvael called from the clearing.

"Aye," he called back.

He still hadn't turned to face her, but he spoke to her nonetheless. "When we get back, we'll finish this discussion."

"Is that what dragons call that . . . a discussion?"

Violet eyes glared at her over those big shoulders. "Don't push me, woman. Not now."

But she did want to push him. She wanted to push him until he took her, until he fucked her raw and left her unable to even beg for more.

She shook her head as she followed behind him. *Nay. That's not normal, Talaith.*

Chapter 9

Briec followed her deep into his brother's cave. The storms had started again before they'd barely taken to the air. It had been a hard, frightening ride as lightning lashed at them and rain poured onto them from the heavens as if the gods were pushing them back to the safety of Gwenvael's cave. Yet he'd barely noticed. Not with Talaith's thighs gripping his neck and her hands tangled tight in his hair. As usual, she squealed all the way back to the cave, but he could barely hear her over the raging winds.

Once they'd made it safely inside, she'd slid off his back without assistance and stormed off. As if *she* had a reason to be angry. He wasn't the one hiding anything. Truly, he'd been honest to the point of blunt.

"What's going on with you two?" Gwenvael questioned, sitting back on his haunches.

"Nothing."

"You're lying, Briec."

He wasn't lying. As far as he was concerned, until he was balls-deep inside that woman, *nothing* was going on. But he was ready to change that. Right now.

"I'm not lying. Leave it be."

"Oi." Éibhear stood beside the cave entrance, staring out

at the pouring rain. "Anyone else a little concerned about this weather?"

Gwenvael and Briec rolled their eyes together, but Gwenvael said, "Uh-oh. Baby brother is *concerned* with the angry weather. It must mean something dire."

Éibhear snarled, his silver eyes glaring at their gold brother. "You can both rot in hell."

Leaving his siblings to their argument, which would probably last a good while, Briec went in search of Talaith. They had much to discuss.

He went to the alcove she'd been using as her bedroom. Each night since they'd been here, she'd gone to bed alone. And each night he'd slept outside her room, feeling this overwhelming need to keep her safe. It had been absolute hell, too. The woman moaned in her sleep. At first, he thought her in pain, so he'd rushed to her side, only to see her hands beneath the covers. He quickly realized she pleasured herself in her sleep.

Not getting into bed and taking up where her hand left off had been one of the hardest things he'd ever done. Somehow, though, he kept the promise he made himself to have this woman. But he'd have her awake and begging.

Her room now stood empty, so he continued on farther into the cave, following her scent. As her scent became stronger, his dragon body tightened in anticipation, realizing where she'd disappeared to.

He finally stood outside the cavern filled with hot springs. She'd been using this place every night to bathe. Apparently that was her current plan. He silently watched her as she untied the bodice of her dress, sighing as the tight material loosened around her flesh. She'd just started to peel the dress off her shoulders when she abruptly stopped, her entire back snapping straight.

Holding the dress up in front of her, she slowly turned and glared at him. "Can I not get five minutes to myself?" she spit out between clenched teeth.

"Not when you're hiding something from me."

Briec walked into the cavern and, using an old trick his mother once taught him, sealed off the cavern entrance. It was a parlor trick. It only looked as if stone blocked the way, but it was effective and powerful. His brothers would never be able to find them unless they went to Morfyd for help. Last he heard, she and his eldest brother's bitch mate were on some battlefield somewhere.

Talaith let out a trembling breath when she realized he'd cut off her only means of escape. Taking a step back, her hands still holding up her dress, she demanded, "Why did you do that?"

"I wanted some time with you alone. So we can talk."

"About what?"

He shifted to human and took a slow step toward her while she took a slow step back. "About Madron soldiers searching for you. About a dead soldier in an alley."

"Why they want me is none of your business."

"It is when they tried to kill me as well."

"Then you should have left me there."

"Aye. I should have. They would have been dead sooner, I think." He dragged his gaze up her body until he reached her eyes. "And the soldier in the alley?"

"He grabbed me. I was defending myself."

Another step forward. "You could have called for help."

Another step back. "He covered my mouth."

"So, you . . . the merchant's daughter, living the last sixteen years in a tiny little peasant village outside Madron as a dutiful wife, easily took down a well-trained soldier bent on taking you?"

"Who said it was easy?"

"You walked from that alley without a hair out of place or sweat on your brow, little witch." Another step forward. "You hadn't even dirtied your gown."

"Wait!" She stumbled back, her entire body trembling.

Placing one hand on a large boulder, she took a deep breath. "Just wait."

"I can smell so many emotions swirling around you, little witch. Rage. Hate. Resentment. Even panic. But you know what I don't get from you, sweet Talaith?" He smiled as her dark brown eyes stared at him. "The scent of fear."

That's when she bolted.

Where she thought she might be going, she had no idea. He'd blocked off the exit with a spell she knew to be as old as time itself and then proceeded to stalk her around the cavern demanding answers. Answers she could never give.

She'd tried once to tell someone what was going on. An old healing woman in the village she thought might be able to give her some help. Talaith barely mentioned Arzhela's name when pain so intense she felt she'd die on the spot racked her young body. For ten days and nights, Arzhela kept her like that. Kept her alive but in blinding pain.

Talaith learned her lesson the first time. She never spoke of Arzhela again, and that was the day she knew she'd always be alone. She'd always fight this battle on her own. That no one would ever be able to help her.

Not even handsome dragons who seemed to enjoy snatching human females from their homes.

Not surprisingly, Briec caught her easily, pulling her body up against his. Her back to his chest. Honestly, why couldn't these dragons shift *into* clothes? As it was, she was weak from the long day and frightening night.

As soon as the soldier grabbed her, Talaith's training had kicked in with a vengeance. It hadn't occurred to her someone might be merely trying to distract the dragon brothers so they could get hold of her. But by the time the soldier pulled her into that alley, she'd already retrieved her dagger from the holster tied to her boot.

"Scream and it'll be the last thing you ever do," he warned

her. But she had no intention of screaming, silence and stealth her weapons as much as her dagger. He lowered her to the ground and his hands loosened around her body. That's when Talaith quickly pulled one of the small pins she kept nestled in the leather wrapped around the hilt of her blade. She spun on her heel, slapped her free hand over his mouth, and stabbed him with the long thin pin. She hit six key points in his throat in less than four seconds.

Her trainers would be proud.

Grabbing his throat, the soldier—who turned out to be older and with only one eye—stared at her in shock, unable to say a word. The poison she'd chosen from her collection ensured quick action. She lightly pushed him on the shoulder once. He fell back like one hard piece of stone, crashing to the ground as the poison worked its way through his system. By the time she slipped the pin back into the secret spot on her dagger and the dagger back into its sheath, he was dead.

Now, her dagger lay off in a corner with her boots. Dammit. *Poor planning, Talaith.*

Especially with Briec's impossibly warm hands holding her close against his naked body while she struggled to keep her gown up above her breasts. It was a battle she was currently losing.

"Let me go, Briec."

"Not until you tell me the truth. Not until you tell me what's going on."

"Nothing is going on."

"You're lying."

"I'm not." She really wasn't. No orders sent to her. No demands for her at all. In fact, the goddess had been frighteningly quiet these days past. Talaith didn't know why, but she'd enjoyed the loss of Arzhela's presence surrounding her . . . smothering her. Holding for ransom the only thing that had ever mattered to Talaith these long, painful years.

He held Talaith easily, her back against his chest. The

bastard was right—she felt no fear. Not from him. Not anymore.

"Let me go, Briec."

His arms tightened around her the tiniest bit. "I need answers, Talaith."

"There are no answers I can give you."

He lowered her to the ground and turned her to face him. His gaze held such confusion. "That's a strange thing to say, little witch."

"Not really."

"Why won't you trust me?" If she didn't know better, she'd swear he sounded hurt. But she did know better. This was Briec the Arrogant. He felt nothing, especially for her.

"Trust you? I trust no one. Why would I trust you?"

The smallest smile curved those delicious lips. "You do have a point I suppose." Violet eyes swept down the length of her and her trembling started again. A look from this male had her shaking with desire.

"Fine. I will leave you to your secrets. It's not like you'll be staying forever." She fought hard not to let him know how much that statement hurt. "But there is still something I must know, Talaith." He swept her hands away from her dress. "And I must know this right now. No more avoiding."

She stared up at him with narrowed eyes. "What?"

"My kin . . . family. I need to protect them as they would protect me. So if they're in any danger—"

Startled, she shook her head adamantly. "No, Briec. I'd never hurt your family. And Gwenvael doesn't count."

Briec finally grinned at that. "You're actually right."

"And Éibhear. I'd never let anything happen to him. He's so cute and sweet and—"

"You can stop now," he growled. Releasing the material of her gown, he allowed it to slip down her body and pool at her feet. "I need no more clarification on that subject. I just needed to be sure."

"Well, in case your old age has caught up with you,

dragon, I tried to leave and you wouldn't let me. *You* brought me here. *You* are keeping me here. I can promise that getting trapped here with *you* and your brothers in this lovely cave was not part of any grand scheme of mine."

One big hand slid across her shoulder and to the skin above her breasts. "Thank you for pointing that out."

She smiled. "Just trying to help you out, you poor old thing. How old are you anyway? Two, three thousand years?"

That's when he shoved her into one of the bigger hot spring pools.

Bastard!

By the time she'd pulled herself to the surface, he was there. Naked, hot, and quite determined.

"Wait—"

"No." He pushed her to the pool's edge, her back against smooth stone. "We're done talking. Let's find other uses for that acid tongue."

She braced her hands against his chest, pushing him away while he grabbed hold of her waist. "Oh, yes, that's me. She of the acid tongue. While you, Lord Dragon are rife with charm."

"Rude cow," he snarled.

"Overbearing bastard," she snarled back.

The only warning she got was the narrowing of his eyes, then he was kissing her.

She tried to fight him off . . . in a way. She knew she punched his shoulder at least once. But as his tongue slid between her lips and he pulled her body tight against his, she really did lose sight of her ultimate plan—whatever that ultimate plan might have been. She didn't know anymore.

All she knew was that she was naked. He was naked. They were alone. The hot water of the spring caressed her body while his strong, rough hands gripped her tight. And it had been so long since she'd been with anyone—human or otherwise.

He released her mouth, only to move down to her throat. Where the noose had bit into her flesh, he licked the still-healing wound gently, causing her to pant and whimper. Then, against her ear, he said, "Tell me to stop, Talaith. Tell me you don't want this."

She frowned in confusion. "Why . . . oh!" Her eyes crossed as the tip of his tongue dipped into her ear. "Why are you saying that to me?"

"Because you seem to always do the opposite of what I tell you." Big hands gripped her breasts, the thumbs dragging slowly around her nipples. "I wanted to ensure your silence."

She laughed and she could feel his mouth smiling against her neck. "Cheeky bastard."

"Aye. You do bring out the worst in me, little witch."

One of his hands released her breasts, but his mouth quickly took the empty spot. His tongue lapped at her nipple, his teeth gently grazed it. So lost in the feel of his mouth on her, she didn't notice where his free hand was until his middle finger slid into her.

She gasped, her head thrown back.

That strong finger moved around inside of her, exploring her. "Gods, you're tight. Exactly how long has it been?"

Longer than she was willing to admit. "None of your business." She winced as he pushed two fingers inside her.

"Well, that statement screams years."

"You know, you keep talking and annoying the living hell out of me."

His fingers never slowed their steady, probing invasion. "You're right. We should be like you—Talaith, she of the few words."

She had a very rude remark at the ready, but he licked his lips and again attached them to her breast. Talaith's head rested against the edge of the pool as her body arched into him.

Digging one hand into his long hair and the other gripping

his shoulder, Talaith held him to her. Her hips moved of their own accord, following the movement of his fingers. Gasps filling the cavern, he played her body effortlessly, making her lose control. But when his finger slid across her clit again and again, Talaith couldn't hold back any longer. Her mouth opened and a long, drawn-out groan shuddered out of her. Then her entire body bowed, a brutal climax slamming through her.

His fingers pushed back inside her, scissoring open several times. "Much better." She didn't know what he meant until he turned slightly and his hands gripped the back of her knees, lifting them up and apart. Horrified at how exposed he'd made her, she tried to pull away from him, but his erection pushed against her sex, demanding entrance . . . and receiving it.

His cock slid inside her and wet heat wrapped around him, welcoming him home. Briec closed his eyes, shocked at exactly how good being inside this woman felt. So soft. So beautiful. So damn difficult.

"We . . . we shouldn't be doing this," she panted out desperately.

Dammit! But that wasn't a firm "no"—so he needed to distract her before she said the word he dreaded. The one word that would make him stop.

Well, she was human. Didn't they usually like compliments and things? It couldn't hurt.

Ignoring his body's demand to pound into Talaith like his life depended on it, he said, "You have very strong thighs."

He felt her entire body tense suddenly. *Uh-oh.*

She pulled back a bit to look into his face. He didn't like the scowl she suddenly had but she no longer looked panicked either. "Sorry?"

Briec cleared his throat. He didn't think she realized it,

but she kept tightening around his cock over and over again.
Clench. Unclench. Clench. Unclench.

It was driving him absolutely mad.

"You have strong thighs and are very, um, handsome."
There. That should work.

"*Handsome?*" she hissed. "Are you fucking me, Lord
Dragon, or buying a horse?" Well, he had wanted to distract her.

"I was trying to compliment you."

She sighed. "Here's a thought, dragon . . . don't speak. I
believe I can go a lifetime without your compliments."

Smiling, he asked, "Is this one of those times I should say
I'm—"

"Sorry? Yes!"

He kissed her neck, enjoying the feel of Talaith against
him. "I'll think about it."

"Oh, well, isn't that—"

He cut off her sarcastic remark by thrusting fully into her
until his balls slapped against her. She groaned, her arms
wrapping around his shoulders.

"Lovely," he panted out between hard thrusts, "I've actually found a way to keep you quiet."

Her arms tightened their hold as she bit the side of his
throat and by the dark gods did *that* feel good. "Some moments I absolutely hate you."

Briec smiled, enjoying his little witch more than he
thought possible. She never backed off, but he liked that. It
made everything a little more fun.

"Perhaps," he groaned out as he thrust into her tight
pussy, forcing her body to accommodate him. Making her
breathless. Making her demand more. "But other moments
you're absolutely mad about me."

Her legs, held wide open and tightly in his arms, began
shaking. Her panting turned harsher and more vocal.

Briec tightened his grip on her, pulling her down hard as
he continued thrusting into her. "That's it, sweet Talaith," he
ordered, barely holding his own climax at bay. "Come for me."

She choked on a sob, while heat and wetness drowned his cock. It was all he needed. Moaning, he released inside her, enjoying the feel of her hands tightening in his hair.

For several minutes the pair stayed locked together—their heavy breathing and the soft gurgling of the hot springs, the only sound in the cavern.

"Talaith?"

"Hhhmm?"

He smiled at how sated she sounded. "Are you all right?"

Lifting her head from his shoulder, she glanced around as if suddenly remembering where she was.

"Uh, um, aye." She leaned back, her hands against his shoulders, trying to push him away again. "I'm fine."

He could see the embarrassment on her face, but he had no idea why. What exactly could she be embarrassed about?

"Talaith?"

"We better get back."

"Back where?"

"Um . . . to . . . uh . . ." With a heavy, defeated sigh, she shrugged. "Somewhere."

No. No. This wouldn't do. No regrets for what they had done. Especially since he planned to keep doing it for quite awhile, over and over again. He had yet to tire of her.

Briec wrapped his arms tight around her and pushed his chest into hers.

Startled, she looked up at him. "What are you doing?"

"Getting you used to the way things are going to be for awhile."

"What do you—" She gasped when, still brutally hard, he began fucking her again. Long, slow strokes now he could take his time.

Stunned, she said, "How did you . . . how can you . . ."

Briec leaned in and whispered softly in her ear, "Remember, sweet Talaith? Not human."

Her own body now matching him thrust for thrust, she moaned back, "Clearly."

Chapter 10

It was the long tongue on the back of her knee that woke her up. Forcing her eyes open, she looked over her shoulder to see Briec, naked and beautiful, stretched across the enormous bed. His big arms placed on either side of her legs, holding his body over her as he leaned forward and again licked the back of her knee, reveling in it as if someone had spread the finest honey on her skin.

"What are you doing?"

"Waking you up." His voice sounded raw and husky from sleep and sex. She liked it.

Nipping the sensitive flesh, he grinned. "See? You're awake now."

"How long did I sleep?"

"Too long."

It didn't feel like too long.

When he'd finally exhausted her in the hot springs, he'd picked her up and carried her back to her bed. After quickly drying her off, he'd set her down and got in behind her, muttering something like, "It's about time you let me in this bed." Too tired to ask what the hell he meant, and enjoying the feel of his strong arm around her as he drifted to sleep, she instead buried her head in the pillow and quickly dropped off.

Now here he was, dragging that gorgeous body up and over hers, his warm, wet tongue leading the way.

"You taste good."

"Coming from a dragon, that compliment can be a little scary."

He nipped one butt cheek, then the other. "Be nice, woman."

She didn't want to be nice. She wanted to play. Especially since she never had before. At least not in bed. "Why should I be nice?" she teased. "You're not nice." And my, but she did enjoy that about him.

He kissed her lower back, right at the base of her spine, then licked it. "I don't know how," he murmured against her warm flesh.

"Perhaps I can show you how easy it is to be nice."

Slowly his eyes lifted to look at her face. "Oh, I think I'd like that," he breathed out huskily.

She pulled from his grasp, raising herself on her knees while he leaned back, his hands flat on the bed, propping him up.

Turning, she moved to his side and placed her hand on his chest. She stroked the hard, smooth skin and marveled at how her merest touch caused ripples across his body. And that was only with her hand.

Leaning forward, she used the tip of her tongue to tickle one nipple. He let out a harsh gasp, followed by a moan when she suckled him into her mouth. She slid her mouth to the other side and did the same. He shuddered and moaned again, making Talaith smile.

Who knew she had this kind of power?

Talaith dragged her hand down his chest and her lips and tongue followed. Before she even reached his straining erection, he'd lifted his hips as if expecting her to take him in her mouth. Her arrogant dragon.

Instead, she licked it from base to tip and back again.

Then she followed the pulsating veins, avoiding the head except to occasionally tickle it with her nose.

"Talaith," he groaned.

"Aye?" Her tongue slithered up the underside of his shaft.

"Don't torture me, woman."

"Torture you? Me? The weak human torturing a dragon of such awesome power and intellect?"

He grinned at her teasing. "Yes, evil witch. You're torturing me. At least have the decency to admit it."

"I'll admit nothing."

"So I noticed," he muttered while he watched her every move.

She ignored his comment, unwilling to ruin the good mood with the reality of her situation. She had no idea how long before the goddess came for her, and she didn't want to waste a second thinking about anything but Briec and how he made her feel.

Talaith wrapped her hand around the base of his shaft, marveling at its length and width while enjoying the taste of it, of him. She licked fluid off the tip, teasing the slit with the tip of her tongue, forcing another broken moan from him.

His hand slid into her hair, massaging the back of her head with his long fingers. "Talaith . . ."

"Mhmm?"

He growled and she fought her desire to laugh.

"Stop teasing me, wench. You're being heartless."

"I find using the word 'please' quite effective at these moments." She nipped the base and his body jerked in response. "Begging would be even better."

When he didn't answer, she glanced up to find him gazing off, frowning.

Leaning back a bit, she stared at him. "Gods, you've never said please, have you?"

"I'm thinking." He was silent for a few more seconds, then . . . "No. I never have." He looked down at her, one eyebrow raised. "And I don't plan to start now."

Anyone else—king or peasant, husband or child—she'd feel insulted. Yet she wasn't because she knew he wasn't being cruel or cold-hearted. Just a dragon who never had to say "please" and "sorry" before. And if she thought for one moment she would end up spending the rest of her life with him, she'd have some real concerns.

Since that wouldn't happen, as he'd reminded her the day before, she wouldn't worry.

"That's a real shame, dragon." She ran her tongue across the tip, blew on the wetness she left behind. "Because without it . . ." Her open mouth hovered over his shaft for several seconds and she heard him swallow in desperation, anticipating her sucking him into his next life. Instead of doing that, she snapped her mouth shut. "I can't help you."

"You evil—"

"Ah, ah, ah. *You* be nice."

Snarling, his hand still tangled in her hair, he pulled her close then pushed her onto her back. He lay across her, his mouth claiming hers.

Wicked, wicked thoughts flowed through her brain while Briec's hands moved across her body, his tongue thrusting against hers.

She moaned and writhed under him, and he pulled back just enough to say, "We both know I can make you beg long before me, sweet Talaith."

"My, my, we are"—she arched into his body as one of his hands slid between her thighs—"sure of ourselves."

"It's a gift."

"A gift for you. A curse for the rest of us."

He smiled as he teased her hard nipple with his tongue. Digging her hands into his hair, she silently urged him to take it into his mouth, but he only chuckled, opting to blow on it instead.

Bastard.

Before she could tell him that sentiment out loud, a movement out of the corner of her eye caught her attention.

She turned her head and Gwenvael, in dragon form, his hair soaked as if he'd been outside in the rain again, lay there. His head rested in the palm of his claw and when she looked at him he bared his fangs—a dragon smile.

She squealed so loud, Briec's whole body jumped. Then, using the buried strength of her people, she shoved the big male off her, scrambling away from him so fast she toppled right off the bed and onto the hard ground. Thankfully out of Gwenvael's view.

She grabbed one of the furs piled on the floor and wrapped it around her body, making sure to cover her head completely.

Éibhear, so deeply absorbed in the third volume on his grandfather's life when a very young dragon—*Darkness's Bones, that dragon was a slag*—he didn't realize Gwenvael had left the room until he returned with an extremely calm Briec. A little too calm, in fact.

Naked, with an erection that could knock down the walls of the Dragon Queen's mountain home, Briec didn't even look at Éibhear as he turned to face his golden-haired brother. "Shift. Now."

Uh-oh. Éibhear closed his book. It was a rare moment when a dragon asked another dragon to shift to human, but apparently Briec didn't want to shift back to dragon.

Gwenvael rolled his eyes but chanted the ancient spell, which quickly shifted him to human form.

"Before you say anything, brother, I wasn't there long."

Briec didn't respond. He simply stared at Gwenvael who seemed hell-bent on ignoring that which was right in front of him. Like Briec's simmering rage.

"I mean, I could see your little Talaith has a way with her tongue."

Éibhear closed his eyes briefly and wondered exactly how

such a brilliant dragon could be such an utter idiot at the most dangerous times.

"And a strong, firm grip with that hand of hers."

So intent on amusing himself, Gwenvael didn't even see Briec's hands lower to his sides. Or see he'd closed his eyes and begun chanting softly.

"Although I always thought of you as the kind to literally force a woman's head onto that rather healthy-sized cock you've got there."

Powerful ancient Magicks flowed between Briec's hands as Gwenvael kept right on talking.

"But to each his own, I guess. Oh, and by the way, brother, she has an amazing body. All lush and curvy. Personally, I could lose hours in that sweet . . . *aaaaarrrggghhhhhhh!*"

Gwenvael slammed into the cave wall with such force, Éibhear was sure he heard something break. Although he doubted it was that ridiculously hard head of his.

Briec hadn't even moved from his spot. Although not nearly as powerful as the Queen or Morfyd, Briec had trained with dragon wizards in his early days. Interested in Magick, but not enough to stray from his path of Dragonwarrior, he had developed some powerful Magick skills.

Clearly, Gwenvael failed to remember that.

Éibhear stared at Gwenvael's prone body, sparks of Magick still coming off him.

"When he wakes up," Briec said, "and that won't be for quite awhile, tell him to stay away from me."

"Aye." Éibhear decided against saying much else.

With a nod, Briec walked back toward where he'd no doubt left Talaith. Sparing his unconscious older brother one more glance, Éibhear shrugged and returned to his book.

Briec walked back into the chamber, his rage still singing through his veins. What he didn't expect to find . . . Talaith trying to leave wearing only a fur covering.

"Where are you going?"

"Outside."

"Outside?"

"Yes. I'm hoping there's still a storm. I'll run in the rain, naked, and hopefully catch my death. Or, if I'm truly lucky, lightning will strike me dead."

"Why would you . . . I don't under . . ." Briec rubbed his eyes with his knuckles. His cock hurt from its need to come and she was babbling. Damn woman. "What are you talking about?"

"You don't expect me to live with this embarrassment, do you?"

"Embarrassment about what?"

She took a step back, her face a riot of confusion. "About your brother watching us."

Now *he* was confused. "Why would that embarrass you?"

"If you're not embarrassed why did you take him out of here and, I'm hoping, gut him like a fish?"

"Because he interrupted me," he bit out between severely clenched teeth. "And I wasn't done."

"Well, we're done now," she barked and actually tried to walk around him. Grabbing hold of the fur, he snatched it off her. Angry, Talaith spun around but froze when she saw his face. He could imagine how he must look. Desperate, most likely. Because he was.

"You're not going anywhere." Not now. Not after last night. Now he knew why Fearghus smiled. If this was normal human fucking, he couldn't believe he hadn't taken a human before. And he wasn't about to let that idiot brother of his ruin this.

"I understand, dragon, that you like to pretend you have some hold over me, but let me inform you quite clearly—"

"What has you so upset, Talaith?" He cut her off, stepping in front of her so she couldn't leave. "Just my brother walking in on us?"

"Oh, come on, Briec. He didn't just walk in on us. I have

no idea how long that big bastard had been standing there watching us, but by the look on his face, it was for quite a bit."

"So what?" He took a step toward her and immediately she took a step back. "You think my brother, especially Gwenvael, has never seen two beings fucking before? Do you think he's never done it?"

"I don't care what he's seen or done. All I care about is—"

"Yes?" he pushed. Still walking toward her, forcing her back into the chamber.

She shook her head. "This was wrong, Briec. I shouldn't have. We shouldn't have . . ."

"Why?"

"What do you mean why?"

"Why shouldn't we have done what we did? Because I'm a dragon?"

She shrugged. "Well . . ."

"Because you have a husband?"

"But I do have—"

"Or because knowing someone was watching us— watching you—made you wet?"

Talaith slammed into the cave wall behind her. "What?"

"Or maybe it's just the fear of being caught, Talaith." He put his hands against the wall behind her head, caging her in. Trapping her. "Knowing someone could walk in on you at anytime. Knowing they might see you with my cock down your throat or my fingers in your ass?"

She slapped his arm. "And don't try *that* again!"

"Knowing that no matter what we're doing, I won't stop. I won't stop until you're screaming and crying and coming all over me."

She crossed her arms in front of her chest and looked away. But he still saw the heat in her eyes. Could still smell her lust. And he simply loved how her nipples hardened and he hadn't even touched them.

"Is that why you feel ashamed, Talaith? Because you like

that bit of danger sometimes? Because it's outside what those horrid little peasants told you was right?"

"I. Hate. You."

He glanced over his shoulder as if he expected to find Gwenvael there again, although he knew the bastard wouldn't be moving for the next few hours. "You know, Gwenvael might come back." He looked back at her. "Or Éibhear. You know how he likes to chat with you."

"Move, Briec."

"As you wish." He dropped slowly to his knees in front of her, ready to grab her should she try to bolt again.

"Wha . . . what are you doing?"

He leaned in, burying his nose in her groin. He took a deep breath, letting the lust-filled scent of her move through him. She was already so wet.

He grabbed hold of her thighs and pried them apart.

"Wait," she begged as he wedged one hand against the blazing heat of her sex.

"We can't wait, Talaith. I don't know when they'll come back here." A flood of warm, fresh juices wet his hand at his words. *Oh, yes,* he moaned to himself.

Taking firm hold of her rear, Briec lifted her and forced her legs onto his shoulders.

"Briec," she whispered desperately.

"Sssh, little witch." He nuzzled her pussy, all dripping wet and perfect. "Get too loud and they'll be sure to come to see what's going on."

He buried his head between her thighs, hearing her voice catch as she tried to hold back a cry. Smiling, ridiculously happy with this strange woman, Briec speared her pussy with his tongue. She gripped his head while he licked her clean, amazed at how wonderful she tasted.

Talaith's legs clamped tight around his neck and he heard her struggling not to moan out loud. Digging his fingers hard into her beautiful ass, he pulled her closer to his mouth, mercilessly lashing her clit with his tongue. Her hips rode his face, her moans getting louder and louder.

He loved how he could make her lose control, how he could make her come apart in his arms like this.

She gave a startled squeak and then she did just that—she climaxed; her body tight and hot around him. Before her muscles could stop their contractions, he dragged her to the floor. Inside her before she could even see straight, Briec pounded into her relentlessly, completely lost to her and what she did to him.

Her hands, still buried in his hair, pulled him down for a brutal kiss. As soon as their lips touched and she tasted herself on him, she groaned and her climax started all over again. Her sex clenching him so hard, she hauled him over that edge with her.

He purred her name as he came, and she never heard it sound so sweet before. Clinging to her as his hot seed poured inside her waiting body, Talaith held back tears she'd never allow to come. Too cruel. All of it. To finally know paradise, only to have the gods snatch it away from her whenever they chose was too cruel for words.

Briec kissed her shoulder, her neck, her chin. Then he was over her, staring down at her. Smiling and never judging her. She truly hadn't seen anything so beautiful before.

"You never fail to amaze me, sweet Talaith." A big palm cupped her cheek gently. "I chose very well, my little witch."

Perhaps. Shame he didn't choose first.

Chapter 11

Gwenvael held his head in his hands and prayed for death. This was worse than any night after hard drinking he'd ever had. Why didn't Briec merely kill him?

Damn spellcasting dragon.

He didn't know what the bastard had done to him, but it took him the rest of the day and night to recover enough to make it to the next day's morning meal. Talaith sat at one end of the table, reading. Briec sat at the other, reading. Neither spoke to each other and, if Gwenvael didn't know better, he might have thought he'd imagined the little festival of fucking he'd witnessed between the two.

Even Éibhear looked confused and refused to speak.

When Briec did finally say something, it startled them both—but not Talaith.

"Where's the bread?"

Turning the page of her book, but not looking at him, she said, "I finished it."

"You didn't save me any?"

"Is that my role now? I'm supposed to save you food? If you wanted it you should have claimed it."

Gwenvael looked at Éibhear and his brother shrugged helplessly. He remembered quite clearly after Annwyl and

Fearghus's first time together, how the two of them fucked constantly and anywhere convenient. Going at it relentlessly.

Perhaps the bedding between these two hadn't been as amazing as Gwenvael first thought.

"Would it kill you to not keep the food all to yourself, like a rat storing for winter?"

"Would it kill you not to eat as if it's your last meal? Is sharing with others so inconceivable to you? Should I add that to the list with 'please' and 'I'm sorry'?"

"Only if you add 'glutton' to your list of 'never shuts up.'"

Talaith gave an almost royal wave of her hand. "I'm done with this conversation." She shoved her chair back and stood. "And I'm done with you."

"Conversation too much of a challenge, m'lady?"

"More like too boring. Kind of like you."

"Now if you gentlemen"—she looked at Briec—"and whatever you are, will excuse me."

She turned and walked out.

"What is wrong with you?" Éibhear snapped.

Briec looked truly confused. "What are you talking about?"

"Why were you so mean to her?"

Briec stood. "I wasn't mean to her. I was arguing with her. Now if you'll excuse me, I need to go discover—to my horror—that the little witch hasn't made the bed."

He grinned and Gwenvael knew exactly what was going on. He shook his head in disgust. Never. He would *never* get this way over any female—*ever.*

Unfortunately, Éibhear was still confused. "You never make your bed, Briec. Mostly because we rarely sleep in beds."

Briec sighed and shook his head. As he walked out, the mighty erection straining the front of his black breeches leading the way no doubt, he tossed over his shoulder to Gwenvael, "Explain it to the pup, would you? I'm busy."

Éibhear frowned. "Explain what to me?"

* * *

She squealed as he threw her back on the bed. "Didn't I say I wanted this bed made?"

Lifting herself up on her elbows, "You most certainly did not. And I'm not a servant. You want the bed made . . . *make it yourself!*"

The dragon growled at her and Talaith squealed again, trying to scramble away. He grabbed hold of her ankles and yanked her to the foot of the bed.

"Get off me."

"No. You need a good lesson, I think. Saucy wench."

He flipped her onto her stomach and dragged her back until only her chest rested on the bed and both of them kneeled on the floor.

She tried to look over her shoulder to find out what he might be up to, but he tossed the end of her dress over her head.

"Och! Briec, you arrogant bastard! Let me go!"

He didn't answer her, but he did pry her legs apart.

Talaith gripped the fur coverings in her hands and bit her lip.

"What are you going to do?" she whispered, working hard to keep the giggle out of her voice.

"Nothing you don't deserve." She felt the head of his erection pushing against her sex. "And definitely nothing you don't want."

"That sure are you, dragon?"

He pushed his cock home with one thrust and she cried out. His big hands ripped the dress open from the back, then deftly stripped it from her body. When he gripped her breasts tight, she moaned and slammed back against him.

"I'm very sure, little witch," he whispered against her ear. "Now tell me how much you want me."

His thrusts started off slow but powerful, forcing her into the bed.

Panting, her body delirious with lust, she said, "I'll tell you anything you want, dragon."

"Mmmhhm. Good."

"As soon as you beg me for it."

He bit the back of her neck, making her wince at the slight sting then moan when he licked the wound. "Evil wench," he muttered against her sweating flesh.

"Presumptuous snake."

Then they stopped talking all together.

Briec intertwined his fingers with Talaith's and pushed her arms over her head. Her eyelids fluttered open and she smiled up at him. "You never let me sleep."

"Why sleep when there are more interesting things to do?" He kissed her neck and nuzzled under her chin. "You're a Nolwenn witch, you have centuries for sleeping."

"In other words I should enjoy you while I have you?"

His grip on her hands tightened and he kissed her chest. "Exactly." He didn't want to give her false hope. In another hundred or two hundred years, he'd be done with her. Or three hundred. He hadn't made up his mind yet. Maybe even four if her already brilliant oral skills continued to improve. Or five if she continued to scream his name at the best times. But no more than that. And to promise more would be wrong.

Briec groaned as Talaith's leg slid up his thigh to wrap around his waist, the sheath holding her knife scraping against his skin.

"Good. I hate to think I'd be stuck with your arrogance for longer than was necessary."

"You're the only one who says I'm arrogant. Most say I'm honest."

"They're afraid to tell you the truth. Afraid to tell you you're difficult and annoying."

"And why aren't you afraid, little witch?" he asked seconds before sucking one of her nipples into his mouth. Her back arched and she moaned, her hands fighting to pull from his grasp.

Briec rocked against her, his cock teasing the soft skin of her thighs but he didn't enter her. Not yet.

Her body picked up his rhythm, her hips pushing back.

"I don't know. I should be afraid. You're a fire-breathing dragon. Your kind hunts my kind for sport."

"Aye, but it's not much of a challenge unless you're in a pack," he mumbled against her breast, unwilling to release it.

She stifled a laugh and Briec grinned. He did enjoy making this woman smile.

"How do you live with yourself, Lord Arrogant?"

In between using the tip of his tongue to toy with her hard nipples, he answered, "Very easily, Lady Difficult. I find myself quite charming."

"All that gives me ease is to know you'll be done with me soon. I'll simply leave when the rains end—"

Briec brought his head up so quickly she gasped in surprise.

"You'll leave when I'm done, little witch. Not before."

Her brown eyes narrowed. "You insist on pushing me, dragon."

"There is no pushing. Merely fact. *I* will tell you when your blood debt to me has been paid."

"Gods damn you, Briec." She tried to pull away from him, but he held tight to her hands. "Why do you have to be such an ass?"

"And why must you fight me all the time?" He rested his lips against her ear. "Why can't you just come when I tell you and be done with it?"

Talaith shook her head. "Briec . . ." She let out an exasperated sigh. "Be grateful for that blood debt, dragon, because I truly believe I would have killed you long ago."

"Now you sound like my mother."

She opened her mouth, he assumed to say something but nothing came out. And was her eye twitching? After several seconds, when she still said nothing, he kissed her.

Talaith's fingers gripped him tight while the rest of her body melted beneath his.

He liked that his mere kiss could do this to her. Make her this wet and ready.

He sunk his cock deep into her drenched sex and shuddered at the feel of her. Of the absolute rightness of his body inside hers. With each powerful stroke, he added more time on how long she'd stay with him. The first stroke led to another ten years. By the tenth stroke, another hundred.

When he finally climaxed and came deep inside her soft body, losing himself to her completely, the word "forever" crossed his mind.

Briec blinked, then stepped back from the cave entrance. His brothers stared, too.

"What the hell just happened?"

Shrugging at Gwenvael's question, Briec took a careful step outside. The two suns shined brightly, no clouds to mar the beauty of the day. Normally not a strange occurrence . . . except for the fact that less than a mere second before, the storm had still been going full blast and had been for days. Black clouds roiled, rain came down in thick sheets to drench the land. And now—nothing.

"Anyone talk to Morfyd?" Briec asked softly.

"No. She's been off with Annwyl."

"You'd best track her down then."

"What about you?"

He scratched the back of his neck with the point of his tail. "I'm taking Talaith home."

From the corner of his eye, he saw his brothers glance at each other. "What?" He whipped his head around, nailing both dragons with one look. "What's going on?"

Gwenvael rested back on his haunches. "You're not going to toss her away when you're done, are you?"

"What?"

"You'll keep her, won't you?" Éibhear asked. Well, it was more like a demand.

"What are you two idiots going on about?"

"We like her."

"A lot."

"And?"

"And, she's not like other women," Éibhear nearly snarled, but Briec already knew that. "Don't simply toss her aside because you allow yourself to become bored."

Briec didn't think he could become bored with Talaith. Not ever. Since the rains hadn't stopped for days, neither had they. Spending most of the day in bed or the hot springs. Only peeking out to get nourishment . . . or argue, which always led back to bed or the hot springs.

It had been amazing. Perhaps the best days of his already long life.

"What I do or won't do, will be my business, brothers. Not yours."

Éibhear, the youngest and most passionate of them all, pointed one black talon at his older kin. "Hurt her, Briec, and it will quickly become my business."

Briec looked at Gwenvael. "Any threats from you?"

Gwenvael shrugged, his smirk well in place. "Just this— get bored with her brother, and feel free to send her my way. I'll gladly take her in. And give her everything she needs."

If Éibhear hadn't jumped between them, Briec would have snapped Gwenvael's neck like a twig.

"Not on your life, dragon!"

Talaith hid behind Éibhear, which seemed to anger Briec even more.

"You're not being rational."

"If rational means any more flying—then you're damn right."

Gwenvael laughed, but it turned into a cough as Briec's violet eyes swung his way.

"You almost got me killed the other night. Can't we walk? Or get a carriage with horses?"

Snorting out another laugh, Gwenvael quickly turned away.

"Talaith . . . come here."

Wrapping the fur-lined cape Éibhear gave her tighter around her shoulders, she shook her head. "No."

"If we leave now, we'll be there in two hours. If we walk, we're looking at days. In this unpredictable weather."

Well, that didn't sound much better. But the thought of flying turned her stomach.

"Can't we stay here?"

Gwenvael smiled. This cave was his. "Why, of course you . . . *ow!*"

His claw covering where Briec's tail had slashed his snout, he yelled, "*What was that for?*"

"Accident."

"Wait, wait, wait." Talaith stepped out from behind Éibhear, who looked ready to blast his brother out of the bloody cave. "Don't fight."

"Then we best leave."

Talaith scratched her head and wished she hadn't had all those sausages for breakfast. "Fine."

"Talaith . . ." Éibhear moved toward her, but she immediately saw Briec wouldn't stand for that.

"It's all right, Éibhear. I'm sure I'll be fine. If I don't fall to my death."

Sighing in exasperation, Briec barked, "Woman, you test my patience."

"And you push mine," she snapped back.

She smiled at Éibhear. "It was lovely meeting you, Éibhear."

"Well, I hope we see each other again."

He could hope, but she knew better. Instead of lying, she reached up, wrapping her arms around his neck . . . or, at least trying. Dragons were so big. "And thank you for all the books."

"I'll send you more," he promised.

She nodded and stepped away. "Now please take care of yourself. Especially in this weather."

"I will."

"And don't let Gwenvael goad you into a fight."

"I won't."

Briec let out a big sigh behind her, but she ignored him. "And be good, Éibhear the Blue." She rubbed his snout with her hand.

"Are you going to tell me to be good as well?" Gwenvael asked.

Talaith rolled her eyes. "Oh, why bother?"

"It's polite."

She turned from Éibhear and walked up to Gwenvael. "Perhaps. But you are not. Polite, that is."

"This is true." He lowered his snout close to her. "Can I get a rub as well?"

Laughing, Talaith reached up and rubbed her hand against the scale-covered flesh between his nostrils, successfully avoiding the fresh wound. "You are a beast, Gwenvael the Handsome. And I can't wait until some female comes along who will make your life absolutely intolerable."

"That's a lovely sentiment. Could you put that into verse for me?"

"I'm waiting," Briec bellowed.

With a resigned sigh, Talaith walked over to Briec. "Perhaps we could—"

"Get on or I'll take you there in my claw."

"You are not a nice dragon at all."

She grabbed hold of his hair and awkwardly hauled herself onto his back.

"Comfortable?"

"I'd be much more comfortable back in my . . . *aaayieeeeeeeeeeeeeeeeee!*"

And she screamed like that all the way to Briec's den.

* * *

"How bad is it?"

Brastias shrugged at Morfyd's question. "It's slowed us down. The mud will make it slow going. Why?"

"Only wondering when we'll get back to Dark Plains." He didn't like the frown of worry marring that beautiful face. He adored everything about that face, but especially the female beneath it. He didn't like to see her upset.

"Before the storms I would have told you not long. I mean, we separated from the other troops to get back quicker. But when Annwyl began circling this general area—"

"We've been going in circles?"

Her angry exclamation startled him. "I thought you knew."

"I've had so much on my mind." She rubbed her forehead. "Where's Annwyl?"

"Sleeping. And please don't wake her up."

"Yes, but—"

"You know how she is when she hasn't seen Fearghus for a long time. And she hasn't seen Fearghus for a *very* long time."

In battle, the queen's forced separation from her mate made Annwyl a formidable foe. But when the battles were over, the men avoided the woman like she bore the plague. Unless Fearghus was near to keep her . . . uh . . . occupied.

"All right. I'll wait until she wakes."

"Is it something you can tell me about?"

Those blue eyes he dreamed of almost every night turned toward him. "It's nothing to worry about, Brastias." She patted his shoulder and his entire body tightened. She had to stop doing that. She kept touching him like a friend or one of her brothers. The last thing he felt for Morfyd the White Dragonwitch of Dark Plains was brotherly.

"You sure? I can be quite helpful."

Finally, she smiled. Good. He loved seeing her smile. "I know you are, my friend."

Friend? "Morfyd, I—"

Lightning flashed and storm clouds suddenly appeared. Morfyd looked up at the sky. "Dammit."

Brastias sensed her concern went beyond getting Annwyl back to Fearghus. "What is it, Morfyd? What aren't you telling me?"

Shaking her head, the woman turned from him and walked off. He watched her until she disappeared into her tent, then the skies opened up and rain poured down on him.

"Hold on."

"Hold on? Why?" Talaith finally lifted her head from where she had it buried in Briec's mane of silver hair. She should have never looked. The dragon was heading right for a waterfall . . . and he wasn't stopping.

"*What are you doing? Have you gone mad?*" she yelled over the brutal storm. It had plagued them all the way from Gwenvael's den to Briec's. The dragon had been able to keep ahead of it until a bit ago.

"Don't you trust me, sweet Talaith?"

"*No!*"

He chuckled as the waterfall—and the stone wall behind it—came closer and closer.

With a screech, Talaith buried her face into Briec's neck, her hands gripping his mane. She knew the moment they hit the waterfall as even more water drenched her and a roaring sound assaulted her ears, then it stopped and she was in complete darkness. She thought it was over, until the dragon went free-falling into the blackness.

His humming during all this didn't help either. It competed with her screams.

When the dragon suddenly stopped, she thought for sure whatever remained in her stomach would come flying back up. He spoke a charm and torches lining the cave walls burst with light.

"Finally. Home."

Without releasing the beast, Talaith looked up and saw the enormous cavern the dragon had dropped down to get to this level. Bastard. He could have warned her he wasn't planning on some kind of poetic suicide.

Briec flew slowly down the cavern and Talaith marveled at the size of Briec's cave. Gwenvael's hadn't been this large.

The deeper they went, the brighter it became with more and more torches lighting the way.

After a good fifteen minutes, the dragon pulled to a stop, gently landing.

"You all right?"

She yanked his hair and he rewarded her with a short grunt of pain. "No. I'm not all right."

He began walking, heading deeper into his cave. "You really need to get used to flying. And stop pulling my hair. It's irritating."

"Why?"

"Because it's attached to my head."

"Not why should I stop pulling your hair, dragon. Why should I get used to flying?"

"Because, it's the easiest way to get out of here. Unless, of course, you'd prefer the long walk out."

Knowing there was another way out, even one, gave her much ease. She'd have to find it later when the dragon slept.

"Do I have to ride bareback all the time? Can't you wear a saddle or something?"

Briec abruptly stopped walking. "Don't ever say that to me again."

She didn't know he'd be so sensitive about it. "Sorry."

He nodded his enormous horned head and walked on. After another ten minutes, Talaith noticed large caverns filled with treasure. Also like Gwenvael's cave. Eventually, he entered an enormous chamber and that's when he finally stopped walking. Briec lowered himself to the ground and Talaith slid off his back. She leaned against him as her legs took a moment getting steady again.

Once she had some control, she pushed away from his body and slowly made her way deep inside. She gasped in surprise. "Briec . . . it's . . . um . . ."

"Yes?"

"It's beautiful." She stared at the tapestries covering the walls. Beautiful ones that told stories of dragon heroes from long ago. He also had an immense dining table, silver-accented chairs surrounding it; couches for lounging, and one of the alcoves from the main chamber held the biggest bookshelf she'd ever seen, filled from top to bottom with books. More couches and chairs littered the alcove as well so one could rest and read.

It was warm. Cozy. And she'd never felt safer in her life. She fell in love with all of it immediately.

"I thought it would be like Gwenvael's. Maybe even a little worse."

Briec moved up beside her, his tail encircling her feet but not touching her. "Gwenvael doesn't stay in his home much."

She could believe that. The few days they all stayed in due to the storms, Gwenvael kept leaving and risking the weather so he could get a few minutes outside. He was not a dragon who liked being away from other beings for too long, unlike his brothers.

"So you do like it?"

"Yes. I love it." She stepped away from him, pulling off her wet cape, and glanced into the different alcoves.

Briec cleared his throat. "If there's something you don't like, we can change it. Get you something nicer."

"Nicer than what?" Everything before her was of the finest quality. Briec was definitely a dragon who liked his comforts expensive. "All of it is beautiful, Briec. Truly."

She stopped at one of the alcoves only to find the largest bed she'd ever seen.

And, for some unknown reason, she felt bitter jealousy at the sight of it.

"What's wrong?"

She shook her head. "Nothing."

She felt heat at her back and knew he'd shifted. So when his big arms wrapped around her shoulders, his hard body pushed up against her back, she wasn't surprised. Although the extremely affectionate gesture confused her to no end.

"You don't sound like it's nothing."

"You can't expect me to sleep there."

His head leaned over her shoulder, staring at the bed. "Why not? I know you wouldn't prefer the floor."

"I simply don't want to."

"I need something better than that, Talaith. What is it?"

She sighed. Might as well be honest. Couldn't hurt. "I won't stay in the same bed with you—"

"Why the hell not?" he demanded, suddenly angry, but unaware she wasn't done.

"—that you've stayed in with other females."

Talaith felt Briec's body relax behind her as his anger receded quickly at her words.

Nuzzling his head against hers, he said, "You have nothing to fear, Talaith. I've never even used that bed. My brothers insisted I had to have one. Plus, I've never brought another female here."

She snorted in disbelief. "You're trying to tell me that you've never had another female here—ever?"

"Aye."

His tongue traced the line of her ear. She worked hard to ignore it, unwilling to let him distract her. "How old are you?"

"Two hundred and sixty-two winters last moon."

"And in all that time you've never brought a woman back to your home?"

One of his hands slid across her collarbone, across her

chest, settling comfortably on her breast. "Not this home. I won't promise my parents' den fared as well. I didn't want any female here, thinking they could take over . . . move in. So I met them in their own lairs."

Yet he was willing to let her make changes if she found anything displeasing. No, no. She wouldn't think too much on what that could possibly mean and instead she focused on trying to control her breathing. Not easy when he squeezed her breast while his fingers tweaked her nipple through the material of her gown. "Well . . . I . . . I guess that's all right then."

His tongue dipped into her ear and her entire body trembled. "Are you sure, little witch? I want to make sure you're comfortable. That you'll be happy here."

"I am." She gripped the arm still wrapped around her shoulder, holding her close, unwilling to let her go.

"We can wait to get a new bed here. It will take some time. I'll have to raid another village to get it. After the storms, of course." His teeth tugged her earlobe and she marveled at how easily this dragon played her body. Like he'd been handling it all her adult life as opposed to just a few days.

"I don't want to wait for a new bed."

"Really? You're sure?"

She wanted to cry in frustration as every tug of her earlobe leapt right to her sex and stayed there. Talaith didn't even know when she'd begun squirming, desperate to feel the arrogant dragon inside her again.

"Yes. I'm sure."

"You don't sound like you're truly convinced."

"You are such a bastard, Briec," she panted.

He chuckled in her ear. "I know. So you do like it?"

She bent her head to the side, hoping he'd kiss her neck. He did. "I thought we already had this conversation. I love it."

"More than Gwenvael's?"

"Well . . ."

He released her and spun her around to face him. "I expected an immediate yes."

She shrugged. Playing with fire, she knew. But she couldn't help it. "But he has the hot springs."

"Is that it?"

"That's very important."

He grabbed her hand. "Come."

"That's what I was hoping for, but you stopped."

He pulled her, leading through the cave. Down into an alcove with a path leading below.

"Where are we going?" She heard noise, but from where she now stood, she couldn't quite make it out.

"You really need to learn to trust me. You act like I'm dragging you off to your execution."

The deeper they went, the darker it became and the louder the sound grew. Finally Briec stopped. "What about this, Lady Demanding?" He said a word and flame lit torches.

Talaith sat down hard right where she stood. "Briec . . ." she breathed out, unable to find words to describe what she saw.

It was a waterfall. Here, inside the dragon's cave. It was enormous, dropping right into a river that snaked and disappeared under rock.

"Briec, it's beautiful." She looked up and saw the pride on his face. Her words pleased him. Greatly.

He tugged her back to her feet. "That's not all." He took her all the way down until they stood right beside it. Their hands still clasped, he held them under the rushing water.

"It's warm!"

"Aye. The waterfall is heated from under the ground and it warms up the river water."

She grinned. "This is amazing."

"My brothers don't know it's here," he remarked offhandedly. "Actually, no one in my family does. They all think I use the lakes outside."

But he'd told her. She now knew more about his home

than his brothers did. The home where no other female, not a relation, had been inside.

"What do they do when they stay?" she asked, working hard to control her pounding heart.

"They use the lakes. If they knew about this, I'd never get rid of them."

He turned to her and smiled, and her heart went back to full gallop.

"Aren't you uncomfortable in that dress, little witch?"

She glanced down at it, grateful for the distraction. "No. It's quite comfortable. That's why I wore it for—" She lifted her eyes and saw him staring at her with one eyebrow raised. "Oh. Uh, I hate it. I feel completely trapped in this dress."

"Then we best get it off you, eh?"

"All right then."

Silently, she watched his hands slowly untie the ribbon holding the front of her dress together. The dragon took his time removing the ribbon and pulling the tight bodice apart, exposing her breasts.

He stared at them for what felt like forever. Merely stared. Finally, she couldn't stand it anymore.

"Perhaps—"

"Sssh. Quiet. I'm concentrating."

She didn't know which took precedence. Yelling at him for shushing her—she really hated that—or asking him why he was concentrating.

Curiosity won out.

"Concentrating on what?"

"You're still talking."

"Briec."

With an exaggerated sigh, he said, "Fine. Once again I have to find ways to silence you."

She gasped as he leaned forward and his warm mouth closed over her nipple. He sucked on it gently, driving her insane. She wanted more.

Talaith slid her hand into his silver hair, pushing him closer to her. "Harder," she gasped. He chuckled, but obliged.

Eyes closing, she leaned back. One of his big arms wrapped around her waist and held her. With his free hand he took hold of her other breast and squeezed the nipple between his fingers. "Gods, Briec. That . . . that feels so good."

He didn't let up, keeping the pressure relentless on both breasts. She felt every suck, every pull down to her sex. Her panting grew worse. Her small cries more intense.

"Briec . . . I . . . I think I'm . . ." At her nonsensical words, he sucked and squeezed harder, and suddenly a climax was coursing up her back, through her groin, out her fingers and toes. She'd never felt anything quite like it.

She gasped and shuddered in his arms as the climax overtook her. In those seconds, everything held still. All she could feel was Briec holding her and his mouth and hands on her body. The cave walls could crumble around them, and she was relatively certain she'd never even notice.

When she came, he almost came with her. It took years of hard-learned self-control to keep his climax at bay. But as soon as her body settled down, he stripped her dress the rest of the way off and tossed it somewhere. He'd have to find her another because he had no idea where he threw it. He picked her up in his arms, her legs wrapped around his waist, her face buried in his shoulder, and walked into the water.

As soon as he had her under the waterfall, her head snapped up and she laughed like a child. Nothing had ever sounded sweeter.

"So, tell me now, little witch. Is my den better than Gwenvael's?"

Arms thrown over his shoulders, legs high on his waist,

Talaith was actually able to look down at him for once. Her hand caressed his jaw, pushing his wet hair off his face. "Oh, aye, Briec. It is."

He smiled and held her tighter until she said, "Of course, I haven't seen Éibhear's den yet. It could be amazing for all I know."

"Treacherous female," he accused and dropped her. She briefly disappeared under the waist-high water, but as soon as he saw her flailing arms he grabbed her and picked her back up.

"That wasn't funny!" she yelled, clawing wet strands of hair from her eyes.

"Oh, come on. It was a little funny."

"No it was not. You vindictive—" He cut off her words with a kiss. Immediately, she melted into him. It didn't take much to distract Talaith from her anger. One of the many things he enjoyed about her.

When he finally stopped kissing her, she finished, "Bastard."

"Such cruel words from such a beautiful mouth."

She blushed and looked away, always a bit uncomfortable when he complimented her. He'd have to get her over that. He loved a good compliment. And there were few beings he felt worthy of receiving them.

Unwilling to wait a moment more, Briec placed her on the rocky ledge. She watched him quietly as he pulled himself out of the water. Grabbing her hand, he leaned back against the ground, positioning her until she was over him.

"Ride me, little witch."

Without an argument—for once—she straddled his hips. Grasping his already hard cock, she stroked it a few times. Briec arched into her hand. "What are you doing?" he choked out.

"I like how it feels in my hand," she replied. "I like how it's soft and hard all at the same time."

"Is that all you like about it?"

Shyly, she shook her head. "I like how it feels when it's inside me."

"Then put it inside you, little witch. Don't torture me."

"Not even a little?" she asked.

"Later. Not now. My patience wanes."

"Fair enough." She lifted her hips, placing the tip of his cock against her pussy. Her juices already ran down her thighs, betraying exactly how wet she was for him. How ready.

Slowly, so damn slowly, she impaled herself with his cock. While her body stretched to accommodate him, she moaned and gasped. When she'd finally taken all of his cock inside her, she looked down at him.

"You feel good."

He groaned. "You're killing me, little witch."

"I don't mean to."

"Yes. You do." But he didn't care. He wanted . . . no . . . he *needed* her to move. "Fuck me, sweet Talaith."

She grinned and he didn't like it one bit. "Say please."

Evil wench! "No."

"Fine. Don't say it." She clenched her pussy—once.

"You evil cow."

"That didn't sound like please to me."

"Fine." He glared at her. "Please."

She stared at him and he snapped, "What?"

"Well, the way you were acting about saying that word, I thought you might burst into flame."

"Talaith . . ."

"Calm down, O' Scaly One." She leaned over, her hands resting on his shoulders.

"Tell me if this feels good." Her husky whisper had him arching into her before she even started the first stroke.

Her hips rose and fell, the walls of her pussy clenching tight on each upstroke. She was milking him, pushing him to come.

She leaned down and kissed him, her tongue sliding inside his mouth.

Gods, she did feel good. All of her. Briec was relieved she did like his cave, because she wasn't going anywhere. She wasn't leaving. Not now.

She dragged her mouth away from his and gasped, "Come for me, Lord Arrogance. I want to feel you come inside me."

Briec grabbed Talaith's hips and drove himself up into her, holding her steady for his pounding thrusts.

She panted and writhed on top of him, saying his name over and over. When he felt the walls of her pussy spasm around his cock, he let go and his whole body arched up as he came.

Finally, Talaith collapsed on top of him. Her entire body limp, her pussy still throbbing in time to her heartbeats.

He pulled her wet hair off her face. "You all right?"

She patted his forehead, which he found annoying. "Don't ask me stupid questions, Briec."

"As you wish, little witch." He wrapped his arms around her, holding her tight against him.

They stayed like that, in comfortable silence, until she said, "Why haven't you gone down yet?"

"I don't know. You'll have to ask him yourself."

She sat up enough to look him in the eye. "I am *not* talking to your . . . your . . ."

"Mighty throbbing manhood?"

"Briec."

"That which brings you much delirious pleasure?"

"Briec."

"That which makes you whole?"

"Stop it, dragon. You're making me physically ill."

He cupped her face between his hands. "You like it here enough to stay? Yes?"

She stared at him with wide eyes.

"What? Why are you looking at me like that?"

"Usually you'd say something like that as a statement. But that sounded suspiciously like a question. Are you asking me something?"

He reached down and swatted her bare ass with the palm of his hand.

"Ow!"

"Be nice, woman. I'm not used to this."

She rubbed her ass and glared at him. "Do that again and you'll lose that which you believe makes me whole."

Briec grinned. "Should I kiss it and make it feel better?"

"No. Just keep that face of yours where I can see it. Cheeky bastard."

"Such a way with words, little witch. I can't believe the men haven't flocked to you."

Her eyes narrowed, but she couldn't hide her grin. "And you with your humble, caring nature. A line of females should be forming outside your cave door as we speak."

"Is this your way of saying no one will put up with us?"

"My husband tried to have me burned at the stake and you brutalize your brothers on an hourly basis, which makes them not want to be too close to you for very long. What does that tell you, Briec the Arrogant?"

"That they're jealous of our greatness."

Talaith laughed hard, her face buried against his neck and her entire body shaking.

"What?" Briec asked in all sincerity. "What's so funny?"

Chapter 12

The storms continued relentlessly. Although there would be moments of sunshine, moments of frightening calm, a few hours or sometimes even minutes later, it would all start over again.

Talaith barely even noticed or cared. For weeks now, there had been no sign of Arzhela. And after so many years of living in fear, she felt peaceful. She knew it wouldn't last. She knew Arzhela would call her to perform her task, and she would go. Until then, Talaith spent her time enjoying Briec and not having that evil heifer in her mind for even a little while.

Briec seemed to enjoy their time together as well. If he wasn't reading or sneaking out to find a cow or lamb, he was with Talaith. True, there were a few times he'd ask her, "Please by the love of all that is holy . . . *stop talking!*" Which, of course, she completely ignored. Leading them into one of their many arguments. They didn't argue because they were angry, they argued because it drove them both wild.

It had become quite the joke. They'd find the most ridiculous things to argue over. One day, she yelled at him because the butter for her toast had gone bad. Another time he growled at her because she left a wet cloth on his cave floor. But no matter what they argued about, they always ended up the same way—fucking. Like two wild beasts in heat.

Talaith felt as if she were making up for the last sixteen years of her life where her husband would lay on top of her, bounce around a bit, roll off and go to sleep. True, it didn't start out that way, but within the year that was the best she could hope for. Shutting off his desire for her with a spell turned out to be absolutely no loss.

Ah, but Briec. For a being not human, he truly understood a woman's body. And he worked hers in a way even thinking about it in passing made her knees weak. Some days, after a particularly hearty argument, they'd couple fast and furiously. Each taking what they wanted and giving back only what was necessary. It was selfish and deliriously fun.

Other times, he'd spend all day in bed with her, taking her slow and long. Toying with her. Teasing her. Like he had all the time in the world. Both worked wonderfully for her and she'd already begun to plan their argument for the night. She had the feeling the fruit he'd brought in the other day wasn't ripe enough.

Aye. That'll work.

Smiling, Talaith crouched beside the cave entrance watching the rain fall. This way in was at ground level by a stream and was not big enough for Briec to enter in dragonform, which could explain why he knew nothing about it. He still thought there were only two entrances into his cave, but she'd discovered five others. When the time was right, she'd tell him about those extra entrances. No matter how this all ended, she'd want to make sure he remained safe long after she was gone.

Looking up at the dark sky, Talaith hoped Briec would be all right. He'd left nearly an hour before with promises of returning with something special for her besides the fresh supply of bread she truly needed. She couldn't begin to guess what his "something special" might be, but she didn't care. Trinkets, gifts, even his treasure meant nothing to her because wealth couldn't buy her what she needed.

The torrent of rain stopped suddenly and she glanced up at the two suns shining brightly overhead. Startled, Talaith looked around. Unwilling to miss this opportunity of getting out of the cave for even a few minutes, she stepped away from the entrance, breathing in the fresh scent of a rain-doused forest.

She'd only gotten a few feet away when she felt the hairs on the back of her neck rise. Her eyes closed and she almost moaned in despair.

"Hello, Talaith. Miss me?"

Shaking with rage and fear and outright hatred, Talaith slowly dropped to her knees and bowed her head before the deity. "My Goddess."

"Guess who?"

Blinded by small hands over his eyes, Briec smiled at the teasing voice in his ear. "Hell and damnation?"

"Well, that was just mean." He turned and his baby sister punched his arm. "You're all so mean to me."

"No we're not . . . except Morfyd."

The beautiful redhead smiled and he marveled at how much she reminded them all of Gwenvael, only female. And a tad bit lustier.

"That's because she lets me torture her. I don't know why she blames me for her own weakness."

"Brat."

She giggled and threw herself into her brother's arms. "I missed you, brother. I haven't seen you in ages."

"Aye. I've been busy."

His sister pulled away, smiling up at him. "And with whom were you busy?"

"That, baby sister, is none of your business."

She pouted and he bet that worked on all the males, human and dragon, who had graced her bed. "You're no fun."

"And you are a spoiled brat. Guess that makes us even."

Keita the Red Viper Dragon of Despair and Death—as one unfortunate town named her after their failed attempt to enslave her with chains so she could be their guardian—twirled around showing off her expensive gown. "Isn't this lovely?"

"And who died to give you this?"

She looked affronted. "No one. But I do have someone for you to meet." She motioned to three knights who quickly headed their way, angrily eyeing Briec.

"They don't know everything about me, brother," she whispered. "So I'd appreciate it if you not mention it yourself."

Briec shook his head. His sister was absolutely shameless and yet she never embarrassed him like Gwenvael often did. He found her entertaining.

The knights strode to a stop beside Keita, surrounding her.

"And who is this, m'lady?" one of them asked, glaring at Briec as if he'd done something.

"This, my loyal knights, is my brother, Briec."

Once they realized he was kin, they all visibly relaxed and nodded greetings.

"Isn't he handsome? As all my brothers are." She winked at Briec. "If you're kind to him, perhaps he'll let us stay in his home."

Briec knew exactly what his little sister was up to. She must have grown bored with these men, but those days of using humans for sport and then dinner were long gone. With Fearghus having a human mate and their queen awarding the Mad Bitch of Garbhán Isle the loyalty of all dragons, it would be in bad taste to toy with them.

Besides, he knew Talaith wouldn't appreciate it one bit. And that was enough to ensure he not get involved.

"Unfortunately, little sister, that will not be possible."

The pout returned. "Oh?"

He looked at the three men. "Perhaps another time."

Keita took his arm. "Would you excuse us a moment, gentlemen?" She walked off, not bothering to wait for their answer. "You have changed, brother."

"Not really. We all have to grow up eventually."

"Why? I'm only a hundred and ninety winters. I have years to go before I have to be as boring as Fearghus or Morfyd."

Chuckling, Briec leaned down and kissed his sister's forehead. "Do be careful, brat. You play with fire too often."

"Ah, but we *are* fire, brother." She patted his chest and trounced off, but as she reached the men, she spun back around. "Should I mention to Daddy that I saw you?"

Only Keita called *Bercelak* the Great, one of the most feared dragons in this region or any other for that matter, "Daddy." And she was the only one he'd allow to get away with it.

"No."

Nodding, she said, "That's what I thought."

She walked off and, like well-trained dogs, the knights followed.

The wind picked up a bit, and Briec knew another storm was coming. He wanted to get back to Talaith. To see her beautiful face and perhaps start another argument over . . . he stopped to think a minute. Ah, yes. The fruit. He bet she ate all the fruit.

He shrugged. That would work for a good argument.

She looked up at the goddess who had been the bane of her existence for sixteen years now. She hated Arzhela, the goddess of light, love, and fertility. Talaith hated the bitch for what she'd made her do, and what she still needed her to do. Talaith hated her for taking her away from her people and leaving her in that village where she would always be an outsider.

But what she truly hated the bitch goddess for most of all? Taking away Talaith's daughter.

"You summoned me, goddess?"

Bathed in gold light, a wreath of gold and white flowers adorning her golden head, the goddess smiled at her. "You always say that with a sneer, my darling girl."

"Do I? I hadn't noticed."

Talaith no longer looked at the goddess. She feared what her eyes would show. So she stared at her neck. Smooth, pale, and long, Talaith dreamed of dragging her blade across it.

"Of course you noticed," Arzhela stated brightly. The goddess always looked bright and cheery. It hid the dark soul beneath. "But it matters not to me. For your time is coming." She clapped her hands together. "And I am so excited!"

"Yes, goddess."

Arzhela pouted. "You don't sound excited."

Cruel, heartless bitch!

"Whatever brings you joy, goddess, brings me joy."

"There's that tone again," she remarked cheerily, but without a trace of genuine humor. "Be that as it may, everything is falling into place just as I planned."

Talaith frowned, her eyes still focused on the bitch's throat. "Sorry, goddess?"

"Well, your presence here. Did you really think a dragon would want *you?*"

Arzhela wanted Talaith to believe Briec was one of her many pawns like her priestesses or Lord Hamish who even now held her daughter in his fortress, and had these many long years—assuring her daughter was so close and yet so very far. But Talaith knew Arzhela's power didn't move past the humans. "If there is one thing I know, it is that you do not control the dragons. *Especially* this one."

She heard the guttural hiss a split second before the goddess used Magick to lift Talaith and throw her against the outside cave wall.

The wind knocked out of her, it took Talaith a bit to push

herself back to her feet. But by then she understood completely what had been going on. Arzhela had no control over the dragons. Her Magick couldn't breech what the dragons considered their very basic defenses. No wonder Talaith hadn't heard from the bitch Arzhela in over a moon—she couldn't touch her when Talaith was with the dragons. But as soon as Talaith left Briec's cave and his protection . . .

"Don't test me, Talaith. I am in no mood."

"Sorry if I offended you, goddess."

Arzhela took a deep breath, most likely working hard to control that monumental rage. Once she'd calmed herself, her voice again took on the light lilting tone Talaith had come to loathe.

"Oh, don't apologize, dear. It's all right. But perhaps I should make some things clear to you. He's noticed her."

Panic, cold and brutal, swept through her limbs, making her immobile. Making her helpless. For the first time in the last five years, Talaith looked the bitch in the eye. "What?"

"Hamish has noticed her. Not surprising, Talaith. She's the same age you were when you had her. Although much more attractive, but you've always been a bit plain. Guess she took after her father, more so than you."

Talaith fought her desire to scream. To fight. To kill. She even fought her desire to wretch.

"Now, don't panic, love. I see it on your face. If you follow my instructions, you won't have anything to worry about."

"You promised you'd protect her."

"And I will. Just as I promised." The goddess's face turned ugly as her true nature swept across it. "But don't think for a moment that you'll be able to get out of this. Don't think for a moment anyone or any . . . *thing* can protect you from me."

The goddess lifted her hand, two fingers out, and it felt as if Talaith's throat was back in that noose, choking her.

Killing her. Her fingers scratched at her bare neck, fighting to remove a noose that wasn't there.

"You know what you need to do, Talaith. And you will do it. And you'll do it well." Arzhela made a fist, and the feeling worsened, getting tighter around Talaith's throat. Not only cutting off oxygen but soon, crushing bone. "Do it well, or your throat won't be the only one I crush. But I'll make sure he has her first. I'll make sure he makes her *love* it."

Fear for her child overrode fear for herself. She no longer cared about her death. She only cared about her daughter. The daughter they'd ripped from her arms before she'd taken her first breath. The daughter she worried about every moment of every day. The daughter whose name she didn't even know.

"Yes," she tried to scream, but was only able to barely choke out.

"Good." Arzhela released her and Talaith dropped to her knees, hands around her throat, taking in deep gulping drags of air. "I'm so glad we understand each other so well. Tomorrow you'll leave here and head toward the rising suns. Understand?"

"The weather?"

"I'll protect you from that." Which told Talaith Arzhela hadn't been responsible for all these storms. Surprising.

"The suns will rise tomorrow. And I'm sure you'll know what to do once you arrive at your destination, yes?"

Talaith shut her eyes. "Aye."

"Wonderful. Wonderful." Arzhela turned and headed off into the forest. "Oh, and I've returned your powers to you. By tomorrow, you'll be back where you were when you pledged yourself to me." Pledged herself? She never pledged herself to anyone or anything. The bitch was insane. "Don't forget, Talaith. Once this is all done and your task complete, you can take your daughter and your Magicks and return to your people and your desert gods. But you mustn't fail me."

She actually still wanted Talaith to believe she'd survive this task. She must believe her truly stupid.

"Sleep well, Talaith. Tomorrow begins a brand-new day."

Then Arzhela was gone.

Chapter 13

Briec stared at Talaith across the dining table. She hadn't spoken since he arrived home, appearing lost and in pain. She'd pulled her bare feet up onto the chair, her chin resting on her knees, her arms tight around her legs.

"Are you not hungry?"

Without looking at him, she answered softly, "Not really, no."

"Talaith? Talaith, look at me." She did, those dark brown eyes turning to him. His chest tightened at the sight of the pain in them. "Gods, woman. What happened while I was away?"

"Nothing. Really." She forced a smile, it seemed as if doing so caused her physical discomfort. "I'll be fine in the morning."

Leaning back in her chair, she took a deep breath before speaking again. "So, how did it go in town today? Is everyone all right with these storms?"

"Aye. It's a little muddy, but surprisingly not too much damage. I feared the river would overflow, but it hasn't."

Her forced smile turned bitter. "The gods must be protecting us then."

Briec didn't know what to do with Talaith like this. She seemed ripped apart from the inside out, while at the same time, she seemed dangerously angry. And the fact that it brought out some unnamed emotion in him, gave him no ease.

"I bought something for you."

"Oh?" She didn't sound the least bit interested.

"Aye." He stood and walked around the table until directly behind her. "I had this made for you."

He slipped the silver chain on her neck, quickly latching the clasp. As he released it, the pendant dropped to hang down her gown, right between her breasts. Talaith grasped the pendant and looked at it carefully while Briec crouched beside her. He'd given her a dragon. Not large at all, but modest in size, ensuring Talaith would feel comfortable wearing it. With wings expanded from a detailed back, fangs bared, its claws and tail holding on to a single jewel he'd pulled from his own treasure.

"Do you like it?" he asked softly.

"Briec, it's beautiful. But why—"

"I wanted you to have something from me."

She stared at him for a long time, almost making him uncomfortable. Then she asked, "Why?"

"Why what?"

"Why did you want me to have something from you? Why do you care?"

"Because . . ." His brain scrambled for some answer he could understand. "I've enjoyed having you here with me." Did she still want to leave him? Did she still plan grand escapes? Or did she realize this was where she belonged?

"For now," she pushed.

He blinked, then nodded, extremely confused. "Um . . . yes. For now. That was what I'd always said."

Her smile turned sad and resigned and Briec had absolutely no idea what to do about it. What he never expected, though, was for her to take his face between her hands and kiss him.

* * *

What did she expect him to say exactly? That he loved her? That he wanted her with him forever? Her mother's words came back to her as she kissed Briec. The words she'd said to her when Talaith told her she was with child.

"Foolish, foolish, Talaith. You keep expecting to find happiness—and you never will. Not for us."

"Us" being the Nolwenn witches. The most powerful witches in Alsandair. And the loneliest. Nolwenn witches had consorts, but only for physical needs or Magicks requiring sex. When the men became too old to perform, the witches sent them on their way. They may have favorites among them, but never enough to care once they were gone.

Talaith loved her daughter's father, which was unheard of. Of course, having her daughter at sixteen was absolutely unheard of, too. Especially since her own mother didn't have Talaith until it was well past her two hundredth winter.

Yet the Nolwenn way of life wasn't what Talaith wanted. Not for herself and especially not for her daughter.

His hands gently gripping her shoulders, Briec pulled back from her. It wasn't easy for him. She saw that in the way his violet eyes watched her. As always he wanted her . . . for now.

"Talaith, what is it? What's wrong?"

"Nothing." She stroked his jaw, loving the rough feel of it against her hand. "Just take me to bed, Briec."

He didn't have the answers he wanted—the answers he'd never get—but knowing the dragon as well as she did now, she knew he expected to get it out of her tomorrow.

He picked her up out of the chair and carried her to the bed they'd been sharing together.

She'd make this night memorable for both of them, because soon memories would be all she'd have.

Chapter 14

Danelin, captain of Queen Annwyl's elite guard, checked his sword carefully for any nicks. It was the one thing that kept him from crying out of pure boredom. Exactly how much more rain and mud could he be witness to? They'd barely moved more than a league in the past week. He wanted to go home. He had a small bit of land Annwyl gave him after she took her brother's throne. On it was a small house with an even tinier garden. But it was his and he loved it.

Yet all the men felt like that lately. They'd been away from Garbhán Isle for too long now. They wanted to see their wives, mistresses, children . . . even their mothers. They were weary of battle and definitely weary of this weather. Although Danelin had no doubt in a few months they'd be clamoring for another battle, another war, they still needed the occasional break from it.

The one who needed the break from it most of all, however, was their queen. They all knew she'd been away from her mate for far too long. The longer they were separated, the sharper her tongue. And woe to the small war party that accidentally crossed their path. Often the rest of them didn't even have to fight . . . she did all the work for them.

Aye, only one was brave enough to face her when she got this way. Only one dared to irritate her.

Morfyd stormed from the queen's tent, but she stopped when a book—thankfully soft of cover—hit her in the back of the head. Swinging around, the dragon in human form yelled, "*You are the most insufferable, difficult bitch I've ever had the displeasure of knowing and I can't wait to be rid of you!*"

Danelin glanced up at his commander and Brastias sighed. With a shake of his head, he stepped in front of Morfyd before she could stomp away. "What is going on with you two?"

Morfyd looked at Brastias, then at the men watching her. After taking a deep, calming breath she shrugged. "Nothing. Why?"

Briec, smiling while still half asleep, reached for Talaith. His hand grasped nothing but bedding and he pulled himself fully awake.

"Talaith?"

He'd been hoping to find her still lying next to him. He had plans for her this morning, and they all involved her legs resting on his shoulders. So finding her already up and about did nothing but irritate him. Plus, he still had many questions to ask the wench. Her sudden mood swings the previous night did nothing but confuse him, and he realized he didn't enjoy that confusion one damn bit.

Briec looked around the chamber and frowned when he didn't find her in one of the chairs reading as he usually did. He sat up, pushing his hair off his face. "Talaith?"

He slid out of bed and left the chamber, heading toward the main area where they ate. She wasn't there and no fire burned in the pitfire since the previous eve.

Sniffing the air, Briec tried to track her somewhere in his home, but there was nothing but her lingering essence.

"No!"

Briec shifted to dragon with a thought and stormed through his cave looking for her, barking her name.

"Talaith, answer me!"

She didn't and he knew. He knew she'd left him. And another, less used emotion reared its very ugly head . . . rage.

Briec made it topside, bursting from his cave entrance with a trail of fire in his wake. He tore through the countryside searching for her. She couldn't have gotten far. He'd find her and bring her back. Even if she kicked and screamed the entire way, he'd bring her back.

He'd bring her home.

Talaith watched the dragon fly overhead. He didn't see her. He wouldn't. True to her word, Arzhela had given her back her powers with a vengeance. Talaith almost woke Briec up as she stumbled from her early-morning bed, her entire body screaming in pain as the Magick was unleashed within her.

Now she used that same Magick to block her presence from the dragon's keen senses, something she hadn't been able to do before. Hearing him call her name, knowing he at least cared enough to search for her, almost sent her back to him.

But her daughter—the most important thing right now.

Besides, why bother going back to him even if she did survive this? If he wasn't tired of her now, he would be one day.

Closing her eyes, and heart, to the sight of him, Talaith turned and headed in the direction of the two suns. Headed toward her destiny and, most likely, her death.

Chapter 15

They'd tracked her for hours, thinking they were being stealthy. Not really. About an hour after they started, she led them where she wanted them to go while watching from a safe distance. She'd take them to a lake she knew of in these parts—her teachers made her learn every map available—and destroy them there. She had no time for games at this point. Besides, after leaving Briec, she had a great desire to hurt something deserving to be hurt.

Perched safely in a tree, Talaith stared down at the lake and cursed. There were two women, alone, naked, and bathing in the lake. She needed them to run. Now.

Using the sturdy branches of the old tree, she quickly climbed down, jumping the last few feet to the ground.

Immediately, the two women turned toward her. They looked so different from each other. One had golden brown hair, green eyes, and a very recent knife slash across her face. The other had white hair, blue eyes shaped like a cat's, and the mark of a witch on one cheek. The witch blocked her, so Talaith had no idea how powerful her Magick. And she had no time to figure it out.

"You must leave. Now."

They didn't. Instead they stared at her. Not in fear or confusion, but in curiosity.

"Did you not hear me?"

"We heard you," the brown-haired one said before dropping her head back into the water.

And that was all either one of them said.

"Unbelievable," Talaith muttered. "Now I have to protect their stupid hides as well as my own." And she was stupid. She could run, in theory. The men would find enough sport with these two so chances were high they wouldn't bother coming for her. But she couldn't do that to any woman.

She heard the men stomping through the trees toward them. She knew a fire spell that should handle them pretty well. And possibly destroy the entire forest. *Oh, well. Can't be helped.*

The men stepped past the line of the trees, but looked past her. Quickly glancing behind her, she realized that both women had gotten out of the lake. *By the gods. Those bitches are huge!*

"Focus, Talaith," she chastised herself.

At least they'd thrown on some clothes. One had on her witch's robes. The other simple leggings, cotton shirt, and leather boots. They didn't appear worried, though. They should. Unless the witch had great power. That would definitely help at the moment.

"Well, well. Look what we have here, lads."

Talaith rolled her eyes. Why these idiots never came up with anything more original before the raping and pillaging, she'd never know.

She counted. Fifteen men. Fifteen to their three. *Eesh.* She would have preferred better odds than that, but nothing she could do about it now.

Her attention on the men in front of her and the chant on her lips, Talaith readied herself to destroy an entire forest— or start a small bonfire, she wasn't quite sure which—when the brown-haired woman walked past her.

"You know what I love, gentlemen?" the woman asked with a big smile. *Good gods, why is she talking to them?* Talaith glanced back at the witch, who gave a helpless shrug. As if this were an unruly puppy rather than a woman who would get them all raped and killed.

"And what would that be, luv?" one of the men in front asked with a knowing smile.

"When the gods throw sport my way."

She moved so fast, if Talaith blinked she would have missed it. Missed the woman ripping the man's sword from his scabbard, expertly hefting the blade, and swinging.

Talaith watched the man's head roll away. It would have been comical if it weren't a bit vile.

Taking a step back, the woman watched the other men, her newly obtained sword raised.

"Come on then, you lot," she encouraged. "You're not going to leave me standing here, are ya?" She looked over the men before her. "Which one of you is man enough to fight me?"

Man enough? Try stupid enough.

That's when other men stepped from the trees. Based on their ages and a distinct lack of bitterness on their faces, Talaith knew these men were not with the ones who had been tracking her. They were with this woman. They wore dark red surcoats over chainmail shirts and leggings. The crests on their surcoats were of a black dragon with two swords crossed behind it.

Well, there went Talaith's brief theory the brown-haired woman was a poor, sole mercenary.

One of the woman's warriors, a tall handsome man who couldn't seem to stop grinning, glanced at her. "Do we really have time for this?"

"Don't rush me, Brastias. You bastards want me relaxed. This will relax me." She turned back to the confused men. "Well?" the woman challenged again. "Anyone?"

The cornered men glanced around and realized the warriors

with the dark red surcoats surrounded the entire lake—and them. They had no choice *but* to fight her.

Two men charged her at the same time. She blocked both their blades with her own, kicked one, knocking him to the ground and gutted the other. She took his sword as her own and finished off the man still on the ground at her feet.

That's when the rest decided to attack the woman as one.

Talaith looked to the warriors to see if they would help. They didn't. Their swords remained sheathed, their sighs indicated boredom. The witch moved up to stand beside her. "This won't take long."

She had a distinct feeling the witch was right.

A grin spread across the warrior woman's face as she blocked a blow with one sword while slashing at another attacker with the other. Blood flew, splattering across her shirt, but she didn't even notice it, instead turning to another man and gutting him from stomach to throat. She took his head, turned, cut another man in half; crouched, slashed, took another man's legs. She moved so fast, Talaith found it hard to follow her. But within seconds, she'd killed them all . . . except one.

The warrior woman cracked her neck as her green eyes locked onto the last man. He raised his sword, but she knocked it out of his hand with one blow from her own. She kicked him in the chest, sending him crashing to his back.

Then she placed one extremely large foot onto his chest and crouched down, pinning him to the ground with her weight.

"So tell me, what were you planning to do with us? Eh? Going to make us scream? Beg for mercy?" She leaned in, forcing her foot into the man's chest, her face filled with utter disgust and contempt. "Should I do that to you? Should I make you cry? Should I make you beg?"

She took a deep breath, and Talaith could see how hard it was for this woman to keep her anger under control. A battle written all over her bruised and damaged face.

"No. I'll not waste my time on the likes of you," she sneered.

Slowly standing, she left her foot on his chest while tossing one of the swords she held into the lake. "A true and honorable warrior loses his head in battle and goes home to his ancestors with pride. But that won't be for you. I curse you, scum. I curse you and your brethren to the never-ending pits of despair and suffering where you'll spend your eternity."

Two hands clasping the hilt, she raised her sword above the man's chest. "I do wish you luck, though," she uttered, almost kindly. Then that rage returned, so fierce it nearly stole Talaith's breath. "For you will surely need it."

With that, she brought the sword down, it seemed, with all the force she could possibly muster. The blade slammed through the man's chest, tearing through cheap armor, and hard bone until it embedded itself in the rocky ground beneath. The man's screams made Talaith wince, but she couldn't look away, even as the woman twisted the blade this way and that to quicken his death.

He made another gasp, blood pouring from his open mouth, then went silent.

The woman stood, leaving the blade in his chest. She examined herself.

"I swear. I clean off one coat of blood, only to have it replaced by another. I wonder why I bathe at all while on campaign."

"Because you don't want to wake to find a pack of wolves licking blood off you . . . again," the witch offered sweetly.

Grimacing, "I thought we swore never to speak of that."

With a laugh, the witch replied, "I don't remember that agreement at all."

"Callous cow."

And that's when they all turned to Talaith.

Uh-oh.

How she could actually find this woman more frightening than the three dragons she'd stayed with for days, she'd never know. But now that her Magick was back, her sense

of this woman's barely contained rage was almost palpable.
It slid under her skin like a living thing.

"You all right?" It took Talaith a moment to realize the
warrior woman had spoken to her.

"Oh." She cleared her throat. "Yes. Thank you."

The woman's cold green eyes examined Talaith from feet
to head as she held her hand out and one of the warriors
handed her two swords in their scabbards. Walking calmly
toward Talaith, she tied them to her back.

"Thank you for warning us."

Never before had Talaith had such an overwhelming
desire to run. This was not like the dragonfear. This was
much worse. "You're welcome."

Standing before her, the woman bent her neck to the side.
Talaith winced as she heard every bone in the woman's neck
and shoulder crack into place. *Ack!*

"Your name?"

Answer her, you idiot. "Talaith."

The woman nodded. "I am Annwyl."

Without thinking, Talaith stumbled back from her. "The
Blood Queen?"

Blinking, the woman looked startled, then . . . well . . .
then she looked *hurt.*

"Oh, shit," the witch mumbled beside her. Then she and
the good-looking warrior passed annoyed glances.

"*Is that what they call me?*" Annwyl threw her hands up.
"That is so unfair!"

The witch shook her head. "Annwyl . . ."

"I work hard to protect the land—"

"Annwyl."

"—to keep them all safe—"

"Annwyl."

"—and this is how they repay me?"

"Annwyl!"

"*What?*"

"Let it go. We need to get back. Or do you wish to keep your mate waiting any longer?"

Good God. This big bitch has a mate? That had to be one brave man.

Annwyl growled. Literally. Then turned on her heel. "Fine." She looked over her shoulder at Talaith. "But don't call me that again."

"Uh . . ." Talaith glanced around at the other warriors and realized they were working hard not to laugh. Some had to turn away. "Of course, my, uh, queen."

She saw the men wince as Annwyl stopped in her tracks. Without bothering to turn around, she barked, "Don't call me that either."

"My liege?"

"Not even close."

Talaith had grown tired of this big bitch barking at her like she were a small child and, as usual, Talaith's mouth ran much faster than her sense. "Is there anything I should call you? Or should I just grunt and point in your direction?"

When the men and witch all stared at her, she had a feeling she might have gone too far—again.

Slowly, Annwyl turned back to her. Talaith had a feeling very few people said much to the Blood Queen of Garbhán Isle.

But, instead of taking Talaith's head or cursing her to those nasty pits she seemed so fond of sending people to, the queen smiled. A really sweet smile, taking Talaith completely by surprise. "I think Annwyl will do, don't you?"

"Uh . . ." Talaith shrugged. "Yes?"

Her smile broadened. "Yes. And you best come with us."

"What? Why?" Well, that was *definitely* not the right response, but Annwyl—nor Arzhela—appeared to notice.

"Annwyl," the witch murmured. "I'm sure that Talaith has somewhere else to—"

"You think this was the only band of scavengers roaming these forests, sister?" Annwyl cut in quickly. "They're one of many. You know that better than most." To Talaith she said, "Come with us now. We'll get you some food and some safety. You can decide what you want to do from there. All right?"

She made it sound like a request, but Talaith knew better. Dread filled Talaith's being. Most of the gods knew she shouldn't go. But she had no choice.

She had absolutely no choice.

Briec stared out over his land. As human he sat at the very edge of the highest entrance to his cave. He knew eventually his brothers would arrive, and when they sat next to him, one on either side, he wasn't surprised. And, he had to admit at least to himself, he was quite grateful.

"What happened?" Éibhear asked.

"What does it look like? She left me."

Gwenvael leaned over to stare down at the sheer drop to ground level. "Planning to throw yourself from here as human and end it all?"

"Of course not." He let out a deep sigh. "I just got home, truth be told. I've been looking for her for days."

Éibhear raised one leg and rested his arm on it. "Why did she leave?"

Briec's head dropped forward in abject misery. "I don't know."

He sensed more than saw Gwenvael lean down a bit to get a good look at his face. "Are you really that upset?"

Bellowing in fury, he turned on his brother, "*Do I look happy to you?*"

His brother held his hands up. "Calm down. I was just asking. I didn't realize you'd become *that* attached."

"How could you not see that?" Éibhear asked. "Lofal the Blind One could have seen that."

"When has Briec ever cared about a female beyond the bedding?"

"Talaith was different," Briec seethed.

"Ah, yes. The woman whose name you didn't even care to know at first."

"Shut up, Gwenvael. Or you'll quickly find out if your human body can fly."

"You sure you're just not mad because she had the audacity to leave *you*—Briec the Mighty?"

Normally Briec would shove his brother's face into the dirt, but he didn't even feel like doing that. For four days he searched everywhere he could think of for her and nothing. Not even a trace of her. Finally, he gave up and returned back to his lair, which suddenly seemed way too big and extremely lonely. He didn't realize how much he'd come to enjoy her very presence. The scent of her. Her voice. Her extremely acid tongue. The way she kept tripping on his tail.

But, he kept reminding himself, she left him. She left him when he hadn't done anything wrong. And she'd actually seemed damn happy when with him. If she hadn't been, she would have told him in that rude way she had.

"Aren't you going to hit him?" Éibhear asked.

"I don't feel like it."

"Good gods." Gwenvael stood. "This is worse than we thought, Éibhear. Up, brother." Gwenvael grabbed Briec's arm and pulled him to his feet. "There is only one answer for this."

"Which is?"

"Drinking and eating. The whoring will keep until we get you good and drunk. By the time we're done, brother, you won't even remember her name that you didn't even care to know in the first place."

Now, why did he doubt that?

This wasn't what she expected. Never, in her wildest dreams.

This . . . *this* was the Blood Queen of Garbhán Isle?

Scourge of the Madron lands? Destroyer of Villages? Demon Killer of Women and Children? She who had blood pacts with the darkest of gods?

This was Annwyl the Bloody?

Talaith watched, fascinated, as Annwyl held onto Morfyd the Witch's wrists. Morfyd—the Black Witch of Despair, Killer of the Innocent, Annihilator of Souls, and all around Mad Witch of Garbhán Isle or so she was called on the Madron lands—had actually tried to sneak up on Annwyl to put ointment on the nasty wound the queen had across her face. But as soon as the warrior saw her, she squealed and grabbed hold of her. Now Annwyl lay on her back, Morfyd over her, trying her best to get Annwyl to stop being a ten-year-old.

"If you just let me—"

"No! Get that centaur shit away from me, you demon bitch!"

"Annwyl, I'm not letting you go home to my brother looking like that. You look horrific."

"He'll have to love me in spite of it. Now get off!" She shoved and Morfyd tumbled back right into Brastias's arms. And he looked damn pleased to have her right there.

"That's it." Morfyd stood, straightened her robes and glared at Annwyl. "You've asked for this."

"Don't you dare—"

But the spell was unleashed, flying across the small campsite, lifting Annwyl and slamming her back against the tree behind her. Then it pinned her there.

Now Morfyd sauntered over to her. "If you'd given me two seconds, we could have been done with this, but you had to be difficult."

"I hate you."

"Join the queue."

"Vicious cow."

"Argumentative harpy."

Morfyd carefully rubbed the cream over Annwyl's fresh

scar. Once done, she spit a counter-spell and Annwyl hit the ground.

"Ow!"

"Crybaby."

No, this isn't what Talaith expected. Annwyl the Blood Queen was supposed to be a vicious, uncaring warrior bent on revenge and power. She let her elite guard rape and pillage wherever they went, and she used babies as target practice while their mothers watched in horror.

That's what she was supposed to be and that's what Talaith expected to find. Instead, she found Annwyl. Just Annwyl. A warrior who spent most of her resting time reading or mooning over her consort. She was silly, charming, very funny, and fiercely protective of everyone. Her elite guard, all handpicked by Annwyl, were sweet, vicious fighters and blindingly loyal to their queen.

And then there was Morfyd. A taller woman she'd never met, with a power Talaith envied. She had monumental control, the kind Talaith had only seen with the older, more powerful Nolwenn witches. Morfyd's beautiful face spoke of many young years. Perhaps no more than thirty winters. If that.

With a sigh, Morfyd sat beside her on the tree stump. "She makes me insane."

"Like family."

Morfyd smiled. "Exactly."

Wiping off the ointment she'd used on Annwyl with a dry cloth, Morfyd asked, "Are you cold, sister?" Morfyd had been calling her sister since she met her. She seemed to know she was a witch. Though not a very powerful one.

"Why do you ask?"

"Because you haven't taken off those gloves in two days."

Of course she hadn't. A witch of Morfyd's power only need take her bare hand and she'd know all there was to know about Talaith's past, from her first breath at birth to her last gasp with Briec. Because she hadn't had any training in the witch arts for the last sixteen years, Talaith had no idea how to keep her out.

"I am very chilled, sister," she lied.

"Oh, I'm sorry."

"No worries."

"No worries about what?" Annwyl sat on the other side of Talaith, handing each some dried beef and a large chunk of bread. The battle she'd just waged with Morfyd already forgotten.

"Talaith is chilled."

Annwyl sighed. "I'm sorry, Talaith. I know we've been living rough these few days, but we'll be home soon enough. All the rooms in the castle have a built-in pitfire. It's nice."

Good gods. The woman wasn't merely taking her back to Dark Plains, she was planning to put her up at Garbhán Isle as well.

"I'm fine, Annwyl. Really."

"When we stop for the night, you can sleep in my tent."

Panic swept through Talaith like wildfire. "That's not nec—"

Annwyl waved her argument away with a scarred hand. The woman had many scars. "It's nothing, Talaith. Really. But, of course, it's up to you."

"She snores," Morfyd warned.

"I do no such thing!" Annwyl yelled back.

"Like a bull in rutting season."

"When we get back to Garbhán Isle . . . don't speak to me."

"Trust me, Annwyl, *that* will be a pleasure."

Talaith would have loved to enjoy their argument, but she couldn't. Not when it took all her strength not to start shaking.

Talaith stood outside the back of Annwyl's tent. Again, she swallowed down her nausea and thought only of her daughter. At the moment, that was all that kept her moving forward. With another quick glance around, Talaith crouched low and burrowed her way between the tent and the ground until she was inside.

She stood and walked over to Annwyl. The woman slept soundly. One arm thrown over her head, the other laying near the floor. Barefoot, she still wore her leggings. And her bindings all she wore on top. Several large blade wounds covered her upper torso and lots of tiny ones covered those. All old and long-ago healed.

The strangest thing was the markings over her collarbone. These marks were of an ancient and intricate design and were light brown against her sun-darkened skin. They resembled a faint tattoo or old brand and Magick radiated off it. Some kind of protection. *Perfect.*

Her long brown hair lay loose around her and she'd kicked the covers off so that they rested on the floor.

She looked peaceful.

Again Talaith closed her eyes, shutting out everything but the thought of her daughter. This sacrifice would save her daughter and that's all that mattered.

Keeping that in her mind, she raised the dagger—tightly gripped in both her hands—over Annwyl's chest. Right over the protective brand on her chest. With a prayer to any god *but* Arzhela to save whatever may be left of her soul, she brought it down with all the force she could muster.

When it stopped short of its mark, she realized she'd closed her eyes. Otherwise, she would have seen Annwyl's arms come up, crossed, blocking her from completing the move. Talaith let out a relieved breath and that's when those cold green eyes snapped open to focus on her.

"I have to admit, I thought you'd be a tad stealthier than this." Annwyl gripped her hands and turned the blade toward Talaith's throat.

* * *

Annwyl watched closely as the blade inched closer and closer to Talaith's throat . . . and Talaith let it. In fact, she lifted her chin in preparation for the cut. Annwyl pushed it so far, the blade actually pierced the skin and all Talaith did was wince a bit. Then nothing. She'd already resigned herself to it; she could see it in the woman's eyes. She'd seen it before during her brother's reign, when Annwyl still lived with him. That resignation when you knew death was imminent and there was no way out. She witnessed it often with those condemned to his dungeons.

Worse, she'd seen it in Talaith's eyes from when they first met her at that lake. So it wasn't that she'd given up because Annwyl had a blade to her throat. The woman was dead when she'd walked into the tent.

With an annoyed sniff, Annwyl pushed the woman away and stood, pacing beside her.

"What . . . what are you doing?"

"Not what you want me to."

"Dammit." Talaith grabbed her arm in a vicious grip. Vicious enough to hold its own in a fight and yet hadn't. "Finish it, Annwyl. Finish it now!"

Annwyl saw the desperation in those dark brown eyes. Knew no amount of rationalizing would help. So Annwyl backhanded her, sending her flying across the tent.

Without another word, Annwyl calmly walked to the tent flap, pulling it back a bit. "Brastias," she called out. "Fetch me Morfyd, would you?"

"Aye."

Annwyl stepped back inside, studying the dagger in her hands. It was plain but sturdy and sharp.

Talaith was just rousing herself from the floor when Morfyd walked in. She frowned at Talaith and turned to Annwyl, but her confusion stopped and she stared at the dagger in her hand. "Where did you get that?"

"What? This?" Annwyl waved it at her battle mage and Morfyd jumped back from her.

"Keep that thing away from me."

"Has everyone lost their mind? I've got her trying to kill me in my sleep and you're suddenly frightened of daggers."

The dagger quickly forgotten, Morfyd placed her hands on her hips. "I *told* you it was her."

"Yes, but you didn't *tell* me she'd practically beg me to kill her, now did you?"

Morfyd glanced at Talaith still pulling herself up off the floor. "I'm surprised you didn't."

"Does she look insane to you, Morfyd?" Annwyl asked calmly. "Does she look like she doesn't have control of all her senses?"

"No, but—"

"Then why would she come at me with a blade? She's not a fool. And only a fool would risk facing *me* in hand-to-hand combat. We've both watched her—she's a well-trained assassin. She could have poisoned my food or water. She could have killed us all and then slipped away without anyone ever knowing. She could have used the poison-covered pins she has stuck in this hilt." Annwyl was pretty impressed with herself for catching sight of the extra dangers that lay in the simple and plain dagger. "Instead she puts a dagger to my throat."

Annwyl shook her head. "No. She's merely the sword, Morfyd. I want the hand that wields her."

"Easy enough."

Morfyd walked over to the woman who still looked a little dazed. Of course, Annwyl had made sure to hit her hard. Taking firm hold of her hand, Morfyd ripped off the leather glove Talaith had been wearing since they met her and took the woman's hand in her own.

"No!" Talaith, suddenly quite alert, tried to pull her hand from Morfyd's grasp, but the dragonwitch merely gripped Talaith's throat with her free hand and squeezed.

"Fight me, sister, and I'll tear your throat out."

Morfyd closed her eyes and everything became quiet.

Annwyl knew if she were a dragon or had any Magick skill whatsoever, she'd be able to see all the colors and flames and whatever else those Magickally inclined could see. But Annwyl was just a warrior with a dragon for a consort. All she could see were two women standing there like two statues. She found it a little odd.

Sighing from boredom, she walked over to her saddlebags and pulled out a flask of water. She took a long drink, but was startled when Morfyd suddenly said, "Oh. Oh."

She turned to look at her and Morfyd was absolutely beaming while Talaith scowled at her intently. Morfyd always wore that expression when she knew an absolutely divine piece of gossip.

"What?"

Clearly trying not to laugh, Morfyd shook her head. "Nothing."

"You lying cow. What's going on?"

"Nothing." She coughed, and released Talaith's hand. "Except you have some powerful enemies."

"Tell me what I don't know, witch."

"Powerful enemies who are gods."

For a moment, Annwyl was shocked beyond all reason . . . then she shrugged. "Now that I think of it—I don't know why I would be surprised."

Talaith sat impassively on Annwyl's bed while Morfyd told of all she'd seen. She spoke of Talaith's first love and how she lost the young soldier before their child had even been born. She told of how her mother and the other Nolwenn witches, blindingly angry at her relationship with the soldier and her soon-to-be-born child, tossed her out of the temple so she would learn a lesson. She knew they'd take her back as soon as the baby was born. What none of them saw was Arzhela. Her priestesses came for her the night of Talaith's daughter's birth. They tore the child from her arms and then dragged Talaith, bleeding and cursing, to their temple. Because Arzhela, goddess of light, love, and fertility was their patron, most of the priestesses were midwives. They cleaned off the blood, healed her, and then told her quite plainly she'd never see her daughter again unless she did what they told her.

Three months later, they took her to the little village outside of Madron and handed her over to a man, telling her he would now be her husband. She would take care of his house, clean his clothes, feed him well and, in return, he wouldn't question where she went every day. Because at those times, she would be in the local temple dedicated to Arzhela. There the head priestess would bring in the best of the best among the local assassins. For sixteen years they'd trained her until the moment when she would have to face a monarch so demonic, so evil, so contemptible in every sense of the word, she would thank the goddess for the chance to be the one to destroy her.

Talaith looked over at that "demonic, evil, contemptible" monarch who, at the moment, was busy blowing her nose into a cloth she'd picked up off the floor. Seemed the constant change in weather was making the evil demoness sneeze.

"So what do you want to do?"

The two women looked at her and Annwyl shrugged. "Well, I can't kill her now. I'm not that big a bitch."

Morfyd raised an eyebrow. "It really depends on who you ask."

"I hate you."

The two women smiled at each other and Talaith briefly hated them for having such a close relationship. For having each other for friends.

Annwyl stared at Talaith for a moment, then asked, "You wanted me to kill you. Why?"

Talaith looked away from Annwyl's direct, steady gaze. She heard Annwyl's strong voice. "She won't answer me."

"She thinks she can't. Because of Arzhela."

She thinks she can't? Talaith repeated in her head. What did this heifer know anyway?

"She can't touch you here, you know." Morfyd walked over and sat beside Talaith on the bed. "She'll never get past me. Past my defenses."

Talaith snorted in disbelief.

"It's true. Stretch out for her. Feel for her."

So Talaith did, and the witch spoke true. She couldn't feel Arzhela within a league. It was like they were in a protective bubble. She hadn't felt like this since she'd left the dragon's protection.

"Arzhela hurt her before," Morfyd explained to Annwyl. "When she tried to tell. But now . . . now Talaith only fears for her daughter. That's why she wanted you to kill her. If she was killed in battle or while trying to kill you, her daughter would be taken to safety. But if she killed herself or told someone to kill her, Arzhela would make the girl pay."

Annwyl sighed as she sat on the other side of her. Two tall, scary bitches surrounding her. *Hell, Talaith, it could be so much worse.* "I'm concerned for her daughter. Especially if she's with Hamish."

"Well, we all know your feelings on that man."

"And you all forget I do *know* the man. I know what he can do. What he's willing to do. And if he thinks Arzhela will bring him power—"

"Which is exactly what I'm sure she's promised him."

"Then we can't leave her there. Not for another second."

Talaith sat between the two women completely confused. Were they talking about getting her daughter back? Why?

"Well, I'm sure Brastias and a few of the—" Morfyd began.

"No." Annwyl stood. "We'll go."

Talaith and Morfyd froze. They immediately looked at each other, then turned back to Annwyl.

"What?" Morfyd asked.

"You heard me. Get off your asses."

"Annwyl, have you lost your mind?"

"Hardly." She walked to the tent flap and motioned to someone. A young boy, her squire perhaps, ran to her. She spoke to him briefly and he ran off.

"You want us to go into Madron territory to retrieve a girl we've never met and have no idea what she looks like?"

"Well, I'm assuming she looks like her." She pointed at Talaith. "Exactly how many desert people do you think Hamish has in his kingdom? It's doubtful there are many because they usually have more sense than to go there."

"Oi," Talaith finally objected.

"You don't count. You didn't have a choice."

Annwyl pulled on a sleeveless chainmail shirt. "Morfyd, you'll need to wear something other than your witch's robes. Leggings would be good."

"Annwyl, wait—"

"What?" Annwyl turned on them both so fast, the witches leaned back a bit. "What are you going to say, Morfyd? That we should leave that girl there? That girl who had nothing to do with this and was merely a pawn? Leave her there for Hamish?" The queen's obvious horror at Morfyd's suggestion spoke volumes. "You know I won't let that happen. So get off your asses, you lazy sows, we leave in quarter hour."

She handed the dagger to a stunned Talaith, grabbed her own two swords, and stormed out. Confused, Talaith looked at Morfyd, who merely shrugged. "Her brother handed her off to Hamish years ago. As a bride, no less. If it hadn't been for Brastias and the others, she'd be his wife instead of queen. Although knowing Annwyl as I do now, more likely she'd be dead after taking half the wedding party with her."

"So she really plans to—"

Morfyd placed her hand on Talaith's shoulder and that's when Talaith felt burning tears flowing down her cheeks. She had no idea when she started crying or why she couldn't stop. "If you were looking for a mindless killer, only concerned with blood and pain, you'll be sorely disappointed. I know that's what they told you. But they lied, Talaith. *She* lied." Long fingers wiped the tears from Talaith's cheeks. "Now, no more crying. We'll need you armed and ready. You'll finally get to properly use those skills of yours."

Talaith nodded. "I understand."

"Good." Morfyd stood. "Now I have to go find leggings." She winced. "Och. That sounds so unattractive."

"You didn't tell her." Talaith stood and tilted her head back to look Morfyd in the eye. "About—"

"Your dragon?" That should sound stranger than it did. But it felt right to Talaith, which concerned her even more. "Are you ashamed?"

Talaith thought on that for a moment, but only a moment. "No. I feel no shame. And I won't start now."

"As you like." Morfyd smirked. "And no. I won't tell Annwyl about your dragon."

"I see she wears their image all over her armor and branded on her arms. Has she actually killed one in battle?"

The witch began coughing and Talaith felt sure she only did it to cover up her laughter.

After clearing her throat, she said, "You might say she's faced down one or two during her reign. One of them, she ripped his heart right out of his chest."

Talaith winced. *Lovely, Talaith. A dragonslayer. Perhaps next you could align yourself with a witchhunter.* "Should I be concerned if she finds out?" She at least wanted to find and save her daughter first before the queen turned on her.

The witch smiled and Talaith felt no comfort from it.

"Concern yourself with your daughter for now, Talaith, Daughter of Haldane. The rest will work itself out . . . in time."

Chapter 16

"Wake up, Briec."

Throwing one arm over his head to block out the glare of light, Briec ignored the voice calling him to get up. He didn't want to get up. In fact, the way he felt at the moment, he planned to never get up ever again.

"Briec. Up. Now!"

Groaning, his head moments from splitting completely in half, Briec forced his eyes open and stared into the beautiful face of his baby sister.

"Keita?"

She smiled. "I was starting to worry you'd never wake."

"I don't want to be awake. So why are you waking me?"

"Fearghus sent me for you. He needs you and Gwenvael and Éibhear to do something for him."

Briec rolled over, resting his dragon head on his scaled forearms. "I'm not his errand boy. Nor am I the errand boy to his bitch."

His sister, still in human form, crouched beside him. He knew why Fearghus sent her instead of coming himself—Briec had a harder time saying "no" to his little Keita. Especially when she said, "What's wrong, brother? You're never this surly to me."

He sighed. A big, long sigh. "She left me, sister."

"The female you had here? Why? Was she unhappy?"

"I didn't think so. But I guess she was." Briec sat up a bit, his claw to his chest. "What is this unbearable feeling in my chest? *It's driving me mad!*"

Fighting her smile, his sister reached over and ran her hand through his hair. "That, my sweet brother, is called heartbreak."

He glanced down at his chest. "Will that be a physical deformity?"

Now his baby sister punched his shoulder. "Briec, you fool. I mean she broke your heart. You cared for her."

"A human? Broke *my* heart?"

"Deny it if you want, but I can see it in your eyes."

Briec pushed himself up. Even still sitting he towered over his sister's human form. "Good gods, the witch has hexed me!"

"No, brother. You simply fell in love with her."

He glared down at her. "Now you're just pissing me off."

Sighing deeply, she said, "As you wish, brother. I'm in no mood to fight you." She stood in front of him. "Now, Fearghus needs you."

"To run errands."

"No. He found one of Lord Hamish's spies at Garbhán Isle. He was planning to kill Annwyl upon her return."

For a moment, he did not forget Talaith, but he pushed thoughts of her back for something a bit more urgent.

"When is her return?"

"She actually should have been there by now, but a messenger came and told Fearghus she and her guard were delayed. Although her army finally made it back about three days ago."

"The spy?"

"Fearghus killed him . . . when he was done."

"And we know it's Lord Hamish?"

"Aye. He's always hated her, but no one ever thought he'd be stupid enough to go this far."

"So what does Fearghus need of me?"

"He wants you three to go into Lord Hamish's lands. Find out anything you can. Especially if his troops are moving out."

Briec nodded. "Aye. I'll go." Annwyl was hardly his favorite human, but once she'd mated with Fearghus, she became kin. Which meant, if one chose to be her enemy, they brought the wrath of the House of Gwalchmai fab Gwyar down on their head. "But I've already been there. I found nothing."

Nothing but the woman who made him insane with lust.

"Look deeper. That's why Fearghus wants Gwenvael to go with you. If there's one thing our brother does well, it's get information."

"True. I'll see what we can find out."

"Good." She pointed to her passed out brothers lying across his cave floor. "Now help me wake these two idiots."

"Perhaps you can poison him. Something that will make his eyes pop out and his tongue grow too large for his mouth."

Talaith again looked at Morfyd. She'd been doing that the last two hours they'd been riding toward Madron. Annwyl would say something particularly odd, and Talaith would look to see if Morfyd found it odd as well. Clearly the witch did, but it seemed she'd gotten used to it.

For once, Talaith found someone who made her speechless.

"I can poison him, if you wish. I've been trained to handle all sorts of poisons."

"I want to see him suffer before he dies."

"Annwyl," Morfyd sighed out. "Seeing him die rather defeats the purpose of getting in, taking the girl, and getting out. I think our goal should simply be that we are not seen. Not how much more violent we can make the man's death."

"Morfyd's right. Hamish has been shoring up his army for quite awhile now. With only three of us, we should err on the side of stealth."

"Shoring up his army? For how long?"

Talaith reached back in her memory to when she began seeing more and more young recruits traipsing through the village on their way to Hamish's castle. "Two years. Maybe a little more."

"Interesting."

"Well, what did you expect him to do, Annwyl?" Morfyd asked. "Wait for you to come and kill him? He knows you hate him."

"I know. I'm just tired of waiting. I still say we should strike now."

"You need more reason than theory."

Annwyl rolled her eyes. "You and your bloody logic."

"It's why you have me around. That and no one else will put up with you."

Pulling tight on her reins, Annwyl suddenly dragged her horse to a stop. She cocked her head to the side. "Do you hear it?"

Morfyd, briefly silent, nodded. "Aye. I do."

"Where?"

"Annwyl, maybe we should—"

"Where?"

With a sigh, "There." Morfyd pointed into the trees. "I think there's a clearing on the other side."

Annwyl turned her horse toward the forest and charged in.

"Damn her!"

"What is it?"

"A battle."

Talaith blinked in surprise. "And she's just going to—"

"Now you know my daily nightmare."

"Well, we can't let her fight alone."

"Not you too," Morfyd groaned.

Talaith snorted. "If she'd asked, I would have suggested

we ride on by. But since she's already galloped in head first . . ."

"Aye." Morfyd nodded. "You're right."

The two women turned their horses and followed the Blood Queen into battle.

"Stay!" Achaius pushed her back, forcing her behind a tree. It wouldn't do much good. They were horribly outnumbered by the men who attacked their small party. Only her and the three men who gave up their homes and army life to protect her. It wasn't the first time her Protectors had battled others in order to keep her safe. But this was the first time they'd come face to face with those they'd once called comrades.

Crouching low, she looked out over the field of battle and winced as her Protectors barely blocked blows aimed for their head or hearts. But as she began to fear all was lost and her friends doomed to a bloody death, she saw her.

A beautiful and scarred warrior woman rode on an enormous black stallion, two swords strapped to her back. She stopped at the edge of the clearing and stared out over the battle. She didn't move until she saw the crest on the enemy soldiers' surcoats. Then with a blood-chilling scowl, she tied the reins to her saddle, ripped the two swords out of their scabbards and kicked her horse into a fierce gallop. As she rode, she steered only with her knees and took heads as she went. One after another after another after another.

While her Protectors stayed out of the warrior woman's way, the soldiers screamed warnings at each other and that's when they focused their attack directly on the warrior woman. Foolish move. She wasn't alone. Two other women rode to the edge of the clearing. Unlike the first, these two wore capes, their faces and bodies hidden. The taller one stayed on her mare. A witch, that one, as she raised her hands and white-hot flames flew from her palms. The men charging the witch turned into a writhing ball of fire.

The other, smaller one, slipped off her horse and silently moved up behind one of the soldiers. One hand under his chin, his head lifted, a blade across his throat. She went from soldier to soldier doing that until seven of them lay at her feet. By then, the others had noticed her too, so she crouched low as two soldiers charged her. One she sliced his inner thighs open. He screamed hysterically as blood flowed. With the other, the small woman removed another blade from the belt around her hips and threw it, lancing his eye like an egg. He dropped his weapon and screamed while covering his face. She cut his throat as she passed him.

So fascinated by the three women fighting on their side, clearly sent by her god, she didn't realize anyone was behind her until the smaller female yelled, "*Down!*"

She dropped to her knees, her arms covering her head. She heard the soldier above her garble a parody of a pain-filled scream, then fall next to her. Slowly, she looked over. A dagger with a plain, leather-wrapped hilt stuck from his mouth.

"Stay in that position and I'm sure those soldiers will find many uses for your ass."

A brown hand appeared before her, the fingers slender and delicate. A few calluses from hard work. She recognized those hands. She'd seen them in visions.

"You going to stare at it or are you going to take my hand?"

Shaking, she removed her glove and put her hand in the woman's outstretched palm. Her fingers were longer than the woman's, her hand stronger. She had her father's hands and his eyes. She got her mother's face and, supposedly, her acid tongue.

Taking a deep breath, she gripped the woman's smaller hand and let her see everything.

* * *

Talaith impatiently waited for the girl—at least, she guessed she was a girl, hard to tell under that cape—to take her hand. Annwyl and Morfyd seemed to have the rest of the battle under control, killing off Hamish's remaining men. They must have still been looking for her and these poor wretched men and this girl got in the middle of it.

As soon as Talaith and Morfyd rode up, they knew why Annwyl hadn't waited for them, but eagerly threw herself into the fray. Annwyl recognized the Madron crest.

"You going to stare at it or you going to take my hand?" she half teased, half demanded.

After a few more intolerable seconds, the girl took off her leather glove and reached for Talaith's hand. Fascinated, Talaith stared at the brown hand slipping into hers. Someone from Alsandair this far north? But before she could say anything, the girl gripped her tight and images flooded through Talaith.

She could see her own face screaming and crying while being held back by Arzhela's priestesses as she reached out in desperation; she saw the gold gates of the Madron castle; the kind face and warm feelings of a maid caring for a child not her own. The images sped up and things quickly turned dark as a large man, a soldier or guard, pulled his hand back to slap, but other soldiers intervened. A fight ensued, lives lost. Then the men—the Protectors— were traveling, from town to town, village to village, city to city. Never staying in one place longer than necessary. Resting briefly. Feeling safe with these men but lost. Protected but lonely.

Instinctually, Talaith snatched her hand back, dropping hard on her ass. Through wide eyes, she watched the girl pull her hood off her face and those eyes . . . the eyes of Talaith's first love and lover looked at her.

"He promised you'd find me," the girl whispered. And Talaith saw all her hopes of the last sixteen years reflected back to her from that face. "He promised you'd never stop until you had me back."

With that, the girl threw herself at Talaith, wrapping her long, strong, warm arms around her.

At first, Talaith had no idea what to do. Not merely because her mother had never been affectionate, nor any of the Nolwenn witches who helped raise her, but because this wasn't how it was supposed to happen. Not in a million lifetimes.

"I'd really like it if you hugged me back."

It was such an innocent statement. And an honest one. Tears welling in Talaith's eyes, she wrapped her arms around her daughter and hugged her so tight she feared she may break her in half. But the girl didn't complain. She said nothing, actually, but the tears falling against Talaith's neck told her all she needed to know.

The brothers landed outside of Madron, their baby sister right behind them. She'd already arranged to have clothes and supplies awaiting them. They would travel into Madron human, hiding who they really were until necessary.

"Are you coming with us?"

Since she had yet to shift, Briec somehow doubted it. "No." Her lips turned into a nasty snarl, which meant only one thing. "Her Majesty has summoned me." Ah, yes. Only the Dragon Queen could annoy Keita this much. Mother and daughter did not get along like father and daughter.

Briec, still recovering from his nights of excessive drinking, tried to figure out how to put the blue surcoat on over his chainmail shirt and leggings. "What happened to those knights you were with?"

Keita burped and all the brothers quickly turned to her in surprise.

"Oh, Keita . . . you didn't," Briec charged.

"You know the rules, Keita. You either eat them or fuck them . . . you don't do both," Éibhear added.

"Not unless you do it right."

Keita and Gwenvael laughed but when Briec and Éibhear merely stared at them, they stopped.

Keita shook her head. "Of course I didn't eat them. I sent them on their way. Sadder but satisfied."

"I don't need to hear this about my baby sister," Briec muttered.

Even as dragon, he could see his sister giving him her adorable little pout. "You're still sad."

"He's miserable," Gwenvael offered as he struggled into his chainmail shirt. "He's starting to remind me of Fearghus before Annwyl."

"None of us are having this conversation." Briec wrapped a cape around his clothes, pulling the hood over his head to hide his silver hair. "She left me. It's over."

Because it was over. Even if he wanted to find her, he had no idea where to start. But he didn't want to find her. She'd left him. Without a word. Without a thought. She'd left him and now he had *feelings*.

For that alone, he'd never forgive her.

Chapter 17

Talaith opened her mouth again to answer her daughter's question, and again the girl cut her off.

"Because as I see it, the gods brought us together. I knew you'd find me. I always knew. I never knew you'd be so pretty, though. I wish I was as pretty as you. But, I'm not. I've had to face that fact and move on with my life. It hasn't been easy. Of course, nothing the past nine years has been easy, but it has been interesting. We've been everywhere, we have. The mountains of Brandgaine and the mines of Maledisant. You see, we've always kept moving. Always on the go. Never stopping except for a few weeks at a time. Except for my Protectors, I've had no friends. Although I think I see them more as uncles as opposed to friends. I think I need friends. Now that we've found each other perhaps I can actually have friends."

Talaith became tired just *listening* to the girl. All these years, they'd accused Talaith of being too talkative, too chatty. But this . . . this was amazing.

From what she'd been able to glean, her daughter's name was Iseabail. And she intended to keep it and she hoped that was all right. True, Talaith didn't give her that name but she was used to it now and didn't want to give it up.

Her Protectors—and that's exactly what she called them—referred to her as Izzy the Dangerous. Apparently while growing into her tall body, she had a tendency to be awkward and clumsy. And there was an incident with a horse she suddenly refused to finish telling.

Talaith still didn't know how these men came to protect her daughter because Izzy hadn't taken a breath long enough to allow Talaith to ask. Glancing at Morfyd and Annwyl, who led them back to Annwyl's elite guard, she could see them looking back at her and laughing hysterically. *Evil cows.*

"How did you learn to fight like that, anyway?"

"Well—"

"You see, I want to learn to fight like that. Achaius has taught me a bit, haven't you, Achaius, but mostly they tell me to run and hide when danger is near. But I'm sixteen winters now and running and hiding seems awfully unseemly, don't you think?"

"Um—"

"It was like I told Achaius, he can't protect me forever. Didn't I say that, Achaius? And what happens if, the gods forbid, he and the others get too hurt to protect me? Then what will I do?"

It took Talaith a moment to realize Izzy actually waited for an answer. "Oh, well, that's a very good point. It's a hard world and you have to learn how to—"

"Survive. Exactly. That's exactly what I was telling them. But do you think they listen to me? Of course not. I'm just She Who Shall Be Protected. As if that's the name I was born with.

"Anyway, I'm just glad to finally know you and meet you, like he promised I would." Talaith wanted to ask, "Like who promised?" but there was no chance as her daughter barreled ahead. "My heart would break if I never met you. You are my mother after all and we should have never been separated. At least that's how I feel and although I will admit, I've been wrong on more than one occasion, it is rare. And I absolutely think I'm right here. You see, it all comes down to . . ."

On and on she went—and Talaith had never been happier.

"Explain to me again why we're at a whorehouse?"

Gwenvael sighed around his ale. "Because, my thick-headed brother, if you want information about human men then you go to the one place all human men come to eventually."

Briec glanced over at Éibhear, but baby brother was too busy watching every woman in the room to notice.

"You sure you're just not hoping to get—"

"Gwenvael!"

Briec leaned back as a round, extremely large-breasted woman threw herself into Gwenvael's waiting arms.

"You've been gone ages."

Gwenvael pulled the woman onto his lap and nuzzled breasts fairly exploding from her bodice.

"Sorry, my sweet. I've had so much to do lately. Couldn't be helped."

"Well, you're here now. And you've brought friends, I see."

"Family, actually. These are my brothers, Briec and Éibhear. This, my brothers, is the fair lady Antha."

"Lords." She dipped her head a bit, but refused to release her hold on Gwenvael's neck. "So, old friend, anyone here that garners your interest this eve?"

Gwenvael pulled the woman close and whispered into her ear, "Anyone who has entertained those of Lord Hamish's court."

Eyes that were once warm and friendly, turned calculating in seconds. "Ah. That would be many, but he and his men do have their favorites. Of course, they are in much demand. Securing their time won't be cheap."

"Good thing I have so much gold to share."

Beaming, the woman slipped off his lap. "Then I shall get them ready for your pleasure, lord." She glanced at Briec and Éibhear. "And for your brothers as well?"

Éibhear eagerly leaned forward, but Briec pushed him back. "No. Just food and wine."

"As you wish." She turned and flounced off.

"Why must I wait down here with you?" Éibhear sounded as if he'd rather chew tree bark.

"This trip isn't about bedding wenches, little brother." Briec turned to Gwenvael. "Get what we need and then let's go."

For more than a week he'd had to put up with his two younger brothers. For more than a week he'd listened to constant arguing, complaining, debating, and whining. More than any one dragon should ever have to endure. True, they'd gotten much information, enough to satisfy Fearghus's needs he was sure. But Briec wanted to return to his den. He had much sulking left to do, and his idiot kin wouldn't give him a moment's peace to get on with it. The sooner he handed off the information and left these treacherous humans to their petty little lives, the better he'd feel.

"I want to give Fearghus what we have and then be on our way," he continued. "I grow tired of both of you."

"Of course, brother." Gwenvael, grinning as always, walked off.

Angry and more than a little frustrated, Éibhear crossed his arms in front of his chest. "He'll be gone hours. You do realize that?"

"Stop whining, baby brother. You'll have more than enough time in this life to find females who will eventually make you miserable."

Staring into the campfire, Talaith sighed softly. She'd tried for ages to get back to sleep, but couldn't. Not with her daughter leaning against her. Not with her daughter right beside her.

"You can't sleep, sister?" Morfyd whispered, sitting beside Talaith.

Talaith glanced down at a sleeping Izzy, whose head rested comfortably in her lap. "Could you?"

The witch grinned. "Good point."

Morfyd tore a loaf of bread in half and handed one side to Talaith who took it gratefully, seeing as she was unable to eat earlier. Her excitement over Izzy too great.

"Tell me, Morfyd," Talaith whispered around a bite of bread, "how did you know I was coming?"

Morfyd almost choked on her bread and Talaith knew she'd been right. Annwyl had been waiting for her. That was why she sent her army back to Garbhán Isle while she, Morfyd, and her elite guard remained. Waiting for her.

"That's what I thought, sister. When you walked into the tent this morning you said to Annwyl, 'I told you it was her.' How did you know?"

Morfyd swallowed her bread and thought carefully on her answer. Talaith knew the witch would only tell her so much. But anything was better than nothing.

"I've committed myself and my Magick to powerful gods. They warn me of danger." That couldn't have been vaguer if she'd said, "I know some people."

"Which gods?"

The witch smiled and put her finger over her own lips. "Dare to be silent," she whispered to her and Talaith couldn't help but smile back. During the dark days of Lorcan the Butcher's reign, before Annwyl killed him, witches lived by that code. It was all that kept them alive.

"Perhaps you'll find out in due time," Morfyd stated in a low voice. "The way you found your daughter."

Find her? Talaith had found nothing. Someone or some-*thing* had thrown Izzy in her path as certainly as Talaith's hair was curly and Izzy talked too much. True, she'd gotten what she wanted without having to kill the Queen of Garbhán Isle or rush headlong into suicide, but that also meant someone else cared about all this. Someone other than Arzhela.

Realizing she'd get no answers from Morfyd this eve, she let it go. At the moment, at least, she was safe. But, more importantly, her daughter was safe. Nothing could make her happier.

Although, she knew, there was one other thing that would make this perfect. But she'd lost him forever.

Brushing painful thoughts of Briec from her mind, she lightly combed Izzy's short, wavy hair with her fingers and, to her utter delight, Izzy giggled in her sleep.

She'd make the worst Nolwenn witch. She's too bloody happy.

Talaith smiled, knowing how that would irritate the very life from her mother. Enjoying the thought much more than she should, she went back to eating her bread, enjoying cautious but sane conversation with her first female friend, and loving the feel of her beautiful daughter tucked in safely beside her.

Arzhela screamed and the priestess who'd approached with the oracle's news dropped to the floor, blood streaming from her eyes, ears, and mouth.

She didn't mean to kill her, but Arzhela's rage knew no bounds now.

That bastard had led the bitch child straight to Talaith. Now they were all one big, happy family under the protection of that dragonwitch. And that dragon was powerful, only rivaled by her evil mother. Arzhela would never be able to break through the dragonwitch's defenses without years and years of work—and she no longer had that kind of time.

For centuries, her oracles had predicted the birth of a blood-drenched queen who would change everything. That queen was Annwyl. But with dragons surrounding her at every turn, Arzhela's only hope was to get a human close enough to cut that scar-covered throat.

Arzhela had chosen Talaith carefully. A human witch of considerable power, but who was still too young to have harnessed it. While the other Nolwenn witches would never bend under Arzhela's will, Talaith's inexperience made her a convenient target.

The constant arguments with her mother and her love affair with the soldier made it almost too easy. Alone, Talaith had given birth to her daughter. By the time her priestesses arrived, the girl had nearly bled to death. Still, she put up quite a fight when they claimed her child.

That child turned out to be Arzhela's only bargaining chip where Talaith was concerned. The only way she could keep any control over this uncontrollable human.

When the child disappeared from Hamish's care, she thought for sure she'd lose her hold over Talaith, but the child never resurfaced. She disappeared with the men who had stolen her; and Arzhela, nor the other gods, could track the little beast down. Eventually she gave up looking for her and continued her focus on Talaith.

At the time, she thought perhaps the child died. Arzhela didn't know or care. All she knew was that Talaith didn't know the girl was gone. Which meant Arzhela still controlled her.

When Annwyl took over her brother's throne and aligned herself with that black dragon, Arzhela knew her time had grown short. With Hamish's help, she cut off all information in and out of the tiny village Talaith lived in. That way Talaith continued to hear only about the evils of Annwyl, a necessity since she insisted on having this sense of honor her trainers had been unable to beat out of her. Arzhela knew she'd have a near-impossible time killing a woman she considered innocent.

Still, all she needed was for Talaith to get one chance at

Annwyl the Bloody. The witch would never survive the battle. Either Annwyl, a mighty warrior, would kill her as her last act or Annwyl's blindingly loyal elite guard would destroy Talaith in retaliation. It didn't matter. As it didn't matter what happened to Talaith's daughter. All that mattered was that Annwyl must die before the next full moon.

And everything was moving along perfectly. All would happen as Arzhela had anticipated.

Then that bastard silver dragon came along, destroying all her plans.

Now Talaith had her daughter back and the protection of the dragonwitch and the Blood Queen.

Still, Arzhela had other options. Another plan that Hamish was already moving on. It wasn't what she wanted. It was messier. But now she had no choice.

And she blamed Talaith and her little bitch whelp for all of it.

The barwench slammed another pint of ale down in front of Briec. She'd been slamming everything in front of him since he told her to leave him alone. She'd not taken it well, but he didn't care. She annoyed him. Everything annoyed him.

Gwenvael had been gone for quite a bit, giving Briec more than enough time to obsess and be miserable about Talaith.

Éibhear sat next to him, equally as miserable for a completely different reason.

"Come on, Briec—"

"If you ask me about getting a woman one more time, I'll tear off all your scales . . . again."

His baby brother slumped back in his seat, but as quickly sat back up. "Gwenvael."

Briec looked up, shocked to see a serious and still fully dressed Gwenvael coming back into the main dining area. He dropped gold on the table and motioned to his brothers.

They glanced at each other before following him out.

"What's wrong?" Éibhear asked as they headed out of town.

"Our paranoid older brother may be right," Gwenvael remarked, his face tense. "We need to get to Hamish's lands."

"We're no more than a day's flight from there. If that much." Briec remembered well the last time he was near Hamish's lands—when he found Talaith. The treacherous, deceiving Talaith.

"Good. I fear there's little time to waste."

There were things about his kin Briec knew. Fearghus was mostly unpleasant unless he was alone. Humans were lucky Morfyd cared about them because with her power she could destroy an entire kingdom without much effort. Keita would never sleep alone if she could help it. Éibhear would always be the nicest among them. And Gwenvael the Handsome only feared an angry female—or angry father of a female—cutting off his cock while he slept . . . until now.

Suddenly the brother who never took anything seriously moved with a purpose Briec had never seen before unless a warm, wet pussy waited at the end of his journey.

"You going to tell us what happened, brother?"

"Aye. When we take to the skies." He glanced at Briec. "Once we're done in these lands, Briec, we head to Garbhán Isle."

"You can head to Garbhán Isle. I'll head home."

"That's your decision, Briec. But if what I found out is right, Fearghus will need all his kin."

The dragon who needed no one suddenly needed all his kin around him?

This was much worse than Briec feared.

Chapter 18

Talaith pulled up on the reins of her horse, stopping the giant beast in its tracks. She stared, unable to do much else.

"What is it?" Izzy asked, leaning around her mother to see why they'd stopped. They didn't have enough horses for everyone, so a few of them doubled up. Talaith didn't mind, though. For five days she'd had her daughter right where she'd always wanted her . . . by her side.

"Look. Garbhán Isle."

"Oh." Her daughter stared. "I guess it's nice."

Talaith smiled. "Seen many castles have you?"

"A few." Izzy shrugged. "Brick and stone aren't what impress me, but the people inside them."

"You're awfully . . . thoughtful, for a girl barely ten and six."

"Not much else to do but think and read these last few years."

"Well, there are worse ways you could have spent your time." *Especially for one who barely takes a breath that doesn't include words.* "We're here because of Annwyl's good will."

"In other words lie and tell her the castle looks fabulous."

"Exactly."

With that, the pair moved on, and Talaith fell in line with the rest of the elite guard. They all looked worn and tired from their journey, and Talaith knew they longed to be home.

It had been a hard five days of constant riding, and nights of sleeping on the cold, hard ground. Annwyl no longer bothered having her tent pitched. Instead, as soon as the suns rose they were up and riding again.

Now that they were close, though, their spirits grew. Within two hours, they entered the town and as soon as the locals spotted Annwyl and her men, cheers arose as the people came out to greet her.

Blushing a bright shade of red, Annwyl took the flowers offered, shook a few hands, and smiled at the babies. But she never stopped moving. Soon, they worked through the throng of people and arrived at the massive gates of the castle of Garbhán Isles.

When Annwyl's brother reigned, Garbhán Isles was a place of horror. Those taken there, not of royal blood, never heard from again.

It didn't look that way now. The castle itself was bright white with silver accents all around the moldings. The grounds of the courtyard were clean, with flowers and trees planted all around the outer edge.

Annwyl pulled her steed to a halt inside the courtyard. Frowning, she looked around. Talaith couldn't tell if she found something to cause her displeasure or if she searched for something.

Shaking her head and sighing, Annwyl dismounted. "Talaith, I sent my squire ahead yesterday and had rooms made ready for you, Izzy, and her Protectors."

Surprised, Talaith and the men glanced at each other. Achaius, as always, spoke for all three men. "Quee—" At Morfyd's quick head shake, he corrected himself, "M'lady, stables will work well enough for the likes of us."

Annwyl snorted. It seemed to be her version of a laugh. "That's unacceptable, gentlemen. You'll all have your own rooms and fresh clothes." She turned and faced Achaius and the others. "You've done your duty, men. And you've done it well. You deserve peace and quiet now."

She pulled her saddlebags off her horse. "Besides, I need loyal men like you by my side, if you're interested." Stuttering, Achaius tried to answer but Annwyl cut him off by holding her hand up. "You don't have to answer me now. I don't know what you men left behind. But if you'd like to stay, there will be a place for you here. If not, you will not leave empty handed."

Too stunned to say anything further, the Protectors dismounted their horses and began to unpack them.

Annwyl looked at Talaith. "And as for you two—"

"Annwyl, I—"

"I'm sorry. Was I done speaking?"

Talaith sighed in mock exasperation while Morfyd chuckled.

"No, my *liege*. Please. Go on."

Not bothering to hold back her smile, Annwyl continued. "I want you both to stay here, under my protection, until you know what you want to do."

"I was thinking," Izzy volunteered, "that maybe I could—"

Annwyl placed her hand over Izzy's mouth and kept right on talking to Talaith. "There's no rush, Talaith. Take as much time as you need."

"Thank you, Annwyl. I really do appreciate that." She did, too, because she really had no idea what she would do. She and Izzy had their whole lives ahead of them. For once, Talaith felt hope rather than despair. It was a new and heady feeling she was simply unused to.

"Now, Iseabail the Dangerous"—Annwyl took her hand away from Izzy's mouth—"you were saying?"

But Izzy was no longer looking at Annwyl and for once she had nothing to say.

"Izzy?"

The loud sound of a big hand making contact with Annwyl's

chainmail-covered ass startled both women away from Izzy's captivated face.

"And where the hell have you been?"

Annwyl turned, her gaze moving up and up and up some more into the handsome face of an absolute bear of a man. "Where have *I* been?" she snapped back. And Talaith wondered if Annwyl had lost all reason, challenging this man. Then she remembered Annwyl had lost her reason long ago. "I've been securing *our* lands. That's where *I've* been."

One very dark eyebrow raised over even darker eyes, a smirk on the handsome man's face. "You were supposed to be back weeks ago."

"Sorry if the war isn't running to your timetable, lord."

"I see," he said, a lock of coal-black hair slipping from under the hood of his cape and across his eyes. "Someone's begging for me to—"

"All right then," Morfyd cut in, taking firm hold of Izzy's shoulders and pushing her in the direction of the Protectors. The girl went, but her eyes stayed glued on what Talaith could only assume was Annwyl's husband.

Looking back at the huge man, Morfyd shook her head. "Hello, Fearghus."

Without turning away from Annwyl's face, the man motioned at the witch. "Morfyd."

Morfyd crooked a finger at Talaith. "Come, sister. Let's get you settled. I fear you and I are much too young for such a display."

The couple hadn't moved any closer to each other, but they didn't need to be any closer. The way they stared at each other was enough to make anyone feel like intruders.

"No need. We're leaving."

Annwyl grinned at Fearghus's words. "Oh? Are we?"

"Aye." He took firm hold of Annwyl's hand. "To Dark Glen with you, wench."

Morfyd turned. "Fearghus, wait. There is much to discuss."

"Later, sister."

"*Much* later," Annwyl added with a very girlish giggle, Fearghus dragging her behind him.

Morfyd sighed in exasperation and walked toward the castle steps, leading Achaius, Izzy, and the other men into the building and to their rooms.

But Talaith didn't follow; too busy staring at the retreating form of Annwyl's husband. Fearghus. The way he moved seemed familiar. *Extremely* familiar. She watched him until the couple disappeared around the corner of the castle.

"No. No," she muttered to herself. If she kept this up, she'd see Briec everywhere. In every man she met until the end of her days. She couldn't live like that.

No. Fearghus was merely a very large man. Perhaps a tad unnaturally large but a mother could achieve that with the proper spells and sacrifices. Besides, that behemoth was what someone like Annwyl needed.

Exactly someone like Annwyl would need.

Convinced she was right, Talaith let out a deep sigh of relief, only to choke on it as a black horned head appeared from around the corner Annwyl and Fearghus had only moments before disappeared behind. Long, *long* black hair brushed the ground. So as not to damage the surrounding buildings, he kept his black wings tucked tight against his body. His *dragon* body. And on that dragon sat an extremely happy and content Annwyl.

Panic and excitement vying for possession of her lungs, Talaith watched silently as Fearghus—and she knew it was Fearghus—took to the air. Her eyes tracked the couple—and they were a couple—until they passed another dragon.

"No, no, no. This isn't happening." Stepping away from her horse, Talaith stared up at the sky. There were so many! Dragons of every color flew above her. Some sat patiently on the silver-tipped spires of the castle chatting with other dragons flying around them.

From a distance, she hadn't seen the dragons because

they didn't want to be seen. Most likely for defense of Garbhán Isle.

Placing her hand over her chest, she realized that yes, her heart *did* just stop in her chest. Didn't she actually need that to beat? "This can't be happening."

Talaith needed answers. And she needed them now. She sprinted into the castle, pushing past soldiers and guards, through the Great Hall where they were already setting up for the evening's feast, and up the stone steps. She found Morfyd and the others on the second floor.

"Oh, Talaith. Good. This will be your room."

"Good." Talaith grabbed Morfyd's arm and shoved her into the bedroom. "Give us a moment, Iseabail," she said to her daughter's surprised face before slamming the door shut.

"What's wrong with—"

"Fearghus just *flew* away."

"Oh." And she watched Morfyd try to hide that smile. *Conniving, betraying bitch!*

"*That's all you have to say?*"

"Don't yell at me, witch," Morfyd snapped back.

"What do you expect me to do? You lied to me."

"No. I didn't."

"You saw everything, Morfyd. You were in my mind. Uninvited if you remember. You knew about Briec."

That damn smirk returned. "Aye. I did."

"*Then how could you not tell me?*"

Morfyd's eyes narrowed. "There's that yelling again."

Talaith's eyes closed as she realized something. "Fearghus called you 'sister.'" And not like witches called each other "sister." But as annoyed siblings.

"Aye."

Which means . . .

Talaith headed back toward the door. "We're leaving." She'd take her daughter and go. She couldn't stay here. Not now.

She had her hand on the metal door handle when Morfyd's voice stopped her. "And where will you go, Talaith, Daughter of Haldane? Where will you take Izzy and think you will be safe? Annwyl seems to think it's over, but we both know it won't be over. Not until Arzhela is somehow dealt with."

Morfyd now stood next to her. "But you'll be safe here. Under my protection and the protection of my people. If you run now—"

"I'll run forever," Talaith finished for her.

"You both will. And hasn't Izzy run enough?"

Talaith laid her head against the door. "But Briec—"

"Briec never comes here." Morfyd stroked Talaith's hair from her face. No one but Briec had ever touched her merely out of kindness. "He hates this castle. Detests Annwyl. And barely tolerates the rest of us. The farthest he'll go is Dark Plains. Fearghus's den. He won't be here. And, if you wish, I won't tell him you're here. If that's truly what you wish."

She didn't hesitate. "No. I don't want him to know I'm here." She'd worked hard the last few days to push him from her mind and her heart. To let him back in now would only lead to her broken heart when he was finally done with her.

"Then I'll never tell him."

Talaith, suddenly drained beyond all reckoning, pulled her door open. "Thank you, Morfyd."

The one she now knew to be one of the rare dragonwitches her mother and the sisterhood spoke of in reverent tones— when they spoke of few beings that way—nodded and walked out. Talaith could hear her showing the men their rooms. But Izzy stepped in before she could close the door.

"Is everything all right?"

Talaith nodded, fairly dragging herself across the room to the big bed in the middle of it. She dropped back on it, ignoring her dirty, travel-worn clothes. "Everything's fine, Izzy."

The door closed, but Talaith knew Izzy hadn't left. The bed dipped as Izzy stretched out beside her.

"I talk too much, don't I?"

Talaith, grateful for the distraction, laughed. "We both do, I think."

"Were you disappointed when you finally met me?"

Talaith turned on her side, propping her head up with her hand. "Of course not." She reached out and took gentle hold of Izzy's hair, running her fingers through the wavy, light brown strands. Her daughter never let her soft hair get too long. It barely touched her shoulders and already she complained it was getting "unruly."

"You remind me so much of your father."

"Is that good or bad?"

"It's the best. I loved him. He was handsome and brave and very tall. Spoke his mind, too."

Izzy, a naturally affectionate girl, reached out and took hold of Talaith's free hand. "You should know," she intoned in mock seriousness, "I have a real problem with speaking my mind."

"Yes. I've noticed you're a shy, retiring girl."

"And coquettish."

Laughing, Talaith reveled in her daughter's good humor. Considering what Iseabail had been through, she admired that.

Still, she didn't want the poor girl shocked to death when she went outside.

"Izzy, there is something I should tell you—"

"By the gods!" Izzy scrambled off the bed and dashed to the large windows. She pushed open the enormous and heavy glass—no arrows would be getting through that thick material—and leaned out. "Look!"

Terrified she'd lure them over, Talaith quickly moved to her daughter's side. "Get inside, Izzy," she ordered while pulling the windows closed.

Izzy stared at her. "You're not scared of them, are you?"

The way her daughter asked that made Talaith extremely nervous, she simply didn't know why. "Aren't you?"

"Why would I be? He who protects me is . . . uh . . . hmmm . . ." Izzy suddenly found interest in the molding around the window.

Grabbing hold of her daughter's arms, she turned Izzy to face her. "Iseabail?"

"Yes?"

"The god who protects you . . ."

"He's ever so nice," she rushed to explain. "And, as you see, he picked only the finest men to protect me and—"

"*Your god is a dragon?*"

"There's no reason to yell," Izzy mumbled. "He's protected me for years. He's never hurt me or asked anything of me. Except not to say who he was. He said people wouldn't understand. Guess I mucked that up, eh?"

"Dammit, Izzy."

"You don't understand. He's taken such good care of me. He's taught me to read and write. Some math and science, although I'm not very good at it. As well as history, which I'm excellent at."

"And he wants nothing in return for all that care? All that protection?"

"He doesn't. He's never asked me for anything."

"Do your Protectors know?"

She shook her head. "He was only a voice to them. Figured it was less scary."

"But you . . ."

She shrugged. "Always dragon. Came to me in my dreams. I never minded. I found him comforting."

"Who, Izzy?"

Frowning in confusion, "Who what?"

"Who's this dragon god that protects you?"

She smiled. "Well, Rhydderch Hael, of course. Who else would be powerful enough to protect me from the human gods?"

Talaith closed her eyes, her stomach dropping with dread. "Rhydderch Hael? He's your protector?"

"Aye."

"The *father* of all dragons is *your* protector? That's what you're telling me?"

"He's oh so very nice," she insisted.

Talaith racked her brain, trying to remember what the teachings of the Nolwenn witches said about Rhydderch Hael. She knew him to be one of the oldest gods on this world and many others. He had a loyal mate. A dragon goddess of equally awesome power who many feared.

Dragons were his domain. He protected them, gave them Magick and skills, and he merely asked they take care of the world they inhabited. For centuries, eons even, it worked. But new gods appeared. Fickle gods hungry for power who brought the humans with them. It changed everything. Especially when the humans insisted on hunting dragons and dragons found humans so very tasty.

Many believed some of the humans' gods, including Arzhela, decided to destroy Rhydderch Hael, hoping they would assume his power and take control of this world, as well as many others. But, as always, they underestimated the rage of a female. Rhydderch Hael's mate fought by his side and rallied the other dragon gods to his cause. They pushed Arzhela and her god kin back into their realm, creating a seal that would keep them out forever while the humans' gods did the same.

Since then, both sides used the humans and dragons as their warriors or pawns in the hopes of obtaining more and more power. So far, the balance remained.

But Talaith knew well that the slightest shift could change everything forever.

"Izzy," she sighed because she didn't know what else to say.

Izzy perked up. "But don't you find dragons fascinating?"

Talaith rolled her eyes. "No." Arrogant and annoying, yes. Fascinating—never.

Izzy stared out the closed window. "Think one of them will take me flying?"

Walking back to her bed, Talaith dropped on it face first and pretended she didn't just hear that.

Chapter 19

"Stop fidgeting."

"Sorry." Iseabail held still for about thirty seconds . . . then began again.

"Izzy."

"I'm sorry. I've never been to a party before."

"Keep this up and you won't go to this one because you won't be dressed."

Izzy the Dangerous stared in the full-length mirror at the reflection of the woman who gave birth to her. She was busy tying up the back of Izzy's dress. It was Izzy's first dress since she was seven. And definitely her first grown-up gown.

She still couldn't believe it had only been two weeks since her life completely changed. She went from homeless, motherless bastard wandering the land with three very poor soldiers to merely a bastard. But she had a home now. And a mother. A mother she loved. She'd loved her before she knew her, but the risk still remained her mother could have turned out to be a horrible, beastly woman. She wasn't. She was amazing. And so funny. If there was one thing Izzy loved to do, it was laugh. Her mother kept her laughing—constantly.

"Finally." Talaith, who told her it was up to her if she wanted to call her mother, gripped her hips and turned her around so that mother and daughter faced each other. She frowned deeply at Izzy's chest. "I don't much like how low-cut this is."

Izzy glanced down. "Why? It's not like I have anything to speak of."

"Yet. If you're anything like me, you're a late bloomer. Still, this is cut awfully low." Suddenly her mother's hands gripped the bodice of her dress and pulled up.

Rolling her eyes in exasperation and batting at her mother's hands, "There will be other girls there my age and they will have similar gowns."

"Don't care. It's up to their mothers if they want them seen as whores."

The two looked at each other. It was Izzy's snort that forced them into a fit of giggles.

"That's a horrible thing to say!"

"Perhaps." Talaith picked up a rose garland from off the bed. Izzy wasn't old enough yet to have flowers threaded through her hair like her mother's. But the garland was beautiful and smelled wonderful. "But just you remember, daughter. Achaius will be watching out for you tonight." Achaius had taken Annwyl's offer of staying, while her two other Protectors planned to return to their homes and families after the feast.

"Any of these lusty soldiers get within five feet and they'll regret it."

"You and Achaius have been strategizing again," Izzy complained. They did that a lot, it seemed.

Talaith placed the garland on Izzy's head and adjusted it until she gave a satisfied sniff. "That'll do."

She stepped back and looked her daughter over. She smiled, but it quickly turned into another frown. Crouching, Talaith lifted the hem of Izzy's dress a bit. "What are these on your feet? Where are the slippers I gave you?"

Izzy looked down at the leather boots she wore, fitted with blades on both sides. Annwyl lent them to her. They both had equally huge feet. "Slippers? What if I have to run for my life or fight an animal to the death? Can't do that in those girly slippers now can I?"

Turning, Izzy headed toward the door, but she could hear her mother mumbling under her breath, "Yes, you're my daughter all right."

Fearghus sighed. "Move your ass, woman."

"Control yourself, dragon," Annwyl called back from the connecting room she kept as her own. She filled it with her clothes, armor, weapons, and books. Always books for his Annwyl. But when they were together, they shared the same bed.

"Explain to me again why we're having this party." He'd much prefer spending the evening eating something hearty and then burying himself balls-deep in his woman until morning. Parties, like most things besides Annwyl, bored him.

"It's not a party. It's a feast. And it's in honor of my men, their families, and whatever else you want to think of."

Stretched out on the bed, Fearghus threw one arm over his eyes. "Can't they have their feast without us?"

"You're whining, Fearghus. Don't whine. Now, how do I look?"

He lowered his arm, his breath catching at the sight of her. Annwyl hadn't even worn a dress at her coronation. Why she decided to wear one tonight, he had no idea, but he'd be eternally grateful. A deep, dark forest green, the dress molded to her every curve, hugging tight across her large breasts. The tight sleeves reached to the middle of her hands, covering his markings, and a piece of velvet looped around the middle finger on each hand, holding the sleeves in place. Her golden brown hair, threaded through with green flowers, reached below her waist.

But leave it to his Annwyl—she still had two swords tied to her back. Of course, they weren't her big battle swords, but a pair he'd had made for her with jeweled hilts—the blades still sharp as sin, though.

"You look beautiful."

After everything they'd done together, everything they'd been through, he still had the ability to make her blush.

"Um . . . thank you."

He held his hand out to her. "Come here, Queen Annwyl."

She took a step toward him, then stopped. "Oh, no. You'll not get me that easy, knight." She still hadn't realized that when she desired him, she always went back to what she originally used to call his human form before she knew the dragon and the man were all the same being. "They're expecting us. We have guests to greet."

Fearghus growled. "I said come here."

With a less than queen-like squeal, Annwyl dashed back into her room. Before she disappeared, Fearghus saw she wore leather boots, blades shoved into the sides. *My Annwyl.* He'd have her no other way . . . except on her back.

He charged off the bed and snatched the door leading from their room to the hall open. She'd just come out of the other room. When she saw him, she squealed again and ran toward the stairs. He followed, both of them pushing past some of the highest human and dragon royalty in the land. A few they knocked into the wall. Neither cared.

"Come here, wench."

"Not on your life, dragon."

She made it downstairs, barely dodging Fearghus's outstretched hand. But his other arm looped around her waist, lifting her completely off the ground.

"Let me go!"

"I've got you now, my queen. The question is what will I do with you?"

"Bastard!"

"Sweet talk will get you everywhere."

The two laughed and struggled until they looked up and found both Brastias and Morfyd staring at them.

"Must you two do that?" Morfyd demanded in a harsh whisper. "In front of *everyone?*"

"Well, actually—" Annwyl began, but Fearghus feared what she'd say, so he covered her mouth with his hand. "Sorry, sister. We'll stop."

"Good."

She and Brastias walked off, but as soon as Fearghus released Annwyl she yelled after them, "We'll do our best to be good little monarchs."

Morfyd swung around so fast, fangs showing, that Annwyl stumbled back and then dodged behind Fearghus.

"My, aren't we the brave queen, my love."

"Shut up, mate."

He was one of the young soldiers in training. He'd bragged about it for the last five minutes while he continually tossed his white blond locks over his shoulder.

Izzy didn't like him. And she had the almost overwhelming desire to shave his blasted head and then stuff her pillow with all that blond hair.

Music suddenly flowed through the hall and dancing started. Izzy longed to dance because she never had before.

Turning from the boy—she'd never consider him a man—in the hopes of finding a dance partner who didn't make her skin crawl, she froze when his hand grabbed firm hold of her arm.

She looked down at the hand holding her and then up at the boy attached to that hand.

"Let me go."

"We weren't done talking."

"We are now."

He gave her an indulgent smile she longed to punch off his face.

"Come. Dance with me." Ignoring her attempt to get him to release her, he headed toward the dance floor. But three large men blocked his path.

"Problem, Izzy?" Achaius asked calmly, but Izzy had lived with the man for nine years. She knew when he might snap and crack open a few heads in the process.

"No. No problem."

The boy was a fool but nothing she couldn't handle.

Her Protectors, in unison, looked down at the hand holding onto her arm and back at her.

"Doesn't look that way to us," Achaius observed.

"Achaius—"

"Perhaps you better get out of my way, old man."

Izzy winced and resigned herself to the boy's fate.

Achaius ignored the boy and focused on Izzy. "What did we teach you, Izzy, when someone placed his hands on you without your permission?"

"But—"

"Izzy?"

With a sigh, Izzy moved around to face the boy, his hand still holding onto her arm. She used her free one to slam her fist into his throat.

Startled and unable to breathe, most likely, he stumbled back.

"Good lass." Achaius patted her on the back. "Now off with you. We'll take it from here."

"Achaius, it really wasn't—"

"Don't make me get your mother over here, Iseabail."

"No, no. Not necessary," she replied hastily.

The boy may not realize it, but he'd be better off taking a beating from these three men in a dark corner than facing off against her mother. She'd seen the damage that woman could do, remembered the bodies lying on the field of battle.

No, it was best not to get her mother involved.

"Then go and enjoy yourself," Achaius said as he gently

pushed her toward the dance floor. "We'll join you in a few minutes."

She glanced at the boy and felt a small pang of regret for him, but he really did bring this on himself.

Talaith barely managed a yelp before a strong hand dragged her off into a deserted hallway. She went for her concealed dagger but quickly realized it was only Morfyd.

"Grabbing trained assassins and hauling them into dark corners is always a bad idea, Morfyd."

Morfyd dismissed Talaith's words with a wave of her hand. "Forget all that. I have something much more interesting."

The two women stopped as a young man with white blond hair dashed by them. He'd been badly beaten, his face a bit of a bloody mess.

Talaith watched him disappear around a corner. "Should I ask—"

"No," Morfyd cut in. "Probably not."

The dragonwitch most likely spoke true. It was much better Talaith *not* know what was going on.

"So, what's so interesting?"

"The captain of the guards finds you quite attractive."

Talaith stared at the dragoness currently in human form—and she kept staring.

"Well?" Morfyd pushed, her excitement evident as she bounced on the tips of her toes.

"Well, what?"

"Go dance with him."

By the gods, she's matchmaking.

"Absolutely not." Talaith turned and headed back to the party when Morfyd's words stopped her in her tracks.

"I thought you were over him."

Talaith swung around to face her new friend and current royal pain. "*We* are never to discuss *him*. Ever."

"Why, if you no longer care for him?"

Talaith shoved the female farther into the dark alcove. "Would you keep your voice down. Honestly, I don't know why you keep on about it."

"I want you to be happy."

"I am happy. With my daughter."

"And that's all you want?"

"That's all I've ever wanted. So leave it be, Morfyd."

Talaith walked off and kept walking even when Morfyd whispered much too loudly, "What about the Duke of Winsley? He's quite cute and has loads of riches."

Annwyl thought about setting herself on fire. Anything had to be better than listening to this man go on and on. Who was he again? Lord Winsley? Duke Winsley? Whatever. He was boring and his nose was excessively long. She desired to break it. Would he cry like a babe? Or take it like a man? She'd wager on the crying. He looked weak. She hated weak men. She hated weak women. She hated weak in general.

Besides, he kept referring to her as queen. True, Morfyd said no head taking during the feast. But what about an arm? Or a leg? Of course, the screaming would start, but she'd prefer the man screaming rather than boring her to death.

Annwyl looked over the man's head—she would tower over him even in her bare feet—and saw Fearghus standing by the entrance to an alcove. When she realized he had her attention, he smiled and motioned to the alcove with his head. Then he disappeared inside.

Knowing what awaited her, she glanced down at the duke or earl or whatever he was and said, "That's fascinating, but I have to go."

Without waiting for him to say another painfully boring word, she slipped through the crowd and went into the dark alcove. As soon as she walked in, Fearghus's hands slipped around her waist and dragged her deeper inside. He pushed her up against the wall, his lips against her throat and his hands pulling up her dress.

She dug her fingers into his hair and bit her lip to keep from crying out. Didn't help, though. Not with Morfyd's personal "battle dog" stalking her every move.

"My liege?"

Fearghus's hands stopped moving and Annwyl felt her rage slowly simmer to the surface.

Through gritted teeth, she snarled, "What, Brastias?"

"Your humble servants await, m'lady."

"And they can keep waiting," she growled back.

"No, my queen, I don't think they can."

"Brastias—"

"Don't make me get Morfyd, my ladyship."

Damn him. He called her those names to irritate her. And irritate it did.

"Fine!"

Annwyl pulled away from Fearghus, ignoring her mate's growl of warning, and stalked out of the alcove.

"Happy now?"

"Aye. I truly am, my—"

"If you give me one more title, I promise I'll cut your throat."

Brastias grinned. The bastard. "As you wish, Annwyl."

"Not really. Otherwise I'd be back in there."

Brastias laughed and glanced into the dark alcove. "And you, my lord Fearghus? Will you be joining us as well?"

A deep sigh came from the darkness and then Fearghus's tense voice replied, "Not at the moment, no."

Annwyl winced. She may be a little slippery between her legs, but her long dress hid it well. But she knew poor Fearghus's chainmail leggings could never hide the erection she'd felt pushing against her stomach only moments before.

* * *

"You know, you really don't look *that* old."

Talaith slapped her hand over her daughter's mouth. Forcing a smile at the duke her kin had just insulted, she dragged the girl away.

"All right, little miss, I need you to get control of that tongue."

Izzy frowned at her mother and nodded. She pulled the hand off her mouth. "I'm sorry. I didn't mean to insult him. It was only, I couldn't believe how old he was."

"And how did you find out his age?"

"I asked him."

Talaith sighed. "You can't do that, Izzy."

"Why?"

Clearly her daughter's dragon protector hadn't taught her much in the way of manners. But now that Talaith thought about it, dragons and manners were not synonymous. Brutal honesty and directness—that was where their strengths lay.

"Because it's considered rude."

"I'm sorry." She appeared horrified she may have insulted the man. "I'll go apologize."

"No." Talaith grabbed her daughter's arm before she could move away—the girl moved like lightning. "I'm sure he won't give it another thought. But point it out to him . . ."

Izzy closed her eyes. "I'm not good at this, am I?"

"Izzy, you've been living with three hard soldiers for the past nine years. You're doing fine." It was merely her eagerness that continually got away from her. "Just watch your tongue and remember to think *before* you speak."

Izzy nodded. Suddenly, she leaned over and embraced Talaith, pulling away only after she'd kissed her cheek.

Mother and daughter smiled at each other before Izzy bounced off in search of more people to accidentally insult.

Brastias watched the partygoers carefully. True, he was supposed to be a party guest as much as any of the others, but the two assassins sent to kill his queen had made him excessively wary.

It surprised him Talaith, one of those assassins according to Morfyd who'd asked for his silence, not only lived but seemed to have become the best friend of the queen and her Battle Mage. He had no idea why. Both Annwyl and Morfyd insisted she'd been the victim of circumstance. Perhaps. Brastias didn't rightly know. But, he grudgingly admitted, he'd grown fond of Talaith, too. He'd especially grown fond of her loud, chatty daughter.

Still, no one had told Fearghus about how Talaith came to join their little party, and so happy to have Annwyl back, he didn't question it.

It won't be fun when he finds out.

He would find out, too. He always did.

"You want to take a bit of a break, General?"

Brastias looked at Danelin. "What do you mean?"

"If you studied the guests any more, sir, you'd be forcing them to strip and bend over."

Brastias chuckled. "That obvious, am I?"

"Aye, sir. Besides"—he motioned across the room—"there is someone I'm sure wouldn't mind if you asked her for a dance."

Following his second-in-command's line of sight, his eyes settled on Morfyd. Tonight she didn't wear her usual witch's robes. Instead, she wore a sparkling white gown, cut low in the front, and her white hair curled and hanging loose around her shoulders and down her back, with white and silver flowers threaded throughout.

Definitely the most beautiful thing he'd seen in his entire existence.

"Go on, sir." Danelin pushed Brastias with his shoulder and Brastias almost struck him down with his sword.

Instead, he gritted his teeth. "I'm going. I'm going. Don't push."

Taking a deep breath, Brastias moved across the floor

toward Morfyd. Tonight he would ask her to dance. The worst she could say was "no." But he would think positively for the moment. She'd say "yes" because he wanted her to say "yes."

He stepped in front of her. "Lady Morfyd."

She grinned. "*Lady* Morfyd? Isn't that a bit formal between old friends?"

Friends? He didn't want to be friends. In fact, he was tired of being friends.

"Well, that's the thing—" But before he could finish a large hand slapped him on the back, almost sending him flying into Morfyd.

"Brastias, old friend."

Scowling, Brastias turned and faced Gwenvael. Bundled up in a cape and furs, his face nearly hidden by the hood, he'd clearly only arrived. "I had no idea there was a party this eve. Good thing we washed before changing and coming here."

Gwenvael, typically unaware of what he'd interrupted, pushed Brastias out of the way so he could kiss his sister on the cheek.

"You look lovely this evening, sister."

Morfyd, always so self-contained and in complete control, practically fell over herself as she grabbed her brother's arm. "*Are you alone?*" she demanded frantically.

Frowning, he said, "No. I've got Briec and Éibhear with me. Why?"

She bounced on her toes. "Where? Where are they?"

He pointed to a spot across the floor. Éibhear, happy and good-natured as always. And Briec, looking as if he wished he were anywhere but here—as always. They both had the hoods of their capes up over their heads, nearly obscuring their faces. But Brastias knew them well enough to see who was who. And, based on past experience, Brastias knew as soon as Briec spoke to Fearghus, he'd leave. Now that he thought about it, Briec had only been there one time before.

When he and his kin came to convince Annwyl to return to her mate after their year-long separation. Any other time the brothers met, it was at Dark Plains. Strange having him here now. The information they possessed must be extremely important for him to make the trip.

The music changed tempo to a fast jig and one of Iseabail's Protectors lifted her up and swung her around the floor. She squealed excitedly as he passed her off to one of her other Protectors who passed her off to the next.

He admired those men. They'd taken good care of that girl for nine years. While they may go hungry, they made sure she ate. While their clothes and armor may need repair, her clothes were always clean and cared for. And from what he heard, woe to the man who came near her, much less hurt her. No, the lass couldn't have been in better hands until she could return to her mother.

One of the Protectors reached into the crowd and dragged a shy and extremely embarrassed Talaith out to join the dance. At that moment, he heard Gwenvael gasp in surprise.

"But, wait . . . that's . . ."

His sister gripped his arm tighter, causing him to wince in pain. "I know. I know!" The toe bouncing became decidedly worse. Morfyd's one weakness—gossip.

Brastias turned back to watch Talaith. Although they didn't lift her up like her daughter, the Protectors swung her once and passed her among each of them. She laughed even as her face turned dark red in embarrassment, knowing everyone watched her. Although some decidedly with more intensity than others.

Especially Briec. He stepped forward out of the crowd, staring so intently at her Brastias found himself holding his breath, waiting for Talaith to notice him.

She did . . . at the moment she slipped and slammed face first into his chest. Laughing, she gripped his arms and pushed herself away. Most likely with an apology on her lips as was her way. But when she looked into the face of the man—or, in this case, dragon—who held her, she froze.

Staring at each other, the pair stayed stuck to that particular spot. Until, finally, Briec spoke.

"*You left me!*"

No angry bark that. Nor a yell. Or even a shout. It was a roar. So much so, it shook the very foundation of the castle. The music stopped. The dancing stopped. Even Fearghus stood in surprise, dropping Annwyl on her ass since she'd been happily sitting in his lap at the time.

"*Well?*" Again that roar.

Recovering quickly and clearly livid, Talaith snatched her arms away from Briec's grasp. "*Don't you dare yell at me!*"

"No word from you. *You just left!*"

"I had a previous engagement that didn't involve you!"

She turned away, but Briec took firm hold of her arm. "So you say nothing? You simply sneak out?"

"Why don't you just say what you mean? It isn't that I left that bothers you. It's that I left *you*. The wondrous Briec the Arrogant. Left by some peasant no less." She snatched her arm back. "How humiliating for you," she sneered with enough venom to wipe out a small town.

"You seem to forget, m'lady . . . *you* belong to me."

Fairly growling, "I belong to no one. *Especially* you."

Pitch black smoke snaked from Briec's nostrils and then his brothers were there. Fearghus took firm hold of the back of his neck. "Let's go somewhere and talk, brother."

"We're not done," he snarled, his eyes never leaving Talaith's face.

"Oh, we are," Fearghus insisted, pushing Briec toward the great doors; Gwenvael and Éibhear following their kin out.

Annwyl motioned to the musicians to begin playing. Then she crooked her finger at Talaith and Morfyd.

Watching Morfyd and Talaith disappear with Annwyl, Brastias sighed heavily.

Will I ever get a moment alone with that woman?

* * *

They walked past the gates of the castle, stopping when they finally hit the forest, and that's when Briec punched Fearghus's hand off his neck. The last thing he wanted right now was for anyone to touch him.

"You need to calm down, brother," Fearghus warned softly.

"And you need to go to hell."

Éibhear, always the peacemaker, stepped between the two. "Everyone calm down. I'm sure there's a logical explanation to all this. Right, Fearghus?"

Fearghus, ever the "calm one" stared at their baby brother as if he were simple. "How the hell would I know that? I don't know what's going on."

Gwenvael leaned against a tree, looking smug. Briec wanted to rip his face off. "Brother has Claimed a woman."

"Talaith?" Fearghus asked, confused. "The human?"

"I didn't Claim her."

Gwenvael crouched beside the tree, picking up blades of grass and ripping them with the tips of his fingers. "You certainly are acting like you did."

The bastard was right. But he couldn't help it. He'd walked into his brother's hall expecting to give him news and go. He'd been in no mood for a party, so he'd had no intention of staying. But there she'd been. Right in front of him—in another man's arms. Several other men, in fact, dancing her around the floor. She wore a dark blue velvet dress clearly fitted to her frame. Her black, curly hair threaded through with flowers the same color of her gown. She looked so beautiful. She looked . . . happy, like she didn't have a care in the world. All the time they'd spent together, she'd never looked that relaxed except when she slept in his arms.

What did he do wrong that some other male did right?

Fearghus crossed his arms in front of his chest. "Who is she anyway?"

"Don't you know?" Didn't seem like his brother not to know who'd come into his den.

"I've asked Annwyl about her, but suddenly the most direct female I've ever known turns surprisingly vague. As does Morfyd. And I haven't had much time to get any details." Most likely because Fearghus had been busy fucking Annwyl blind.

"Briec found her in a little village outside of Madron." Éibhear pulled the hood of his cape back. "He took her."

"I rescued her. Get it right at least."

"Why did she leave you?"

"Do you think I know that? Do you think I have any idea why I woke up and found her gone?"

"Perhaps she had another man all along." True, he could kill Gwenvael, but their mother would never forgive him. "Perhaps she left simply to get back to him and she merely waited until you trusted her enough."

"She left for no man," a female voice said from the safety of the trees. "She left for me."

Gwenvael grinned. "This just got interesting."

"I will kill you where you stand, brother."

"Don't yell at me because your woman . . . has a woman."

"I want you two to stop this conversation right now," Fearghus ordered softly. "I mean it."

The trees rustled a bit and a tall, but extremely young, brown-skinned girl stepped forward. Even in the dark night, the nearly full moon blocked by the forest trees, Briec could still see the girl clearly. He sucked in a startled breath.

"By the gods . . ."

Fearghus motioned to the girl. "It's all right, Izzy. They're harmless." The girl moved closer and Fearghus introduced her. "You degenerate lot, this is Iseabail . . . Daughter of Talaith."

How could she not be? She looked exactly like her.

Except her eyes were a much lighter brown as was her hair and she was a good bit taller. Other than that, they were mother and daughter.

"She never told me of a daughter."

Gwenvael snorted. "I see you built up a wonderful level of trust there, brother."

"That's not fair," the girl snapped. She looked at Briec. "She couldn't tell you. She *really* couldn't tell you."

"Why?"

She moved closer and Briec saw exactly how young she was. "She was protecting me. And, to a degree, herself. She would have hurt her if she told you anything."

"Who would have?"

"Arzhela."

Gwenvael stood. "The goddess?"

She nodded. "It's complicated."

"It's not like we had any plans this eve," Éibhear teased. Iseabail smiled but her eyes grew wide as the moonlight suddenly peeked out and spilled across Éibhear.

"Is your hair blue?"

"Uh . . ."

"Can I braid it?"

"No!"

"Izzy." Fearghus easily drew her attention back to him. "Focus, girl."

She sighed. "Do you really want me to tell you?" The dragons nodded. "You won't like it." Her light eyes flickered to Fearghus. "*You* especially won't like it."

"Why especially me?"

"Because it was your mate she was sent to kill."

"You . . . and Briec?"

"That's the eighth time you've said that."

"But it's just . . ." Annwyl stared at her with her mouth open. "You . . . and *Briec?*"

Talaith, shaking her head, stalked over to the window of Annwyl's bedroom. It had to be the most enormous bedroom she'd ever seen. Obviously it took much to get Fearghus the Destroyer to spend time at Garbhán Isle.

"Well, what's he like?"

"Don't you know? He is your *family*." Plainly there was much more to Briec than she knew. She thought Morfyd, Fearghus, and Briec were merely all dragons. The same breed. It never occurred to her they were *all* family. Kin, as Briec would say.

Annwyl laughed. "You must be joking. He hates me."

"You did hit him," Morfyd chastised.

"He was in my way."

"No, he wasn't."

"Close enough."

Talaith buried her face in her hands. "This is a nightmare." She turned accusing eyes on Morfyd. "You said he never comes here!"

"Normally, he doesn't. And don't yell at me."

"So you hate him?"

Affronted, Talaith whirled on Annwyl. "I do not hate him."

Confused, Annwyl scratched her head. "Then what's the problem?"

"Everything."

"Why are you making this so complicated, Talaith? If you still want him, be with him."

"I can't. I have to think of Izzy."

"Exactly how much longer are you going to use her as your excuse?"

Talaith turned away from the window to face Morfyd. "Pardon?"

"She's sixteen winters, Talaith. Soon she'll be trying to figure out what she wants to do. Maybe help here or she'll meet someone and want to start a family. Let's face it, even with her Nolwenn blood, she'll never be a witch. She has absolutely no powers."

"That's my fault," Talaith sighed. "There were spells I should have cast. Sacrifices I should have made."

"Haven't you sacrificed enough?" Annwyl asked, silencing Talaith.

"Well," Morfyd continued, "she doesn't seem to miss it, so I wouldn't concern myself too much. But you can't build your life around hers because she'll be starting her own life soon. Then what will you do? Stay here and be lonely? Perhaps become the wife of one of the knights? Is that what you really want?"

What she wanted was Briec. She'd always want Briec.

"Briec is not an option."

"Why not?"

She glared at Morfyd. "Because he made it clear I was only temporary. Something to pass his time with."

Annwyl threw herself into a large, winged-back chair. "He didn't act like you were temporary. He acted like you broke his heart."

Talaith shook her head. "That's not possible."

"He looked like you ripped his heart out of his chest, threw it to the ground, and stomped all over it while singing a jaunty tune." Annwyl shrugged at Morfyd's bemused expression. "I might have seen that look before on his brother."

"Perhaps when you stabbed our father?"

Annwyl laughed. "No. Then he just looked proud."

"He'll never understand," Talaith sighed out. "He'll hate me for what I was sent to do to you."

"I'm fairly certain he honestly won't care. The only one who'll care is Fearghus. And I have no intention of telling him anything, so—"

The three females jumped, Annwyl's words cut off, as Fearghus kicked the door in.

Annwyl stood. "What the hell is wrong with—"

"Everyone out! Now!"

Morfyd didn't hesitate. "Night, all." Then she was out the damaged door like a lightning strike.

Talaith could guess what Fearghus now knew and she wasn't about to stand there waiting for him to focus his rage on her. With a nod to both, she hurried past them and out the door. But as soon as she stepped into the hallway, Briec took her arm and dragged her off. The last thing she saw was her daughter—*good gods, what could she have told them?*—waving at her with one hand while making a grab for Éibhear's blue hair with the other. Startled, Éibhear slapped her daughter's hand away before practically running down the hall.

Then Briec pushed open a door and shoved her into a bedroom. By the time she turned around, he'd locked the door and thrown the key into the fire blazing in the small pit built into the wall.

Bastard.

Chapter 20

"You open that door right now." She wasn't going to panic. She wouldn't allow him to make her panic.

"Not until we talk."

Talk? Ack! Panic! "Talk? About what?"

"About why you left me. About your daughter. And about all these . . . these . . ."

"These what?"

"*Feelings!* I never had them before until you. And now I've got them. What exactly did you do to me, little witch?"

"Me? I didn't do anything to you. I told you to let me go."

"And because I didn't let you go, you hexed me with these feelings?" He said his accusation like she'd gutted him while he slept.

"I didn't hex you with anything, you idiot." She walked to the large window and stared out over the now-deserted courtyard. One look at the dragon lord's face must have sent all scurrying for cover from his rage—even his family.

"Then why do I feel like this?"

"Feel like what?" she asked absently.

"Like you ripped my heart out, threw it to the ground, and stomped all over it while singing?"

Eyes wide, Talaith turned to face Briec. "What?"

"My chest hurts. It's never hurt before—until you. Make it stop," he begged. "I can't stand it."

Unable to form words, much less coherent thoughts, Talaith slid down the wall, sitting hard on the floor.

She closed her eyes, fighting her desire to sob. "I didn't want to hurt you, Briec. I swear." She pulled her legs up tight and dropped her head onto her raised knees. "I didn't want to hurt anyone. I just wanted my daughter back." Finally, tears flowed. "I had to get her back."

After a painfully long silence, Briec sat on the floor beside her. She had the castle wall at her side and back, and Briec on her other side. She should feel trapped, smothered, but she didn't. Not with him.

"Your daughter is beautiful," he said softly. "Just like her mother."

Wiping her tears, desperate not to look as pathetic as she felt, she asked, "What did she tell you?" Knowing Izzy as well as she did now, probably everything.

"Everything."

"Of course, she did." After several shaky deep breaths, Talaith once again had control. "So I guess you feel pity for me now." Which would explain why he was suddenly being so nice. "The poor peasant used by a goddess."

"Maybe I should feel sorry for you, but I don't. You're too much of a pain in the ass to be pitied."

Against her desire to feel morbidly depressed, Talaith chuckled. "That's very kind of you."

Briec moved a bit, and the material of his wool cape rubbed against her arm. "Why didn't you trust me, Talaith?"

"It had nothing to do with trust. Whether I trusted you or not, I couldn't risk Izzy." And she couldn't risk *him*. Although Arzhela may not have been able to use her Magicks on Briec, that didn't mean she wouldn't send men to kill him. To sneak into his lair and destroy him while he slept. "I wasn't willing to risk anyone I cared about."

"Am I someone you care about?"

Talaith didn't answer. She didn't dare.

Briec rested his head on her shoulder, his silky hair rubbing against her neck and jaw. "Answer me, Talaith." She didn't. Instead, she turned her head away from his.

"Then tell me to go."

"And you would?"

"If that's what you want. But you have to say the words, Talaith." His gloved hand slid over her leg, resting on her knee. "Tell me to go."

Say the words, Talaith. Say them before he breaks your heart. But the words . . . she couldn't force them out. And she tried. She really did. But it felt so good having him by her side again. She'd missed him so much. Annoying, rude, bastard dragon that he was.

When she said nothing, Briec let out a barely audible sigh. Briec the Arrogant had actually been worried she'd send him away. Well, that felt nice.

"You look beautiful tonight."

Talaith cleared her throat. "Thank you."

"And your daughter is very brave. Just like her mother."

"Brave? Is that what they call it? Or blindingly stupid?"

"Brave seems much more fitting." Briec turned his head, his lips brushing her bare shoulder where her dress tugged down a bit. "I missed you, Talaith. And I don't like that feeling. I hate it when I'm miserable."

Giggling—to her horror—Talaith pulled back to look in Briec's face. "Oh, no. You being unhappy. Can't have that, now can we?"

"You're right. We can't," he responded in serious tones. "An unhappy Briec is an unhappy universe."

The giggling became decidedly worse, because she knew Briec was actually serious.

"You think it's funny? My misery?"

"You needed to be a little miserable. To know how the rest of us feel most days."

He shuddered. "The nightmare of being human." Sitting

up straight, he adjusted his body so that he faced her side, his powerful legs on either side of her body. Then, he began slowly removing the flowers threaded through her hair. She let him. It felt nice.

"So you're a trained assassin."

She bet other people at this moment weren't having this odd a conversation. "Um, yes."

"Are you good at it? When you actually *try* to kill your prey as opposed to taunting them into killing you?"

"Aye."

"Do you enjoy it?"

"No. Not at all. Because I can kill people doesn't mean I enjoy doing it."

"I see." He took his time, slowly removing each flower and letting them drop to the floor, making sure to constantly touch the skin on the back of her neck or her shoulders. Carefully, he moved her where he wanted her, so that he could remove all the flowers from her hair. It felt so good having him care for her. Eventually, dark blue flowers covered the floor around them and her body trembled at every sweep of his hand.

Briec leaned in close, his lips brushing her ear. "Stand up, sweet Talaith. Let me help you out of this dress."

Briec stood, gently bringing Talaith with him. He kept all his movements deliberately slow. He didn't want to push her too quickly. He didn't want her to run again.

When he'd spotted her at the feast, his rage took over. He'd had all his words planned. Knew all the things he'd say to her so she'd understand exactly how much she'd hurt him. But then little Iseabail told them everything. The only one not moved had been Fearghus, but that didn't surprise any of them. Fearghus's only concern, as always, was for his mate. His Annwyl.

Now Briec understood, because he felt the same way about Talaith. His Talaith.

"Did you miss me, Talaith?" he asked as he untied the back of her dress.

"Ha! You wish." But he could hear the shake in her voice.

"Not even a little? Not even at night, when you slept alone?"

"Who . . . who said I was alone? Perhaps I've had a myriad of lovers since I've been with you."

He had a momentary stab of jealousy and then he remembered who he was dealing with. Talaith whose favorite phrase seemed to be "Get your bloody hands off me."

"Really?"

"Aye. Many, many lovers. Good ones, too. All human."

"Like who?"

She tensed. "Who?"

"Aye. Give me names. Or, at the very least, rank."

He finished unlacing her dress, but didn't pull it off yet. Instead, he ran his fingertips lightly across the exposed flesh of her back. Her trembling grew much worse, but so did the smell of her lust.

"I'm waiting."

"Well, there were so many. I'm not sure I remember all their names."

"My, you've been busy since last we met."

Pushing her hair to the side to kiss her neck, Briec froze at the sight of a silver chain. He hadn't noticed it before. He walked around until he faced her. She stared up at him, her cheeks flushed; her eyes wide.

"What? Does my disloyalty shock you?"

"Your disloyalty?" Briec took gentle hold of the silver chain and lifted it, pulling the pendant from under her bodice. She grabbed for it, but his hand closed over it first. "Disloyal, and yet you still wear this."

Tugging the death grip her fingers had on him loose, he

opened his hand and stared at the dragon pendant he'd given her the last night they were together.

"I . . . I wear that because it looks so nice with this dress."

"Except it was hidden *under* your dress. You wear it close to your heart."

She looked away from him. "It's a bauble. It means nothing to me."

"That's a lie, Talaith." He gently grasped her chin and forced her to look him in the eye. "We both know that's a lie. You would have never kept this, much less wear it, if it meant nothing to you."

Her panic now vied with her lust, but Briec knew why. She didn't want him to know how much he meant to her. She still wanted to maintain distance and, in the end, control.

"Don't be foolish. No one's ever given me jewelry before. I couldn't simply toss it away, now could I?"

Briec shook his head. "Talaith, exactly how good an assassin could you be when you are such an incredibly bad liar?"

"I'm not a bad liar. I mean, I'm not lying. I mean—"

"Sssh." He held onto the necklace and used it to pull her closer. "For the love of all that's holy, woman," he whispered, "stop talking."

Staring at his mouth, "But I still have so much more to say, you selfish bastard."

He grinned, unable to help himself. Then he kissed her, keeping it simple at first. His lips touching hers. But she moaned and went up on her toes to get closer to him. That was more than he could handle.

He released the necklace so he could dig his hands into her hair—his gentle control gone. He licked her lips and she opened her mouth to him. Now he moaned as her tongue touched his, sweeping around it, stroking against it.

Unwilling and unable to wait any longer, he slipped his fingers under the dress, pushing it off her shoulders. He pulled away, easing the dress down her body as he knelt in front of her.

"Step out of it."

She did with no argument, and he quickly tossed the dress into the nearest chair.

As always, she had her blade tied to her upper thigh. "Still keeping this around, eh?"

"Oh." Talaith went to grab the sheathed dagger, but Briec caught hold of her hand.

"No. Leave it." He smiled up into her startled face. "I like it."

Nothing made him lustier than the thought of her legs wrapped around his waist with that damn blade tied to her thigh. Besides, he trusted her.

He stood before he could toss her to the floor and fuck her within an inch of her life.

"Get on the bed, Talaith," he ordered while he nearly ripped his own clothes off.

One eyebrow perked up on that beautiful face. "Should I get on all fours, lord? Or merely lie there? Like a forest animal awaiting slaughter."

Laughing, his upper body now bare, Briec lifted her up by the waist. "Must you argue everything, woman?" She squealed as he tossed her back on the bed. "Can you not just lie there and take it? Like a good little lover?"

Her eyes narrowed. "Oh, that's nice. How some female hasn't snapped you up already—I'll never know."

"I think that's because I've been waiting my whole life for you. And no one else would do." It was an honest answer, and one she in no way could handle as she made a strange little "eep" sound and tried to climb off the bed.

"No, no. You're not going anywhere." He pushed her back, covering her body with his own. "Now kiss me, you chatty cow."

"Go to—" He kissed her before she could finish that lovely little statement.

Pushing her legs apart with his knee, Briec settled himself comfortably in the vee of her body, allowing his hands to roam freely over her soft skin.

"Hell!" she finished when he finally pulled his mouth away from hers.

"Now is that any way to talk to me?" He kissed her neck, his fingers circling her hard nipples. "Especially since you so clearly adore me."

"Is it nice in your dream world, dragon?" she gasped out, her body arching into his hands, then his mouth as he moved down. "Are there fairies and elves there to keep you company?"

"Who needs old wives' tales about fairies, when I've got you—an old wife?"

He felt that punch to his shoulder long before it arrived. Still, it made him laugh more. Sitting up, he stared down at her. She tried glaring at him, but her uncontrolled panting as well as her flushed cheeks and body made it much less intimidating.

Briec grinned, grabbed both her legs, and flipped her onto her stomach.

"Oi!"

"Up on those knees, love." He pushed her legs up, raising her lovely ass quite nicely. "I need access to this ridiculously wet pussy of yours. Have many plans for it this evening, you know?"

She started to say something, but he didn't hear her and she stopped talking as soon as he buried his face between her thighs. He thrust his tongue inside her, enjoying the taste of her wetness sliding down his throat.

Talaith groaned and so did Briec. Did he really think he'd ever be done with this woman? Did he really think he'd ever be able to walk away from her? Unable to wait a second longer, he nearly destroyed his chainmail leggings as he pushed them down his legs to his knees.

He leaned up, resting against her back. Getting a strong

grip on her wrists, he held her in place as he drove his painfully hard cock inside her. She hissed, her legs spreading farther apart to allow more of him in. He obliged, shoving into her until his balls slammed against the soft cushion of her ass.

"Gods, you feel good," he gasped, her muscles tightening around his cock. "You're strangling me."

"I would," she panted back. "But you have my hands pinned."

"Callous cow."

"Irritating bastard."

Yes. Now *this*, this was home. Right where he belonged. Where he'd always belong. With this rude, sarcastic woman. And he knew *she* felt the same as soon as he stroked himself in and out of her sweet pussy. Without even realizing it, she moaned his name, begging him not to stop.

"I won't stop, little witch." He picked up his pace, unable to keep any semblance of control while inside her. "I won't ever stop." Because he couldn't. Not where she was concerned.

Using his free hand, he reached around her waist and slipped his fingers in between her thighs. He found her clit and stroked it, desperate to bring her to climax before he lost all reason. She must have been close, she panted and moaned his name into the pillow, her pussy spasming around his cock, dragging him deeper inside her wet heat. And, with a relieved sigh, he came hard inside her.

Panting, sweating, and momentarily exhausted, the pair crashed onto the bed. Her hand grabbed his, removing it from her clit. "You're killing me."

"Not yet. But that could change any day."

Laughing, she punched his thigh while he kissed her neck. He pulled out of her gently, slowly turning her so that she faced him.

He kissed her forehead. Her cheeks. Her nose.

"I missed you," he murmured against her lips. "Don't do that again."

Her arms wrapped around his neck, pulling him close. "Don't do what again?" she sighed, his lips moving to her throat. He knew she loved when he kissed her throat.

"Leave me. Don't leave me again, Talaith."

Her body stilled in surprise, but before she could say anything, he kissed her. Long and deep, enjoying the sweet taste that belonged only to her.

Just as he belonged only to her.

Chapter 21

Annwyl knew she was in trouble when she woke to find Fearghus standing over her, his arms crossed over that massive chest, and his jaw clenching and unclenching.

"We need to discuss your assassin situation, mate."

Somehow she'd managed to put him off the night before. It must have been when she wrapped her mouth around his cock. But clearly that tactic wouldn't work this morning. She guessed he'd been up for awhile . . . seething. Partly mad she found it so easy to distract him. Partly because it still angered him she'd kept something like this from him. Fearghus really hated that. But telling him about Talaith would have just upset him unnecessarily. Not that he'd ever understand that.

"Fearghus, there's nothing to tell. So let it be." She tried to turn over and go back to sleep, and that's when she realized he'd tied her to the bed.

"Oi! You bloody bastard! *Let me go!*"

His fingers brushed against the inside of her leg. "Not until we have a nice long discussion about you keeping things from me. We've got all morning. And I have unlimited patience."

Uh-oh.

* * *

Talaith's eyes snapped open when she heard the queen of Dark Plains cry out, "Gods! Oh, gods! *Fearghus!*" Since she sounded extremely far from actual pain, Talaith didn't worry.

Instead, she grinned. *Those two.*

Stretching, Talaith enjoyed the feel of Briec's arms around her. In fact, since she was in no rush this particular morn . . .

Turning over, she said huskily, "Time to wake up that great, big coc—Izzy!"

Standing at the end of the bed was her only daughter. The girl grinned at her.

"How did you . . . how did you get in here?"

"Picked the lock."

Pulling the fur coverings she'd thankfully already had around her even tighter, "Nice to know you have that skill." She elbowed Briec awake.

"What?"

"Look who has come to wake us up." Perhaps the floor would open up and drag her to the pits of hell rather than waiting until she officially died.

Briec scratched his head and yawned. "Good morn, Izzy." He rubbed his eyes with his knuckles. "Now as you may have realized, you're upsetting your mother. So why exactly are you here?"

"Making sure you treated her right." Her daughter grinned and Talaith remembered seeing that expression on Izzy's father's face more than once. That's probably what snagged her heart in the first place. "And it looks like you have."

Embarrassed, Talaith yelped, "Iseabail! Out!"

"No need to yell." She sauntered toward the door, no longer in a gown but leather leggings, boots, and a green, soft cotton shirt. "I'll have the servants bring up food and hot water to bathe."

The servants? Seemed her daughter had quickly gotten used to court life.

Izzy easily pulled open the heavy wood door. "And no need to rush."

The girl, who Talaith was seriously considering disowning at the moment, stepped out into the hallway, but before she closed the door, she heard her daughter say, "I told you I could get past any lock, Gwenvael. Now you owe me ten gold pieces."

Talaith buried her face in her hands, but unfortunately she couldn't block out Briec's voice. "I like her."

"Shut up."

Hours later, Talaith found Annwyl asleep on her throne. Her legs thrown over the arm of the chair, her branded arms crossed in front of her oh-so-ample chest . . . and she snored.

Yes. That's very attractive, Queen Annwyl.

Unwilling to wait for the woman to wake up, Talaith tapped her shoulder. But froze when she felt the tip of Annwyl's dagger against her throat. The queen hadn't even opened her eyes yet. When she finally did, she blinked several times. "Oh. Sorry, Talaith." She placed the dagger back in the sheath at her side.

Yawning and stretching, she said, "What is it?"

"Wondered if you wanted to go for a ride with me?"

She had to get out of this castle while she had the chance. Briec had kept her in bed for another four hours before he'd finally taken a quick bath and disappeared. She knew if he found her anywhere near that room or any bedroom, he'd have her flat on her back before she could blink.

Annwyl sat up, but winced. "All right. I'll go. But no trotting or galloping. I'm sore in my—"

"Really, my queen. I don't need anymore detail than that."

* * *

"How much time do we have?"

Gwenvael sat back on his haunches. "Weeks. His army's large. He won't be getting it this far quickly."

Fearghus had sent them into Madron lands to find out exactly how far Hamish was willing to go in his quest to destroy Annwyl. Apparently quite far. They soon discovered his army was on the move, heading toward Dark Plains and Annwyl.

"Still," Briec cut in. "We should be ready by the time he gets here."

Fearghus glanced at Gwenvael, then back at Briec. "We? Planning on staying?"

"As long as she's here—I'm here."

Sighing, Gwenvael stepped away from his kin, knowing this would get very ugly, very fast.

"Well, I no longer want her here. I want her gone."

Briec shook his head at Fearghus's order. "No. She stays."

Gwenvael usually enjoyed a good fight between his siblings, especially when no one paid him any mind. But this felt different. It felt . . . dangerous. He hadn't seen Fearghus this angry since their father tried to kill Annwyl. Nor had he seen Briec this determined about anything ever.

"She tried to kill my mate."

"You act like that's a first."

"Don't play with me, Briec."

By a stream deep in the forest, the four brothers had returned to dragon form for this meeting and even spoke in the ancient language of their kind. Which made this feel even more serious to Gwenvael.

"I'm not. But I'll be damned if I let you push her from this place. She's happy here. She feels safe here. As does her daughter. So they both stay."

"You barely know this bitch, and yet you protect her like—"

"Take care, brother, how you speak of her."

Gwenvael looked at Éibhear who had been surprisingly quiet during this conversation. He could tell by the expression on his baby brother's face he felt no better about the course of this discussion. They may not get along very well, his family, but they always protected each other. Gwenvael would hate to see some female get between them.

"This is my kingdom, Briec," Fearghus growled out. "I'll speak of her any way I like."

"She stays."

"She goes."

"Perhaps," Éibhear finally piped in, "we should ask the women."

"Why would we do that?" the two eldest asked in unison.

Éibhear motioned with his head. "Because here they come."

All four of them looked at the rough trail that led through this forest. They could see Annwyl on her pitch-black war stallion, Violence, and Talaith on a much smaller brown mare Gwenvael didn't recognize. Not surprising really. No one caught him trying to eat the brown mare like Annwyl caught him with Violence.

The women walked slowly through the trees, speaking softly. But it was Talaith who saw them first. Well, actually, she seemed to see Briec before she saw any of them. Again, not really surprising, as her horse reared up, almost unseating her.

Violence, however, was quite used to dragons by now.

Annwyl caught sight of the brothers and her eyes narrowed in suspicion. "And what goes on here, I wonder?" she called out.

"Nothing to concern yourself with, mate."

"Really?" Annwyl rode her horse closer as Talaith worked hard to control her much more skittish mare. She wasn't doing a half-bad job either.

"Why don't I believe you . . . *mate?*"

"I don't know. Maybe because there's been so much lying going on here of late."

"I never lied to you, Fearghus."

"You didn't tell me the truth."

"Because I knew you would act this way. And if this is about Talaith—she stays. As does her daughter. Until I say differently."

"This is our kingdom to rule together. Remember?"

"Dragons are your domain. Humans are mine."

"She tried to kill you, Annwyl."

"So did your father and yet he's welcome here for meals."

Gwenvael snorted out a laugh. "She's got you there, brother."

Fearghus's tail slapped him so hard in the snout, he actually saw stars for a moment.

"*Ow! What was that for?*"

"Accident."

Annwyl rode up to Fearghus. "Did you stop trusting me, Fearghus?"

"Of course not—"

"Then trust me now."

The mated pair stared at each other for a long time, until Annwyl's hand finally reached out and brushed against Fearghus's neck. "Walk with me, Fearghus."

He nodded and silently the two walked off. Briec headed toward Talaith, but his dragon form was apparently too much for the beast she rode. The mare reared back, throwing Talaith off, and bolted into the woods.

Talaith waited until she could breathe again before she forced her eyes open. What she didn't expect was to look up at three dragon snouts staring down at her.

Like something out of a nightmare.

"She breathes!"

"Of course she does. She just got the wind knocked out of her."

It was now official—*Even my nightmares are getting ridiculous.*

Talaith pushed herself up until she sat. It was very hard not to cringe when all those snouts brushed against her.

"Could you all move back a bit? You're crowding me."

"Sorry, m'lady."

She grinned at Éibhear. "You insist on calling me that, Éibhear."

"You seem like a lady to me."

"Only because he's been around Annwyl too much," Gwenvael joked.

Talaith grabbed a talon from the two younger brothers, barely able to get her entire hand around them, and allowed both to haul her to her feet. She now stood in front of Briec. He'd kept his dragon form, and she studied him carefully.

Annwyl seemed so comfortable with Fearghus, whether dragon or human. But the dragon part of Briec still disturbed her a bit.

It's probably those scales . . . or the fangs.

"Are you all right?"

"Aye." She rubbed her backside. "Just a little sore, is all."

Gwenvael bowed low, his dragon snout scraping the ground, his eyes focused on her rear. "Perhaps I can help you with that, m'lady."

Briec didn't even look at him as he slammed his tail into Gwenvael's chest, sending him flying back into the trees.

Éibhear shook his head as he walked off in the opposite direction toward a clearing. "He really does bring that on himself."

Briec waited until his brothers were away, then he focused on Talaith. "I'm scaring you, aren't I?"

"What gave you that idea?"

"I can smell it."

Eek!

"Don't be ridiculous—" she began to lie.

"Talaith."

"Oh, all right. I find you a bit . . . intimidating when you're like this. You're so very large and fangy."

"Is that even a word?"

"Probably not."

"Then what would give you ease, Talaith?"

She frowned. "What do you mean?"

"How do I make you comfortable with who I am? Because nothing will change the fact that I am a dragon. I can shift to a human form, but I am in no way human. And to be quite honest, I have no desire to be."

"Does it matter whether I'm comfortable with you or not?" she asked carefully.

"Aye, Talaith. It matters greatly."

Talaith let out a trembling breath, refusing to read any more into that statement than what he actually said.

"It's just that so much of you looks, um, dangerous."

"We are predators. We hunt. We kill. We feed."

Talaith took a step away from Briec. "If that is supposed to make me feel better . . ."

"It's supposed to let you understand who and what I am. But I'm not a monster, Talaith. I would never hurt you. Or anyone you care for."

"I know."

"Do you?"

"Aye," she replied with all sincerity. "I do."

"Well, that's half the battle then, isn't it?" It took Talaith a moment to realize he'd begun to walk around her in a circle. "The question is, sweet Talaith, what do we need to do to ease your other concerns?"

"Well . . . eek!" She jumped as his snout brushed against her back.

"Well, what?"

"I . . . uh . . . I really don't know . . . uh . . . what are you doing with *that?*"

The tip of Briec's tail slid down her back, across her ass, and slowly down her legs. She wore leggings, but they weren't made of thick material. So when his tail wound itself around her leg, she felt it to her very core.

"Briec, I—"

"Continue, Talaith. Tell me what scares you."

Everything? "Well, that's a vast list."

"I meant about me, or my kind, specifically. We'll have to deal with the litany of your other fears another day."

She glared at him. *Arrogant bastard.* "Well, your fangs are a tad unsettling."

Briec's head swung down until they were nose to snout. Then he pulled back his lips to reveal those huge, white fangs.

"What *are* you doing?"

"Go ahead," he said through his teeth, "touch them."

"Not on your life."

"Talaith, you have to get over this fear."

"No, I don't. I can run away. Screaming. Like a girl."

His tail tightened around her leg and she knew he wouldn't let her go until this insane nightmare was over to his satisfaction.

"Touch them, woman."

Closing her eyes tight, she reached and felt around. Considering these were fangs, she couldn't feel anything that hard.

"Talaith . . . that's my nostril your hand is in."

"*Oh, by the gods!*" Desperately wiping her hands on her trousers and squealing, her body now shook in disgust as opposed to fear.

"Try that again, shall we? With your eyes open this time."

"Don't you have some kittens to torture? Or some town to destroy?"

"Talaith," he said with an exaggerated sigh, and she

knew she was dealing with Briec the Arrogant. "You and I—*I* feel—are destined to be together."

"Oh, good gods," she groaned.

Briec went on as if he hadn't heard her. "So in order for us to make this work, we need you to get over your tiny little insecurities."

"Your arrogance makes my eye twitch."

"Only because I'm challenging you."

"No. I'm relatively confident it's because you're arrogant," she barked. "No, no. Forget it, dragon. I'm not sticking my hand in your mouth."

Sighing heavily, he sat up. "Fine. How about this then . . ."

Again she squealed as the tip of his tail unwound from her leg and suddenly appeared in front of her face. "Would you watch that thing. You're liable to take off my nose or something!"

"Touch it."

"Actually, I like my fingers attached to my hands."

"Fine. How about touching my horns?"

"Well, this conversation just went horribly wrong."

"You're making this difficult."

"I'm not sure what you're trying to show me."

Frustrated, Briec shifted to human and walked up to her until they were mere inches apart. "That you and yours are safe with us. You have nothing to fear. Nor does your daughter. And you never will."

Her expression softened and a smile began to form on her gorgeous lips. Of course, the timing couldn't have been more perfect for Éibhear to run past the forest entrance. Normally, not too odd. He was a young, playful pup. Yet it was the fact that he had Iseabail hanging onto his tail that had panic hitting Briec's system.

"Uh . . ."

"What's wrong? You just went more white than usual."

Éibhear shook his tail. "Get off! Get off! Get off!"

Laughing, Izzy continued to cling to him.

"Is that Izzy?" Talaith turned to look behind her, but Briec grabbed her shoulders and forced her back to face him.

"You know how I feel about you, Talaith," he nearly yelled, desperate to keep her distracted.

"I do?"

"Of course you do."

"Since when?"

"Since last night."

She shook her head. "I don't have time for this. I promised Morfyd I'd meet her over at the groves." She again turned to walk down the path to the clearing, but Éibhear reappeared, this time slamming his tail on the ground, trying to dislodge an unrelenting Izzy.

Briec took firm hold of her shoulders and spun her back to face him. He had to think of something fast or all his "you have nothing to fear" work would be lost. So he said the first thing that came to his mind . . . "I love you."

Both shocked at his words, they could only stare at each other.

Finally, she spoke first, "You what?"

Now that he'd said it, he realized something. "I love you. I actually do." He grinned. Who knew loving someone would feel so wonderful?

"You love me?"

"Yes." So happy about this, he barely noticed Éibhear taking flight and dragging Izzy through the trees trying to knock the girl off. "Now you say it back to me."

"Pardon?"

"Say it back to me. Say you love me. Because we both know you do." How could she not?

"Och!" She pushed his hands off her shoulders. "Do we now?" Reaching up, she grabbed one of his nipples and twisted.

"*Ow! What the hell did you do that for?*"

"*Accident*," she bellowed, then stormed off.

Stunned, Briec shifted to dragon. Which was good, because Izzy landed right on his back.

Panting from the exhilaration, she yelled up to Éibhear, "You're being unreasonable!"

"Stay away from me," Éibhear barked. Briec had never heard his brother sound so unnerved before.

"Your brother is a big baby."

"For a dragon he actually is a baby."

"What's wrong? You sound sad."

"I told your mother I love her and she walked away."

Izzy scrambled up his back. "I wouldn't worry about it. She's simply frightened of her feelings for you." The girl sat on his shoulders. "Give her time."

"What if I don't want to give her time?"

"Your risk. But I know she's well worth the wait." He knew she spoke more of herself than of anything else.

"I know she is."

"Good. Now will you take me flying? Your brother is an unreasonable crybaby."

"No. I will not take you flying."

"Why?" she whined the question, but instead of irritating Briec, she got him to smile. Especially when she dramatically slumped down against his neck.

"Because your mother doesn't want you flying anywhere. And I'm going to respect that. But I will walk you back to the castle."

"Fine. Besides, I think I saw Gwenvael around."

Briec had only taken a step when he immediately stopped. "Stay away from Gwenvael."

"Why?"

"Because he'll only get you into trouble. And no more bets with him." He'd have to talk to his brother, too. He wasn't about to take the risk Gwenvael would start having those long conversations he'd been known to have with young males Izzy's age where he insisted on discussing adult matters.

"Oh, all right."

"Good." Briec started off again, but her next words almost had him tripping over his own claws.

"So when can I start calling you Daddy?"

Chapter 22

Morfyd looked up from the herbs she'd pulled. "Are you all right, Talaith?"

Brows drawn together in a dark frown, her lips mashed into a thin line, she shook her head.

"What's wrong?"

"Nothing."

Morfyd leaned back, wiping her brow with the back of her hand. "Lying will only irritate me."

Digging around certain roots so as not to ruin them for Morfyd's spells, Talaith grumbled, "Your brother told me he loved me."

"And?"

"And he must be lying. He can't love me."

"Why not? Is there something wrong with you I wasn't made aware of?"

"You're enjoying this, aren't you?"

"Of course I'm not." Actually, she was. "But as arrogant and irritating as my dear brother is, I don't think you should dismiss him so easily."

"I wish I could dismiss him. I wish I could walk away."

"Why? So you can be *this* miserable all the time as opposed to occasionally?"

Talaith finally looked up at her, and her eyes narrowed with suspicion. "Gods, you're treating me like family, aren't you?" she accused. And she sounded terrified.

"You are family."

"I am not."

"You are."

"Not."

"Are."

She could see Talaith preparing herself to get good and frothy when Annwyl rode up. She easily jumped down from that mammoth stallion Morfyd knew would look wonderful on a spit with a little bit of seasoning and walked over to the two women. She dropped to her knees and on to her back, her arms flung wide.

"I feel strange today."

Talaith shook her head and went back to gathering the roots while muttering under her breath, "That is simply *too* easy."

Morfyd worked hard not to laugh and, instead said, "Perhaps you're under the weather, my queen."

"No. I don't feel sick. And don't call me that anymore."

"It's probably the full moon. It's the time of dragons tonight, but it still affects us all."

"Is that why you two witches are out here? Doing your evil work?"

"You seem to appreciate my evil work when it helps your army."

"That's because as a monarch, I can be that ridiculous."

"Good to know, my liege."

Talaith put more roots in a basket she had beside her and showed Morfyd what she had. Morfyd indicated two more and Talaith went back to digging.

"So, am I leaving?" Talaith asked softly.

Annwyl frowned. "I don't know. Are you?"

"I'm asking you. Fearghus seemed determined that I go."

"Don't worry about Fearghus. I reasoned with him and we came to an understanding that satisfied us both."

Morfyd glanced at her oldest brother's mate and queen of the land. "You forgot to put your bindings back on after having your dirty, disgusting way with my brother."

Annwyl's hands immediately went to her chainmail-covered, but unbound breasts. "Shit."

"No, no, Annwyl. Truly." Talaith reached over and patted Annwyl's shoulder. "I do appreciate the sacrifices you've made for me."

Annwyl threw one forearm over her eyes, ignoring Morfyd's laugh. "Sarcastic cow."

Talaith relaxed back in the tub, the water steaming around her. By the time she and Morfyd finished gathering all the supplies, she was a little sore and covered in dirt and sweat. Yet nothing a hot bath couldn't cure.

She wished she could go with Morfyd tonight and do some spellcasting, but it had been much too long. Although Arzhela had returned her powers to her, Talaith's skills were still extremely weak. Get on the wrong side of one of Morfyd's spells and she could end up someplace she'd rather not be with no way home. Or open a doorway she could not close. No. She'd wait. Actually, Morfyd had given her a few books to get her started and promised she'd train her in those basics she'd most likely forgotten.

When Talaith finally thought long and hard about it, she realized she wanted to be the witch she was born to be. She wanted to heal the sick, protect the weak, destroy those who would bring pain and destruction to those who were unable to defend themselves. What she definitely didn't want to do anymore . . . kill for a goddess. Her days as an assassin were over now. She no longer wanted that in her life and she wouldn't have Izzy subjected to it.

To be quite honest, she had enough scares watching Izzy

watch Annwyl. That wasn't merely admiration or awe she witnessed in her daughter's eyes. That was envy. And, to Talaith's horror, it had nothing to do with Annwyl being queen. No, her daughter watched her while she trained with her men or rode that giant of a horse.

Talaith had a sinking feeling her daughter's ambitions had nothing to do with court life or catching the eye of the cutest knight.

Sighing, Talaith slipped farther into the tub, not surprised when a few minutes later her daughter knocked and walked in.

"Is it all right if I have dinner in my room tonight?"

Talaith looked up and couldn't help smiling at how beautiful her daughter was. And how lucky Talaith was. Not only to have finally gotten to meet her after all these years, but that her daughter survived with her wits and heart intact. Unlike Talaith, there was no bitterness in Izzy. No callous distrust of everyone. A glowing, happy girl who loved life but didn't fear death.

How did I get so lucky?

"Of course you can. Is everything all right?"

"Aye. Just don't feel like smiling and being polite tonight."

She knew exactly how the girl felt, but if Talaith didn't go, she knew Briec would think it was because of him. Of course, he'd be right.

"I understand. Feel free to eat in your room. You know, Izzy, you don't actually have to ask me that. I'm sure you can decide where you'd like to eat without my help."

Izzy shrugged. "I know." She rubbed her hands against her leggings. "It's just . . ."

"It's just what?" she prompted when Izzy stopped.

"I don't know what I should and shouldn't be asking you. I mean, this is all a bit new to me."

Talaith held her hand out and her daughter took it gratefully, crouching beside the tub and holding Talaith's hand close to her heart.

"I have no idea what I'm doing either, love. So we'll figure it out together. You and me. Does that sound about right to you?"

"Aye. Except. . . ."

"Except what?"

"What about Briec?"

It took all Talaith's strength not to pull back her hand in shock. "What about him?" Damn. She didn't mean to sound so angry. A bit of a clue something was wrong.

"Shouldn't you both be making decisions together?"

"And why would we do that?"

"Because he loves you."

Dammit. "Does he now?"

"Aye. And it hurt him you didn't tell him that after he told you."

Now Talaith did snatch her hand back. "And how do you know that?"

"He told me after I fell out of the sky."

Briec . . . quickly forgotten. "Pardon?"

Now Izzy showed true annoyance. "Well, you can blame Éibhear for that."

"I can?"

"Aye. If he'd just taken me flying when I asked him to, I never would have grabbed on to his tail which led him to drag me through the trees trying to get me off."

All those muscles Talaith had unknotted when she first got in the tub were now tight and painful.

"*You did what?*"

"Why are you yelling at me? You should be yelling at Éibhear."

"You ask me if you can eat dinner in your room, but you don't ask me if you can torture Éibhear to take you flying?"

Truly perplexed, Izzy asked softly, "Why would I ask you that?"

* * *

Éibhear lifted up the heavy bed, with Briec facedown on it, and checked again.

"What are you doing?" his big brother asked, voice muffled by the bedding he'd buried his head in.

"Looking for my sword. The one Annwyl gave me. I was going to wear it at dinner."

He dropped the bed back down and Briec grunted.

"Exactly how long are you going to mope over this, Briec?"

"Until I die of old age. Now you won't have to ask me that damn question again."

Éibhear opened his closet and rifled through there. "I hate seeing you like this."

"Aye," Gwenvael agreed from his safe position on the windowsill. "You are quite pathetic."

"I will kill you," Briec warned without lifting his head from the bed.

"Well, what did you expect Talaith to say to you?"

"I expected her to tell me she loves me."

"Maybe she doesn't . . . ow! What the hell was that for?"

Éibhear shook his hand out. It was true. Gwenvael *did* have an amazingly hard head. "Accident."

Gwenvael's body tensed and Éibhear prepared himself for a fight when a loud banging at his door stopped them both. They figured it was Fearghus from the sound of it.

"Come."

The door opened and his worst nightmare walked in, pushed by her mother who had firm hold of her shoulder.

"What do you want, little girl?"

"Be nice," Briec growled without lifting his head from the pillow—until he heard Talaith's voice. Then his head snapped up and he stared at her.

Aye, his brother truly did love her. Éibhear could see it in the dragon's violet eyes.

"Say it, Izzy," Talaith snapped.

"I don't think I should . . . ow!"

Éibhear bit back his smile when Talaith tugged her daughter's hair.

"Don't make me tell you again."

The girl's light brown eyes locked on his and he raised an eyebrow, thoroughly annoying her. But it seemed she didn't want to test her mother. "I'm sorry . . ." Her glare became worse when he gave her a huge, taunting grin.

"Finish it," her mother ordered.

"I'm sorry I grabbed on to your tail."

"And . . ."

Sighing, "And I'm sorry I harassed you about taking me flying."

"Good." Since Talaith was behind her daughter, she never saw the spoiled little brat stick her tongue out at him. "Now to your room."

Practically frothing at the mouth, the girl stomped off. Talaith shook her head. "I'm sorry, Éibhear."

"Not a problem." No point in telling Talaith, a woman he adored, that she'd spawned a demon.

Talaith turned to go and that's when she saw Briec. He used his arm to prop his head up.

"Lady Talaith. Is that what you're wearing to dinner tonight?"

Talaith looked at her dressing gown. Clearly she'd just gotten out of the tub. Her hair, soaking wet, reached down her back in big curls and she hadn't put shoes on.

"And exactly when did I start owing you an explanation for anything I do?"

"She's got you there, brother." The pair turned on him so fast, Gwenvael stumbled back against the window, almost falling out of it. "Don't bother. I'll accidentally hit myself in the head later."

Muttering to herself, Talaith glared at Briec and left.

Growling, Briec jumped off the bed and followed.

Once the couple were gone, Éibhear headed back to the

closet, but Gwenvael's next words caused him to hit himself with the closet door.

"What I don't understand is why everyone keeps hitting me."

"Talaith, wait."

"No."

He caught up to her, grabbing her arm and turning her around. "Please."

By the dark gods, did he actually say "please"? Ignore it, Talaith. Ignore it. "Why did you tell Izzy what you said to me?"

"To be quite honest, her timing was impeccable."

"I know. She'd fallen out of the sky." Talaith pointed an accusing finger. "That's what you were trying to hide from me, wasn't it? Her and Éibhear."

"Talaith—"

"So what you said was merely to distract me. I should have known." She tried to walk away again, but he yanked her to him, pinning her arms behind her back.

"I meant every word I said to you, Talaith, Daughter of Haldane. And don't ever suggest again that I didn't. I don't say things lightly or merely to get someone into bed. I love you, Talaith. You might as well get used to it."

"I don't want to get used to it or you."

"What are you so afraid of, little witch? Of losing your heart? Of falling in love with me?"

Falling? She'd fallen. Face first off the highest spire. But she'd dare not tell him. She dare not speak the words that would hand her heart over to this dragon for the next six or seven centuries.

"Let me go, dragon."

He pulled her closer, leaning down a bit to let his lips brush against her forehead. "Why do you keep fighting me, Talaith? We both know you love me. Why won't you admit it?"

"Is there ever a time you're not an arrogant bastard?"

"Is there ever a time you're not a difficult bitch?"

"No."

"Then I guess that makes us perfectly matched, now doesn't it?"

He grinned and she couldn't help but smile back.

"Look at that smile. Now isn't that a thing of beauty."

She'd never had anyone say such things to her before. It thrilled her and made her uncomfortable all at the same time. She tried to turn her face away, but Briec wouldn't let her.

"Look at me, Talaith." She did, and he rewarded her with a soft kiss on her nose. "You are beautiful. And I'll tell you that every day if you let me."

"Not sure I can handle that kind of pressure."

"Guess you'll have to learn," he muttered as he kissed her cheek, then her jaw. "Stay with me, Talaith. Stay with me until our ancestors call us home."

Sighing, even with her arms still pinned behind her back, she leaned into Briec, letting his mouth move slowly up her chin toward her lips. "That's a very long time for both of us, Briec."

"Aye. If we're lucky."

He kissed her, his mouth taking hers gently. Coaxing her to trust him, to allow him in to her life and become part of it as she let his tongue slide in and claim her mouth.

Briec released her arms, allowing her to reach up and wrap them around his neck, bury her hands in his hair. Not until her dragon had she realized exactly how pleasurable kissing could be, how wonderful.

Pulling out of their kiss, Briec's lips traveled down to her neck. He bit her gently and she moaned.

"Let's go to your room, Talaith. Let me show you how good we can be."

Smiling, she managed the impossible and pushed him away. "No, dragon. I promised Annwyl I'd be at dinner tonight."

"She'll understand," he growled, reaching for her again.

She moved away from him, walking backward toward her bedroom door. And Briec matched her pace for pace.

"No. We'll go to dinner tonight." She arrived at her door, her hand grasping the handle.

"Why?"

"Because"—she pushed the handle down and made ready to move—"I want to watch you squirm thinking about me sucking that huge shaft of yours into my mouth later tonight."

He went to grab her, but she had the door closed in his face before he had the chance. She locked it and leaned against it, smiling even as he banged on it from the other side.

"Open this door, wench!"

"No. I have to get dressed. Go and play with your brothers, dragon. I'll see you at dinner."

"Evil tease." She heard his body lean up against the door, and his whispered words made it into the room like a warm, caressing wind. "I'll make you pay for this tonight, sweet Talaith. I promise you that."

As always, he moved silently in his human form, but she still knew when he'd walked away from the door.

Talaith took slow, easy breaths and tried hard to get her body under control. She couldn't go down to dinner with her nipples burrowing through the dress and her wet sex leaving marks on her chair.

"It would be unseemly," she said to no one in particular, then she laughed and it felt so good.

Briec sat back in the chair, staring at Talaith as she did her best to ignore him and continue to listen to Gwenvael tell a completely inappropriate tale about himself and several young maids whose poor father caught them in his stables.

It had been a long, painful meal. At least for his cock.

Although he did have to admit, if he weren't so rock hard and desperate to get inside Talaith, it would have been a pleasant dinner with his kin.

At first, though, Briec wasn't so sure that would be the case. Fearghus kept glowering at Talaith over his wine. But by the third time, when Briec thought for sure he'd have to beat his brother to death, Annwyl's hand slipped under the table. Briec quickly realized that without breaking conversation with Morfyd who sat on the other side of her, Annwyl had taken a rather firm hold of her mate and apparently had no intention of letting go. After that, Fearghus paid attention to no one *but* Annwyl.

Morfyd shook her head in disgust. "That poor man."

"What?" Gwenvael demanded with a smile. "They couldn't remain virgins forever."

"Oh, that's it." Morfyd stood. "I've heard enough. The full moon rises, I have things I must do, and I'm finding you, brother, quite vile."

"You know you love me."

"Only because our mother insists upon it."

Morfyd grabbed hold of her satchel and headed out. They never questioned their sister's witchcraft, they simply appreciated it.

"I'll see all of you on the morrow."

Éibhear stood as Morfyd walked from the Great Hall. "I have this intense urge to go flying. Like to come, Gwenvael?"

"No, little brother. I have some other plans."

Now sitting on her mate's lap, Annwyl leaned forward. "Take care you oversized slag. I hear one more complaint about you and I'll—"

"And you'll what, dear sister?" Gwenvael challenged. "You'll what?"

Her eyes narrowed. "Perhaps you should ask your father that."

Fearghus really should stop looking so proud when she

mentioned that past incident. It did nothing but offend their parents.

"Evil wench," Gwenvael teased.

"Shameless dragon."

Gwenvael stood. "Shame is for the weak and the humans. No offense, Talaith."

"None taken." She laughed.

"But it's such a stupid emotion, don't you think?"

Annwyl snuggled back into Fearghus's body, wrapping her arms tight around his waist. "Then it fits you perfectly, eh Gwenvael?"

Giving an arrogant snort, Gwenvael followed his sister and younger brother out. That left the few servants cleaning up and the two couples.

Briec stared hard at Talaith. He'd grown bored with his kin. He wanted her.

"You ate all the dessert," he accused.

"Was that entire cow not enough of a meal for you, dragon?"

"I barely got any. Between you and my brothers. Besides, you should have made sure I was well fed. Isn't that one of your duties?"

Her eyes narrowed, but he saw the lust in them. "I have no duties, you scaly bastard. And I never will."

"Well . . ." Annwyl interrupted, although Briec never turned from Talaith. "As entertaining as this is, we're off. Oh, and Talaith, let Izzy know she can stop at the practice field after mid-meal tomorrow."

Talaith's eyes turned from lust to panic in a heartbeat, her head swinging around to freeze Annwyl right where she was. "*What?*"

Annwyl sat back down in Fearghus's lap. "What what?"

"Why does Izzy want to come to the practice field?"

"Arrow in the dark . . . to watch us practice?"

"Don't get sarcastic with me, my liege. My daughter will *not* be watching anyone practice anything."

"Why are you so upset? It's not like I asked your brat to join my army."

Talaith pointed a finger at the one woman who could legally have her beheaded. "And you just keep it that way."

"Are you threatening me? I just want to be clear. Are you threatening me?"

Rolling his eyes, Briec glanced at his brother who appeared equally bored. But when Fearghus's eyes looked past him, a deep frown dragging his black brows low, Briec turned to see what he was staring at.

It was moonlight. But, for some unknown reason, it wasn't white or silver, it was orange and yellow . . . like flames. And it spread throughout the room, filling the Great Hall.

The brothers continued to watch as their women argued. Until Talaith's gasp caught his attention.

"Look at that," she whispered, staring at the oddly colored moonlight. "I've never seen anything like this. It's beautiful." Talaith glanced at him then . . . and grinned.

Like a battering ram, that smile snatched his breath away and destroyed his ability to think. He gripped the arms of his chair and fought hard—so very hard—for control. But he sensed it was a losing battle.

Talaith's smile faded. She stared at him in wide-eyed silence. She knew something was wrong, she merely didn't know what.

Of course, neither did he. All Briec knew was that he had to have her. Not just have her either. He had to Claim her. Make her his own. He had to bury himself inside her until the two suns rose. He needed to fill her with his seed until it lubricated her eyes. His desire for it overwhelmed his logic. No matter what his rational mind told him, he couldn't stop his body's response to her.

"Fearghus, wait!" He tore his eyes away from Talaith to see his brother standing up, Annwyl tight in his arms. He looked at Fearghus's face and both dragons realized they were feeling the same thing. The overwhelming desire to lay claim to what they considered theirs.

Growling, Fearghus carried an arguing Annwyl out of the Great Hall.

Briec locked his sights on Talaith, who stared at him with wide brown eyes. He watched her closely as she pushed her chair back and carefully stood. He continued watching her while she slowly moved toward the stairs. He expected this was how humans acted when they were around a wild jungle cat or a vicious dog. Thinking that if they didn't startle the beast or make any sudden movements, they'd make it back to the safety of their homes.

Too bad it wouldn't be that way for Talaith.

Talaith made it as far as the bottom step, before she stopped. As soon as she'd seen that strange light coming from the moon, she knew something was very wrong. Not deadly, but not right either. She sensed it had taken over the entire castle. Then when Fearghus dragged a struggling Annwyl from the room, she knew she'd been right.

Now she glanced back at Briec. But she realized that had been a mistake. Because he growled and she squealed and took off. Up the stairs and toward her room, but he was right behind her. She could feel him closing the distance between them, reveling in the chase. The bloodlust pounding through his ears and his system.

She made it back to her room and had barely enough time to slam the door shut, but his hand was there, shoving it open. She stumbled back, watching Briec move into the room. His eyes locked on her like a lion's locked on a deer.

He kicked the door closed with his foot and turned the key, trapping her. "Come to me, Talaith."

"Oh, you must be joking." She moved around the bed, although she knew it wouldn't really keep him from her.

"Talaith. I need you." Nice words, except he was already

pulling off his surcoat and chainmail shirt. "Don't deny me. Not tonight."

"You're not yourself, Briec."

"Sorry, love. That's not quite true." He walked toward her, while yanking off his boots at the same time. "My body's human, but at the moment you're dealing with pure dragon."

"I find that a little scary."

"I need you, Talaith," he said again. "Tonight I Claim you. Tonight I make you mine."

Her mind screamed at her to run away, to take the blade she had hidden under her dress and cut his soft human throat. But her body . . . her body wanted to lay on the bed and open up to him like a sacrificial offering.

"Briec, it's just—"

"No, Talaith. No words tonight. Just say 'yes' and leave the rest to me." He stood before her naked now. *Eeeck!* True, it was all her imagination but his shaft looked ten times bigger. He held his hand out to her. "Please, Talaith. Please."

She knew he fought his own body's urges. She knew he was desperately fighting whatever had control of him so he didn't terrify her. She wasn't terrified, though. Not of Briec. Not even when he was like this.

Knowing that, she walked up to him and placed her hand inside his much bigger one. He let out a sigh, taking firm hold of it and tugging her closer. It looked like he was about to kiss her, but he suddenly stopped. His eyes closed and he once again fought for control.

"You know I love you, don't you, Talaith?"

"Aye."

"As you love me?"

Now or never, Talaith. "Aye."

His eyes opened. "So please, when this night's over . . . please remember that."

Then he ripped the dress from her body.

* * *

Suddenly feeling exhausted, Morfyd sat against a large tree, overlooking one of the biggest lakes on Garbhán Isle. It was getting late. She had important protection spells and rituals to perform. The powerful Black Moon of the Fire Dragon would only be full for a little while longer. But she was so tired.

She didn't understand it. She hadn't walked that far from the castle.

"Mind some company?"

She looked up to see Brastias standing over her. Anyone else she'd tell them to leave her be, but this was Brastias. She never seemed to get any time alone with him. She moved over a bit and patted the ground near her.

"Please."

He sat beside her, his chainmail shirt brushing against her arm. She caught his scent and closed her eyes to enjoy it fully. He smelled wonderful.

"I hope I'm not interrupting anything."

"No. I was going to do a few things, but I'm suddenly so tired."

"Are you all right?"

She nodded. "Aye. It's been an extremely tense few months. I'm sure my body is simply exhausted from it all. I think I need to sleep a few days to make up for it."

Brastias smiled, his arms resting on his raised knees. "More like a few weeks."

"You're probably right." She looked at his face. "You look tired, too."

He leaned his body back against the tree. "All of a sudden, I am." He shrugged. "And I came all the way out here just to get a chance to talk to you alone."

Morfyd barely stifled a yawn. "About what?"

Closing his eyes and resting his back against the tree, he muttered, "It can wait."

"Good." Morfyd relaxed against him and rested her head on his shoulder. "You don't mind do you?"

But he was already snoring and she soon followed him to sleep.

Éibhear silently watched Talaith's daughter almost slice her face open with the sword she'd been playing with for the last half hour. He'd been flying when he caught her scent far from the castle. Worried someone had taken her, he tracked her to this rather open glen where the light from the full moon gave her enough illumination to play warrior.

His only plan had been to sit back and watch her, then make sure she got back to the castle safely. But at this rate, she'd cut her own throat. *Who gave her that thing anyway?* Then it suddenly occurred to him it was the sword he'd been looking for. "Dirty, thieving, little cow," he snarled.

When she got the blade stuck in a tree trunk, he moved forward silently. He waited until his snout was barely inches from her neck, before he shouted, "*And what the hell do you think you're doing?*"

Screeching, the young girl spun around and punched Éibhear dead in the snout. It didn't hurt as much as it startled him, but he still moved back from her. But as soon as she saw who he was, she immediately calmed down.

"Oh," she said with obvious lack of interest, "it's you."

"Yes. Me."

"I thought it was someone scary." And with that, she went back to trying to get the sword out of the tree trunk.

Spoiled little heifer.

"Are you going to stand there and stare at me or are you going to help me?" At this point, she had both her feet planted on the tree while desperately pulling on the sword's hilt.

Éibhear had to admit, she must have some strength if she got it stuck in that far.

"I'd prefer you tell me what you're doing out here . . . alone?"

"Have we lost track of my mother, that you feel the need to fill in for her?"

Why you little . . .

"Look, I care about Talaith. And for some unknown reason she'd actually care if something happened to you. So I'm here to make sure you're safe."

"Care about her do you? Well, I hate to dash any of your hopes, but Briec got to her first. And I like *him*. He's perfect for her. You, however, are not."

Éibhear took a deep breath to calm his growing rage, when the blade suddenly dislodged, flew from her hands and skittered past him. Another inch it would have embedded itself in his forehead.

"*That is it!*" he roared, uncaring if he woke up all of Dark Plains. "I'm taking you back right now!"

When the blade dislodged from the tree, she'd lost her footing and landed flat on her back. Now she stared up at him with wide light-brown eyes.

"By the gods, are you all right?" She scrambled to her feet. "Did that cut you?"

He heard the concern in her voice, but chose to ignore it. "Move."

"All right. No need to yell at me. I didn't throw that at you on purpose."

She easily picked up the sword he'd seen grown men struggle with and headed back toward the castle.

"And when we get back, you'll put my sword right back where you got it."

"Oh, don't get all moral on me. I was only borrowing it."

"Don't even try to explain it. There is no 'borrowing' where dragons are concerned."

"Fine. You know, dragon, this would go much faster if you flew me there."

True, the trek back to the castle was not a short one, but there was no way he was placing this spoiled brat on his back.

"Forget it and keep walking."

"Fine."

She picked up her step and Éibhear glanced up to judge how far the castle actually was from them and how much longer he'd have to endure her presence. And that's when he saw it. The moon hovered over the castle, orange and yellow light bathing the white stone so that it appeared as if flame surrounded the building. He didn't need anyone to tell him something was very wrong with what he was seeing. Magick of some kind, yet he didn't feel any sense of pain or suffering. Actually, when he allowed his senses to expand out, he felt something else all together. Something that made his loins tighten.

He looked down at the young girl he'd gamble his treasure was still a virgin. He rolled his eyes. He couldn't let her go back there. At least not tonight.

"Wait." He slammed his tail on the ground in front of her. "Perhaps I'm being—"

"Oooh. Can I play with your tail again?"

She reached for it and Éibhear yanked it back. "*No!*"

"Well, you don't have to yell at me."

All he wanted to do was throw this girl back at her mother and fly away, hopefully never to see her again. But that wouldn't happen anytime soon. So, he steeled his already taut nerves and stared down at her.

"No. You cannot play with my tail. But if you really want to go flying—"

Before he even finished the words, she squealed, grabbed hold of his mane and scrambled up onto his back.

Stunned, he sat there for a moment. He'd never known a human so immediately comfortable with who and what he was. Even Annwyl took a little time to get completely comfortable with Fearghus.

"Go, go, go! I want to fly!"

"Calm down!" *This is going to be a long night.*

He turned and walked off the other way.

"Aren't we going to the castle?"

"That'll be too short a trip. I thought I'd take you out for a bit." *At least until that moon goes back to wherever it came from.* "But no screaming or anything. People are trying to sleep."

"Yes, sir."

Éibhear grunted, pleased he'd finally gotten her to calm down at least a little.

"You have gorgeous hair, you know. I love the color."

"Thank you."

"Can I put warrior braids in it?"

"*No you can not!*"

"I was only asking."

Then he heard the little brat giggle and as he took off, heading away from Garbhán Isle and that moon, he debated whether to spin over onto his back and let her take her chances. But that seemed wrong.

Damn his morals.

Chapter 23

Still waking up, Brastias held Morfyd tight against him. Her body warm, she smelled wonderful. He kissed her forehead, her cheek. She moaned and snuggled closer to him, her lips brushing his jaw.

With a smile, he kissed her. Her hands clutched at his shoulders, tugging him closer. One of her long legs wrapped around his waist as he gently moved her to her back, his tongue lazily exploring the wet warmth of her mouth.

Sighing, her hands buried in his short hair, Morfyd teasingly sucked on his tongue, playfully torturing him with a mere taste of what she could do to his cock.

Pulling back slightly, he licked her lips. He could spend hours merely kissing this female. Although he was sure he couldn't last hours. He pushed his erection against her mound and she groaned . . . then she froze. He felt the change in her down to his toes. Forcing himself fully awake, Brastias leaned back and stared down into Morfyd's beautiful blue eyes. And that's when he saw pure panic.

"Morfyd?"

"Oh, gods!" She pushed him off her with one good shove, and scrambled out from under him. Somewhere during the night, the majority of her clothes went missing. She grabbed up her robe and satchel.

"I . . . uh . . ." She looked at him one more time. "Well . . . see ya," she screamed, her face flush with embarrassment and horror. Then she ran. He didn't know the dragon could move that fast as human.

Brastias dropped back onto the hard, unforgiving ground and stared up at the two suns.

Stared and wondered when last he may have seen his leggings.

It was late morning when Talaith finally opened her eyes. The insistent knock at the door forcing her awake.

"Hold," she squeaked.

She looked at Briec. On his stomach, his face turned away from her, Briec's arm still held her captive at his side. She reached over and poked him with a finger. He didn't even move. Not surprising. Not after last night.

She pushed his arm off and slowly swung her legs off the bed. She winced and shuddered from the pain. Her entire body sore and well-used, sticky from sweat and other fluids, she wasn't sure she could actually make it to the door. After a few moments of sitting, she grabbed one of the furs from the bed and wrapped it around her. Shuffling slowly she made her way over to the door, unlocked it and let the servants in.

Like every morning since she'd been at Garbhán Isle, they brought hot water for her bath. She waited while they filled the tub and then she dismissed them.

Talaith closed the door and made her way to the tub. Dropping the fur at her feet, she stepped into it and eased herself into the water, her body screaming in protest the entire time. Once she was in, she dunked her head under the water and proceeded to scrub herself clean.

Her exhaustion bone deep, every muscle sore. Her lips,

nipples, sex sensitive to the touch. She had no idea what happened last night, but she'd be feeling its effects for days.

Over and over again, Briec took her. He was relentless and she was demanding. Sometimes he'd take her four or five times in a row. As soon as he'd climax, he'd flip her over and, still erect, start again.

She wished she could say the whole thing was some kind of horrible experience, but she'd be lying. Except for the aftermath to her body and the accidental burning of her back during the night, she enjoyed every second, and quickly lost count of her climaxes. The few times he did stop, the break wouldn't last long. And just as she began to slip into a deep sleep, he'd start kissing her again, fucking her again. Making her beg for everything he had to give.

Finally, when the first rays of the two suns peeked out, he'd climaxed one last time before passing out on top of her. Thankfully she had enough energy left to heave herself out from under him before dropping off to sleep as well, or he would have awoken to a crushed Talaith.

After soaking until the water turned cold, Talaith dragged herself from the tub and dried off. She bit her lip to keep her moans and groans in as her muscles screamed at all her movement. She knew enough of healing to know if she went back to bed, as much as she may want to, her body would cramp up and she would be unable to walk or do much of anything for days.

Somehow she managed to pull on a soft black dress, since the thought of anything touching her sex, even leggings, almost sent her into a crying tantrum. She brushed her hair off her face, and headed toward the Great Hall. She got halfway down the stairs when she stopped and sat down heavily, unable to go a step farther.

Talaith had no idea how long she was sitting there like that when Morfyd found her.

"Gods, sister. Are you all right?"

She couldn't hold back the tears any longer . . . her entire body hurt more than she could say.

"No." Talaith shook her head as tears streamed down her face.

Morfyd crouched beside her. "What is it? What's wrong?"

"My entire body hurts. I can't walk."

"You mean sore? Or something else?"

"Sore." So very, very sore.

"All right. I've got something for that. Come, sister." The witch slipped an arm around her waist and lifted her up. Being that she was actually a dragon, Talaith didn't worry she might be too heavy for Morfyd. The female basically carried her to the Great Hall.

It surprised her to find it deserted. Usually, this time of morning, the Great Hall fairly buzzed with activity. But today it was merely the two of them.

"Where is everyone?"

Morfyd sat her in a chair at the dining table.

"Recovering, I suspect."

"Something happened last night. What?"

"I don't know. I passed out by the lake last night. I woke up with . . . um . . . I woke up and had no idea where I was or how I got there. Although I think I'm glad I left. I'd hate to think what would have happened if I were actually here."

Morfyd dug into her satchel and pulled out several jars of herbs. She grabbed a bottle of wine, poured some into a chalice and then mixed in some herbs.

"Here. Drink this. Straight down."

With shaky hands, Talaith took the chalice from Morfyd and did as she ordered.

"Good." Morfyd took the now-empty chalice from her. "Give it a few minutes and you'll be amazed how well it works."

"What about everyone else here?"

"Those who lived away from the castle are fine, although from what I can tell they slept quite deeply. The few servants who've been bustling around this morning are all those who lived with their families off the castle grounds."

"And the ones who live here?"

Morfyd winced. "Aren't much better than you, I'm afraid. But I've already made them a batch of what I just gave you."

As Morfyd said the words, a soft warmth spread throughout Talaith's body, and the brutally painful soreness seemed to wash away like so much sand during a high tide.

Morfyd studied her closely. "Feel better?"

"Aye." Talaith smiled in relief. "Aye, I do. Gods, thank you, Morfyd."

"You'll have to drink some more tonight before you go to bed. But by tomorrow you should be completely fine."

Talaith wanted to hug the woman, but decided against it. Instead, she stood and took several tentative steps. Her smile turned to a grin. Even the soreness between her legs had melted away.

"I'm getting the ingredients to that miracle concoction, Morfyd."

Morfyd laughed as she rose to her feet, watching Talaith walk around in front of her. "Of course. With your skills I have no fears you'll make it wrong."

"Mmmhm. It even helped with this burn." She very lightly reached back and brushed her fingertips along the burn marks peeking out from under her dress.

"I have to admit . . . that did surprise me."

"Why? Have you never accidentally burned one of your lovers during a lusty bedding?" she joked.

Morfyd took the chalice back from Talaith. "Accidentally?"

"Aye. Do you have something for burns? I'd prefer not to have to live with the scars if I don't have to."

Coughing out an uncomfortable, awkward laugh, Morfyd pulled the shoulder of Talaith's dress down a bit. "Uh . . . Talaith. This was no accident."

"What do you mean?" That didn't make sense. Briec had

never hurt her, intentionally or otherwise. Even last night, when his lust got the best of him, he still made her feel cherished, cared for, and so very loved.

"I mean Briec marked you last night. He Claimed you as his own."

He'd Claimed her. Briec's desperately spoken words floated back to her, "Tonight I Claim you. Tonight I make you mine."

"Didn't he tell you?"

"*Does it look like he told me?*" Talaith screamed in fury, the full weight of what he'd done slamming down on her. "That arrogant bastard. I'll kill him!"

"Talaith, I don't think it was anything he could control."

She stalked up to Morfyd, ignoring the fact the female towered over her. "Are you saying if the kitchen maids were with him last night, he would have done the same? Are you telling me this is meaningless?"

"No. That's not what I mean at all. What I think is that Claiming you was something he'd already planned. Knowing Briec he'd planned to wait. To discuss it with you first. At the very least tell you he was going to do it."

"Really? Is that what you *think*, sister? How fascinating your load of centaur shit is."

"Perhaps you should calm down."

"*Perhaps you should fuck off!*"

Talaith stalked over to the open archway of the Great Hall and stared out over the courtyard. Trying to get control of her enormous panic. He'd Claimed her. Gods, what did that mean? Exactly what would he expect of her? She wouldn't lie to herself, if Briec had asked her, she would have said "yes" and stayed with him forever. Not hard, because she loved him. But, more importantly, it would have been her choice. That's all she wanted these days. To have a choice. But he'd taken that from her.

Trying desperately not to cry, she watched the soldiers

prepare for the presence of Lord Hamish and his army in a few weeks time.

Talaith stared and debated what she would do. And that's when they came around the corner. Éibhear in chainmail shirt and leggings and Iseabail in the leather leggings and the soft oversized cotton shirt she'd been wearing the night before.

Iseabail, talking non-stop as always, followed behind Éibhear like a puppy. They reached the steps of the Great Hall entrance and Éibhear stopped, turning around to grab Izzy by her shirt and pulling her onto her tiptoes.

"Please. For the love of all that's holy, woman—*stop talking!*"

"Well, you don't have to yell at me. I was merely saying . . ."

Éibhear, growling like an enormous bear in the woods, released her daughter and stalked up the stairs. Izzy still behind him. Still talking.

As Éibhear walked past her, muttering, "Good day, Talaith," she briefly wondered when everything turned a bright, blood red.

Thoroughly branded, thoroughly fucked, and thoroughly pissed off, Talaith let the full range of her anger loose . . . and she let it loose on Éibhear.

Talaith grabbed Éibhear by the front of his chainmail shirt and, using the strength of her ancestors, swung him around and slammed him against the wall.

One hand shoved against his throat, she pinned him to the spot, while retrieving her blade with the other and placing the point of it against his jugular.

"*What did you do?*" she shouted in his face.

"What? What are you talking about?"

"*To Izzy! What did you do to Izzy?*"

"Nothing." Éibhear stared at Talaith, his silver eyes desperate. "I swear!"

"Mother, let him go!" She could hear her daughter pleading

with her, but barely. The rushing in her ears drowned out almost all other sounds.

This . . . *this* was the final straw. If these dragons thought they'd get her daughter too—not in her lifetime.

"*Tell me what you did!*"

"He only took me flying last night," Iseabail fairly screamed.

Talaith glared at Éibhear. "*Is that what you told her it was called?*" she yelled in his face.

"*No!*"

Morfyd stood on the other side of her, "Woman, get your hands off my brother."

"Not 'til he tells me what he did to her. This way I'll know whether to cut off only his balls or the entire bloody thing!"

Éibhear's eyes darted to his sister's. "Morfyd . . ."

She sighed. "Éibhear, tell us what happened."

Éibhear kept his focus on his sister, then spit it all out in a rush: "I was out flying last night when I saw this one alone, far from the castle. I was going to make her come back here, but when I looked I saw the moon and it just didn't look right and it was hovering over the castle as if suspended there. I was afraid to bring her back here, so I took her flying. I showed her around Dark Plains until I grew tired. We were near Dark Glen, so I took her to Fearghus's den, because I knew it would be safe. We stayed there the night, but I swear I never touched her!"

"It's true, Mum," Iseabail pleaded. "I swear it."

He spoke true. She could see it and sense it. But she still hated all dragons at the moment. "Then you best keep it that way, dragon."

Finally she pulled away from him, lowering her blade to her side.

Talaith turned and took several steps away, when she heard the pair arguing in hushed whispers.

"See what you got me into? I'm never helping you again, brat."

"I should have let my mother skewer you."

Without looking at them, she snapped, "You two stop that. Right this minute."

They both stopped.

She motioned to the stairs with her head. "Iseabail get up to your room and take a bath. I'll be up in a few minutes to discuss why you left the safety of this castle in the middle of the night."

"But, I—"

"*Move!*"

Giving one last glare to Éibhear, her daughter stormed off, brushing past a slow-moving Annwyl who practically crawled down the stairs.

Somehow the warrior queen managed to dress in what Talaith now knew to be Annwyl's everyday wear as opposed to her battle wear—sleeveless chainmail shirt, leather leggings, and leather boots.

"Morfyd," she whined.

"It's all right, Annwyl." Morfyd's voice sounded tight and angry, but clearly she decided not to push a confrontation. Good plan. Talaith may not be dragon, but at the moment she could kill anything mortal.

As Annwyl slowly made her way to the dining table, Morfyd quickly mixed up another chalice full of her brew, using her finger to stir all the ingredients. A servant passed her when she was done, so she handed it to him and motioned to Annwyl.

Annwyl took it, but before drinking said, "Well, I know I like finger with my wine."

"Drink it, you whiny cow."

"Someone's in a bad mood." Annwyl swigged the wine back with one gulp, wiping her mouth with the back of her hand. She dropped the chalice to the table. "How long before this works?"

"Couple of minutes."

"Good." Using both hands, Annwyl leaned against the dining table.

But it seemed fate played against Annwyl this beautiful morning as one of her soldiers stepped into the Great Hall. "Annwyl, we need you."

Annwyl sighed and, even though the drink most likely had not worked yet, somehow forced herself to straighten up and walk toward her soldier. Talaith guessed it wouldn't do for the queen to be indisposed because her mate fucked her silly the night before.

Talaith admitted the woman had some mighty strength, though. Where Talaith cried and simpered like a babe, Annwyl simply pretended it never happened. *Better woman than me.*

Annwyl slid past Morfyd and Talaith who'd kept their backs to each other.

But as soon as Annwyl passed the women, they both knew. Startled, they turned and looked at each other, their moment of anger quickly forgotten. They watched Annwyl make her faulty way toward the archway. Once she got there, she suddenly grabbed the wood molding and doubled over.

Morfyd and Talaith ran to her side, but by then she was throwing back up everything she'd drunk. Not surprising. Talaith saw the kind of herbs Morfyd had in that drink. Ones that, among many other things, would prevent a woman from becoming with child.

Too late for that.

Morfyd took hold of one arm while Talaith grabbed the other. Morfyd motioned to the soldier. "Find Brastias or Danelin. They must help you. The queen is ill."

The young soldier nodded and ran off while the two women dragged Annwyl back into the castle.

They sat her down at the dining table and Morfyd crouched in front of her. "Annwyl? Can you hear me?"

Annwyl frowned at the witch. "Of course I can hear you. Gods, Morfyd, I'm only sick from last night's antics. And you can blame your virile brother for that. So stop looking as if I'm at death's door. I already feel better."

Morfyd rubbed her eyes with two fingers. "All night, Annwyl? You were with him all night?"

Annwyl's frown deepened. "Of course, I was. Where else would I be? Besides," she muttered softly, "he wouldn't let me go."

She looked between the two women. "All right, witches. Fess up. What's going on? Why do you both look like that?"

Morfyd took Annwyl's hands within her own. It seemed a caring gesture, but Talaith guessed it was because Morfyd wanted to control where those hands went when Annwyl found out the truth.

"Sister—"

"Spit it out, Morfyd. I grow more annoyed by the second."

"Fine. There's something you should know."

"Which is?"

"Annwyl . . . you are with child."

Annwyl snorted. "Of course I am. I lay eggs in two days time." She chuckled at her own joke until she realized the two witches weren't laughing. She glanced between them. "You're wrong, of course."

"No, sister. I'm not. You're with child."

Pulling her hands back, "So what are you saying? That I betrayed your brother? That I was with another? Because that never happened."

"I know. Yesterday you weren't with child. And today, after the entire night with Fearghus, you are."

"You said humans and dragons could not breed. *You* said it was impossible."

"And, normally, it is."

"Normally?"

Morfyd shrugged. "The gods sometimes change their minds."

The two witches barely moved in time, Talaith finally having the chance to experience the full extent of Annwyl's rage as it exploded around them.

Briec sat on the end of his bed. Freshly bathed and dressed, he held his head in his hands.

By the dark gods of fire, what had he done last night? What had he done to Talaith? Would she ever forgive him? Could he ever forgive himself?

He wasn't surprised when his door slowly opened and Fearghus stood in the doorway. His black hair hid half his face and he could barely meet Briec's eyes.

Fearghus shook his head. "So this is shame, brother?"

"Aye . . . and I like it even less than heartbreak."

Éibhear appeared beside Fearghus.

"Your woman is insane."

Fearghus frowned. "Annwyl?"

"Not your woman. His woman. She almost cut my throat."

Briec's eyes narrowed. He felt more protective of her now than ever before. Of course, before he hadn't taken her like an animal from night until well into the morn. "Why? What did you do?"

"I protected her daughter."

Briec groaned. "Oh, gods . . . Izzy. Tell me she wasn't here last night."

"She wasn't. I found her off playing with my sword."

Fearghus finally laughed while Briec's eye twitched. "What the hell does that mean?"

"She stole the blade Annwyl gave me. I found her training with it. Her words, mind you. I'm surprised she didn't cut her own throat."

Briec let out a breath. The thought of even one of his kin

taking advantage of his woman's daughter made him feel like Bercelak when it came to Keita and Morfyd. More than one dragon had lost his wing to Bercelak's protective nature. And humans . . . well, Bercelak the Great had enjoyed many good meals made of his daughters' human suitors.

"But before I could explain what happened, your woman put a blade to my throat. And I didn't appreciate it."

"My heart bleeds."

"And how's Annwyl?" Fearghus asked softly.

"Crawling. Gods, what did you do to her last night?"

Fearghus slammed his head against the doorframe. "She's going to hate me."

"Don't worry, Fearghus. We'll live together, bitter and alone. Like the Doane brothers," Briec feebly joked.

Glaring at Briec, Fearghus snarled, "Never say that to me again." No one wanted to end up like those two bitter old dragons.

"Well, I'm going to bed." Éibhear sighed. "It was a long night putting up with that evil little cow."

"Watch what you say about my—" Briec stopped speaking but his brothers were quicker than they usually acted.

Fearghus grinned, enjoying the demise of Briec's less than loyal ways when it came to females. "Gods, brother. Were you about to call her your daughter?"

"What if I was?"

"Come on, Briec," Éibhear begged. "You can't make that annoying harpy part of this family. Don't I suffer enough with you lot?"

"Too late, brother. I Claimed Talaith last night."

"That was fast work. How did you get her to agree?"

When Briec looked at the floor his brothers laughed incredulously. "You Claimed her without her permission?" Fearghus demanded. "Have you lost your mind?"

"And she's mean, brother. I didn't realize how mean until she threatened to take my balls. I felt like Gwenvael."

"Don't make me feel worse than I already do."

"What do you think she'll do when she realizes what it means?"

"Kill me." If he were lucky. Leave him, if he weren't.

"Give her time, Briec. I'm sure she'll come around." Fearghus stood up straight, tossing his hair off his face. "Well, I best go find my woman. Make sure she hasn't—"

The roar rang through the castle, cutting off Fearghus's words and startling the three brothers.

They knew that sound. Annwyl's war cry. They'd all heard it more than once since knowing her. But with Hamish's armies nowhere near Dark Plains . . .

As one, they moved. Out of Talaith's bedchamber, down the hallway, and down the stairs to the Great Hall where they all stopped by that last step. They stopped and stared.

Morfyd stood beside the archway leading outside. She looked torn between bolting for her life and shifting right there, taking the castle and its contents with her.

Briec's eyes quickly searched for Talaith. He found her. She crouched on top of one of the dragon statues that littered the hall, her blade held firmly in her right hand. He had no idea how she got up there, but he was grateful.

Slowly, Fearghus moved toward Annwyl. Brave dragon his brother, since she'd just picked up one of the dining tables made of solid wood and threw it against the wall as if it weighed no more than a twig.

"Annwyl?"

"Stay away from me, Fearghus." She *sounded* reasonably calm. That couldn't be good.

"Annwyl, talk to me."

Roaring, the crazed warrior kicked the chair at her feet up, grasping it in midair with her hands. Then she turned and let it fly. Fearghus calmly stepped out of its way while Briec and Eibhear dived for cover.

"Calm down."

"Go to hell."

Briec found it fascinating how calmly the couple spoke to each other, although the rage coming off both practically washed the rest of them from the room.

"Someone mind telling me what the hell is going on?" Fearghus asked the entire room.

Green eyes flickered to Morfyd. "Tell him, witch. Tell him what you told me."

Morfyd, not moving away from her one chance at freedom, looked at their older brother. "Annwyl is with child." Fearghus's eyes narrowed at the implication of that statement and Annwyl snorted. Morfyd held up her hand before either could say anything. "I believe it's yours."

"You *believe* it's mine. Why does that not fill me with confidence?"

"It's definitely yours."

They all turned at the sound of Iseabail's voice. "And 'it' is 'they' . . . twins, my queen."

Her hands in tight fists at her side, Annwyl's rage-filled gaze focused on Izzy seconds before Briec stepped in front of her.

"Don't even think about touching her," he growled.

"No, no, brother. I want to know how this little girl seems to know so much." Annwyl leaned over to look at Izzy, a cat keeping an eye on a mouse.

Talaith climbed down from the statue and circled around toward Izzy.

"I'm waiting for an answer."

"You can wait until the earth crumbles beneath your feet. Stay away from her."

"Stop. Please. You're all looking at this the wrong way." Izzy stepped around Briec, moving away from him when he tried to grab for her.

"Izzy," he warned but she waved him off, her entire attention focused on Annwyl.

"Don't you see? You've both been chosen, Annwyl. You and Fearghus. Both chosen by a god."

"What god?" Fearghus demanded.

"Rhydderch Hael, of course."

Briec and Morfyd looked at each other. Good gods. The girl's protector was Rhydderch Hael?

"What do you mean 'of course'?" Fearghus snapped.

But Annwyl had bigger issues. "Chosen by Rhydderch Hael to do what, Izzy?"

The girl grinned. "Create the future."

Annwyl moved so fast, they barely had time to even register, much less move out of her way. Luckily, Annwyl still took her rage out on the furniture. She lifted up another chair and slammed it into the floor, smashing it to pieces.

"*Annwyl!*"

"No, Fearghus. Stay away from me." She walked toward the stone wall and away from Fearghus. "You did this to me. You and all your kin!"

"Me? Do you think for a moment I had anything to do with this?"

"How could you not know? Last night . . ." Annwyl turned from her mate, her arms wrapping around her body. "You took me again and again and again all night. And it was only to—"

Fearghus, his anger finally spilling out, reached Annwyl in two long strides. He grabbed her arm and swung her around. "*Is that what you think? Do you actually think I'd do that to you?*"

"*What am I supposed to think?*"

"You're supposed to think it's a gift from the gods," Izzy said in that calm, happy way she had.

Annwyl and Fearghus looked at her and said together in complete exasperation, "*Shut up, Izzy!*"

Talaith should be angry the way they spoke to her daughter, but she would have said the same thing to Izzy. She knew the gods and their selfish ways, and she dreaded the day

Izzy found out her god differed in no way from Arzhela or any of the others.

Placing her hand on her daughter's shoulder, she said, "Leave it be, Izzy."

"I can't. He needs me to tell them."

"Are you his messenger now?"

"No." She shrugged. "I think I just happen to be here."

Gods, Izzy. Talaith would laugh if she didn't feel for Annwyl. It had all fallen into place, hadn't it? Rhydderch Hael ensured Annwyl's arrival back at Garbhán Isle before the Black Moon. In order for this to work, the couple needed to be together. It could have easily been Talaith as well except she'd had her "one." *Thank the desert gods for something.*

Still, that all begged the question of what part Izzy and Talaith played in all this. It was Annwyl and Fearghus Rhydderch Hael needed. Little Izzy couldn't merely be the messenger of his less-than-happy news.

Fearghus seemed to calm down first. Gently, he pulled Annwyl into his arms. Her body shuddered with each breath.

"Gods, Fearghus . . . what the hell is in me?"

Fearghus looked to Morfyd who could only shrug.

"They're your children, Annwyl," Izzy piped in cheerfully. Before Talaith could yank her back, Izzy walked up to Annwyl and Fearghus. "Don't you see? He didn't choose you two because you were convenient. Or even because you were loyal to him—which, you're actually not. But he chose you because he could think of no other strong enough to not only bear these children, but to protect them until they could protect themselves. Many will want them dead, Annwyl. Many have already started."

"Arzhela?"

Izzy nodded at Morfyd's question. "She's the goddess of birth, among other things. She doesn't want your children to live and she wasn't above killing you to stop this."

"Are they dragon or human?" Fearghus asked, his arms tightening around Annwyl. Holding her close and under control all at the same time.

"They're both. They're both of you. But nothing this world has seen before." Izzy stood right in front of Annwyl. "He didn't choose lightly, Annwyl. Your bravery, your strength . . . even your rage, all played a part in his choice. He likes you," she finished simply.

Suddenly Annwyl laughed, pushing Fearghus's arms off her body, and Talaith winced at how insane it sounded. All she wanted to do was grab her daughter and run for their lives. But she knew making any sudden moves could set Annwyl off.

"He can't make the choice for you, Annwyl. Nor can he force you to do this. As you know, there are ways to . . . end this if you so choose." Izzy glanced at Morfyd and, thankfully, walked back to her mother's side. "But he does ask you to think on it first. Before you do anything."

They all stared at Annwyl, waiting for some kind of answer. All but Éibhear. He stepped away from the wall he'd plastered himself against and cocked his head to the side.

"Anyone notice . . . no birds," he muttered. Then he yelled, "*Down!*"

The dragons moved fast. Like lightning. Briec grabbed Talaith and Izzy around their waists, pulling them close into his body while turning his back. Morfyd pushed Éibhear and herself up against the wall near the doors. Fearghus stepped back and to the side as a volley of arrows flew threw the open windows and doorways, flooding the room.

Talaith looked up to see that the only one who didn't move was Annwyl. She simply stood there, watching as the arrows landed all around her.

Either she's the bravest woman I've ever met or the craziest bitch ever created.

Screams and war cries came from the outside courtyard

as Brastias stumbled in to the hall, an arrow-riddled shield in his hands.

"Annwyl . . ." he puffed out. "It's Hamish."

Annwyl only stared at him.

Briec released Izzy and Talaith but still used his body to shield them. "Where is he?"

"Outside the castle gates."

Fearghus shook his head. "That's impossible. He shouldn't have been here for weeks."

"One of my men just told me. One second he and his woman were alone in the fields—the next, Hamish and his full army were there. He barely got them both away in time."

"Full army?"

Morfyd stepped away from the wall. "Only a god could have gotten them here like that."

"Arzhela's pet," Talaith sneered. "Her most loyal servant. He only allowed her temples to be built in Madron. She'd originally sent Izzy to him."

"We don't have much time," Brastias went on. "They're headed this way. The troops are scrambling now."

Annwyl silently headed toward the doors.

"Annwyl, wait," Fearghus called after her.

She stopped but didn't look at him. Or any of them for that matter.

"You have two choices, Fearghus," she said quietly. "We can stand here and . . . *discuss* this with the way I'm feeling at this very moment. Or . . . I can go out and have my discussion with Hamish and his troops first." She glanced back at him, golden brown strands of hair falling across her scarred face—but nothing could conceal the rage burning in those green eyes. "Choose, dragon."

Fearghus made a sweeping gesture with his hand. "Hamish."

She nodded and headed toward the door, Brastias behind her, but Fearghus's dark voice followed her out, "But when you return, my mate . . . we'll have much to discuss."

Turning to his brothers, he said, "Call to the other dragons, then take to the skies. Destroy their supply wagons and as many of their troops as you can manage. But they know we're here, so be careful. Morfyd . . ." He looked at his sister. "Go with Annwyl. Protect her as best you can. But don't get close."

"I had no intention of it, brother."

Now those dark, dark eyes fell on Talaith. "Do you have healing skills?"

"Aye."

"Then set up this hall to receive our soldiers. The servants will help you. There are other healers who will come to lend their aid."

Talaith nodded, relieved he'd given her a task rather than telling her to get out. For whatever reason, it seemed the dragon had decided to forgive what she'd almost done to his mate. Then again he did have much more pressing concerns than some little assassin with a god on her tail. "It's done. Should we set up another place for enemy casualties?"

"There won't be any," he said simply, before walking away.

Talaith understood why the dragon and Annwyl were together. Well matched those two, because no mere female could handle a dragon like Fearghus and no human male would ever be able to sleep soundly in a bed next to Annwyl.

Briec took her hand. "Talaith—"

"Wait." She looked at Izzy. "Go to your room. Lock the door. You are only to let me, Briec, or Achaius entry. Understand?"

"But—"

Talaith narrowed her eyes at her daughter. "Don't play with me, little girl. Do. You. Understand?"

Izzy gazed at the floor. "Aye. I do." Poor thing. Talaith had been ordering her out of the room all day.

"Then go." With that, Iseabail disappeared up the stairs,

and Talaith turned back to Briec who hadn't released her hand. "Go. Do what you need to do. And when you get back, *this*"—she waved dramatically indicating her back and new brand—"will be discussed."

He smiled, leaned over, and kissed her shoulder. She felt it all the way to her toes.

"As you wish, my soft and defenseless damsel."

He left her. And Talaith didn't stop watching him until a confused, half-dressed Gwenvael stumbled up next to her. "Is it me . . . or did I miss something?"

Chapter 24

She was pregnant. With twins, no less. How was this possible? True, she loved her Fearghus. More than she thought she could love anyone or anything. But still . . . he wasn't human. Did he betray her for his loyalty to the dragon gods? No. Not Fearghus. If there was one thing she could say about her mate, he obeyed no one but himself.

Besides, he'd been uncontrollable the night before. Not that she didn't enjoy it, but her dragon had been unable to stop himself.

No, the dragon gods had used him as much as they'd used her. While the human gods preyed on Talaith and Izzy.

She'd really begun to detest the gods.

"Annwyl?"

Annwyl looked at Brastias. "What?"

He cleared his throat. "There are more over there."

She glanced at the battalion of troops fighting her men. They'd been trying to run away . . . from her. But her men had swarmed over them before they got too far.

One of the thirty bodies at her feet moved and she realized she hadn't killed him. She raised the blade in her hand and slammed it down with raging force. She assured herself this one had moved on to his next life, yanked her sword out of his body, and used the cloth Brastias handed her to wipe the blood off her face.

"Come," she said calmly, handing the cloth back to him. "I want them all dead before the two suns are in the western skies."

She headed toward the battling troops, watching her enemies flee from her giving her so little satisfaction.

Talaith ripped the large cloth into strips as other servants set up beds. They prepared for many wounded, although she hoped it wouldn't get that bad. She was to blame for all this. Arzhela sent Hamish here to avenge the fact that Talaith didn't do what Arzhela had sent her to do.

Now they'd all suffer for her disobedience. Still, she'd risk everything for Izzy. Absolutely everything.

Having changed into comfortable leggings, boots, and shirt, Talaith was ready for anything. She finished ripping up the cloth and handed a large pile of the material to one of the healers. *Nearly done*, she thought with some quiet pride. Then she felt it. It was almost a physical thing.

The power of the dragons receding. Like a warm fur pulled off her naked body in a cold room. Frantically, she looked around. No one else noticed it. Not surprising. The only ones left were the humans—because the dragons had all gone out to fight against Hamish.

She remembered Morfyd telling her she'd passed out at the lake the night before. Which meant she'd been unable to reinforce any of her protections. Which meant . . .

"Gods . . . Izzy!"

She'd never moved so fast before in her life, dodging around soldiers, guards, and servants as she tore through the Great Hall and up the stone stairs toward her daughter's room.

She'd gotten within mere feet of the door, when it burst open from the inside. Achaius flung out and against the wall.

"*No!*"

She ran into Izzy's room in time to see her daughter, stomach down on the floor, literally dragged from this world into another.

Desperate, Talaith dived for her, landing on her stomach, her hands lacing with Izzy's. She saw her daughter's frightened, tear-streaked face and then she was gone.

"*No!*" she screamed again. "*No! No! You bitch!*"

Talaith didn't cry. She didn't allow herself that luxury. Instead, she jumped to her feet and charged from the room.

She ran down the stairs, barking at one of the healers to go to a thankfully still-moving Achaius, and then out of the Great Hall past the other healers asking her questions and for further assistance. She stormed out into the courtyard, nearly getting herself trampled by a young soldier on horseback. Angry, the soldier pulled his horse back and glared at Talaith.

"Be cautious, wench. You'll get yourself killed."

Snarling, she reached up and dragged the soldier off his warhorse. She put her foot in the stirrup and hauled herself up into the saddle. She turned the horse toward the gates leading to the battlefield. "Take me to, Annwyl."

With those few words, the horse bolted.

Brastias could feel Annwyl's growing impatience with the battle. Soon, she would turn toward Hamish and go after their leader. He didn't know what happened in that hall before he arrived, but something had brought back the Annwyl he remembered so well. He hadn't seen her like this since they first found her in wedding clothes and heading toward Madron to be Hamish's bride.

Although she remained a brutal warrior—he knew that would never change—she'd calmed down a bit since meeting Fearghus the Destroyer.

Whatever happened couldn't be good. She'd annihilated most of the Madron army by herself while the dragons destroyed troops and supplies from the rear. Even Morfyd, who usually fought by her side as battle mage, kept to the air this day.

As it was, a little while longer, Annwyl's army would have Hamish surrounded and then Annwyl would finally get her chance to destroy the man.

"General."

He looked at his next in command. "What?"

"Talaith."

Brastias followed Danelin's eyes and watched as Talaith rode up to them on a warhorse most of the men stayed away from.

"Why is she here?"

"I have no idea."

Brastias called to Annwyl, "Talaith approaches!"

Annwyl pushed the body off her sword and turned to face the woman originally sent to kill her. The horse slid to a stop in front of the queen and Talaith dismounted like she'd been born in a saddle.

"Arzhela's taken Izzy."

The queen's green eyes darkened with intent. "What do you need?" Annwyl never wasted time with useless questions like "What happened?" or "When?" Those questions would come later.

"I need Hamish." She looked at the hundreds of troops between themselves and the Madron leader. "He has the key that will take me to Izzy."

"I doubt he will just hand it over."

"He will to me . . . when I'm done with him."

Annwyl nodded. "Then follow me. And prepare to put your skills as a killer to use, witch. Brastias, Danelin. Stay behind Talaith."

Annwyl faced the hordes of warriors, her two swords at the ready. "Anything not in our colors . . . dies."

With those last words, Annwyl moved forward and destroyed all in her way.

* * *

In the time it took Annwyl to cut through the line of men to get her to Hamish, Talaith had only killed three soldiers. The rest who dared to approach them, the queen dispatched with a swipe of her steel.

No wonder Fearghus didn't stop her from going into battle. Her rage combined with her battle skills made her one of the deadliest warriors Talaith had ever seen.

Good. She needed this deadly warrior to take her to Hamish. Then she would take it from there.

"Take him, witch. We'll need to deal with them."

Hamish's soldiers attacked the small group, forcing Annwyl to focus her attention elsewhere.

Talaith looked up to see Hamish, in full armor, standing on a high battle carriage so that he could survey the battle around him. He called out orders to his commanders and they called orders to runners. It was a good system, but no one counted on Annwyl's desire to kill absolutely *everything* at the moment.

"Well, well. The Betrayer." Hamish leaned over, staring down at her with a smirk she couldn't wait to slap off his face. "What's wrong, love? Missing something?"

His commanders surrounded the carriage, protecting him from the ground soldiers. She had no doubt as soon as the dragons reached this far, he'd move his location. But for now, he was feeling extremely safe.

"You cross worlds to get to your goddess. I need the key that allows it," she said simply.

"I'm sure you do, but you won't be getting it from me. Perhaps if you beg her or—"

Unwilling to waste her time, Talaith slashed the throat of the guard nearest her. Another moved on her, but she slipped out of his reach and slashed the throat of another. She went low, slicing the inside thighs of two guards. The back of the ankles of two others. She stuck her blade in the kidney of another, then grabbed hold of the side of the carriage. The blood-covered blade between her teeth, she climbed quickly using only her arms.

Talaith reached the top, but she had to release one hand and lean back to avoid the sword of another soldier. He extended to grab her, allowing Talaith to take hold of his arm and yank him off the carriage. She easily swung herself over the top with her one arm, landing in a crouch in front of a startled and clearly frightened Hamish.

Finally, he went for his sword, but it was too late. Talaith removed one of the pins from the leather of her dagger hilt.

Talaith stuck the pin into key points on Hamish's face.

Surprised, he only stared at her. Then he dropped, the sound of his armor crashing to the carriage floor harsh even as the sounds of battle and cries of dying men filled her ears.

She slipped the pin back into her dagger and her dagger back into its sheath. "Tell me where the key is and I'll kill you quick. Play with me and I'll let you suffer like this until the poison kills you. And I assure you that will be hours from now. Choose."

He didn't answer as his body instinctively fought the effects of the poison. But she knew it would only be a matter of time until Hamish would become completely paralyzed, blood streamed from his eyes, and green fluid poured from the side of his mouth.

"Tell me," she ordered.

"Me," he puffed out between gasps of excruciating pain.

"What about you?"

"Me," he said again.

Guessing at what he meant, Talaith went to him and proceeded to remove his armor, cutting the leather strips that held the pieces in place. She reached his chainmail shirt and pushed it up under his chin. Arzhela's talisman hung from a gold chain, both of which she'd seared into Hamish's flesh.

Taking her dagger, Talaith touched the blade tip to the

chain. No, she'd have to dig it out. So she did. Burying the blade right under his skin and ignoring Hamish's gurgling screams, she worked the chain and talisman from their resting place. Once she had enough to get a good grip on, she grabbed hold and ripped up. Flesh split apart and blood flew as she tore it from his frame.

Once she had it, she stood.

"Wait," he demanded when she started to walk away. "Kill me," he begged. "Promised."

"Did I? I must have been lying. Enjoy your death, Lord Hamish. May it be long and oh so very painful."

Now that she had what she wanted, Talaith wasted no more time. She went over the side of the carriage, expertly working her way down until her feet hit land. Most of the soldiers who'd come to help Hamish were dead, Annwyl standing in the middle of bodies and their corresponding pieces.

"I need Morfyd."

Annwyl leaned her head back and let out a blood-curdling war cry that had the dragon turning in mid-flight and returning to them.

She landed beside Annwyl. "You bellowed?"

"Arzhela's taken Izzy," Talaith barked as she strode toward the white dragon. "I need your help."

"Come." Morfyd lowered herself so that Talaith could grab her mane and haul herself up.

"And Hamish?" Annwyl asked, although it no longer sounded like she cared.

"He's still up there. In about two hours, his body will begin to decay . . . four hours after that he should die. It's up to you if you want to end his suffering sooner."

Annwyl raised an eyebrow. "He can stay up there and suffer. Maybe I'll sell tickets." She reached up and patted Talaith's foot. "Good luck, sister."

Talaith nodded, holding onto Morfyd's mane as they took to the skies.

* * *

Briec caught the spear in his hands seconds before it would have slammed into his shoulder. He glared down upon the soldiers who fired it at him. They used a similar device Annwyl used to throw boulders at castles. He saw the men stare up at him and, with a snarl, he headed toward them. The spear still tight in his grasp. As he got close, he threw it, impaling the closest one to the device, then he sprayed row after row of the enemy soldiers with white flame.

When an entire battalion was no more than ashes, he landed on solid ground and Fearghus landed next to him. His older brother surveyed the damage he wrought and turned to him.

"Subtle."

"They almost wounded me," he growled.

"Don't be weak, Briec. I'm sure if you'd been hurt Talaith would have kissed it and made it better."

Gwenvael landed in front of them. He spat out a pair of soldier's boots—actually several pairs—and burped.

"I love a good meal."

Fearghus rolled his eyes. "You'll be hacking all that up later tonight."

"No, I won't. Because *I* cooked them. I only get ill when Morfyd cooks. Speaking of which . . ." Gwenvael's gaze traveled up and he frowned. "If I didn't know better I'd swear that was Talaith riding on our sister's back."

Briec's head snapped up. Gwenvael saw true. Talaith, who'd rather eat nails than ride a dragon anywhere, clung to his sister's back as they headed off away from battle.

More of Hamish's troops took that moment to attack, but Fearghus motioned him away. "Go. Find out what's wrong. We'll take care of them." He sneered at the soldiers before letting loose a stream of flame. Briec wasted no more time. He took to the skies and followed his sister to one of the many lakes that dotted the lands of Dark Plains.

He landed as Talaith slipped from Morfyd's back.

"What is it? What's wrong?"

Talaith glanced at Morfyd. "Get started," she ordered. Then she walked over to Briec. "I have to go," she said to him, so calmly it made his blood run cold.

Behind them, Morfyd began chanting, calling on the most powerful of Magicks. He didn't want to know why. He wanted to grab Talaith and take her home. Back to his den where he could keep her safe.

"Go? Go where?"

"She's taken Izzy, Briec."

He knew Talaith meant that bitch goddess, Arzhela. Briec shifted and, as human, grabbed Talaith by the shoulders. "You can't face her alone."

"I can. And I will. You can't protect me from this, Briec. No one can."

"Just listen—"

"Shhh." She placed her hand gently against his mouth. "There's nothing to discuss. Not when it comes to my Izzy. We both know that."

Gods, he was going to lose her. *Again.* "Talaith, please . . . please don't do this."

She smiled and he felt his heart rip apart in his chest. "I want you to promise me something."

"Anything."

"Take care of Izzy for me. No matter what happens, protect her."

He cupped her cheek in his hand. "She's my daughter as you are my mate, little witch. She'll always be protected by me and my kin. You'll never have to worry about that."

She nodded. "I know." She removed the necklace he'd given her, unable to take it with her, and pressed it into his palm. Then she said the words he never thought he'd hear from her. "I trust you, Briec."

He kissed her, pouring every ounce of feeling he had for this difficult woman into that one kiss, hoping she'd understand how much she meant to him. How much she'd *always* mean to him. Her kiss back was just as strong, her hands desperately clinging to him.

He held on until she abruptly pulled back, taking several shaky steps away from him. "I love you, Briec," she choked out. "I'll always love you. Never forget that."

She turned and walked away from him, into the middle of a circle his sister had drawn in the wet, lake-side dirt with the tip of her tail. Talaith quickly removed her clothes, tossing them out of the circle.

She stopped briefly to take her dagger from its sheath. Then she kicked her boots and the sheath away from the circle as well.

Naked, Talaith knelt in the sand and raised her arms above her head. Morfyd walked around her three times, chanting. When she stopped, the circle roared to life with flame.

Ignoring the fire surrounding her, she cried, "I give you my life's blood!" The winds suddenly whipped up, pushing Briec's hair across his face as he watched his woman slash her forearm. Her life's blood poured down her brown skin, pooling in the sand.

"*Take me!*" she screamed to the howling wind.

And then she was gone.

Briec sat hard on the ground, his head in his hands. But he could hear his sister's soft words through the dying wind . . .

"Peace go with you, my sister."

Chapter 25

Izzy pushed herself as close to the tree as she could manage as Arzhela walked closer to her.

She was beautiful, Izzy'd give her that. Especially here in Arzhela's natural home. If she weren't terrified, Izzy would roll in the tall grass or climb the enormous trees with the thick branches overloaded with green, gold, and red leaves. She'd swim in the rushing river or lie under this place's one sun and sleep like her old dog Gruffy used to—belly up and snoring.

But she wasn't with her Protectors, safe and cared for. Or torturing the blue dragon she thought so adorable. And she definitely wasn't safe with her mother and her dragon love, Briec.

Izzy was very much alone with a very angry goddess who hated her mother beyond reason.

I could definitely be in a better place at the moment.

Still, she reminded herself to be thankful for the little things . . . at least she was fully dressed since she came to this beautiful world with the goddess herself. Being naked now could be quite awkward.

Especially with Arzhela kneeling in front of her. Her gold waist-length hair hung in thick ringlets and she wore a garland of yellow and white flowers. Izzy didn't think she was evil, simply a god who existed in fear. And that's why she ruled with fear. It was all she knew.

"Tell me, little one, all these years I could not find you. Why?"

Did she really expect her to answer that question? Lying. Yes, at the moment, lying was her best friend.

"I don't know, my . . . my goddess." She stammered over the words because Arzhela would never be a goddess she worshiped. Not ever.

The goddess's crystal blue eyes narrowed on Izzy's face. "Lie to me if you'd like, little one. It won't stop me from destroying your mother."

"Why do you hate her so much?"

A small white hand reached out to stroke Iseabail's cheek. Somehow she managed not to cringe away from that touch. Instead she focused on something else. She thought of Briec and his brother Gwenvael. Yesterday, they'd caught her trying to mount one of the warhorses. After warning her how dangerous it was—especially with dragons around, which often led to unsteady horses rearing—Briec grabbed her under the arms and swung her around. Then he tossed her to his brother, and Gwenvael threw her in the air. She laughed and screamed until her mother came and almost took off poor Gwenvael's head. Even funnier was how Briec lied and said he was just telling Gwenvael to put her down.

There she was safe. There she would be again. She had no doubt about that. She would believe it until the Old Ones of Alsandair called her home. As long as she believed it, Arzhela couldn't touch her.

"She's coming for you. Nothing you can do about it," Arzhela gloated.

Izzy already knew that. She knew it like she knew the depth and dimensions of the scar on her leg she obtained when she found herself nearly impaled on a fence when she was ten.

Her mother would come for her. And when she did, Izzy would hide until the battle was over and her mother took her home.

"You are bleeding to death."

Slowly, Talaith rolled on her back. "I know."

"Why would you cut yourself like that?"

"I had to get your attention."

A black talon passed over her body. A black talon as big as her. Normally something she'd cringe about and at, but nothing scared her at the moment. Nothing but the thought of losing her daughter.

"You can get up now."

Talaith pushed herself up. The weakness she'd been feeling when she cut the vein in her arm was gone. She felt strong. Powerful. She stood and raised her eyes to the awesome being before her.

"My lord," she greeted while bowing her head in respect.

He snorted. "You couldn't make that sound right if you tried."

Damn. Even worse . . . she *had been* trying.

"Please. My daughter . . ."

"I know, Talaith. I know. I always know where my Izzy is."

She lost her ability to look contrite and fearful in front of a god. Her eyes snapped up to Rhydderch Hael's and she no longer bothered to hide her anger.

"Then why the hell did you let her go? Why did you let Arzhela take her?"

Rhydderch Hael revealed rows and rows and *rows* of fangs. A smile, she now knew. "Now where did my scared little god-fearing mouse go?"

"She trusts you."

"She trusts you more." She wondered if that upset him, but he didn't seem upset.

"What do you want from me?"

Rhydderch Hael sat his black dragon body back on his haunches. She'd thought Briec and his brothers were enormous. Not even close. She couldn't even see where his body ended. She'd glimpsed the tip of his tail, which resembled a spiked broadsword created for a giant. She also noticed that unlike the dragons she now knew, he didn't have two horns, but twelve. His hair, although primarily black, had every shade she'd ever seen in nature rippling through it. But his eyes . . . his eyes were thoughtful and wise beyond the ages. They were also a bright violet. Just like her Briec's.

"You've wondered something since Izzy came back into your life. Ask me now."

She controlled her urge to tell the beast to stop testing her and help her get her daughter back, but she'd dealt with Arzhela long enough to know when to push a god and when not.

Taking a deep breath, she asked honestly, "Why didn't you just kill me when you knew what Arzhela was up to? Why did you protect Izzy when you could have killed me and just ended it? And killed Izzy for that matter."

"Because that wouldn't have ended it. By having you, she didn't bother with other attempts. If I'd killed you it would have gone on and on until she killed Annwyl. And when Annwyl and Fearghus found each other, I knew . . . knew they were the ones."

"The ones to breed your . . ." She shrugged. "What exactly *are* you having them breed?"

"Nothing she can't handle the birth of," he vaguely answered. "That woman won't let anyone or anything hurt what she loves. And she loves like she hates—passionately and until the end of her days."

"And I still live because . . ."

"Even gods need to sleep every once in awhile, Talaith. No, I needed Annwyl to live until my Moon was full in the sky. Then I let the Magick do the rest."

"Huh. Aye. Thanks for that by the way."

There went those fangs again. "As if you didn't enjoy it, Briec's *sweet* Talaith."

Talaith blushed and looked away from the smirking bastard.

"I knew if I protected Izzy, blocked her from Arzhela's sight, I'd keep her safe while forcing Arzhela to focus solely on you until she knew exactly who she wanted dead. She couldn't risk you meeting your daughter before then. She just never expected Briec to be in your village that day."

Talaith's eyes snapped to Rhydderch Hael's gold ones. "You sent Briec?"

"No. I don't send anyone. Unlike you humans, my people are much more . . . independent. I can open doorways, but it's up to them to walk through. No. I only made it rather necessary for one of Fearghus's brothers to go. When I realized it was Briec, I knew the only way I could ensure he would take you was if you were in danger. And even then, there were no guarantees."

"*You* turned my husband against me."

"Oh, he's always hated you. All I need do was light the flint. Of course, I never knew Briec would *keep* you." The god chuckled. "I thought he'd drop you off in the nearest town. Izzy and her Protectors were already headed that way and Annwyl was heading home to Fearghus. Everything was in place as I'd been planning for years. But when that arrogant bastard wouldn't release you, I had to scramble for ideas." He looked Talaith up and down. "Although I can see why he would keep you."

At her glare, he continued. "I warned Morfyd of your coming—because I knew with you still thinking Izzy was in danger, you'd continue to be a true threat to the queen—and started the storms to slow everyone down until you were on the move again. We had a wee bit of extra time, so I didn't worry much. I assumed Briec would tire of you quickly. But he didn't, did he? You must be quite the fantasy come to life to hold on to our dear Briec."

She knew it now—she really and truly hated gods.

"All that's fascinating, but it still doesn't explain—at least to my satisfaction—why I still live."

"We can't cross realms, Talaith. Not like you humans—with your soft, pliable skin."

"You need me to get you into Arzhela's realm."

"Someone as strong as you anyway. I could have used Annwyl, but I have other plans for her. Besides, she'd never be able to get Arzhela's talisman. It would have killed her merely to touch it. But you've been chosen by Arzhela herself, and she still wants you alive—even if it is for revenge at this point."

His giant dragon head cocked to the side. "You *do* have the talisman, don't you?"

Talaith held up her hand, the blood encrusted talisman still clutched by her fingers.

"Good. Good. Now we can get this underway. But first, you must give yourself to me freely, Talaith, Daughter of Haldane."

If she'd followed the Nolwenn path she wouldn't have called a goddess or god to enter her until she was well into her three hundredth winter. She wouldn't have had the power, strength, or guts to do it beforehand. But Arzhela, damn her, made it impossible for her to wait now.

Because Talaith would do anything, give anything, to make sure her daughter made it back alive. And Rhydderch Hael knew it. He knew if Arzhela got her hands on Izzy, Talaith would stop at nothing to get her back. That's why he allowed Arzhela to take her.

At least now, Talaith had no fear as she had before. Because she knew Rhydderch Hael would destroy Arzhela and then he would send Izzy back to Briec. And Briec and his kin would take care of Izzy until her daughter's final days.

Hell, that was more than she would have hoped for two moons ago.

"I give myself to you freely."

"Good." Then Rhydderch Hael took that talon that had

healed her only minutes before and tore her open from bowel to throat.

Arzhela smelled the little bitch as soon as she walked through the portal. She couldn't wait to have fun with this one.

She couldn't wait to pull her heart out through her mouth. No one betrayed her. *No one.*

And if Talaith, Daughter of Haldane, thought she'd be grabbing her little scum spot and taking her out of here alive, she and that light-eyed freak were sorely mistaken.

Besides, she needed Talaith's body. With it, she could get past Rhydderch Hael's protections and destroy Annwyl the Bloody with her bare hands before the bitch ever had a chance to breed anything.

But first . . . first she would savor this bitch's screams.

Plastering on her best and softest smile, she turned and faced Talaith. Naked, which was required to pass from her world to Arzhela's unless escorted by a god as Iseabail was, Talaith stared at her blankly. Already terrified and Arzhela hadn't done anything to her yet. Or her whelp.

"You don't have to be afraid, Talaith," she lied. She never felt honesty was all that important when it came to the humans. "I merely want to talk."

She walked toward Talaith, glancing at the woman's daughter still cowering by her favorite tree. The girl stared at her mother as if she'd never seen her before.

She stood a ram's length from Talaith. "Come, my daughter. Let us sit. And talk." She held out her hand and Talaith looked at it blankly. "Just talk, Talaith. I promise."

Talaith grabbed hold of Arzhela's hand and that's when Arzhela yanked her close and wrapped her free hand around the woman's throat.

"Betray me, you little bitch?" she snarled. "For that, you'll get to watch your daughter die."

Talaith said nothing as she took her own free hand, grasped the one at her throat and slowly pulled it off by bending Arzhela's fingers back.

Confused, Arzhela tried to fight back, but Talaith's strength was formidable. She dragged the goddess's hands from her body. Once free, she grabbed both sides of Arzhela's head and held her.

"My sweet, sweet Arzhela. I've waited so long for this. So long for *you*."

And that's when she knew. Arzhela knew what that betraying little bitch had done.

"No!" She struggled to get away but Rhydderch Hael, who'd finally found a way into her realm, merely smiled Talaith's smile.

"No, no. Don't fight, my sweet. There's no point in fighting."

"Release me, Rhydderch Hael! My brothers and sisters know you're here. They'll come to protect me!"

The god shook Talaith's head. "No. They don't know and they won't. Talaith's lovely body hides my presence nicely, does it not?"

"Bastard," she spit at him in her rage.

Rhydderch Hael snorted. "Thousands and thousands of years and you still haven't changed, you worthless little bitch."

"Go to hell!"

"You first." He threw her—in her own realm—and she slammed into one of the trees she loved. Landing hard on the ground, Arzhela looked up in time to see blue, black, and orange flame shoot out from Talaith's every pore, before it smothered Arzhela in its embrace.

Izzy watched Rhydderch Hael walk up to her in her mother's body.

Tears streaming down her face, she watched him crouch in front of her.

"What is it, my little Izzy?"

"I want my mother." She sounded like a child. But at the moment, she really didn't care. "You promised me I'd have her."

"And you did."

Her tears turned to sobs. "You can't take her from me now. Please. Don't take her from me now."

The god tilted Talaith's head. "I do this for you, what will you give me, my little Izzy?"

Now she understood what her mother had been trying to tell her all this time—with gods there was always a price to pay. But for the woman who gave her life for her there was no other choice.

"My undying loyalty. That is all I have to offer. All I can willingly give."

The god smiled her mother's smile. "That is all any god can ask, my little Izzy."

Her mother's body stood and the god held out her mother's hand. "Then take my hand, little Izzy. Your dragon kin awaits you."

Morfyd dropped her arms. "It's no use."

Briec rubbed his eyes with his knuckles. "Try again."

"I can try until the end of time, brother. But Rhydderch Hael will do what Rhydderch Hael wants."

For hours he and his kin waited. Morfyd had healed everyone's wounds. The lot of them shifted to human and put on their clothes. Then they waited for Talaith and Izzy to return. But still nothing. Even when Morfyd tried again and again to call on Rhydderch Hael, hoping he'd send them back, nothing happened.

"So now what?" Even Gwenvael's frustration was showing. "We can't leave them there."

Frustrated herself, Morfyd growled, "I wasn't planning to."

"Then do something!"

Angry, Morfyd stood, the hood of her midnight-blue cloak hiding her white hair, but not her angry crystal-blue eyes. "If you have any brilliant ideas, little brother, then please feel free to share them. Otherwise, shut up!"

They barely glanced up as Fearghus glided to a stop beside the lake. "Well?" he demanded.

Briec, who'd been leaning against a tree, sighed. "Nothing yet."

"I'm sorry, brother." And he knew Fearghus meant it. For once, the two brothers understood each other perfectly.

"And the battle?" Gwenvael asked.

"Fought and won." None of them were surprised. Not with Annwyl in *that* particular rage.

"And your mate?"

"I'm not sure. I haven't seen her. I think she's still hoping to find some troops left."

Morfyd paced impatiently between her brothers. "Maybe a sacrifice," she said to herself. "My blood may—"

"No, Morfyd." Briec shook his head. "That's unacceptable."

"But, Briec, if it works—"

"Wait." Éibhear stepped forward. "Hear that?"

They all became quiet, staring at the burned circle that now marked the last spot Talaith stood.

Éibhear's head snapped toward the trees. "In there. I hear crying."

Briec moved first, following the direction Éibhear pointed. His family right behind him, except Fearghus who flew over the treetops.

As Briec moved, he could hear the crying. *Izzy.*

He found them quickly. Izzy, sobbing hysterically over her mother, and Talaith, laid out under a tree.

Briec knelt beside Talaith as Izzy looked up at him. "I

can't wake her up." Those simple words felt like a knife through his heart. Everything that meant anything, gone.

Morfyd moved beside them, motioning to Gwenvael to take Izzy. Telling her it would be all right, Gwenvael picked the girl up. Like a young child, Izzy wrapped her arms around his neck, her legs around his waist and openly sobbed into his shoulder.

Moving quickly, Morfyd grabbed hold of Talaith's wrist, then put two fingers to her throat. Frowning, she bent down over the other woman's face.

"She breathes." The brothers sagged in relief while Morfyd looked to the skies. "Fearghus!"

"What's wrong?"

Watching Fearghus lower himself to the ground, Morfyd said, "She's freezing." She quickly removed her cape and wrapped it around Talaith. "I need to get her back to Garbhán Isle and warmed up."

Lifting Talaith in her arms, Morfyd rushed toward Fearghus. "Meet us back at the castle."

Briec watched his sister climb onto Fearghus's back and his brother lift into the air. He was about to follow, ready to yank off his clothes and shift, when Gwenvael stopped him. "I don't think it's me she wants."

Confused, Briec turned and realized Izzy was blindly reaching for him. He moved closer and immediately she wrapped her arms around his shoulders, burying her face into his neck.

He stared at his brothers, unsure of what to do with a sobbing girl in his arms.

Gwenvael leaned into him and whispered in his ear, "Tell her it'll be all right."

Holding her tight and rubbing her back, Briec said out loud, "It'll be all right, Izzy."

"Don't . . . worry . . . about . . . anything," Éibhear whispered against his other ear.

"Don't worry about anything," Briec said softly and Izzy

held him tighter. He closed his eyes and hugged her back. "We'll take good care of your mother, Izzy. I promise."

She gave a little nod. "All right then," she said through her tears.

His brothers walked off and he followed, Izzy still clinging to him. "Let's get you home, little Izzy."

Chapter 26

She woke up, but didn't move for a good five minutes. It was in her training. Sometimes it was smart to pretend you were dead or unconscious until you knew exactly how horrifying your situation.

No sounds, except for snoring. Relatively loud snoring, too. Must be fierce, blood-thirsty monsters with that level of snoring.

Talaith opened her eyes and looked around the room. Candles and a lit pitfire illuminated everything quite nicely without hurting her eyes.

Morfyd slept in a chair, curled up like a cat. Fearghus leaned against the wall, staring up at the ceiling. Éibhear slept flat on the floor, his arms and legs stretched out. She didn't envy the female who would have to sleep next to him for the next eight hundred years. Surprisingly, he wasn't the one snoring. That honor went to Gwenvael. Asleep in a big chair, his big, long legs stretched out in front of him, his head thrown back, he snored like a giant bear. Grinning, her gaze moved to the form of her daughter. Izzy sat on a bench by the window, her legs pulled up, her chin resting on her knees. Awake, she stared out the window into the dark night.

And sitting right next to her, Briec. Like Izzy and Fearghus, he was awake, but he stared straight at Talaith, waiting for her to notice him probably. *Arrogant bastard.*

They stared at each other silently. For once, Talaith knew words were unnecessary. She could see everything she needed to see in Briec's face. In the way his eyes watched her and his relief at seeing her awake.

"Mum?"

Talaith again looked at Izzy and smiled.

"Mum!" The girl scrambled off the bench and dived across the bed, landing in Talaith's outstretched arms. She hugged her daughter tight, letting the girl hold on to her and cry into her neck.

Morfyd stood. "It's good to see you awake, sister." She pushed Gwenvael's shoulder. "Wake up."

Startled, Gwenvael sat up screaming, "*I never touched her!*"

Morfyd rolled her eyes and headed toward the door. "You are a constant source of embarrassment, little brother. Fearghus, follow me."

Fearghus nodded at Talaith and followed his sister out. Gwenvael stood and stretched. "Talaith, my love."

"Gwenvael, my pain."

Chuckling, he reached down, grabbing hold of Éibhear's hand, and dragged the still-sleeping dragon from the room.

Finally, Briec stood. A soft smile on his lips, he headed toward the door, his eyes never leaving Talaith's face. He stopped at the doorway to look at her one more time before he walked out, softly closing the door behind him.

"Izzy?" Talaith forced her daughter back, staring intently at her. "Are you all right?"

Tears streaming down her face, she nodded.

"Are you sure?"

She couldn't remember much after talking to Rhydderch Hael.

"I'm fine, Mum. I am."

"Arzhela?"

A strange expression passed over her daughter's features, but was gone so quickly, Talaith wasn't sure if it was a play of the shifting light or not. "Gone now. I don't think she'll be back."

"Did she suffer?"

"Yes. I believe she did."

Talaith pulled Izzy back into the safety of her arms. "Good. That makes me smile."

"Me, too, Mum. Me, too."

Annwyl leaned back in the tub, sighing heavily. She'd finally worn herself out. Somewhere during her fight with that last battalion and setting fire to the still-decaying and screaming remains of Hamish, she'd lost her energy to continue fighting. She'd left her men to clean up and rode back to Garbhán Isle with her elite guard. After removing most of the blood using the well near the stables and cleaning the blood and gore off Violence, she'd returned to her room. The servants filled her tub with hot water and quickly disappeared. They wouldn't look at her, mostly because they'd seen her decimate the Great Hall hours before.

The bedroom door opened and Fearghus walked in. He didn't look at her either. He simply walked into the room, placed a bottle of wine on a side table by the window, and proceeded to remove his clothes.

"What's that?" Annwyl motioned toward the bottle of wine.

He barely glanced at her. "It's from Morfyd. Should you need it."

She'd suffered no wounds during battle. At least nothing that needed anything more than some of Morfyd's ointments. Unless it was for her other "problem."

"How's Talaith?"

"Awake."

"Good." She probably should apologize to Talaith. She

wasn't sure, but she may have thrown a chair at the woman's head. And a table.

Fearghus dropped his clothes to the floor as was his way. She expected him to go to bed but instead he walked over to the tub and stared down at her.

"You're not going to shove me under the water, are you?"

He finally smiled. "Move up a bit." She did and he got in behind her, his long legs on either side of her. "Back."

She leaned back, relaxing against Fearghus's chest.

"Feel better?"

"Now that I've decimated an entire army and set Hamish's rotting corpse aflame . . . I don't feel half bad."

"Good." Big arms wrapped around her and Annwyl let herself relax with the only being she ever let herself relax around. "We've got decisions to make, love."

"I know," she sighed out. "I know we do."

"Before you met me did you want a family? Children?"

"To be quite honest, I never thought I'd live this long. So I never thought of it as an option. You?"

"Sometimes. But nothing that ever kept me up nights. I do know I don't like to be used."

And that was Annwyl's biggest problem with all this. Gods having fun with her body and with her and Fearghus's love for each other. "Aye. That pisses me off as well."

"Still . . ."

"Still what?"

"Imagine the kind of children we would have."

She'd been doing that all day, in between the killing of course. "Bloody nightmares is what we'd have, Fearghus."

"Aye."

"Killers," she added.

"Destroyers."

"Warlords."

"Definitely."

"So what's your point, dragon?"

"They'll be ours to raise as we see fit. They'll be *ours*, Annwyl."

"Aye. They'll be part Fearghus the Destroyer and Annwyl the Bloody. Two of the most violent and vicious beings known in recent history as I was told the other day by an old wizard passing through town."

"Aye. We are that."

"And do you really want to release the unholy product of *our* union on the world?"

"No, Annwyl." He pulled her wet hair to the side. "I want to release the unholy product of our union on them."

Annwyl tried to sit up, but Fearghus kept a tight grip on her with his arms while he kissed her neck. "You can't be serious, Fearghus."

"Why not," he muttered into her neck. "They play games like this, Annwyl, and they risk the outcome. They risk losing."

"So what are you saying?"

"I want to raise them with one goal in mind. One purpose."

"You want them to challenge gods?"

Fearghus didn't answer her, but instead kissed his way down her neck and to her shoulders.

"You can't be serious," she said again. No, no. This was wrong. There had been a few in history who'd challenged gods. Some lost. Some barely survived. And very few ever won.

"It's what they deserve."

Annwyl pulled herself away from Fearghus. She had to. His kisses were completely distracting her. She turned her body in the large tub so she faced her mate.

"You want us to raise the killers of gods?"

"No. I want to raise warriors who aren't afraid to challenge gods."

"Have you lost your mind, dragon?"

"No, I haven't lost my mind. Think about it, Annwyl. They're already being hunted—apparently by everyone. As are you. If for no other reason, we need to make sure they can protect themselves. And eventually us in our doddering old age."

"Fearghus"—she gave a weak smile—"you've gone mad." But already the idea had grown on her. Even as she knew the wrongness of it—she didn't care.

"They'll be feared," he insisted.

"More like hated."

"Respected. No one will ever use them. They won't be killed. They'll be too mean to die."

"I thought that was your father."

Grinning, Fearghus grabbed her around the waist and dragged her onto his lap. She felt his erect cock pressing against her. "Imagine, Annwyl," he teased as he stroked her body with his hands and set it on fire with his tongue, "hatchlings even my father will fear."

"Now, dragon," she moaned, arching into him as he slowly pushed his cock inside her, "you're just trying to sweet talk me."

Briec felt the tap on his shoulder and forced his eyes open. Izzy stood over him.

"Is everything all right, Izzy?"

"Oh, yes. Everything's fine. I just wanted you to know I was going to bed."

Rubbing his eyes, Briec sat up. Very early morning light spilled through the windows. He glanced down at himself, relieved to see his exhaustion so deep the previous eve, he'd dropped on his bed fully dressed and immediately fell asleep. Good. Otherwise this could have been a very awkward situation. "You're going to bed now?"

"We talked a lot last night. So I'm exhausted."

"All right." He still didn't know why she felt the need to tell him this information.

"So I'm going to my bed now and I'll be asleep there for *hours*. I left Mum alone."

"Izzy!" Briec laughed.

She held her hands up. "I'm merely making sure everyone knows exactly what's going on. And what's going on is I'm going to bed—*my* bed—and have left my mother *all alone*."

"Iseabail."

She gave him that smile that always reminded him of Talaith, kissed him on the cheek, and skipped toward the door.

"Izzy?"

She stopped right at the door and looked at him over her shoulder. "Yes?"

"I'm glad you're back."

"Me, too—Daddy." She winked at him and left. He always detested precocious children . . . until now.

No, he'd definitely be proud to call that mad little girl "daughter." She already fit in so well with the rest of his kin, and his mother would love her . . . and not as a meal either.

Briec rolled off the bed and went straight to Talaith's room. The fur coverings pulled up to her chin, Talaith slept soundly. Not surprising with all she'd been through over the last two days. Trying not to wake her, but needing to be near her, Briec removed his clothes and slipped into bed with her, wrapping his arms around her waist and snuggling her from behind.

"Izzy?"

"That's just ridiculous," he growled.

She glanced at him over her shoulder. "It could have been worse. I could have said Gwenvael."

"And forced me to kill my own brother."

She was safe. She was home. She had her daughter. And she had the most arrogant dragon in the universe. She had her Briec.

Gods, is that happiness I feel? No, no. Best not to question it. That would only bring disaster.

"And what exactly are you wearing?" Briec demanded.

"A nightdress. You can't expect me to traipse around naked with my daughter now can you?"

"Of course not. But she's gone to her room to sleep."

Lifting herself up so that Briec could remove her nightdress without ripping it, which she knew he would do, she frowned. "How do you know that?"

"Because she came to tell me she was going to bed—her own bed—to sleep for many hours."

Talaith covered her face with her hands. "Why does that girl insist on embarrassing me?"

"She wasn't trying to." Briec threw the nightdress across the floor, dangerously close to the pitfire. He pulled the silver chain he had around his neck off and returned it to her. Making sure that once it was on, the pendant fell right between her breasts and against her heart. "She wants you to be happy, Talaith. And she knows I'm the only one who can do that for you." He pushed her back on the bed.

"Tell me, Lord Dragon, does your arrogance ever take a holiday?"

"No. Does your mouth?"

He stared down at her now naked body and purred. No, she'd never get tired of that particular reaction from him. "Much better. I don't like you in those things."

Briec's violet eyes focused on her face. "When we share a bed, which will be forever, you will not wear anything like that."

"Well, I happen to like 'that' and I will wear it whenever and wherever I . . . would you get your hand out of there while I'm yelling at you."

"No. Now put your hands over your head. I think I'll tie you to the bed."

"No, I will not put my hands above my head. And don't think for a second I intend to let what you did to me, go."

"I have done nothing to you"—he raised an eyebrow—"yet."

"Oh? What about this . . . this thing?" She waved at her back. She and Izzy had spent an hour positioning mirrors so she could get a good look at the mark Briec branded her with. The body of a dragon, outlined in black, stretched from her right shoulder and across her back, its tail snaking seductively around her hip, the tip pointing right at her sex—which she looked at discreetly while Izzy went to get food and water. Once she got over the initial shock of seeing her body marked in such loving detail, she had to finally admit to Izzy, "It's awfully nice, eh? Bastard did a nice job."

Not that she'd ever tell him that. Honestly, his enormous ego took up more than enough room in their bed.

He shrugged at her question. "I've Claimed you."

"And?"

"And what?"

She pushed his shoulder. "You never asked me."

"I had other things on my mind at the time, if you remember correctly, woman. Besides"—he leered at her—"would you have said no?"

What a cocky little . . . "I might have."

He snorted and lounged back against the headboard. "Try again."

"You obnoxious, son of a—"

"I grow tired of this. Come"—he motioned to his lap and steadily growing erection—"ride me."

"No." She sat up on her knees, facing him. "We're not done."

The sigh was loud and filled the room. "What is there to discuss?"

"You made the choice for me." He opened his mouth to speak and she held her hand up to silence him. "I know it was out of your control at the time, but I want to make sure we get this clear now. If I stay with you—"

"*If?*"

She ignored his roar of disbelief. "*If* I stay with you, that will not happen again. No one makes decisions for me anymore, but me. We can discuss and work together as a team, but I will accept nothing less. If that is a problem for you, Briec the Arrogant, then we best find that out now."

She waited for his answer, but he stared up at the ceiling. "Well?" she pushed.

He looked at her. "Oh, were you speaking?"

"Briec!" She punched his shoulder.

Laughing he grabbed her around the waist, forcing her onto her back. He brought his body over hers, pinning her with his weight while gazing down into her face. "Do you really think I want some docile, brainless weakling for a mate? I'll leave those for the human males."

"Are you sure? I don't want you regretting this three, four hundred years from now."

He scowled and she knew two moons ago she would have run screaming from that look. Now, however, she felt nothing but lust. "Are you going to argue everything with me?" he snarled.

"Yes," she snarled back.

"Forever?"

"Yes."

Briec's scowl gave way to a soft smile. "Promise?"

Talaith reached up, her hand brushing against his jaw. "Yes, Briec. I promise that I'll spend the rest of my life arguing every point with you, regarding every issue, every moment until the end of our days."

"Stop, Talaith." He kissed her until he had her moaning and giggling at the same time. "You're driving me wild with your anger and resentment."

She leaned up and whispered in his ear, "Then you'll love when I tell you to get your bloody hands off me and get the hell out of my room."

Chapter 27

Morfyd, so busy thinking about a thousand different things now that her brother had informed her he and Annwyl planned to keep their offspring, never noticed Brastias until she slammed right into him. And even then, it took a bit.

"Sorry," she muttered, still distracted.

"You've been avoiding me."

Her head snapped up at the sound of that deep, soul-invading voice. "Oh. Brastias. It's you."

"Aye. It's me."

"Sorry. In a bit of a rush." She tried to pass him, but he grabbed hold of her arm and dragged her back.

"You can't keep avoiding me, Morfyd."

"I'm not." Except that she couldn't look him in the eye. "There's just many things going on right now. I don't have time—"

"Was our kiss that unpleasant?"

"What? Uh . . . no." Unpleasant wasn't the problem. Waking up, writhing against a human male like a drugged snake was the problem.

He took several steps, still holding onto her arm, forcing her to move back. "Interesting. If the kiss wasn't unpleasant, then I can only surmise that something else is bothering you. Something about us."

She felt the cold stone wall at her back. "Look, Brastias, I—"

"No."

She blinked. "No? No what?"

"No more discussion. There's no point, is there?"

"You're right," she admitted with resignation. "There's no point."

He framed either side of her face with his big hands. "That's what I thought." Then he kissed her. His warm mouth claiming hers. His hard body forcing her back into the wall.

And just as Morfyd melted against him, he stopped.

"When you're ready, Morfyd. You know where I am."

Startled and aching, she watched as he pulled away, but before he got three steps from her, she grabbed his arm and dragged him back. She leaned into him and let her lips brush over his.

"I'm sorry, Brastias. I didn't want you to think I was a slag . . . or like my sister."

He grinned. "I could never think that. I've caught your sister with my knights."

She winced. *Damn her.*

"But none of that matters." He stepped forward, pushing her into the dark corner. His big hands caressed her face. "All that matters is you and me."

"There's a you and me?"

"There will be." He kissed her and all those feelings she'd been denying since she woke up by the lake with him, came rushing forth. So intense, it nearly strangled her.

Gripping him tight, Morfyd whimpered into his mouth, enjoying the feel of his hand taking hold of her breast through the thick wool of her robes. If it felt this good with clothes on, imagine how wonderful when they were completely naked.

Seconds from dragging him to her room or his—whichever was closer at the moment—she let out a startled cry as her wrist was grabbed tight and she was yanked from Brastias.

"*Oi!*" Brastias snapped, turning around and clearly ready to fight. But he stopped and stared and Morfyd looked up . . . into the face of Gwenvael. And, by the dark gods, he was angry. Extremely angry.

"You. Keep your hands off my sister."

"Excuse me," both she and Brastias said at the same time.

"You heard me. Both of you. She's not some slag, human. So keep away from her."

Morfyd didn't know what to say. Gwenvael had gone drinking with Brastias on many occasions over the last three years. They'd always been good friends, it seemed. And not only that, but this was *Gwenvael*. To quote their own mother, "Not a pussy he hasn't loved."

"Gwenvael, have you lost your mind?"

"You're my sister, Morfyd. Not some whore he picked up on the street . . . or Keita." It suddenly struck her—Gwenvael felt protective of her. She didn't think he felt protective of anything or anyone. Once again . . . *this was Gwenvael!*

Her younger brother pointed a warning finger at Brastias with his free hand since he seemed bound and determined not to release his hold on her. "You just stay away from my sister. Or we truly will have problems, General." She winced at the way he sneered that last bit.

Gwenvael walked off, dragging Morfyd behind him. She looked back at a shocked Brastias and prayed he could read lips since she couldn't risk Gwenvael hearing her.

She mouthed, "Later."

Based on his relieved smile, he read lips just fine.

"Stop it!" Talaith skirted around the bed, trying to keep it between her and Briec. "They're waiting for us."

"They can wait. Come here." He moved again and so did she.

"It's in our honor, Briec." Annwyl insisted on throwing this feast in honor of their union. It was a sweet gesture from her friend. "We can't miss it."

"Who said anything about missing it? I'm just talking about making a dramatic entrance . . . in an hour or two." Again he moved, and again so did she.

"This is ridiculous." She stood up straight. "I'm a grown woman with a daughter nearly seventeen winters."

"In another six moons."

"And I refuse to allow myself to be chased around a bed like some untried virgin."

"Good." He went for her again and Talaith squealed and ran. He caught up with her by the door and she knew if he got his hands under her dress she was doomed. But before he could get his hands anywhere, a knock at the door pulled them up short.

"Piss off," he barked at the door.

"Come in," she yelled over him.

She batted at his hands as the door swung open. When Izzy's smirking face came around the corner, Briec stepped away from Talaith. "I told you to get your hands off me, woman . . . I'm a respectable dragon. Not some whore you picked up on the street."

"Briec!" She slapped his shoulder. "That's not funny."

"I'm sorry to interrupt Briec's mauling, Mum."

"Iseabail!" The two of them together were absolutely impossible.

"But I need to talk to you about something. Something important."

"Of course. Come in."

"Do you need me to leave?"

"Oh, no. Not at all." Izzy shook her head at Briec's question. "Actually, I'd like to talk to you both." She closed the door and walked into the room.

Briec sat on the bed and Talaith continued to stand by the door. She could see Izzy getting up her courage for this discussion, which worried Talaith more than a little bit.

Finally, with a deep breath and after wiping her hands on her leggings, which Talaith now realized was her daughter's nervous habit, Izzy turned and faced them. "I'm just going to say this."

"It's probably best," Talaith encouraged, working really hard not to panic.

Her only daughter smiled. "I've joined Annwyl's army."

"*You what?*"

Briec stepped between mother and daughter before Talaith could get her hands around the girl's throat.

"Perhaps we should discuss this calmly."

"Calmly? What is there to discuss calmly?" She pushed Briec aside. "You go down there right now, Iseabail, and you tell Annwyl you made a mistake."

Swallowing, her daughter again shook her head. "No."

"What do you mean, 'no'?" Talaith fairly growled. Had she risked everything so this little whelp could give her life on the field of battle to that insane wild woman who had recently become one of her best friends?

"I mean, I'm old enough to make this decision. I hope to become part of Annwyl's elite guard one day. Her squire to start if I'm lucky." Her daughter stood straighter. "And I start training tomorrow."

"No, you will *not* start training tomorrow. Tomorrow I'm sending you to a temple somewhere to become a priestess. Or something equally safe."

"There is nothing safe in this world. I have no Magick like you, Mum. All I have are sturdy thighs, a spine made of steel, and approximately six hundred years to fill. If you think I plan to do that bowing and scraping as an accolade, you are sadly mistaken."

"I will have no daughter of mine being the squire of that bloodthirsty bitch!"

"You were just laughing and eating with her this morning."

"We're not talking about me."

"You're being unreasonable."

"It's in the blood, luv. Get used to it."

"A year."

Mother and daughter looked at Briec who coolly leaned back against the bed.

"What?" Talaith snapped, unable to stop the images of her daughter with a sword through her chest from invading her mind.

"Give it one year. That seems fair, don't you think, Izzy?"

"Aye," she replied eagerly.

"Talaith?" He looked at her and she felt her eyes narrow. She could physically kill him from this distance.

If she argued now, she'd seem like a right prat. And the arrogant bastard knew that. "Fine. A year then."

"Yes!" Iseabail hugged her mother, giving her a big, wet kiss on her cheek. Then she ran to that traitor who called himself her mate and kissed him on the forehead.

"I have to get dressed. I hope there's dancing tonight!"

As soon as the door closed, Talaith turned on Briec. "Why did you do that?"

"Because it made sense."

"What difference will a year make?"

"Now that Annwyl's decided to keep her and Fearghus's demonspawn, she won't be traipsing off to any battles in other territories at the very least for the next year, more likely two."

He had a point there . . . *the bastard.*

"And what about after the year?"

Briec stood. "Be realistic, Talaith. If this isn't right for her, then she'll know that in a year, if not sooner."

"And if it is right for her?"

"Then you best let her do this."

"But—"

He took her hand. "If you don't, you'll lose her. Just like

your mother lost you. And like you, Izzy will get what she wants even if she has to find another army to join. But it won't be Annwyl's where they'll treat her like the daughter of royalty she truly is."

Right again. *Bastard*. But she still had to laugh. "My family's not royalty."

"No, but mine is. And she's one of us now . . . as are you."

"Oh."

Briec took a step toward her. "You did know that, didn't you?"

Talaith took a step back. "Um, well, I hadn't really considered it."

"You've been marked by me, Talaith. Claimed. Which means we're mated. For life. Izzy's my daughter. I may not be her father by blood, but she's mine. To protect and cherish."

"Oh."

"You keep saying that."

He kept advancing and she kept retreating. "I simply didn't see the full ramifications of our, uh, relationship."

Her back slammed into the wall and suddenly Briec's arms were on either side of her, caging her in. "Do you see the ramifications now, *princess?*"

"Uh . . ."

Before she could answer another knock came on their door, and she thought for sure Briec would set the castle on fire. Instead, he yelled, "*What?*"

Éibhear stuck his head in. "Where's Izzy?"

"She went back to her room. Why?"

"No reason. She just has something of mine." He grinned at them. "Carry on."

The door closed and Briec looked back at her. "That's it. We're leaving."

"What? Where?"

"My den. We'll leave tomorrow."

"I don't think that—"

"Not forever, Talaith. But I need some time alone with you. I grow weary of my kin. Very, *very* weary."

"Well, when you put it like that . . ."

"Good."

"But we can't be gone long. I want to be here for Annwyl. I fear what she may do to others if she's not kept calm."

He rolled his eyes. "If you must."

"And Izzy—"

"Another reason for us to leave for a bit, don't you think? It would be a bad idea for you to be here when she starts her training."

The dragon definitely had a point there. "Fine. But like I said. Not for long."

"Good. Now"—he leaned into her—"kiss me, woman."

"Briec," she stretched his name out by whining it. "We can't." But his hands were already under her dress, smoothing up her legs and across her bare hips. For him, she wore nothing under her clothes while alone in their bedroom except for her dagger and sheath—which he insisted upon—and he grinned his overwhelming appreciation. Holding her thighs tight, he lifted her up and settled her legs around his waist. At some point the overeager dragon pulled his leather leggings down to his knees. She felt his cock press against her, hot, hard, and pulsating. Her hands went around his neck, her forehead resting against his.

Gasping, they stared into each other's eyes as he slowly impaled her with his shaft. Taking her, inch by slow delicious inch. She moaned and he "shushed" her. "You don't know who may be on the other side of that door, little witch," he whispered, pushing more of himself inside her willing body. "Anyone could be listening."

His words made her shudder and hold him tighter. She bit her lip to stop from making noise, even as he slammed the last inch of his erection inside her.

"Remember," he growled in her ear, "you'll need to be quiet."

Not likely when he pulled his hard erection out of her grasping depths, only to ram it back in. Again and again and again.

Hoarse sounds unwillingly burst from her throat, which only goaded her dragon on. As usual, he showed her body no mercy and it felt wonderful. She dug the heels of her bare feet into his lower back and her hands into his hair. Her climax crawled up her spine, moving through her body like fire. Unable to hold it back, she opened her mouth to scream but Briec was there, covering her mouth with his own. His tongue tangling with hers, groaning as she exploded over the edge and came. Briec held her tight, rocking with her and, she sensed, enjoying the way her sex gripped him tight, spasms clutching him.

He kept on until a second, more powerful climax took hold of her and that's when, with a loud groan of his own, Briec came. He shot hot and hard inside her, whispering her name into her neck, shaking as the climax drained his body and, for the moment at least, his strength.

"Look what you've done to me, little witch." Briec nuzzled her cheek. "You've weakened me."

She laughed. He held her as easily as he would a babe. "I don't think I weakened anything, dragon. You still seem quite strong to me."

Smiling, he kissed her nose and her forehead, gently lowering her to the ground. "Don't move." He stepped away from her, but only for a moment to get a cloth and fresh water. She held her dress up as he took his time cleaning her. Then she returned the favor. Before she knew it, he'd pinned her against the wall again.

"Oh, no you don't." She slid under his arm and went toward the door. "We're not starting that again. I'm sure they're all waiting on us."

She snatched the door open, only to find Gwenvael quickly pulling his ear away from where he had it against the wood. He grinned at her and she knew he'd most likely heard everything.

"Oh," he said, trying to act surprised. "Hello, sister. I was looking for Briec. I think we need to talk about Morfyd and Bras—*ow!*" He grabbed his bleeding and broken nose. "*What the hell was that for?*"

Turning to face her mirror, Izzy studied herself in the dress Briec had specially made for her. She shook her head and gently pulled the left shoulder of her gown down, wincing as pain danced through her system. She stared at the still-healing dragon brand burned into the flesh of her shoulder. She really didn't know if the dress was doing a good enough job blocking the damn thing.

Although it was hurting much less than it did when she first returned, hiding it from her mother would not be easy.

"Oi!"

Izzy snapped around as Éibhear kicked open her door and marched in. "Where is it, you little brat?"

"Where's what?"

"My blade. Gwenvael saw you steal it. So don't bother lying."

"Why would I lie? It was simply another bet Gwenvael lost. He said I couldn't get it from you again. As always, he failed to have any faith in me."

"Give it."

"Don't snarl at me because I took your blade from you. If you paid more attention—"

"Hand it over. I've got plans tonight with Gwenvael before he heads to the Northern Lands and I won't waste my time with you."

"Fine!" She marched to her bed and reached under it, hauling out the extremely heavy weapon. "How you didn't notice I was taking this, I'll never know. I dropped it three times."

"I was in the middle of a conversation."

"With that rich whore?"

Éibhear didn't bother answering, simply snatched the sword from her. "Stay away from my things, demonspawn."

"Leave. You bore me already."

She turned away from him, but he grabbed her arm and yanked her back. Izzy was seconds away from pulling her knife from her boot until she saw that her dress was still down over her shoulder.

"Izzy, where the hell did you get this?"

She tried to pull her arm away. "None of your business."

Éibhear shook her and she stopped squirming. "Answer me."

Izzy lowered her eyes. "It's the mark of Rhydderch Hael."

"Why do you have it?" When she didn't answer, Éibhear pushed her away. "What the hell have you done?"

She had no answer, but he wasn't waiting for one. "I'm getting Talaith."

She grabbed him before he reached the door. "You do, and I'll make your life a living hell."

"You already do." He shoved her away, but she'd always been quick and jumped between him and the door before he could get it open.

"Please, Éibhear."

"I can't keep this from your mother, princess."

"Don't call me that." He'd started calling her that a few days ago and she had no idea why. She just knew she didn't like how he said it.

"Move," he ordered.

"She'll run!" she blurted out, desperate.

Éibhear stopped.

"We both know she will. And she'll take me with her." When Éibhear didn't move, she kept going. "Right now she feels safe because she feels *I'm* safe. She's finally happy. Briec makes her happy as she makes him happy. But if she thinks for a second I'm in danger or that she may lose me to another god . . . she'll run. Back to Alsandair. And you'll never find us."

"You think so, do you?"

"She may be learning the healing arts now, Éibhear, but don't fool yourself a moment about my mother. She's still a trained assassin who will do anything to survive. And she'll do absolutely anything to protect *me*."

He finally released the door handle. "Why did you do this, Izzy?"

"I had no choice. It was the only way to bring her back alive. But she can't ever know that."

"What did you promise him?"

She shrugged. "Everything."

Éibhear let out a deep sigh. "Dammit, Izzy."

"I know. But what could I do? She's my mother."

Éibhear nodded. "I understand."

"Then you won't say anything?"

He shook his head and she so wanted to run her hands through his blue mane. He'd look so adorable with warrior braids. But anytime she tried to touch him, he practically threw her across the room.

"Thank you."

"Hear me well, though, little girl. If he tries to claim anything from you before your eighteenth winter, I will go to your mother and Briec."

She nodded. "Fair enough." Somehow she knew it would be years before Rhydderch Hael called on her. He wanted her trained and ready. And she would be.

"Go on, then. Fix your dress. Make sure that thing doesn't show. And I'll see you downstairs."

He opened the door and Izzy asked, "Will you save a dance for me then?"

His shoulders tightened and without even turning around, he muttered, "Maybe in another sixteen years, princess."

She waited until he was out in the hallway before she answered. "Not a problem. I can wait."

Grinning, she closed the door, but not before she saw him slam face first into the wall.

Briec barely grabbed her in time. "No, Talaith."

"I'll kill him."

He rolled his eyes. He shouldn't have slept in. By the time they made it downstairs to head back to his den, Izzy's training had already started. Seeing her daughter trying to handle a shield and staff, only to get shoved into the ground over and over, was making his sweet Talaith much less than sweet.

"You can't go over there, Talaith."

"But he's not even one of the trainers."

True. They were probably trying to find out Izzy's strengths before they figured out which class to send her to, so they'd teamed her up against one of the older boys. A youth with white blond hair and an almost permanent sneer. Someone who, Briec was guessing, his little Izzy had rejected or mocked. The boy seemed to find great pleasure in shoving Briec's daughter in the dirt.

Annwyl, who'd been sitting on the fence watching the training, saw Talaith and immediately called a halt.

"Iseabail, Daughter of Talaith. Go say good-bye to your mother."

Izzy dropped her shield and staff and ran over to the pair. For a girl who'd been eating dirt most of the morning, she looked surprisingly happy. Talaith would *not* be happy when she realized Izzy's year would last much longer than that. Clearly the girl had found her true path.

"Good travels." Izzy hugged and kissed her mother. "I'll miss you both." She stood on tiptoes to reach up and hug Briec, rewarding him with a quick kiss on the cheek.

"Izzy, are you sure—"

Izzy groaned and again hugged her mother. "You promised me a year, Mum."

"All right. All right. Well, just remember, I'm only a

thought away. You need me for anything, Morfyd can get in touch with me. We won't be gone long."

"Take your time. I'm sure you two need some time alone." She winked at Talaith and he thought his poor mate would come out of her skin with embarrassment.

"Iseabail."

Laughing, Izzy stepped back before her mother could cuff her on the head. "Only teasing."

"Iseabail," Annwyl called. "Return to the field."

"I have to go. Have a safe trip."

Izzy took one step away, but Talaith grabbed firm hold of her daughter's arm. Briec groaned inward. He thought he'd finally convinced her this was the right course sometime after he'd made her come for the fourth time last night. He should have known better.

"Mum"—Izzy glanced over her shoulder at all those waiting for her return—"please."

Talaith took a deep breath and said, "The boy you're fighting. He's weak on his left side. Take the little bastard out at the knee."

Glancing at her mother then Briec, Izzy shrugged. "Uh, all right then." She smiled. "I'll do that."

"Good. Now go and good luck."

Izzy nodded and walked away. She was halfway back to the training field, when she turned around and ran over to her mother. She threw herself in Talaith's arms, and Briec could hear her fierce whisper as she hugged her mother tight. "I love you, Mum."

With that, she released Talaith and ran to the training field, immediately picking up her staff and shield to begin again.

Briec wrapped his arms around his woman's body. He felt her regret, but also her pride. Especially when Izzy faked out her opponent on his right, only to take out his left knee with her staff. He went down screaming.

"Let's go before I yank her out of there."

"Good idea." He grabbed hold of her hand and walked

toward the stables. It wasn't until he passed the stables that she started fighting.

"Oh, gods. Not the flying!"

"I heard you mounted my sister well enough."

"I want you never to make *that* statement again."

"You don't expect me to walk back to my den, do you?"

"But there are horses."

"I have horses."

"You do?"

"Of course I do. They're one of my favorite meals."

"Now you're simply trying to irritate me beyond all reason."

"Is it working?"

"Yes."

"Good. Then my work here is done."

He made it to the clearing and quickly shifted, without bothering to remove his clothes, before Talaith tried to dart off. Good thing he was quick, too. His tail almost didn't catch her in time.

Picking her up, he dropped her on his back. "Get comfortable, my love."

"I hate you."

"Keep that feeling, sweet Talaith. You'll need it when I get you back to my den and take you again and again and again."

"Just so we're clear, dragon. You are one of my least favorite beings."

He turned and looked at her over his shoulder. "But you do love me? Right, Talaith?"

She rewarded him with a warm, beautiful smile. And it was a reward. "Of course I love you. You mean the world to me, Briec."

He smirked. "Well, of course I do. I'm Briec the Mighty."

She snorted a laugh as she got comfortable on his back. "I walked right into that, didn't I?"

"Aye, my sweet Talaith. You most certainly did. Like a brutal ambush on a snowy mountaintop."

She cleared her throat. "You've actually done that, haven't you?"

"Oh, I have. Want me to tell you about it?" Briec asked as he took to the skies.

"No!"

"Fine. You don't have to be nasty about it. Are you going to be like this when we get home?"

"Yes. As a matter of fact, I am. I'm going to make your life a living hell."

"What makes you think you haven't already?"

"Maybe the way you moan my name, O' Arrogant One."

He soared by trees and Talaith didn't even notice she was so busy arguing with him. Good. By the time he got her home, she'd be so wet and ready for him, they probably wouldn't even make it to the bed.

"That's not a moan, little witch. It's more of a complaint."

"Ha! You only dream of having control in this relationship, my love."

"We'll see who has control when I get you back and tie you to the bed."

"You'll have to catch me first, dragon. And I'm quite stealthy. It's one of my skills."

"I thought complaining and getting lost were your skills . . . ow! Don't pull my hair."

"Then you best make sure you don't make me angry, Briec the Arrogant."

Briec laughed. "And where would the fun be in that, my love?"

Epilogue

Gwenvael sighed in overwhelming boredom, his talons scraping along the rocky, snow-covered ground.

There were a thousand things he'd rather be involved in. But Annwyl had asked this favor of him and he couldn't turn her down. Well, normally he could and would turn her down, but the woman had become a viper the longer her current "state" went on. Large with her Demon Twins, as Briec so eloquently put it, the past seven months had not been easy on any of them. Morfyd received the worst of it and Fearghus learned that there actually *was* too much fucking to be had. Apparently the human female had become absolutely insatiable and Fearghus was no longer safe walking down the blasted castle hallways or hunting in the surrounding forests. The woman stalked the poor dragon like an elk at High Season.

Gwenvael offered to assist Fearghus with his current "burden" and nearly lost his head in the process. Gods, his family never knew how to take a joke and until Annwyl birthed whatever grew in her belly she too would no longer be any fun.

So, when Gwenvael really thought about it, this was all

probably for the best. A nice trek up to the Northlands and away from the Blood Queen.

True, he'd been into the Northlands many times before in the last few months, but never this far into the Mountains of Despair or this close to the Ocean of Death and the Sea of Pain and Suffering. Ah, yes, these barbarians had such pithy names for their landmarks.

Gwenvael could smell the fresh ocean air and he longed to dive in and swim far, far away from this place.

The Reinholdt Fortress. A dank, depressing place if he'd ever seen one, but the Northland barbarians weren't known for their elegance. Even the local dragons—all descendents of the lightning gods and at one time his kinds' mortal enemies—fought hard and lived harder.

It seemed to be the way of this cold, forsaken land and those who lived within it.

To stop the flow of depression threatening to overtake him, Gwenvael reminded himself he could be back at Garbhán Isles dodging another sword thrown at his head for some inconsequential thing he said.

Instead, he was here to meet the legendary Sigmar Reinholdt and his thirteen strong sons, one of whom everyone referred to as The Beast. According to local gossip, The Beast was the scariest thing on two legs and had built quite a name for himself. As Gwenvael traveled through the Northlands these many months, he often heard the name mumbled in whispers and even the women he bed with for the night refused to discuss the man—even when Gwenvael was at his most persuasive.

But that no longer mattered, because now he stood in front of the fortress, a line of Reinholdt troops the only thing between him and the gates inside the compound.

Gwenvael sighed again and barked, "I grow tired of waiting."

"Dragons ain't much for patience, is they?"

"No, they *isn't*," Gwenvael mocked back. Normally he

tolerated humans—especially Annwyl—better than any of his kin, but he was tired, extremely hungry and bored. Bored being the worst of it. As his mother always said, "A bored Gwenvael is an entire town destroyed accidentally."

Many more minutes passed, until Gwenvael considered mowing them all down with his flames just to see them burn when a short, but powerfully built man pushed past the men guarding the entrance. Gods, the man had no neck to speak of. He went from head straight into his shoulders.

"I be Sigmar," the human said as a form of greeting and Gwenvael worked hard not to laugh out loud. These Northerners made his father seem downright warm and cuddly.

"King Sigmar." Gwenvael dipped his head, the most a human could ever expect from a dragon in way of respect—unless the human was female. Gwenvael had been known to roll on his back like a dog for the right female.

"I be no king, dragon. There are no kings in the Northlands. I'm The Reinholdt and clan leader of these lands."

Whatever. "So you asked for me, Reinholdt."

"No. I asked for your Annwyl."

"Well, she's indisposed at the moment, so she sent me as her emissary."

"A dragon emissary for a human?"

One more second of this and Gwenvael had every intention of killing them all. "Aye."

Reinholdt shrugged but said nothing else, preventing the potential carnage. The only problem was Reinholdt stopped speaking all together.

It took all of Gwenvael's strength not to roll his eyes in annoyance. He wanted this over with so he could get some food, ale, and a female or two to warm his bed for the night. Standing out in the cold was annoying him and the snow was freezing his scales. He hated that.

"Again, Reinholdt, you wanted to see me or someone from Dark Plains?"

"Nay. Not me, dragon. The Beast made that request."

Patience, Gwenvael. You're known for your patience.
"And may I meet The Beast?"

Reinholdt passed glances among the other men before looking back at Gwenvael. "You sure about that, dragon?"

"Yes," Gwenvael hissed. "I am."

Reinholdt nodded and looked at the men lined up in front of the gates. As one, they separated into two lines and Gwenvael's eyes widened as "The Beast" stepped forward from the throng of men and walked up to him.

Gwenvael stared down at the sight for several long seconds and then, unable to stop himself, he burst out laughing. He couldn't help it.

This? This was The Beast? Terrifying scourge of the Northlands? Battle Lord and Destroyer? *This?*

"Something amuses you, dragon?"

Round pieces of glass held between a wire frame rested upon The Beast's small nose and cold grey eyes stared at him. The pieces of glass slipped down a bit only to be pushed back by a well-placed finger.

"You?" Gwenvael managed between bouts of laughter. "You are The Beast?"

"That is what they call me."

Gwenvael stared down at the tiny woman before him. Smaller than even Briec's Talaith, there was nothing about this female that said warrior or assassin or witch or anything of any threat whatsoever. She wore a painfully plain, long-sleeved grey dress and fur boots. She had a small eating dagger attached to the girdle on her hips and waist-length brown hair tied into a plait.

The woman couldn't be more plain or boring or uninteresting if she actually put effort into it. And Gwenvael couldn't help it but he laughed harder. So hard he finally laid out on his back and rolled around for a bit, his dragon limbs flailing.

For months he'd heard about this female as a male and he

didn't half expect another Hamish or Annwyl's brother, Lorcan. Or, at the very least, his mother.

Something dangerous and blood-covered. This woman looked like she never left the library.

After several minutes, Gwenvael somehow got himself under control. He stopped laughing but didn't get back up because she stood right beside him. That impressed him. Most humans went out of their way to avoid him when he was in dragonform.

She stared down at him with those cold grey eyes made larger by the glass over each one. He did find those interesting. He'd never seen anything like that before. He wondered why she wore them.

"Are you done?" she asked coldly.

"Sorry, uh . . . Beast." He snorted out another laugh, but choked it back.

"Dagmar will do. Dagmar Reinholdt. Thirteenth child of The Reinholdt and his only female."

Northerners mostly bred males, often forced to steal their females from the south. Even the lightning dragons mostly hatched males. It was as if the land was too cold and desolate for females to be born here.

"I asked your queen here because I have news that may save her life and the lives of her unborn whelps."

Gwenvael frowned, not appreciating anyone referring to his brother's little bastards as "whelps."

"Tell me, *sweet* Dagmar," he mocked. "And I'll tell her."

The female blinked. Once. "No."

Gwenvael pushed himself up a bit so that his snout was barely inches from her nose. "What do you mean, no?"

"I mean, you've insulted me. You've insulted my kin. And you've insulted The Reinholdt. So you can return to your bitch queen and you can watch her die."

With that, Dagmar Reinholdt turned on her heel and walked away from him. She stopped after a few feet, glancing at him over her shoulder, and said, "Now that, dragon . . . *that's* funny."

She walked back into the fortress and the soldiers closed rank. Gwenvael scrambled to his feet and stared at Sigmar Reinholdt, but the no-neck clan leader only shook his head.

"You are a bit of a dumb bastard, aren't ya, dragon?" he said without a bit of pity. "We don' call her The Beast 'cause we're bored, ya know? She'll tell ya nothin' now."

With a resigned sigh, the man followed after his daughter and his sons followed after him.

The soldiers closed up ranks with their weapons drawn. They now blocked the gates and Gwenvael knew they'd never willingly let him enter.

Not sure what else to do, Gwenvael took to the skies, his mind racing. He couldn't go back to Dark Plains and his kin with, "I pissed her off so much she wouldn't tell me anything." Fearghus would have his ass for supper. Not only that, but he wouldn't allow anyone to harm Annwyl or her children. No matter what they might or might not be, they were still his kin and he'd protect the little bastards like he would any of his siblings' hatchlings.

Unfortunately, he had only one option. He'd wait until dark and then snatch the little bitch from the fortress. She was female after all, and if there was one thing Gwenvael the Handsome knew how to do—it was how to handle a female.

Gwenvael grinned, his fangs showing as he headed for the safety of the mountains and nightfall. A few hours with him and he'd have The Beast begging to tell him what she knew—and then he'd just have her begging.

Did you catch DRAGON ACTUALLY,
the first book in G.A. Aiken's dragon series?
Turn the page for a preview . . .

"Hold, knight." She stared at him, taking a deep breath to still her rapidly beating heart. *By the gods, he's beautiful.* And Annwyl didn't trust him as far as she could throw him. Which wasn't far. He had to be the biggest man she'd ever seen. All of it hard-packed muscle that radiated power and strength.

She tightened her grip on her sword. "I know you."

"And I know you."

Annwyl frowned. "Who are you?"

"Who are *you?*"

Her eyes narrowed. "You kissed me."

"And I believe *you* kissed *me.*"

Annwyl's rage grew, her patience for games waning greatly. "Perhaps you failed to realize that I have a blade to your throat, knight."

"And perhaps you failed to realize"—he knocked her blade away, placing the tip of his own against her throat— "that I'm not some weak-willed toady who slaves for your brother, Annwyl the Bloody of the Dark Plains."

Annwyl glanced down at the sword and back at the man holding it. "Who the hell are you?"

"The dragon sent me." He lowered his blade. "And he was right. You are too slow. You'll never defeat Lorcan."

Her rage welled up and she slashed at him with her blade. But it wasn't one of her well-trained maneuvers. It felt awkward and messy. He blocked her easily, slamming her to the ground.

Her teeth rattled in her head. Good thing her wound had already healed, otherwise Morfyd would be sewing it up once again.

The knight stood over her. "You can do better than that, can't you?" She stared up at him and he smiled. "Or maybe not. Guess we'll just have to see."

He wandered off. Annwyl knew he expected her to follow. And, for some unknown reason, she did.

She found him by the stream that ran through the glen. It took all her strength to walk up to him. She really wanted to run back into the dragon's lair and hide under his massive wings. She wasn't afraid of this man. It was something else. Something far more dangerous.

As she approached, he turned and smiled. And Annwyl felt her stomach clench. Actually, the clenching might have been a bit lower.

She'd never known a man who made her so . . . well . . . nervous. And she'd lived on Garbhán Isle since the age of ten; all she'd ever known were men who made it their business to make women nervous, if not downright terrified.

"Well," she demanded coldly.

He moved to stand in front of her, his gorgeous smile teasing her. "Desperate are we?"

Annwyl shook her head and stepped away from him. "I thought you said something about training me for battle, knight." *For the dragon.* She would only do this because the dragon asked her to. And she would damn well make sure he knew it, too.

"Aye, I did, Annwyl the Bloody."

"Do stop calling me that."

"You should be proud of that name. From what I understand, you earned it."

"My brother also called me dung heap. I'm sure he thought I earned that too, but I'd rather no one call me that."

"Fair enough."

"And do you have a name?" He opened his mouth to say something but she stopped him. "You know what? I don't want to know."

"Really?"

"It will make beating the hell out of you so much easier."

She wanted to throw him off. Make him uneasy. But his smile beamed like a bright ray of sunlight in the darkened glen. "A challenge. I like that." He growled the last sentence, and it slithered all the way down to her toes. Part of her wanted to panic over that statement, since it frightened her more than the dragon himself. But she didn't have time. Not with the blade flashing past her head, forcing her to duck and unsheathe her own sword.

He watched her move. Drank her in. And when she took off her shirt and continued to fight in just leather leggings, boots, and the cloth that bound her breasts down, he had to constantly remind himself of why he now helped her. To train her to be a better fighter. Nothing more or less. It was *not* so he could lick the tender spot between her shoulder and throat.

Annwyl, though, turned out to be a damn good fighter. Strong. Powerful. Highly aggressive. She listened to direction well and picked up combat skills quickly. But her anger definitely remained her main weakness. Anytime he blocked one of her faster blows, anytime he moved too quickly for her to make contact, and, especially, anytime he touched her, the girl flew into a rage. An all-consuming rage. And although he knew the soldiers of Lorcan's army would easily fall to her blade, her brother was different. He knew of that man's reputation as a warrior and, as Annwyl now stood, she didn't stand a chance. Her fear of Lorcan would stop her from making the killing blow. Her rage would make her vulnerable. The mere thought of her getting killed sent a cold wave of fear through him.

Yet if he could teach her to control her rage, she could turn it into her greatest ally. Use it to destroy any and all who dare challenge her.

The shifting sun and deepening shadows told him that the hour grew late. The expression on her face told him that exhaustion would claim her soon, although she'd never admit it. At least not to him. But he knew what would push her over the edge. He grabbed her ass.

Annwyl screeched and swung around. He knocked her blade from her hand and threw her on her back.

"How many times, exactly, do I have to tell you that your anger leaves you exposed and open to attack?"

She raised herself on her elbows. "You grabbed me," she accused. "Again!"

He leaned down so they were nose to nose. "Yes I did. And I enjoyed every second of it."

Her fist flashed out, aiming for his face. But he caught her hand, his fingers brushing across hers. "Of course, if you learned to control your rage I'd never get near you." He brought her fingers to his lips and kissed them gently. "But until that time comes, I guess your ass belongs to me."

She bared her teeth, and he didn't try to hide his smile. How could he when he knew how it irritated her so? "I think we've practiced enough for the day. At least I have. And the dragon now has a scouting party for his dinner. But I'll be back tomorrow. Be ready, Annwyl the Bloody. This won't get any easier."

And don't miss the next book in the series,
coming in September 2009 from Zebra. . . .

Putting her feet between the lower slats, Dagmar pulled herself up and leaned over the fence . . . and looked straight into gold eyes.

He was staring up at her, looking guilty, with his hand around the back of Canute's neck.

"What are you doing to my dog?" she asked.

"Nothing?"

"Why are you saying that like a question?"

"I wasn't?"

"Yes you were. And unhand him."

He had a handsome face, whoever he was. Even when he gave a little pout at her order. He looked down at the dog again and then, with a shrug, unclamped his hand. Canute charged back and started growling and barking again.

"Quiet," she softly ordered.

Canute stopped barking but he didn't stop the growling.

"What do you want?" she asked the stranger, curious as to who he was. He couldn't be from the Northlands. His skin was too golden from exposure to the suns, and his gold hair that reached past his knees was loose and wild around his face. The Northland men didn't wear their hair that long or free from the single braid they wore down their backs except when they slept.

He slowly stood . . . and he kept standing until he towered over her more than her brothers did and that said something. Unlike their father, The Reinholdt's sons were all tall, strapping men. But this one was unreasonably tall. And big. Large, powerful muscles rippled under his chainmail shirt and leggings, the dark-red surcoat tight across his chest.

Oddly, he stared at her in such a way as to make her feel . . . but no. No one looked at Dagmar like that. No one. But there was something so undeniably familiar about him. Had she met him before? Long ago?

While she tried to remember where she'd seen or met him before, he grinned.

And it was the grin she recognized. That damn mocking, rude grin.

"You."

His brow went up in surprise. "Very good. Most humans never put the two together."

"I thought I made myself clear earlier."

"Yes, but I have needs."

She blinked, keeping her face purposely blank. *He has needs?* What did that even mean?

"Your needs are not my concern."

"But are you not lady of this house?"

Dagmar glanced around. He did have a point. Without a new wife for her father, the task fell to Dagmar.

"And as lady of the house, isn't it your job to care for your visitor?"

"Except I asked you to leave."

"I did leave. Then I came back. As I'm sure you knew I would." He rested his elbow on the gate, his chin in his palm. "I'm hungry."

The way he said that . . . honestly! Dagmar simply didn't know what to make of this dragon.

He glanced over her shoulder. "Think I can have one of those?"

Dagmar looked over her shoulder and she saw her dogs snarling and snapping in their direction while poor Johann stood around, completely confused. For once the dogs ignored his commands and he had no idea why.

"Have one?" she asked, also confused but for another reason entirely.

"Aye. I'm hungry and—"

Her head snapped around and she slapped her hand over his mouth. "If you say what I think you're about to say," she warned softly, "I'll be forced to have you killed. So stop speaking."

She felt it. Against her hand. That damn smile again. She ignored the feeling of another being's flesh against her own. It had been so long that it felt disconcertingly strange to her.

She pulled her hand away and blatantly wiped her palm against her dress. "Leave."

"Why?"

"Because the mere sight of you frightens my dogs."

He leaned in closer to her. "And what does the mere sight of me do to you?"

She stared up at him and stated flatly, "Besides disgust me, you mean?"

His smug smile fell. "Pardon?"

"Disgust. Although you can hardly be surprised. You come to my father's stronghold disguised as a human when in fact that's nothing but a lie. But I wonder how many unsuspecting females fell for that insipid charm you believe yourself to have only to later realize they'd done nothing but bed a giant slimy lizard. So you, as human, disgust me." She sneered a bit. "Now aren't you glad you asked?"

Actually . . . no he wasn't glad. How rude! She was rude! Gwenvael liked mean women, but he didn't much like rude ones. Slimy. He was *not* slimy!

And if she wanted to play this way, fine.

He leaned in closer, studying her face. He could tell by the way her entire body tightened at his approach, she wasn't remotely comfortable with him getting so close. He knew he could use that to his advantage if necessary. "What *are* those things on your face?"

Beyond a tiny little tick in her cheek, the rest of her face remained remarkably blank. "What exactly are you talking about?"

Gwenvael's head tilted to the side a bit, not sure what else she thought he could mean. "The glass." He went to poke one but she slapped his hand away.

"They're my spectacles."

"Do you mean like a spectacle of bad? Spectacle of horror?"

"No," she replied flatly. "They're so I can see."

"Are you blind?" He waved his hands in front of her face. "*Can you see me?*" he shouted, causing all those delicious-looking dogs to bark and snarl louder.

That constantly cold façade abruptly dropped as she again, but more viciously, slapped his hands away. "I am not blind. Nor am I deaf!"

"No need to get testy."

"I don't get testy."

"Except around me."

"Perhaps you bring out the worst in people, which is not anything one should be proud of."

"You haven't met my family. We're proud of the oddest things."

Her lip curled. "There are more of you?"

"None quite like me. I'm unbearably unique and, dare I say, adorable. But I do have kin." He shrugged. "I'm so very sorry about earlier," he lied. "And I'm hoping you'll help me."

There went that flat expression again. She had this constant expression of being unimpressed. By anything, everything. Yet he was beginning to find it kind of . . . cute. And annoyingly intriguing.

"I'm sure you'd rather I help you, but I delight in the fact that I won't."

That was her delighted expression? Eeesh.

Gwenvael pulled back a bit. "And why wouldn't you help me even after I apologized? So sweetly too!"

"One, because you didn't really mean that apology and two . . . I really don't like you."

He sighed. "Everyone likes me. I'm loveable. Even those who start out hating me end up liking me."

"Then they're fools. Because I don't like you and I won't like you."

"I'm sure you'll change your mind."

"I don't change my mind."

Gwenvael frowned a bit. "Ever?"

"Once . . . but then I realized I was right the first time, so I never bothered to change my mind again."

She was not going to be easy this one. His skills in seducing the most difficult females to do his bidding were legendary. But this one wasn't being very cooperative. Yet she wasn't resisting him as much as simply not responding to him. No matter how he taunted her, she refused to rise to the occasion. He couldn't be more irritated by that!

"Fine," he snapped. "I'll talk to your father then. See if he can convince you to act like a true and proper hostess."

"You do that."

Gwenvael continued to stand there, staring down at her, until she was forced to ask, "Well . . . ?"

"Don't know where he is."

"Find him."

"A proper hostess would show me the way."

"A proper hostess wouldn't have your kind in her home."

"That was mean."

"Yes."

"So you're not going to help me?"

"No."

"Why?"

"I already explained this. I don't like you. True, I don't like most people, but I especially dislike you. I could start my own religion based on how much I dislike you."

Out of ideas on how to handle this wench, Gwenvael went with one of his tried and true methods. He sniffed . . . and then he sniffed again.

The Beast blinked, her expression confused, but then her eyes widened in horror when she saw that first tear fall.

"Wait . . . are . . . are you . . . *crying?*"

It was a skill he'd taught himself when he was barely ten winters old. With brothers like his, he needed it in order to get his mother to protect her favorite son as much as possible. He rarely used the technique now, but he was desperate.

"You're so mean to me," he complained around his tears.

"Yes, but—"

"*Why won't you help me?*" he wailed.

"All right. All right." She held her hands up. "I'll take you to my father."

He sniffed more tears away. "You promise?"

"Do I . . ." She sighed and stepped down from the fence. She didn't jump down, nor did she step down daintily. It was a carefully, plotted step. He bet she took lots of careful steps in her life.

She came out of the gate and closed it behind her. "Canute, here." The tasty morsel that had almost been his afternoon meal immediately went to her side, his yellow dog eyes watching Gwenvael closely.

"And you," she said to Gwenvael. "Come along."

Gwenvael watched her walk away. Her clothes were bulky and plain. He couldn't make out a bit of her body, and he couldn't help but wonder what she looked like without all those clothes. Was she thin like a rail or did she have some curves? Were her breasts big handfuls or something to be tweaked? Was her ass flat or would he be able to grip it tight while he rode her? Did she moan or was she a screamer?

She stopped and glared at him over her shoulder. "Well . . . are you coming?"

And she didn't seem to appreciate it much when he started laughing at her again.

GREAT BOOKS,
GREAT SAVINGS!

When You Visit Our Website:
www.kensingtonbooks.com
You Can Save Money Off The Retail Price
Of Any Book You Purchase!

- **All Your Favorite Kensington Authors**
- **New Releases & Timeless Classics**
- **Overnight Shipping Available**
- **eBooks Available For Many Titles**
- **All Major Credit Cards Accepted**

Visit Us Today To Start Saving!
www.kensingtonbooks.com